Sue Featherstone & Susan Pape

A FORSAKEN FRIEND

Dreams, Dramas

and

Damned Friendship

A Forsaken Friend

Copyright © Sue Featherstone and Susan Pape

First Published by Lakewater Press 2018

All Rights Reserved.

Cover Image by Diana Pinguicha

Cover Design by Emma Wicker

No part of this publication may be reproduced, distributed, or transmitted in any form or by any means, or stored in a database or retrieval system, without prior documented approval of the publisher.

This book is a work of fiction. Names, characters, places, and incidents either are the products of the author's imagination or are used fictitiously. Any resemblance to actual persons, living or dead, businesses, companies, events, or locales is entirely coincidental.

ISBN-10: 0-9944512-9-6

ISBN-13: 978-0-9944512-9-3

I hope you enjoy reading this book, the second in our Friends trilogy. Book 1 - "A Falling Friend" was published in April 2016 and the final instalment - "A Forgiven Friend" - will be published spring 2019.

If you've had a good read, both Susan and I would be grateful if you could take the time to leave a review on Amazon.

Best wishes

Sue x

For Megan and Annie, and Dandy

CHAPTER 1

TERI

I've seen a fair number of naked men, and had my share of lovers. More recently, I've been spoiled. Declan O'Brien – that bastard – had what I can only describe as the leanest, tautest, most ripped body of any of them. His chest was so tight I could beat out a drum on those pectoral muscles. He had slim hips and a perfectly formed bum, which appeared clenched even when relaxed. He claimed never to exercise, always too busy at the Evening Leader newspaper where he worked; but frankly, what he was busy doing was juggling a wife and kids plus laying an assortment of lovers – sadly, me included.

My ex-husband Dan Caine was a suave TV presenter who prided himself on his lightly tanned, good-looking face and a body that would eventually succumb to midlife spread, but not while I was in charge.

But Duck's Arse? No, he certainly wasn't the type of man I'd usually go for.

Duck's Arse – or, now that we're more intimately acquainted, I should call him Richard Walker – had chubby cheeks and rounded, pink lips and overall he was definitely the worse for bodily wear. As he removed his crisp light-blue shirt, it was as if his upper body had been released and his belly sagged gently in the open air.

I've nothing against plump men, it's just that I've never bedded one before, and judging by the man-boobs being proffered, I wasn't sure I wanted to start.

A fold of flesh hung over the belt of his trousers, and I wondered if it wasn't too late to back out of this. Whatever *this* was.

CHAPTER 2

LEE

It really bothered me that Teri wasn't returning my phone calls.

'Why?' Dan asked.

What a stupid question. I'd just spent five minutes telling him.

But he clearly had more important things on his mind as he turned from the stove where a rich aroma of tomatoes and basil and beef bubbled from a pan of bolognaise sauce. 'I think this is almost ready. What do you think?'

Honestly, I think if he's cooking he should make the key decisions, but I slipped off the breakfast bar high stool where I'd been nursing a pre-dinner glass of wine and, taking the wooden spoon from his hand, dutifully peered and poked. 'Just watch it doesn't dry out while the pasta cooks.'

'Pasta?' He seemed surprised. 'I thought you were doing the pasta?'

'Me?'

'Well, I need to keep an eye on the sauce. I can't watch the pasta as well.'

No, poor darling, how could he possibly manage two simmering pans at the same time?

It was tempting to point out he was cooking tea for two rather than feeding the five thousand, but I resisted. Easier just to heat the water and plunge the spaghetti in once it had reached a rolling boil.

'Wait!' Dan grabbed my hand as I dipped the first strands into the pot. 'Aren't you going to add a drop of olive oil to stop the spaghetti clumping together?'

I shook him off. 'No.'

'But…'

'Old wives tale,' I said. 'The oil will make the pasta greasy and the sauce won't stick.'

'My mother always added oil.'

Heaven forbid I should correct the kitchen paragon who'd failed to teach her son how to stir two pans of food at the same time but… 'No.'

Dan shrugged. 'I think you'll find I'm right.'

I don't think so.

'Hmmm,' Dan said twelve-and-a-half minutes later when I placed the food on the table. 'Must be non-stick spaghetti.'

I rapped his knuckles with the serving spoon. 'There's no such bloody thing!'

'That hurt,' he whined.

'It was meant to.'

We ate in silence for a few minutes. 'If the boot was on the other foot she wouldn't be beating a path to your door,' he reasoned, picking up the earlier conversation where we'd left it.

Tell me something I don't know. 'I'm not Teri,' I said, 'and I'll do what I think is right rather than what she'd think was right.'

Yep – first prize for sanctimonious claptrap goes to…

Dan leaned across the table and, pulling his sleeve over his fist, made a circular motion above my head.

'What are you doing?' I asked.

'Polishing your halo.'

I punched his arm aside.

Eventually, I cornered Declan, the man she'd declared the love of her life – *while* she was still married to Dan – after Sunday Mass.

'Couldn't you give her a call?'

'No,' he said, trying to edge away. 'I'm done with Teri.'

I clutched his sleeve. 'That's not fair,' I said. 'She wouldn't be in this mess if it wasn't for you.'

He looked over his shoulder, checking for his wife, Marnie. 'Keep your voice down,' he hissed.

I followed his gaze. 'She's talking to your mother and mine,' I said. 'She won't get away from them in a hurry.'

He scowled. 'Makes no odds, she's seen us together so she'll want chapter and verse afterwards.'

'She can't imagine you and me…?'

'I know. I'd rather slit my wrists but she's suspicious of everything in a skirt.'

I dug my nails into his arm as hard as I could. '*You'd* slit your wrists?'

He winced and I guessed would have tried to prise my hand away but was clearly hampered by a desire not to attract undue attention from Marnie. I gave her a little wave and tucked my arm securely into the crook of Declan's elbow. 'Tell her you're on the shortlist for an honorary doctorate and we're discussing the details.'

The silly so-and-so grinned. 'I'm not, am I?'

'Of course not! But she won't know that.'

'It's not such a daft idea. I've given years of service to the community.'

'Servicing members of the female population doesn't count.'

He frowned. 'There's no need to get personal.'

'Then, stop being ridiculous and answer my question.'

'What do you expect me to do? I didn't encourage her to skip classes, or fall down drunk in front of her students. Or cook the mark books. And, nor,' he paused, 'did I seduce her ex-husband.'

'Don't try and blame me,' I said. 'She'd still be with Dan if you'd kept your pants zipped.'

'Don't be so crude.'

'It's true though.'

As ever, any conversation with Declan rapidly degenerated into a playground war of words. The man's been getting under my skin – and not in a good way – since we were at primary school together.

'But,' he said, 'if she was still with Dan, who would *you* be with?'

So, now he wanted brownie points for his philandering?

'Please,' I said. 'I'm worried about her. I've been ringing her on and off for the last couple of days and'– I let out a deep, theatrical sigh –'don't you care for her just a teeny bit?'

Yes, he did, quite a lot. But Marnie had made it perfectly clear she wasn't prepared to tolerate any more of what she called his 'monkey business'.

'More than my life's worth,' he said.

In the end, though he allowed himself to be guilt-tripped into calling Teri. He said it was because he was a nice guy. I said it was because he wanted a second go at getting into her pants.

Neither of us had any luck. 'She's thrown all her toys out of the pram,' he said when he telephoned to let me know how he'd got on. 'Leave her to cool down, Lee.'

I wasn't surprised Declan advised leaving Teri to stew in her own bile, but, when I reported back to Dan I thought *he* might have been a bit more sympathetic. After all, he'd loved her enough to marry her. Would he chuck me overboard as easily?

He put down the newspaper he was reading.

'Don't be ridiculous,' he said. 'You and Teri are like chalk and cheese.'

I gave the chicken breasts I was tenderising for the griddle pan an extra bash or two. 'And am I the chalk? Or the cheese?'

He scratched his head.

I thumped the chicken pieces again. 'Chalk,' I said. 'Dry, powdery indigestible. Or cheese, which might best be described as curdled milk.'

He said nothing.

Can't say I blamed him. He'd have only dug himself in even deeper. And I was wielding a meat mallet.

He scratched his head again. 'What are you going to do?' he asked. 'Knock the door in with that mallet and tie her to a bedpost until she hears you out.'

I wished he hadn't said that – I'd seen the pair of fur-lined handcuffs Teri kept in her bedside cabinet. 'Naughty but nice,' she'd said. I got the picture. So, I think, did Dan. He blushed.

'You didn't!'

His Adam's apple convulsed.

'Forget it,' I said. 'I don't want to know. None of my business. But, let's get this clear.' I prodded him between the ribs with the mallet. 'I don't need handcuffs to get what I want.'

CHAPTER 3

TERI

Life never ceases to amaze me. You set out to do one thing, and you end up doing something completely different. I'd started the day determined to have it out with Dan – whatever 'it' might have been. And I'd ended up seeing rather more of Duck's Arse than I'd bargained for.

I'd gone down to the Ridings Today studios and without breaking my stride, pushed open one of the two glass front doors that opened out into the wood and chrome reception area of the television studios.

A group of five tee shirt and jeans-wearing television types were gathered in a tight knot just inside the doors. They wore serious expressions to show they were having a non-hot-desk meeting about some important documentary or other.

I ignored them and marched to the reception desk.

A woman wearing too much make-up and a tight, black two-piece skirt suit – polyester by the cheap sheen of the jacket – stared at the computer in front of her, no doubt checking her Facebook status but pretending to be busy working and enjoying the fact she was keeping me waiting.

I sighed loudly and beat out a light rhythm with my fingers on the desktop. The over-made-up dolly didn't even glance up. I was tempted to lean over and switch the bloody monitor off when a voice behind me said, 'It's Teri, isn't it?'

I turned and found myself staring straight into the plump face of a man who was standing just a little too close for comfort. Some instinct warned me not to use my finger to push him back and say as icily as possible, 'Do you mind…?'

Just as well.

It was Duck's Arse, or, rather, Richard Walker, managing director of Ridings TV where my ex-husband was one of the talents.

I'd met Richard before, most notably at a Royal Television Society event that I'd gone to on one of my first dates with Dan. It should have been a fabulous occasion with me draped glamorously on Dan's arm, being introduced to gorgeous celebrities. But what a self-regarding party it turned into: not much by way of celebrity, and lots of television types awarding themselves shiny gongs for simply doing their jobs – best documentary featuring singing parrots riding in motorbike sidecars. That sort of thing.

Dan had left me while he went off to lark it up with a group of television boys and girls, and I'd been toying with the idea of ringing for a taxi and leaving, when Richard plonked his plump arse next to me. I remember thinking then that Mr Boss Man was not my type. I'd named him Duck's Arse because of the dark hair gelled into little peaks on the top of his head. Frankly, hair gelled into a duck's arse on the top of a man's head is ridiculous on any bloke over the age of twenty-two, and even odder on someone in his late forties.

I don't go for duck-arsed podgy guys, especially not when dating someone as gorgeous, sophisticated and generous as Dan Caine. At least, that's what I thought of Dan then, but that was before I realised what a selfish bastard he was. And don't get me started on Victoria, his feckless, snivelling daughter. Or his affair with Lee Harper, my supposedly best friend – ex-best friend.

And now, here was Richard Walker, plumper than life, in the foyer of the television company he ran.

'How lovely to see you,' Duck's Arse said, kissing me first on one cheek and then the other, all the time running his right hand up and down my left arm.

'You too,' I said hesitantly, wondering if he'd notice if I took a tissue from my bag to wipe off any excess slobber.

'What're you doing here? Are you here for the convention?'

'Oh…er…yes.' It sounded weak, and Duck's Arse frowned, examining my face closely.

'Oh, good,' he said. 'I'll give you a lift. Come on, the car's outside.'

CHAPTER 4

LEE

I'm not a love-struck teenager, and nor am I an idiot, so I didn't expect falling in love and getting engaged to automatically equal HAPPY EVER AFTER. On the other hand, nor did I expect Dan to turn into a colossally irritating prick. It was as if he thought the ring – which was pretty but only a ring, for goodness' sake – changed the ground rules. No, Dan. What you see is what you get, and I haven't reached the age of… well, let's say an age where I no longer believe in Prince Charming and knights on white chargers, without feeling able to say NO.

'I don't think it's a lot to ask.' Dan rubbed his eyes with the tea towel. 'Phew! These onions are sharp.'

'Spanish,' I said, replacing the tea towel with a piece of kitchen paper.

'How many more do I need to peel?'

I looked at the mounting pile. 'Depends how many quiches you're planning to take with you.'

It was Saturday morning, and he was making his world-famous quiche Lorraine for an afternoon garden party at the country bolt hole of one of his Ridings colleagues.

'Two, maybe three…' He hesitated. 'I wish you'd come with me.'

He might, I didn't.

'I'm sure you'll enjoy it once you get there.'

I was equally sure I wouldn't. Rain was forecast.

'We'll decamp indoors,' Dan said.

And that would make it better?

'You're just a misery guts,' Dan said, slashing at the onions in a way that didn't augur well for the safety of his fingers.

I scribbled something on the essay I was reading and patted the stack spread out across the breakfast bar. 'Yes, but one who just happens to have rather a lot of marking to finish off.'

Never thought I'd be grateful to the Level Two students and their tediously awful essays on contemporary themes and issues in African American literature.

'That's just an excuse,' Dan accused with more justice than he realised. 'I don't think it's a lot to ask,' he repeated.

Unfortunately, I did. I'd nothing against a good party – who doesn't enjoy good conversation and good food and wine with like-minded people? But, with one or two exceptions, Dan, I suppose, and possibly his boss, Richard Walker – the bloke Teri insisted on calling Duck's Arse – the Ridings TV crowd were a bunch of shallow-minded show-offs who couldn't string a sensible sentence together without the aid of an auto-cue.

So, no, Dan. I'm not going to glam up and slip into a slinky JK Fennick dress and a pair of Jimmy Choos and tag along to your swanky television parties as a bit of arm candy. Not least because I don't possess either.

'Perhaps another time,' I said, knowing full well that next time there'd be another excuse.

Dan didn't reply. He was concentrating on easing his pastry into the flan dish.

'And even if I could spare the time, I don't really have anything suitable to wear.'

He couldn't argue with that. Only yesterday he'd had the temerity to suggest my comfy, cosy duffel coat was looking a little worse-for-wear. And, the way rain clouds were gathering, a warm coat would be a necessity this afternoon.

Dan downed his rolling pin and wrapped his arms around me. I leaned back into him. 'Maybe next weekend I'll take you shopping.'

Lord, I hoped not. Dan was a proper girl when it came to clothes shopping. It was the one thing he and Teri had in common – both of them thought a day at the shops was a day well spent. I thought it was a day sadly wasted.

But, sometimes, compromises have to be made and next weekend saw us stepping into the northern branch of Harvey Nicks to buy a little birthday something for the PA he shared with Duck's Arse.

Dan, being Dan, couldn't help extending his browsing beyond the make-up and perfume counters and had wandered into the women's wear department where he fingered a belted cashmere military-style coat. 'You should splash out on something a little more luxurious,' he said.

It did feel rather gorgeous – just the sort of thing Teri would love – and then I saw the '£2,425' price tag. I yelped and jumped back, almost knocking over a mannequin.

'If you wanted a Teri look-a-like you should have stuck with the original model,' I said.

'No, no,' he said. 'I love you just the way you are.'

Good, because I'm sticking with the duffel coat, purple Dr Martens and eco-friendly smocks.

CHAPTER 5

TERI

Duck's Arse ushered me out of the building towards a sleek black Jaguar parked by the main entrance.

'Perks of the job,' he said, nodding towards the chauffeur sitting in the driving seat and taking a couple of steps ahead of me to open one of the back passenger doors.

'Hi Jim,' he said, leaning in to address the driver. 'We've got a guest today. This is Teri.'

Jim inclined his head in my direction. 'Hi Teri.'

I slipped onto the cool leather upholstery as Duck's Arse gently closed my door and strode around the front of the car to climb in the back next to me.

'Well, this is a surprise,' he said. 'Didn't realise you were into the Digital Realisations of Mainstream Media on Synergetic Platforms.'

He registered the confusion on my face.

'No, thought not,' he said, patting me on the knee. 'Never mind. The convention's just for media types, but there's a good lunch first. Come and eat, and then I'll get Jim to drop you back home.'

The car accelerated smoothly and quietly onto the main road while I considered my options: go along with whatever farce into which my life had just descended or open the door and leap out?

Duck's Arse glanced across at me and his expression softened.

'Not a good idea, lovely lady,' he said, shaking his head slightly.

'What…?' I wondered if he'd read my mind and was warning me against yanking open the door and flying out into the A615.

'I rather get the feeling you were planning on seeing Dan? And I rather get the feeling you were going to create some sort of scene with him in the newsroom?'

'How dare you?' I glared even though he was absolutely right.

Four days ago I'd had to listen to Lee wittering on the phone about how she and Dan had fallen in love; how they couldn't help it; how they didn't mean to hurt me.

Dan and I are divorced, but he still loves me and wants me back – and Lee knows this. So what does she do: moves in on him with a 'I'm just a lovely little Catholic girl who wants to look after a nice man', and Dan, the poor sap, falls for it.

What's worse is that Lee didn't have the balls to tell me face-to-face. She rang me. Why didn't she just text me, the silly bag? She could have put: 'Hving it off with yr ex. Hope u don't mind.'

She knew I was in trouble at work. We're both lecturers at the University of Central Yorkshire – or rather, she still *is*, I'm not. Sacked!

Lee had helped me get a job there and now, instead of standing up for me she rubs salt in the wound. Oh, I can just hear her bleating about how unprofessional I'd been with that miserable little squirt of a student, David Greenspan. The boy clearly fancied me – and not her – so she made up some story about how I threatened him with poor marks if he didn't do what I wanted. Me! As if I have to bribe a man. Well, okay, I did explain to David that students' marks could be changed if a tutor decided to consider them again. But that's hardly bribery, is it?

Then that snivelling Peter Heron – so called university dean – comes up with all the business about my marks not being consistent. Well, show me a lecturer who hasn't skimmed over dozens of tedious undergraduate essays and thought, 'Oh give them a 2:1 and be done with it.'

And then there was the ridiculous accusation that I failed to turn up for lectures and tutorials. Oh, for goodness' sake. If something comes up which means I'm a teeny bit late or miss a day here and there, what's the problem?

Hah! Where's the support the university is supposed to offer its staff when they have problems at home? And, boy, do I have problems at home. They'd be shocked if they knew the truth: that their star lecturer, Miss Goody Lee Harper, wrecked my life by stealing my husband.

Ex-husband.

She probably knew that plonker Heron was going to sack me. What she didn't know – and what I'd been meaning to tell her – was that Dad's business had gone belly up, which meant the end of my allowance. I was flat broke.

But she was so full of her own news about her and Dan.

I told her to sod off and threw my mobile – with some force – across the room where it hit the wall with a thunk. Even in my emotional state, I realised that wasn't a sensible thing to do. I picked it up, but, of course, it had switched itself off and wouldn't come back on. So I threw it down on the oak wood floor with as much force as possible and then, for good measure, stamped on it.

The thing was completely buggered.

So, sacked and humiliated by my ex-husband and ex-best friend, I'd spent the last four days numb, deadened further by the endless stream of tedium that is daytime and weekend TV.

I hardly moved. I limped from bed to sofa and back again, refusing to answer the landline. The thought of going into town to replace my mobile was beyond me. Barely eating, the days were relieved only by bottles of Sauvignon.

Waking this morning, my first instinct had been to go straight round to the studios and confront Dan.

My second was to ignore him and Lee, rise above it and get on with my life.

No chance. I went with the first instinct.

And now here I was, trapped in a black Jag with a man I'd always known as Duck's Arse going God knows where.

'Well,' he said, smiling kindly. 'Dan and I are friends, we talk, you know, and he's told me a lot about what's been going on over the last few days. I saw you in reception and knew straight away something was up.'

'What on earth do you mean?'

'Your body language. Do you think I'm daft? Anyone could tell you were angry, and I'm afraid whatever I think of Dan – or of you – I'm not having a nuclear explosion in one of my newsrooms. I mean, that's what you were planning, wasn't it? A showdown with my main presenter?'

'Oh.' I glanced down. Guilt written all over my face.

'Never mind, love,' he said, playfully nudging me on the arm. 'Come and have some lunch, and let's see how the world looks after a decent bottle or two of Chablis.'

CHAPTER 6

LEE

'I think it's time I got my own key,' Dan said as he swept past me into the hall, dumping his briefcase next to the umbrella stand.

Oh! I hadn't thought about that.

'It's ridiculous I have to knock on the door to be let into my own home.'

His home? I shut the door and followed him into the kitchen where he extracted a couple of wine glasses from a cupboard and filled them both with a bottle from the fridge.

'I didn't know you thought of this place as home.'

He passed me a glass – the one, I noticed, that was slightly less full – and wrapped his spare arm around my shoulders. 'Of course,' he said. 'Home is where the heart is.'

He went to drop a kiss on the top of my head, but I shrugged him off. Things were moving a bit fast; I was still coming to terms with being in love with my best friends' ex without moving him in lock, stock and barrel. Especially as, Dan's demand for a key to the door notwithstanding, we weren't near as loved-up as you might expect. Shame Teri didn't answer my telephone calls or respond to my text messages. She'd have loved – absolutely loved – how many of our rows duplicated ones she'd had with Dan. Like the one about shifting our status from semi-regular stopovers to fully-fledged cohabitees.

We'd been skirting around the issue for a couple of weeks since Dan first suggested buying a house together. I was cooking dinner – all our best discussions seem to start in the kitchen – when Dan first mooted the idea.

'Why?' I'd asked, opening the oven door to baste the chicken.

'Don't you think it's time?'

No, I didn't. Yes, I thought Dan might well be THE ONE but he'd already had two other halves, and while I had my fingers crossed it was three times lucky, I wasn't burning my boats yet. Where would Teri have been, for instance, if she'd done as Dan suggested and sold her precious duplex to buy somewhere bigger so there was more space for his daughter? Homeless, that's where.

Besides, the ink had barely dried on their wedding certificate before the marriage was declared null and void.

'That's wasn't my fault,' Dan pointed out.

True, but who's to say someone better wouldn't come along for me too?

He looked hurt.

'I'm not suggesting I'm looking for anyone else,' I said hastily.

'But you haven't ruled it out?'

Oh, for goodness' sake. 'I just don't think we should rush things. Look where that got you and Teri.'

He couldn't argue with that – although he tried. 'I just thought since I stop here most nights…'

Now he mentioned it… 'It might be nice if we gave ourselves some space now and again.'

That went down like a lead balloon.

Yes, Teri might well be enjoying the moral high ground, but, by not answering my phone calls, she was also depriving herself of multiple opportunities to say 'I told you so…' and 'Serve you right.'

It was a bit rich though – Teri objecting because I'd nicked *her* bloke. How many times had she done that to me?

Except, of course, the Teri and Dan show was long dead and buried before I came on the scene, and, if I'd ruled out all Teri's ex-lovers and boyfriends as potential love interests, I'd have been fishing in a very small pool. So small, in fact, the only fish left in the water would have been Mike Orme, my immediate boss and deputy dean at the university. Teri wouldn't have touched him with a bargepole. Sadly, I'd had less sense. But, that's all water under the bridge and the bargepole with it.

Dan interrupted my musing. 'So,' he said, raising his wine glass, 'a toast to us and new beginnings.'

Pardon?

'We'll get a key cut at the weekend.'

What?

'And a spare one for Victoria?'

I choked into my wine. Steady on! It was, perhaps, time to give Dan a key but his daughter? Now that was a step too far.

Dan clapped my back. 'Are you all right?'

I thrust my glass at him. 'I need a re-fill.'

He opened the fridge and removed another bottle. 'Okay, but go easy, you shouldn't drink too much before supper.'

Supper! I don't care what they call the evening meal in TV La-La Land; in my Yorkshire kitchen, it's dinner!

I took the roasting pan out of the oven – chicken again – and hurled the par-boiled potatoes alongside the bird, sending little splatters of fat flying.

Dan sniffed appreciatively. 'Smells divine.'

'No, it doesn't,' I snapped. 'It smells like a perfectly nicely roasted piece of meat. Only God is divine.'

'Semantics,' he said.

Pah!

He settled himself on a bar stool. 'Anything I can do?'

Make yourself a little less at home?

I stirred the red onion gravy, releasing little wafts of deep, sweet balsamic vinegar.

Oh, why was I being such a moody cow? I'd been lucky enough to meet a lovely guy who clearly thought I was the bee's knees and I was getting my knickers in a twist because he wanted to spend more – not less – time with me? It didn't make sense.

'Yes,' I said. 'The dishwasher needs unloading.'

He grimaced. 'I'm still not sure where everything goes.'

'Time to find out,' I suggested.

If he wanted squatter's rights and a key to the door it was time to start pulling his weight domestically.

If it was a test – and, yes, I think it was – he passed with flying colours. Teri had often grumbled at his inability to perform the simplest domestic tasks. Now, she wouldn't have recognised him. Every pot, pan and plate back in its rightful place. I wondered what she'd think of the new, improved Dan? It would probably add further fuel to her beautiful dreams of a romantic reconciliation.

Well, she couldn't have him. I might still be struggling to adapt to having a man permanently about the house but, next time we spoke, I'd tell her she could whistle. Her plans for a re-match were so 'pie in the sky' they didn't even rank as pipe dreams.

Silly me. I couldn't tell her. She wasn't answering the phone.

CHAPTER 7

TERI

The convention was being held at the King's Hotel in the centre of town. As Jim pulled up by the entrance, Duck's Arse leaned forward in his seat. 'Go enjoy yourself for a couple of hours, Jim. I'll ring you when Teri's ready to be collected.'

'Right, boss,' Jim said, touching his right temple with an index finger.

'Do all your chauffeurs salute you?' I asked after we'd got out and shut the car doors. Duck's Arse placed an arm across my back to usher me up the short flight of steps to the hotel entrance.

'Hah!' he said. 'Jim's an old mate.' But he didn't elaborate.

The dining room was buzzing. There must have been about a hundred people, some in suits, but many in jeans or chinos with sweatshirts or tee shirts – the television-type combo, I assumed. When I turned to take a proper look, I realised Duck's Arse was wearing a well-cut suit with a crisp, pale-blue shirt and what looked like expensive lace-up leather brogues. He caught my glance. 'Do I scrub up okay?' he said, grinning.

'I was thinking I'm not dressed for this.' I'd put on my new red JK Fennick dress and had taken even more care than usual with my hair and make-up. If you're going to have a showdown, you must look your best. And be in red.

'You look pretty fantastic to me,' he said, his eyes moving slowly up and down my body in the way men do with me.

I'd actually been thinking I was over-dressed for what was a television-types gab-fest. But best not to say anything.

We sat at a round table for eight, and Duck's Arse introduced me to the head of regional digitisation, the head of mediatronics, the head of something else with another nonsense job title and others whose titles I didn't get but who were all full of themselves.

But it was strange how, as the levels in the bottles of Chablis went down, conversational interest went up and I found myself joining in with talk about viewer-receptivity and multi-audience agencies.

I was enjoying myself.

My humiliating sacking from the University of Central Yorkshire four days ago seemed a world away.

Duck's Arse was clearly host at our table as he kept reaching for the bottles and refilling everyone's glasses. Mine especially.

'Right,' he said, lifting an arm and placing it around the back of my chair. He nudged heavily against me so that I could feel the weight of his body. I stared straight ahead, fearing what he was going to do or say. The warmth from his face inched closer, and for a moment I thought he was going to nibble my neck. Instead, he breathed into my ear and said in a low whisper, 'Got to earn my keep. Stay here. Back soon.' He stood, sprinted to a low platform at the top of the room and leapt up the two small steps with an energy that was unexpected in a man not only the wrong side of plump, but who'd polished off the best part of a bottle of white wine.

'Okay, you people,' he said authoritatively into a mic handed to him by a be-jeaned minion. 'The conference starts at two – in five minutes – so I want you all to make your way to the Majestic Room where Mike Rowhampton, head of regional digitisation will give the keynote address…'

Mike Rowhampton, sitting opposite me, jolted. 'What…?' He shot a look at Duck's Arse then quickly back at the wine cooler in the centre of the table as though the empty and upturned bottle of Chablis inside would offer answers, if not inspiration.

Duck's Arse strode back to our table, and before he had chance to sit, Mike Rowhampton launched into him. 'Bloody hell, Dick. I thought you were doing the keynote address.'

Duck's Arse reached into an inside pocket of his suit jacket, pulled out a folded wad of A4 paper and handed it to Mike across the table. 'It's all on here,' he said, smiling as though he was enjoying a private joke. 'Just

read it. You'll be fine.'
'But you're coming in, aren't you?'
'No,' said Duck's Arse. 'Something's come up.'

CHAPTER 8

LEE

'You're a scaredy-cat,' Teri rebuked once when I'd been dithering about something she considered inconsequential – like losing my virginity to the bloke who, at the time, I thought was the love of my life. 'And scaredy-cats never get what they want.'

'But I like to make sure I know what I want,' I said.

Which as it turned out wasn't the bloke in question because he slept with Teri first, and there was no way my bits were going near his bits if they'd been near her bits.

And, yes, Teri had definitely been an elephant in the bedroom the first time I slept with Dan. I kept wondering if…no, better not go there.

It had taken a lot of positive thinking though to erase mental pictures of the pair of them naked together, kissing and stuff, and there were still moments when I felt a bit inhibited. Teri's fluffer story is indelibly printed on my psyche.

Perhaps it would have been different if my own most recent sexual relationship with Mike Orme had been less of a disaster? Not that there was any comparison between the two men – Dan didn't own a single knitted waistcoat – but I'd rushed into taking things too far, too quickly with Mike and was in no hurry to repeat my mistakes.

Apart from one: when I first met Dan I'd just discovered I was pregnant with Mike's child. Under pressure, I'd had an abortion – a decision I'd been regretting ever since.

Dan offered a second shot at motherhood. Or, he might have done had he been so inclined.

'No,' he said when I first broached the subject. It was his turn to cook and while the lasagne, which he'd made a couple of days beforehand, warmed in the oven he was mashing garlic and parsley and unsalted butter together to spread on slices of thick Italian ciabatta. 'I do think garlic bread goes nicely with lasagne,' he said, slathering the cut slices with the butter mix.

I poked at his burgeoning belly. 'Steady on,' I said. 'Beware middle-aged spread.'

He sucked in his tummy. 'I'm feeling a little bloated today. Too much mineral water at lunch.'

'Not like you to admit to being full of gas and hot air,' I teased.

He laughed and feinted with the garlicky knife. 'Hussy!'

'So,' I said, as he turned his attention back to the ciabatta, 'what do you think?'

'I think,' he said carefully, 'that you don't know what you're asking.'

How stupid. Of course I knew what I was asking.

'Wouldn't a dog do instead?' he suggested.

'No, it wouldn't.'

'Finlay Baxter, one of the younger reporters, has just bought a labradoodle. He says they're very affectionate and don't smell too much.'

Oh well, if Finlay Baxter recommends them…

'Good with children too.'

That's settles it, we'll get a labradoodle to play with the children we don't have.

'No,' I said.

He finished wrapping the ciabatta in aluminium foil and popped it on the bottom shelf of the oven. 'But why not? Baxter says they're no trouble at all.'

I picked up the buttery knife and bowl and opened the dishwasher. 'Define no trouble.'

Dan shrugged. I've noticed he does that a lot when he's not one hundred per cent confident he's on solid ground.

'Well, they don't need much exercise,' he offered.

I closed the dishwasher and, pulling my mobile phone from the back pocket of my jeans, tapped in a question. 'How much exercise is not too much?' I asked Dan.

'I don't know!'

I did. I'd just Googled labradoodle: thirty to sixty minutes a day. 'Need to be mentally and physically stimulated,' I read aloud, 'or may become destructive and hard-to-handle.' I waved the phone under his nose. 'See for yourself.'

He swatted the phone aside. 'We'd just have to take it for plenty of longs walks.' He was determined to think positive. 'And it would do us both good to get a bit more exercise.'

Speak for yourself. Personally, I thought I got more than enough exercise, especially as Daddy had recently decided he wasn't working up enough of a sweat with his golf and thrice-weekly games of squash so had added jogging to his itinerary. And, worse, co-opted me to join his pre-golf Saturday-morning five-mile circuit of the back lanes where he and Mammy lived.

I hated it. I hated getting up at seven on a Saturday morning to drive over to his and Mammy's house. I hated every single blasted step of the interminable circuit. And I hated Daddy beating me home every time. 'It's my asthma,' I panted on the steps of the house after the first run.

'Excuses,' Daddy said, shutting the door in my face as he went in to shower and change before golf. So, I went home and, still stinking of stale sweat, undressed and crawled back into bed and didn't get up again until I felt more like a human being, albeit a rather smelly one, and less like a washed-out old rag.

But not too washed out to try for a baby. Dan though had other ideas. 'You could take the dog with you when you go running with your dad,' he suggested helpfully.

'Don't be stupid.'

Well, no point beating about the bush. But he wasn't the only one to have an idea or two. 'Of course, if we had a baby I could get one of those all-terrain buggies and take the baby for a breath of fresh air…'

He picked up a newspaper and, spreading it out on the breakfast bar, pretended not to hear.

I put my phone back in my pocket. Okay, I'd leave it for now but, just one more thing… 'Who the hell is Finlay Baxter when he's at home?'

CHAPTER 9

TERI

Blame the Chablis, but during lunch when Duck's Arse had stepped off that platform, strode back to our table and put poor Mike Rowhampton on the spot, I realised how powerful this man was. Okay, Ridings Today was only a tin-pot regional station, but Richard Walker was MD and very much in charge.

When he waved off his colleagues as they left the dining room for their no doubt scintillating conference, he turned to me and said quietly and confidently, 'Let's you and I go somewhere else.'

There was no question in his voice; just authority. He'd decided that's what we were going to do. There's something about the presence of a man who knows what he wants, and Richard had that presence and he wanted me.

With Declan, sex had been fast, frantic and furious. It was a passionate love affair that often started in the hallway of my duplex apartment and ended in disaster.

With Dan, our first encounter had been a flop – quite literally. Dan, poor sap, had been so psychologically screwed up by his scheming cow of an ex-wife that he couldn't perform. It took a lot of patience on my part to get things moving again.

Plump and podgy Richard? You would expect this man, who looked like an overgrown school kid, to be a fumbling boy scout on his first physical encounter. But the softness of his belly, the chubby jowls and the width of his chest were a surprising delight to nestle into and the man's approach to sex was the same: soothing, gentle, quiet and slow.

Well, what a pleasant surprise.

CHAPTER 10

TERI

It was a strangely relaxing afternoon. Blame the Chablis – I did that before, I know. Blame Richard's plump and comforting body, but we had gentle podgy sex with much snuffling and other equally delightful contented noises. God! What was wrong with me? This was not the sort of man I fancied.

There was none of the frantic yelping that Declan and I had engaged in. There was none of the familiarity I had with Dan.

Richard and I had quiet, comfortable sex. I couldn't believe it. And then we slept and when I awoke he was making me a cup of tea. Tea!

'There's Earl Grey, if you'd rather,' he said, standing totally at ease in his nakedness beside the hotel's courtesy kettle, waving what I could see even from the bed was a pale sachet of weak witch's piss.

'Ugh! No.' Reminds me too much of that duplicitous cow Lee Harper, who drank nothing but the feeble stuff. 'And be careful with that kettle,' I warned as steam started to cloud perilously close to his naked, plump buttocks.

We sat side by side in bed, drinking tea until Richard glanced at the bedside table, reached for his watch and said, 'Oh, shit. It's six o'clock.' He turned back to me. 'Sorry, damn. Got to go. But you don't have to rush. The room's paid for – stay the night if you want or I'll ask Jim to come and collect you.'

I'd nothing to go home for. 'I might just stay here,' I said. 'Will you be coming back?'

'Sorry. Can't,' he said.

I assumed he was rushing back home to his wife; although, thinking about it, I'd never heard mention of a Mrs Walker.

Perhaps she was one of those shy, introverted types who didn't have a social life. More likely she was one of those inverted snobs who claimed to hate television and everything to do with it. They say things like, 'I never watch anything on TV…' then go on to tell you who's doing what to whom on *Celebrity Big Brother*.

Going to Ridings Today functions would be beneath a woman like Mrs Walker. She'd prefer to spend her days with her horses and the county set in rural North Yorkshire rather than have anything to do with the part of life that provided the money and lifestyle she enjoyed.

Momentarily, I felt sorry for Richard having a wife like that.

But he was busy tapping into his phone. 'Jim? Yeah…can you pick me up outside the King's in about five minutes…yeah. Thanks, mate.'

He climbed out of bed and dressed quickly – for a plump man he was nimble. He strode over to the wardrobe door mirror to tweak his hair. It went straight up into the duck's arse. No gel. That was surprising.

Finally ready, he leaned over the bed to where I was lying back against the pillows. He seemed about to say something but decided against, planted a kiss on my cheek and was gone.

As the hotel room door shut, I wondered what had just happened. Yes, I know. I should have asked questions.

As I lay in a deep, hot bath, I reasoned it had been a one-off, fuelled by a good lunch and far too much wine.

Richard was obviously married – to the North Yorkshire, county-set woman – but had the occasional fling, paid for a hotel room, then disappeared in a puff of Jim-driven Jaguar fumes.

Knowing my track record, what did I expect?

I dressed and, feeling hungry, picked up the room service menu. But the thought of eating alone in a hotel room was too sad even for me in my sad state.

Maybe I'd go downstairs to the bar and have a drink and a snack there.

I wasn't sure if Richard had left an open tab for me, so I checked my purse. I had about ten pounds. My final salary would be going in the bank at the end of the month, but after that, what?

The week's other little bombshell – along with my sacking and my ex-best friend stealing my ex-husband – had been Dad's telephone call.

His steel business, which had kept us financially secure since I was a little girl, was bankrupt thanks to his complete incompetency and a scheming manager's fraudulent activity.

That, my sacking and Lee's sneaky behaviour with Dan meant the knife was firmly stuck in my professional and private life.

I thought I had enough cash for a small wine and maybe a burger, and made my way downstairs.

The bar was all but deserted apart from a bartender talking to a young man sitting on a stool with his back to the room. Even though I couldn't see his face, there was something familiar about him: the closely cropped, black hair, the white tracksuit bottoms, the box-fresh trainers tucked around the stool legs, the long, lean fingers cradling a pint glass of pale liquid.

The bartender stopped mid-polish and motioned to the young man who turned on his stool. 'Oh…' he said, his eyebrows puckering as he focussed on me.

I ignored his pained expression – not the usual reaction I get from men – because I'd recognised him.

'It's Shayne Brickham isn't it?' I said.

'Er…' He clearly didn't remember me, but something had unsettled him.

'We met at Ridings Today. You were being interviewed by my husband – ex-husband – Dan Caine. You're a footballer, aren't you?'

The bartender barked out a mocking 'Hah!' as though I'd uttered some banality. 'Only the best player the Jukes've ever had,' the little squirt said, nodding at Shayne.

'Oh, sorry. I don't know much about football.' I slid onto the stool next to Shayne.

'S'all right.' Shayne leaned back and eyed me warily.

'The Jukes are the main team in the city,' the bartender said, failing to keep the sarcasm from his tone. I gave him what I hoped he'd see as an evil-eyed look.

Turning to Shayne, I tapped the side of his glass with an extended index finger. 'And are you supposed to be drinking?' I asked teasingly.

'Eh? Oh this. It's lime juice,' he said. 'Can't drink when I'm training.'

'And are you training tonight?'

'Supposed to be.'

'Bit late for training,' I said, looking at my watch and seeing it was nearly seven-thirty.

'What're you, my manager?' Shayne said, rather sharply.

'Oh sorry…'

Shayne shook his head. 'Nah, sorry love. It's me. A bit tense. We lost on Saturday and me manager blames me –'

The bartender jumped in. 'It wasn't your fault. It was that bloody penalty –'

'Own goal, more like.' Shayne faced me and added hesitantly, 'So I'm taking t'night off. Are you my date?'

Lightening responses flashed through my brain. After the extraordinary events of the last few days, could I simply say yes and go on to have what would probably turn out to be a drunken, sexually active and fun night with an up-and-coming, very fit footballer who was at least twenty-five years younger than me?

I took the sensible option. 'No, love,' I said, hoping not to disappoint the poor boy. 'I'm here with someone else. Or, rather, I was here with someone else.'

Blow me, but he looked relieved. 'It's just that me mates have set me up on a blind date,' he said. 'And she's supposed to be wearing a red dress.'

I looked down at my JK Fennick dress. 'Oh…I see. And you thought…'

'Yeah, but you're old – I mean older. She's only about nineteen.'

Well, thanks, Shayne.

I suddenly felt tired – and old. I wanted to go back to my duplex. 'Well, nice talking to you, Shayne.' I rose. 'Have a nice date.'

'Yeah, thanks, love.'

I returned to the room to check I'd not left anything, closed the door and headed down to reception to hand in the key. 'Not staying?' the receptionist enquired.

'No. Thank you,' I said. 'But could you call me a taxi? I'll wait in the foyer.' Might as well spend my last tenner on a cab.

I sat on a well-stuffed sofa opposite the foyer doors and watched as people came in and out.

Then a flash of red on the pavement outside caught my eye. Something familiar about the figure striding up the steps. Something determined about the woman as she pushed open one of the glass-fronted doors.

Something icy ran through my body.

She stopped in front of me. 'Teri,' she said, her eyes wide as though she'd seen something she'd rather not.

'Victoria.'

CHAPTER 11

LEE

'Don't go,' Dan said, curling his fingers around mine as I reluctantly unpeeled myself from under the duvet. He peppered my hand with butterfly kisses. 'Stay and have a little bed boogie.'

Bed boogie? Talk about gilding the lily.

'It'll only take a minute,' he cajoled, voice growly with desire.

Gee whizz, only a minute? Some inducement.

He sucked my fingers. 'Or maybe a little bit longer.'

I bent to kiss his forehead, citrus and sandalwood from yesterday's aftershave teasing my nostrils.

'It had better be a good bit more than a minute,' I said, wrapping my arms around his neck.

Later, while Dan was downstairs making a post-coital cuppa, I wondered how Teri would react if she knew that every time I got between the sheets with Dan I had to mentally kick her out of the bedroom? 'Perhaps we need to practise more often,' I said aloud.

'Practise what?' Dan asked, placing the two mugs on the dressing table.

So, I told him, and he said he'd be happy to oblige anytime. 'In fact, no time like the present.' And before I could say a word, he was hunkered back under the duvet and, in next to no time, the tea was stone cold.

'Shall I make another cup?' Dan asked.

I leapt out of bed. 'No, I'm already late.'

'Late for what?'

'Teri,' I shouted from the bathroom. 'I'm going to doorstep her.'

He propped himself against the door jamb. 'Why?'

I massaged coconut and almond shampoo into my hair and tried to think of a good answer. 'Because…' I said eventually.

'Exactly,' he said. 'There is no reason.' He shook his head. 'I wish you'd let it go.'

Which was an unfortunate phrase because the princess from *Frozen* immediately popped into my head and the refrain 'Let it go, let it go' echoed around the bathroom.

'I can't,' I said.

Dan rolled his eyes. 'Please yourself,' and he stomped down the stairs. 'I'm having a cup of tea.'

Dan's delays meant I was on the wrong side of the rush-hour traffic – a mollusc with purpose could have travelled faster. Stop-start, stop-start; sandwiched between a bus belching dirty diesel fumes and impatient commuters gesticulating and honking horns at one another, I inched towards Teri's duplex.

Inevitably, my mind started wandering. Teri, I reckoned, would be tickled pink that she was casting a long shadow over my bedroom – although she might not be quite so happy that I thought of her as the *elephant* in the corner.

The driver behind me flashed his lights; the traffic ahead was on the move. I waggled my fingers in thanks and pulled forward a couple of paces. Hardly worth the effort.

It was raining slightly and the wiper blades made an ugly rasping noise as they swiped backwards and forwards. I'd get Dan to have a look at them when I got home. Thinking of Dan reminded me of Teri and elephants. She might, just about, appreciate the irony. After all, there's barely enough flesh on her to cover a miniature poodle let alone a pint-sized *Dumbo*. But she'd definitely be distinctly huffy that I'd used her name and elephant in the same sentence. And then she'd ask, 'If I'm an elephant, what are you, a f***ing Tyrannosaurus Rex?'

A rhetorical question, since she *must* know T-Rex was dead and buried twenty-five million years-or-so before the elephant started swinging its trunk across pre-historic swamps. And, if she didn't know? Well, I'd just *have* to tell her, which she wouldn't like because she hates it when my 'head gets stuck up its know-it-all butt-hole'.

The driver behind honked – a long angry blast. Oops! Sorry, I waved in apology and, releasing the handbrake, moved forward the tiniest distance. Not even an elephant's length. Mr Bad Tempered shook two fingers in reply. How rude.

Back to Teri...once we'd agreed to disagree about the historical disconnect between dinosaurs and elephants, I felt fairly certain she'd rub my nose in the fact that a) I was several dress sizes larger than her and that b) sleeping with your best friend's ex was a recipe for a relationship mash-up.

So, of course, I'd have to point out that my dress size was irrelevant and, if by some gigantic leap of imagination it did have any bearing on the case, being an English dress size fourteen didn't make one a mammoth. Not by a long way.

I'd also remind her that the size gap wouldn't be half as great if she had the body of a normal woman rather than a concentration camp escapee.

The traffic lights were green again and, before Mr Bad Tempered could remind me, I slipped into gear and drove, oh, at least three car lengths before, once more, coming to a standstill. I looked in my rear view mirror; Mr Bad Tempered was huffing and puffing at a cyclist who was trying to steal up on the nearside. Good luck to the poor chap. I wouldn't risk life and limb on a push bike in this traffic.

I smiled to myself imagining Teri's outrage at the suggestion she'd benefit from a little more meat on her bones. She'd dance a furious tango that would make Mr Bad Tempered look almost mild-mannered.

Now how would she respond? I glanced again in the driver's mirror. Mr Bad Tempered was trying to head off the cyclist by inching nearer towards the kerb. Yes, attack was the best form of defence. No doubt Teri would take great delight in quoting the sixth commandment: 'Thou shalt not commit adultery.'

And, then we'd argue about whether sleeping with Dan was technically adultery since he and Teri were long divorced before we even had our first kiss. I'd tell her that in my opinion he was a free agent, and she'd spout some stuff about me being Catholic and, therefore, by definition, anti-divorce and that would segue-way into a discussion about whether Dan was even married in the eyes of the Church since his marriage to Teri had been a register office affair and his first wedding to Victoria's mother Sara had been conducted in a non-Catholic church.

Which hopefully would shut her up.

Not for long though. Knowing Teri, she'd come full circle and say I wouldn't be getting all worked up about elephants in bedrooms if I hadn't already conceded the moral high ground.

And round and round we'd go again.

Except, of course, I'd finally reached Teri's doorstep and was sitting there, watching her windows for signs of life and gripping the steering wheel so tightly it was a miracle it didn't snap. I'd lost count of how many times I'd rehearsed my introduction and Teri's reply and my reply to her reply and her reply to… Round and round it went in my head – I said, she said, I replied, she retorted…nothing ever resolved. I could imagine away until the cows came home but unless, and until, we actually had a face-to-face conversation, we'd both be minus the best friend either of us ever had.

Loins finally girded, I let myself into her apartment building using the spare key she gave me ages ago, and which she'd certainly have demanded back if she'd remembered I still had it. Which reminds me, I think she still has a spare key to my house?

There was no answer when I rang the bell and a quick squint through the letter box at the mail piled up behind the door confirmed there was no-one at home. I *could* have use my key to open the door but, somehow, it's one thing to enter uninvited into a communal building and quite another to take up residency on Teri's settee.

This sort of explains why I ended up sitting on her doorstep, knees hunched, back against the wall. Sooner or later she had to come home. Good job I brought sandwiches and a flask of tea – weak Earl Grey, of course – my iPad, a copy of *The Guardian* and my knitting bag because I was parked there nearly all day.

CHAPTER 12

TERI

It was just as well I didn't stay at the King's for a drink. Just imagine the scene had I been tucking into a burger with Shayne Brickham as Victoria – the child from hell – walked in.

Victoria is Dan's daughter, his priceless little princess and a thoroughly spoilt brat.

She was the only child from Dan's first marriage to the grasping Sara, a real piece of work who used sex as a voucher system in that Dan got to have a voucher (sex) if Sara was in a good mood. Trouble was, her good moods were linked to life's treats and luxuries, which Dan, even on his television presenter's salary, found hard to provide.

By the time Victoria was ten, sex between her parents was limited to Christmas, but after Sara had a miscarriage, it stopped completely. When Dan and I got together, Sara had so thoroughly screwed up Dan that he suffered sexual PTSD. It took some patience – and some knowledge of the work of a fluffer – to help him start performing again.

I suppose it was because both parents felt so guilty about their own relationship that they lavished everything on Victoria. And she didn't want anything upsetting her gravy train. So, when I came on the scene, she did her best to break up Dan and me. She would be forever texting her daddy, wanting to know where we were and what we were doing, demanding to see him, insisting he came to watch her ridiculous school concerts, or begging him to buy her the latest Smartphone or take her on holiday. And he, poor sap, fell for it every time to the extent of cancelling dates with me because darling little Victoria wanted him to do something else. Although I was invited to go to whatever teenage nonsense she dreamt up, I refused. There was no way I was going along with her game.

And there she was, striding into the King's in a red dress, intent on hooking up with one of football's promising, young newcomers clearly out for a shag and becoming a WAG.

The grimace of embarrassment on her face as she came into the hotel foyer and saw me was priceless. I could just imagine the thoughts whirring through her tiny brain.

'Nice dress,' I said, eyeing her up and down. 'Meeting someone?'

'Yes, as a matter of fact,' she said, pulling her features into what she hoped was confident superiority.

'Oh, you're not Shayne's blind date, are you?' I put just enough of a mocking tone in my voice to unsettle her.

'Oh…er…'

Yes, that unsettled her.

'Don't worry, dear,' I said, standing and heading for the foyer doors. 'I've known Shayne for ages…and I know all about his *little* blind dates.' I swept past her, glancing over my shoulder to give a cruel laugh. 'Enjoy,' I said.

Just as well I didn't have that burger as I wouldn't have had the taxi fare home.

CHAPTER 13

LEE

I'd read the newspaper from cover-to-cover, sports pages included, and was concentrating on picking up the heel stitches on one of the socks I was knitting as a Christmas present for my father – when I heard the tippity tip-tap of a pair of impossibly high heels and the sound of someone uttering a short laugh, which sounded like, 'Hah!' Bloody miracle she could walk a step, let alone climb two flights of stairs. I jumped up to confront her. Correction, I attempted to jump up but my knees couldn't take the strain, and I ended up in an undignified scramble to look her in the eye.

Just as well I wasn't expecting a warm welcome. 'What the bloody hell are you doing here?' She swayed ever so slightly. It was either the heels or…

'Have you been drinking?'

'None of your sodding business,' she snapped, propping one shoulder against the doorpost while she hunted for her keys.

I folded my arms and waited. She growled and continued digging through the handbag detritus. Funny, she's obsessively tidy in every other area of her life, spends a small fortune on designer totes, yet her bags are a cess pool of dog-eared receipts, half-used lipsticks, grungy eye liner and bleeding ball points.

She gave the bag a vicious shake and flung it at me. 'I can't find the bloody keys.'

I peered into the murky depths, not sure I really wanted to start rooting around in there. "Oh, for goodness' sake,' she snarled, grabbing the bag and upending the contents. The keys rattled to the ground. She knelt to pick them up and, after placing one hand on the lobby carpet, made to push herself upright. And collapsed back on her heels.

'I can't get up,' she giggled.

She held out a hand. 'You're drunk,' I said, hauling her to her feet.

'I am not,' she enunciated rather too carefully for someone who was stone-cold sober. 'Or rather,' she amended, 'I was a little bit squiffy at lunchtime, but I'm perfectly all right now.'

She made a futile stab at the Yale lock. 'Oops,' she said, dangling the bunch of keys. 'I don't think I'm going to be able to do this.'

I took the keys and let her in, and she wobbled into the hallway, jerking her head in the direction of the handbag debris. 'Could you get that lot for me?'

She didn't wait for an answer. Instead, she slipped out of her shoes and made her way carefully into the living room where she flopped onto the sofa and wriggled her toes. 'Oh,' she sighed. 'That feels good.'

I dropped her tote on the coffee table.

'Thank you,' she said. I thought I detected a note of sarcasm. 'I'd ask what brings you here, but I can guess.'

Good, that would save a bit of time.

She waved a hand vaguely in the direction of the kitchen. 'I suppose you'd like a glass of wine?'

Silly question.

'I don't have any chilling in the fridge, but you'll find a couple of bottles in the wine rack.'

Great. I love lukewarm wine.

'I'm afraid I haven't got any of that Muscadet muck you drink,' she called as I rinsed out a couple of glasses. 'But there's a rather nice Chardonnay. Or a Sauvignon.'

Nice and Chardonnay are not words that belong in the same sentence. I opened the Sauvignon Blanc instead and poured two large servings.

'Chuck a couple of ice cubes into each glass,' Teri suggested. 'It'll take the edge off.'

I could see where this evening was heading.

CHAPTER 14

∽

TERI

I was still giggling to myself as the taxi pulled into the car park in front of my duplex. I was even happily muttering something about Victoria being a stupid little cow as I climbed the stairs to my front door. I could use the lift, but find a bit of exercise does wonders for the glutes.

So pleased with myself remembering the look of embarrassment on Victoria's face, I even uttered a happy 'Hah!' as I reached my floor. So it was something of a shock to see a bundle sitting, head bowed, leaning against my front door.

The bundle raised its head.

'Lee?' I said. 'What the bloody hell...?'

'Ah, Teri…' She scrabbled to her feet, dropping a knitting needle and big ball of blue wool, and knocking over her bag so that a Thermos flask and a book fell out.

She studied me closely then accused me of having been drinking.

I glared. She muttered something about trying to get hold of me and me not answering calls.

It crossed my mind to say I didn't know how she'd the nerve to come round here, but the concern on her face and the sight as she ducked to shovel together wool, needles, flask and book irritated more than angered me.

Lee followed me into the apartment and immediately set to work looking for some wine. How that girl can drink.

I wasn't sure what I had in – I'd drunk a few bottles during my 'lost' weekend. I could hear her scrabbling around in the kitchen and then saying something about a bottle of warm Chardonnay.

'Oh, put some ice cubes in it,' I said impatiently, kicking off my shoes and dropping on to the sofa.

I regretted smashing my mobile phone. All my contacts were on it – not that there were that many I wanted to stay in touch with: double-dealing Dan, plonker Heron, damn David Greenspan or any of those other deceitful idiots from university. I'd have added Lee-treacherous-Harper to the list but, as she was busy sorting out the wine, I had to talk to her.

I felt lost without the Smartphone lighting up with texts and calls. I pulled myself up from the sofa and padded in my stockinged feet to the hallway where the landline sat on a distressed cream side table. It had rung several times over the weekend, but I'd been in depression mode and hadn't bothered answering it.

Now it was blinking with five answerphone messages.

I knew most of them would be from Lee Goody-Goody Harper feeling guilty about wrecking my life.

I tapped the message button and, sure enough, there was Lee's voice. I hit delete without bothering to listen. The second message, also from Lee, also deleted. The third message. Lee. Delete. The fourth message, Declan. Oh God, no. Don't even go there, I told myself. Delete.

Declan, who had played his fancy games to get me into bed even though I'd been married to Dan. I'd never have left Dan if it hadn't been for that manipulative Irish bastard.

And once he'd had his fun, what did he do? Go back to his damn wife and all the little brats they'd spawned. And the wife, Marnie, had the temerity to warn me off; came waddling round to my duplex, six months' pregnant with bloody twins, to tell me – me! – to leave her precious husband alone.

I was so upset just thinking about that little encounter that when Lee came into the hallway proffering a glass of wine, I took it and knocked most of it back.

'Er, steady…' she said.

'I need it,' I told her. She gave me one of her doubtful but patient looks. The sort you'd give a recalcitrant elderly relative.

I couldn't do with Lee's moralising, which is one of the reasons I stopped myself from telling her about my encounter with Duck's Arse. Normally – before she stole my husband – I'd tell Lee everything. I mean, the poor girl had little in the way of a love life, and I think it gave her hope that if I could land so many men, she could too. And, guess what? She landed my husband. Ex-husband. Although what Dan sees in her with her leggings and knitting, I don't know.

And that's one reason why I didn't tell her about Little Miss Prissy Pants Victoria and her date with a super, studded footballer. I decided to hang on to that little nugget. It could be useful later.

'I'll just get this last message,' I said, indicating the answerphone. Lee nodded and went back into the lounge.

'Hi sis.' It was Charlie, and he hadn't called me 'sis' since we were children. This must be serious. 'I've tried your mobile, but it's switched off. So I'm ringing the landline. Can you ring me back?'

It was obviously about Dad's bombshell.

I'd never really understood the arrangements with the factory other than that our family lived off the profits. We'd all get a nice fat cheque every month, which paid my mortgage, kept my mother in booze at her one-bedroomed apartment in Lanzarote, helped Charlie run a smallholding in Suffolk with his boyfriend, Denis, and, no doubt, kept Dad in cheese and red wine in rural France.

What a family. We weren't what you'd call close.

When Dad retired to France a couple of years ago he left the running of the mill to his right-hand man, Edward Pranks. But Pranks had been dodgy dealing, draining the profits and the pension fund and had now disappeared. According to Dad, we were broke.

I dialled one-four-seven-one, and luckily the last number had been Charlie's so I was able to ring straight back. He answered immediately as though he'd been sitting by the phone and not tending the four goats he thought so much of.

His 'Hello?' was hesitant, questioning – and tearful.

'Hey, Charlie. It's me.'

'Oh, thank goodness you've rung,' he said and started crying.

'Come on, Charlie. It isn't that bad…' Although I couldn't think of much worse than losing one's trust fund and being completely broke.

'The police'll find Pranks and we'll get our money back…' The words were to reassure Charlie, but *I* wasn't convinced.

'Nurgh,' he said, spluttering through tears. 'It's not about that…'

What could be worse?

'Denis has left me.' And with that the sobs came louder.

Love's young dream had been so vibrant and alive in Suffolk nearly two years ago that Charlie hadn't been able to drag himself away to attend my wedding to Dan. He and Denis had taken delivery of the goats and couldn't leave them, apparently. Now, it seemed, I was confidante number one in the dream love stakes.

'What? Have you two had a row?'

'Oh, Teri,' he cried. 'It was awful. Philomena was pregnant, and Denis said to get the vet…'

'Philomena is a goat?'

'Yes, of course,' he was able to snap despite being heartbroken. He took a breath and went on. 'But I thought it was too early, and Denis was going to Norfolk to an allotment convention, and I said I'd stay with Philly, and he said, no, get the vet, but I didn't and…oh Teri…Philly died and Denis came home and blamed me and he's stormed out…'

'The goat died?'

'Yes,' he snapped again. 'There was a problem with the pregnancy. It was –'

'Agh, no. Spare me the details,' I interrupted. Anything to do with human pregnancy makes me heave. But goats? 'Surely it isn't that bad? Denis'll calm down and come back –'

'Oh no. He's taken the other goats…he's gone for good.'

'What? He's stormed off in a huff with three goats? How the hell did he do that?'

'He loaded them on to the trailer and said I wasn't to be trusted with them.' Charlie started wailing again.

'Well, where has he gone?'

'I…I…I don't know. Oh Teri…what shall I do?'

'Right.' Blame what had been happening over the last forty-eight hours: Dan, Lee, the sacking, being left penniless, Duck's Arse, seeing Victoria, because all I said was, 'I'm on my way.'

CHAPTER 15

LEE

Remind me never again to get in a car with Teri. Especially one she's hurtling down unfamiliar, narrow country lanes in driving rain when she's gagging for a drink.

Teri glanced left. 'Why are you clutching the edge of the seat like that?'

'Like what?'

'Like that.' She tapped my clenched fist. She tapped again. 'Look,' she said, 'your knuckles are blanched white.'

I shook her off. 'Keep your hands on the wheel.'

She raised an eyebrow. 'There's no need to shout.'

'And keep your eyes on the bloody road.'

'Ooh,' she taunted, waggling her fingers at the windscreen and poking her tongue in my direction.

I flicked her fingers aside. 'Don't be so bloody stupid. You haven't a clue where we're going, and I swear to God we've passed that pub at least twice already.'

She peered backwards. 'The Knife and Hand?'

'Yes, the Knife and Hand…will you watch the bloody road!'

'Perhaps we should stop at the next pub,' she said. 'I could kill a large glass of red, and you could do with something to calm your nerves.'

She'd got that right.

'I'd rather carry on,' I said. 'And I don't think it's a good idea to mix drinking and driving.'

'One wouldn't hurt,' she said. 'I think I deserve it. You've done nothing but whine ever since I picked you up.'

Not true. My teeth were gritted as tight shut as a redundant snow plough. It was the only way to stop myself from whimpering like a baby. We'd had our first near miss fifty yards from home when she pulled out in front of a big yellow school bus carrying half the neighbourhood's primary school kids. And the second came just minutes later when she overtook a tractor on a blind bend.

I was beginning to regret offering to come with Teri to Charlie's. It was one of those offers one sometimes makes in the sure and certain knowledge it will be rejected. But peace had barely been partially restored when Charlie rang and after she declared her intention of coming to his rescue in deepest, darkest Suffolk it seemed only natural to say 'You can't go on your own. I'll come too.' And, bugger me, she said yes. S***!

'It'll give us time to talk,' she said, rather ominously, I thought. I wasn't altogether sure talking would improve things between us, but she rang Charlie straight back to let him know he was getting two for the price of one. Of course, I couldn't hear his end of the conversation, but from what I could hear of Teri's responses, he didn't seem too keen.

'No, no, she won't be in the way,' she assured him.

More mumbling from Charlie.

'She can bunk down with me.' Teri grinned in my direction. 'And she won't mind if things are a bit higgledy-piggledy.'

What did that mean?

'And she's very easy to please.'

I might be, but fingers crossed things weren't too rough and ready, because nobody could describe Teri as anything other than pernickety.

Satisfied that Charlie was okay with his uninvited guest, she said her goodbyes and turned to me.

'And now I suppose you'll need to get permission from your lord and master.'

Who?

'Dan,' she said, rolling the wine glass between her fingers. 'He used to get very shirty if I wanted to go away for a night or two on my own.'

'Perhaps that had something to do with the fact you were usually gallivanting with lover boy, Declan?'

'Nonsense! He didn't find out about Declan until much, much later.'

It didn't seem worth pointing out that Dan wasn't a fool, and if he didn't *know* something was going on, he'd certainly had his suspicions. But I did anyway.

'Pshaw!' Teri said.

She was impatient to set off straight away, but I managed to talk her out of it.

'I don't have a spare pair of knickers.'

'I'll lend you…' She paused, clearly picturing me in her lacy, wispy derriere pieces of nothing. 'Okay, tomorrow morning. I'll pick you up at eight.'

Dan frowned and pursed his lips when I told him about the proposed jaunt. 'You'll regret it,' he predicted.

What did he mean? I'd been regretting it almost before the words 'I'll come too' were out of my mouth.

'I'll miss you,' he said, opening his arms for a hug. He smelt, as always, of citrus and sandalwood and powder-fresh deodorant. Inhaling deeply, I thought I might miss him too.

Teri, surprisingly, was bang on time – evidence, perhaps, of her missionary zeal to be a comfort and support to her brother.

'Haven't you got work to do?' she asked as I climbed into her car.

'Yes, but this is more important,' I told her, without adding that the students were on a reading week and, so long as I was on the end of a phone, I didn't need to be physically in the building.

I tried to relax, but there was a tense silence that lasted until Teri put on a seventies CD and we started singing along to 'Dancing Queen' and 'I Will Survive' and 'Maggie May'.

Just like the old days. Perhaps our friendship could do a Gloria Gaynor?

The atmosphere nose-dived again when we reached our destination – an ex-local authority semi-detached house in suburban Cambridgeshire.

'Oh,' Teri said when we'd knocked at the door and introduced ourselves to the householder, a granny in a pinny who couldn't have looked less like Teri's brother Charlie if she'd tried.

'It's the sat nav,' she said as we got back in the car. 'Wrong postcode.'

I'd worked that out.

'So what's the right postcode?'

No answer.

'Do you fancy a drink?' she asked eventually.

'I fancy reaching our destination more.'

'Slight problem,' she said.

You don't say?

'You know when I broke my phone –'

'Smashed it to smithereens.'

'When I broke my phone, I lost my address book as well.'

I knew what was coming next.

'I thought I remembered Charlie's address'– she gave a girly giggle –'but I remembered wrong, which is why we ended up here in lovely Cambridgeshire.'

Yes, but, lovely as it looked, it was also several dozen miles from where we wanted to be.

'Do you have Charlie's address?' I asked.

'Well,' she prevaricated. 'I have a rough idea.'

'I've got a rough idea,' I said. 'Somewhere in Suffolk.'

'At least we're agreed on that.'

She shuffled in her seat and turned the ignition key. 'So, which way to Suffolk?'

Hours later, after a brief stop for lunch when I'd flatly refused to allow Teri 'one for the road', we were still arguing.

'I'll bloody kill you if you don't slow down,' I said, looking at the speedometer. 'This is a thirty mile-per-hour zone.'

'Is it? I didn't see any road signs.'

'No? What about the great big number thirty on a bloody great pole stuck on the kerb-side back there?'

'Nope.' She shook her head. 'Missed it completely. Good job I've got you with me.'

At least one of us was happy.

The sat nav interrupted with instructions to prepare to turn left.

'Slow down,' I shrieked, one hand clasping the passenger armrest, the other clutching the seat belt strap.

She gave a wide-toothed grin. 'I'm braking.'

'How?' I bellowed. 'Braking usually involves removing your foot from the accelerator and pressing the brake pedal.'

'Look,' she said, wiggling the toes now delicately hovering somewhere in the right vicinity. 'And we slow down…'

Not by much. And, once again, we took the corner on two wheels.

I put my face in my hands. It would be a miracle if we got to Suffolk in one piece tonight.

CHAPTER 16

TERI

After I'd spoken to Charlie on the phone, I felt better than I'd felt for a long time. Charlie, my own brother, whom I hadn't seen or heard from for years, had given me something to feel positive about. He needed help, and I was the one to help him. It made me feel worthy.

Charlie persuaded me against driving down to Suffolk that night. 'It's a long way from Yorkshire,' he said. 'Come in the morning. Oh, it'll be good to see you.' And he started crying again.

Lee – full of concern – listened patiently as I told her Charlie's tale, and then she announced, 'Right. I'm coming with you.'

That took me by surprise.

'You can't go driving all that way on your own,' she said.

I couldn't think of an argument, so took another giant slurp of wine and said, 'Okay then.'

It might be quite fun.

In the morning, the idea of being a good Samaritan hadn't dulled, so I pulled my case from the spare room and opened it on my bed. I swung open my wardrobe doors and considered the range of dresses, skirts and silk shirts. What would I need for rural Suffolk? Would there be parties, smart restaurants, clubs and bars?

Think this through, Teri, I told myself. Charlie's just been dumped. He's not going to feel like going out. He lives on a smallholding, growing vegetables and tending goats.

I packed my jeans and sweaters. But threw in a couple of dresses and some nude heels. You never know.

I hadn't been to Charlie's place, but he'd given me the postcode and some rough directions. How hard could it be?

Of course, Princess Lee spent the entire drive white-knuckling and complaining I was driving too fast. I slowed down a bit, remembering that on my drive to the studios yesterday the damned speed camera on the A615, which got me last Wednesday as I was leaving uni after my sacking, got me again. That was twice in a week. Would it count as one given that there wasn't much time in between? The wretched thing got me back in August, and I had to pay a ludicrous fine and got penalty points. Oh, shit, that would be another fine and more points. And how would I pay it now I was out of work?

To take Lee's mind off the road, I put on a seventies CD and got her singing.

Five hours later we were still on the road having keyed the wrong code into the sat nav.

I re-entered the address and set off again and finally Suffolk appeared. By then, we were both too tired to care – or argue.

It was late afternoon and getting dark when we pulled up at the gate by the entrance to Charlie's place. A rough, potholed drive led up to a long, low, single storey building that I remember Charlie once saying had been the stables of a grander house further up the road.

A large four-by-four with a trailer attached was parked across the front of the building but there were no lights on and everything looked quiet, dark and spooky.

I parked next to the four-by-four and glanced across at Lee. She had her Lee-looks-concerned face on, but got out of the car when I encouraged her. 'C'mon. We've got this far.'

The wooden front door of the cottage stood ajar and, as I knocked, it swung open further to reveal a gloomy sitting room.

'Charlie?' I called, poking my head into the dimness.

I could smell wood smoke, and, as my eyes adjusted I made out an open fire to the left with the last embers glowing faintly in the grate.

But all was silent. I stepped into the room, brushing my hand down the wall to my right to flick the light switch.

With the light on, the room sprang into life. 'Wow,' breathed Lee.

And wow it was. Three walls had been painted in a light mushroom, but the fourth – a feature wall against the chimney breast – was covered in what looked like Oriental wallpaper, full of reds, greens and yellows, and decorated with swirling peacocks and fruit-laden trees.

On either side of the fireplace were two heavy, dark wood side tables, each holding matching gold-painted lamps with bright, white shades.

Two two-seater sofas, in bright yellow, covered in even brighter yellow cushions, sat opposite each other by the fire. I could tell they would be expensively comfortable.

Charlie had obviously been spending his allowance. His former allowance, that is.

Lee was busy gazing round.

'Hello. Anyone here?' My voice echoed against the beautifully designed walls.

Silence.

Then I heard what sounded like a stifled giggle from the next room.

'Charlie?'

And then an explosion of laughter.

'Charlie?' I shouted, sternly this time.

My brother appeared in a doorway at the far end of the sitting room, wrapped in a small towel but otherwise naked. 'Oh, sorry, sis,' he said, now unable to conceal his hysteria or most of his bare body.

Behind him, a man emerged. Apart from a boyish grin and a duvet which he'd somehow managed to wrap around himself, he was naked too.

'This is Denis,' Charlie said, indicating the other man, and both of them erupted in snorts of laughter.

'But I thought you two…'

'We had…we did…' Charlie laughed. 'But Denis saw the error of his ways and he came back.' He gave Denis a quick glance and they both snorted again.

'But I've just driven for sodding hours to get here to be with you,' I shouted.

'I know,' Charlie said, collecting himself long enough to stifle a giggle. With some difficulty, he twisted his mouth to prevent another grin appearing. 'I rang your home number but you must have set off. And your mobile's not switched on.'

I must replace that damn mobile.

'Oh, for God's sake,' I snapped but then I heard Lee giggling behind me and I had to admit it was funny: two naked men interrupted mid-reconciliation having to appear from the bedroom and make polite conversation.

'This is Lee,' I said, waving in her direction. 'And you must be Denis?' I said, holding out my hand. 'Charlie's told me a lot about you.'

'All good, I hope,' he said, looking at Charlie, but moving forward with his right hand extended, his left hand clutching the encircling duvet to his chest. As he did so, he stepped on the bottom edge of the duvet, tripped and fell against Charlie who put his arms out to try to save him from falling, dropping his towel in the process. The two men, giggling and floundering against each other, fell backwards on to one of the sofas, a windmill of naked arms, legs and – I couldn't help noticing – penises flapping in an effort to gain traction and balance.

*****

Once the boys were dressed they piled wood on the fire and poured a large glass of Merlot for each of us before sitting side by side on one of the sofas, while Lee and I took the other one.

'Right,' I said, business-like. 'What's been going on with you two? I thought you'd split up?'

'We'll tell you all about that,' Charlie said, flicking his hand impatiently and leaning forward. 'First, what do you know about Dad and the factory?'

I glanced at Lee. This was going to be news for her too. Then I looked at Denis, and Charlie put his hand on the other man's thigh and squeezed it. 'Don't worry,' he said. 'I've told Denis everything I know – which isn't much.'

I took a breath. 'It's a small steel foundry – not a big factory.' Denis nodded. 'But Dad set it up when we were kids, and it got more and more successful and we lived off the proceeds…that is, until the last few months when our allowances got more and more erratic.'

Taking a swig of Merlot, I swallowed and went on. 'Then a couple of days ago, Dad rang – from France, where he's been hiding for years – and said we'd been shafted by Pranks.'

'Pranks?' Lee and Denis asked in unison.

'Yeah,' Charlie said, nudging him. 'I told you. Edward Pranks, Dad's right-hand man at the factory. Started off as a chauffeur-cum-handyman but gradually did more and more – accounts, organising wages and pension stuff – until Dad took himself off to France, leaving Pranksy in charge.'

I nodded at Charlie. 'It turns out that once Dad was out of the way, Pranks started playing fast and loose with the finances. He made a couple of bad investments in new machinery at a time when orders were drying up because of competition from cheap foreign imports.'

'Didn't your father realise what was going on?' Denis asked.

'No, he thought the business was just going through a bad patch, and he trusted Pranks,' I said. 'Trouble is, Pranks started laying staff off to save costs and then, of course, when a big order came in, he didn't have enough people to process it. Dad said the order book has been empty since then – so everyone's been given the boot – and there's no money to pay any redundancy.'

'But there must be some money left in the business,' Denis said. 'I mean, the building alone must be worth something?'

'Pranks sold it off two years ago,' I said. 'The idea was to capitalise on the property by releasing equity to put into the business and then lease the building back, but it seems Pranks didn't put any of the capital into the factory, and nor did he pay any rent or rates for the last eighteen months.'

Lee scrunched her eyebrows and tightened her lips together in an over-concerned look of puzzlement. It's a face she occasionally pulls when she disagrees with something I've said, only this time, she was sharing her amazement.

Denis turned to Charlie and opened his mouth in a silent 'Oh.' Then he added, 'What a bastard.'

'Exactly,' I said.

'And your Dad didn't know what was going on?' Denis asked.

'Well, yes and no,' I replied. 'Pranks discussed selling the building, and Dad thought it was the right idea at the time, but stupidly, he left him to get on with it, gave him the power. He was a complete idiot.'

'And where is Pranks now?' Denis, who seemed to be asking all the questions, shuffled forward in his seat in anticipation.

'Ah,' I said. 'That's the thing. He's done a bunk.'

'Done a bunk?'

'Yes, he's buggered off somewhere, with all the money from the sale of the factory, plus what he should've been paying in rent and rates, and the entire company pension fund.'

I heard a sort of 'Urgh' from Lee.

Denis was more articulate. 'Bummer,' he said, sinking back into the sofa as though it was him who'd seen his monthly allowance disappear. 'And there's nothing the police can do?' he asked, sitting upright again. 'Get hold of his bank account?'

'No.' I shook my head and reached for my Merlot. 'Dad said Pranks has been planning this for years. The police said he's probably gone abroad, created a new identity for himself, and opened accounts under a new name. They doubt we'll ever find him.

'Meanwhile, the creditors are circling, Dad's been made bankrupt and worse, our monthly allowances – Charlie's, my mother's and mine – have stopped. God knows what I'm going to live on.' I looked into my glass and studied the wine, rich and red, as if Merlot held some answers.

'What I don't understand,' I said later, 'is, what happened to the goats?'

Denis looked at Charlie and smiled. 'Oh, the girls. I was in such a bad mood, I drove as far as Ipswich and then realised there was nowhere I could leave them. So I came back to the big house –'

'The big house?'

'Yeah. The big house up the road. Used to belong to some titled chap who owned the whole estate. But when he died a few years ago, his son sold off the various bits…outbuildings, fields…'

'Which is how we bought this part, the old stable block,' Charlie said.

'Anyway, a friend of ours –'

'Andrew,' Charlie interjected by way of clarification.

'Yes, Andrew,' Denis went on. 'Andrew bought the big house and has an orchard. So I threw myself on his mercy, and he let me put the girls in the orchard, and I had a room in the west wing.'

'Sounds grand.' I imagined a stately home with style, servants and a cook.

'Not really.' Charlie took a sip of Merlot. 'The place was pretty run down, and Andrew got it for a song, but he's only been able to renovate part of it so far. The idea is to do up the whole place and rent it out for weddings and such.'

'And where are the girls now?' I asked.

'Oh, Beatrice, Hermione and Daphne? They're still at the big house. I was in too much of a rush to get home this morning to round them up.' Denis glanced lovingly at Charlie and pouted his lips. 'We'll have to go get them tomorrow. You can come with us and meet them – and Andrew.'

CHAPTER 17

LEE

I have a horrible feeling I gaped like a shell-shocked goldfish when Teri revealed her dad's business had gone belly up – actually, I know I did, because Teri stretched out a hand and pushed my chin upwards. None too gently either. 'Don't gawp,' she reprimanded. Bet she'd have gawped if I'd made a similar announcement.

It explained something that had been puzzling me though: Teri's uncharacteristically mad dash to her brother's side. The Meyers have never been the sort of family to hang out together; in fact, the last time all four of them, Mama, Papa, kid brother Charlie and big sis Teri, had been in the same room a blue moon had been shining in the night sky and pink pigs were flying past.

I suppose Mama and Papa must have been close once – well, twice, at least – but for years the only tie binding the quartet together was a mutual dependence on profits from the family firm to keep the wolf from the door. In Teri's case, it wasn't always enough to fill the gap between what she earned as a senior lecturer and what she spent at the Yorkshire branch of Harvey Nicks and other equally exclusive retail outlets. Fortunately, her bank manager shared her elastic approach to overdrafts.

She was quids in when she met and married Dan. The poor besotted fool set up a joint bank account – he paid in and she took out – and she continued to dip into it during her brief fling with Declan.

'He promised to love and protect me until death do us part,' she said when I suggested it wasn't, perhaps, quite ethical to use the debit card Dan had given her on their honeymoon to pay for furniture and fittings for Declan's new flat.

'Yes, but not after the ink is dry on the divorce papers.'

'Bollocks,' she said.

So, it was anyone's guess how she'd manage without salary or allowance or the bank of Dan. He'd finally posted the CLOSED sign after Teri got careless and treated herself to a spa weekend. Even someone as fiscally imprudent as Dan, whose mega TV salary immunised him from most economic realities, had spotted the rogue payment to the well-known, and outlandishly pricey, temple to beauty, relaxation and self-indulgence. More importantly, his accountant was on the phone faster than a fat lady chasing an ice-cream van. 'This is one luxury you can't afford,' he told Dan, and Teri's name was promptly removed from the joint account. She was not pleased. 'Miserable git' was one of her milder comments. Most of the others were asterisk-rated.

Thankfully, all this happened before Dan and I hooked up. While there was a reasonably good chance she would eventually forgive my 'treacherous' liaison, money matters were a completely different ball game.

And, that, almost certainly, explained why she'd hightailed it to Charlie's Suffolk idyll. No doubt she'd hoped to draw on Charlie's reserves before his coffers were bare. Seems Denis had beaten her to it.

CHAPTER 18

TERI

The spare room was tiny. It held two single beds, a large and heavy dark-wood chest of drawers and a tall, narrow wardrobe. With its plain, whitewashed walls, it clearly hadn't been given the lavish treatment the living room had.

'Denis is the interior designer,' Charlie said proudly. 'But we haven't got round to the guest bedroom yet.'

'Watch that wardrobe door,' he advised. 'It doesn't open properly unless you give it a good pull, and it doesn't shut unless you put your weight behind it.'

What style my brother has.

I pulled open the door and surveyed the half dozen wire coat hangers that jangled against each other and considered getting back in my car and driving home. I haven't used wire coat hangers since…well, since never. They are atrocities. All my clothes are hung on padded hangers or wrapped in tissue. I felt slightly nauseous as I unfolded a silk shirt and draped it over the wire.

'It'll be fine for a couple of nights,' Lee said, looking round. 'We're only going to sleep in here.'

My bed was surprisingly comfortable for what I can only assume was horsehair, this being the country. It was lumpy, but soft, and it was strangely reassuring to feel as though I was sinking into it. I slept well for the first time in ages – at least since the Declan and David episodes.

CHAPTER 19

LEE

My expectations concerning the level of creature comforts to be expected at Charlie's place had been pretty low when we set off. They'd plummeted even lower when we pulled up outside what an optimistic estate agent would describe as a 'characterful bijou property convenient for local amenities'. In other words, it was old and falling down but ideally suited to a contortionist with a growth hormone deficiency who was happy to run to and from the shops as part of his or her training for the London or New York marathon. Take your pick.

One look at the guest bedroom was enough to kill the small shred of optimism that had survived stepping over the threshold.

'We like the exposed beams,' Charlie said, opening the door.

Well, that was one way of putting a positive spin on 'the plaster fell off the ceiling during the storms last winter'.

I waited for Teri to say something. No need for me to demand alternative accommodation, when there was a ready-made diva standing next to me. She exhaled slowly. 'It's very light and airy.' What? The wind was practically blowing a gale through the gaps in the window frames, and there was precious little light from the bulb dangling half-heartedly from between those exposed beams.

But, if Teri wasn't going to fight my corner I'd just have to put up with things. 'I'm sure it will be okay for a couple of nights,' I muttered but, honestly, I was planning my escape before the words were out of my mouth. Bedroom? I've seen bigger broom cupboards. There was barely room to swing a full-sized field mouse let alone a scraggy moggy. God knows how Charlie and Denis had managed to squeeze in two beds and a wardrobe that didn't look big enough for a pair of wire coat hangers let alone Teri's extensive haut couture country collection, which, let me tell you, included at least three JK Fenwick frocks, two pairs of Jimmy Choos and a Mulberry tote. Well, she needn't think she was borrowing my wellies.

And I wasn't much looking forward to sleeping on either one of the rickety beds; both of them looked like something my granddaddy might have scavenged from *Steptoe and Son*. As for the sunshine yellow polyester eiderdowns…the last time we'd slept under one of them we'd been billeted in bunk beds in a hostel dormitory somewhere near Bamburgh Castle.

I wondered if Teri remembered. She raised an eyebrow – yes, she did. It was hard to forget.

It had been so exciting; the first time I'd been allowed to go away without Mammy and Daddy and, for the first twenty-four hours-or-so, even the lack of home comforts – such as warm showers, clean toilets, fluffy duvets, lavender-scented pillows and a room of one's own – couldn't detract from the wonderfulness.

Then reality hit in. I thought we'd chosen Northumberland as a holiday destination so we could have adventures together in between exploring the unspoilt moorlands, the beautiful wild coastline and the rich historical and cultural heritage. Silly me. We'd come north because Teri had had a one-night stand with the shaggy-haired lead singer of a third-rate rock-and-roll band and promptly conceived a cunning plan to join the boys in Bamburgh where they'd secured a summer residency at a dance hall.

It could have been worse; at least we were in a youth hostel, and I could hang out with the other girls in our dorm while Teri spent her evenings getting wide-eyed and legless on cheap barley wine and lager, and snuggling up to lover-boy in between sets.

Who am I kidding? It was ghastly. The other girls were nice enough but we had next to nothing in common and, to add insult to injury, they were almost as boy crazy as Teri, but without her dry wit. As a result, they bored me stupid, and, after one particularly excruciating stroll along the promenade ogling the local talent – not! – I developed phantom period pains and headed back to the dorm early, climbed onto my top bunk and snuggled down with a book.

It was the first proper bit of peace and quiet I'd had for days – and nights too. Who'd have thought half a dozen teenage girls could snore louder than a chorus of fire-breathing dragons? Not me.

But warm as toast and in the company of handsome John Reed and the beautiful Lorna Doone, I drifted off into a lovely doze only to be woken abruptly by…more snoring? No, these noises were snuffly and squeaky and interrupted by half gasps and moans and…the bunk was bobbing up and down like a rubber dinghy, surfing the waves at high tide. Christ Almighty! Should I say something? What *should* I say? 'Excuse me, I'm feeling seasick.' Or maybe, I should cough discreetly? Probably not, I'd need to cough up at least a lung or two to attract the attention of the bonking pair below. Instead, I clapped my hands to my mouth and prayed the humping and bumping would end before I threw up. Too late. As the bed stilled and Teri gave a long, low sigh, I leaned over the edge and a shower of bile spewed onto the rug below. 'What the f***,' Teri said.

She winked at me now. 'Your bunk or mine?'

Charlie looked puzzled. 'Pardon?'

'An old joke,' Teri said.

'It wasn't a joke,' I said. 'And there'll be no bunking.'

Charlie turned to leave the room. 'I haven't a clue what you're talking about.'

'Don't worry,' I told him. 'She does.'

'Lee,' she said, eyes wide in mock horror. 'What are you suggesting?'

I flopped down on one of the beds and waited for Charlie to shut the door behind him. 'I know, and you know, that if there's a fanciable man within a twenty-mile radius, you'll find him. And, if you do, you are not bringing him back to this room – at least not while I'm sleeping next to you.'

She plonked down beside me. 'Shove over,' she said. 'I'm having this one.'

I gave up.

****

It was a bit of a disappointment to learn the cottage lacked both wi-fi and broadband. Teri might be embracing the joys of living without twenty-first century necessities, but I wasn't keen to go back to basics. For one thing, although I'd told her it was reading week and I didn't need to be at work, I ought to keep in touch. And I'd promised Dan I'd let him know we'd arrived safely.

'You can sometimes get a mobile signal at the top of the hill,' Denis offered, pointing in the direction of a pin prick. If that was his definition of a hill, he'd best stay away from Yorkshire. His calves wouldn't stand the strain. 'But, not often,' he added.

I wasn't surprised.

'Use the house phone if you need to make a call,' Charlie said.

'There's an honesty box on the table,' Denis added.

'Thanks,' I said, thinking it might not be a good idea to whisper sweet nothings to my lover in front of his ex, her brother, and his lover.

And, I also needed to find someone to cover Teri's classes. She'd definitely be delighted to know we were struggling to find a replacement, but it wouldn't be good for her soul to give her reason to gloat. 'Couldn't you...?' Mike had asked the last time we discussed it a couple of days ago.

'No.' What I knew about Teri's speciality – the life, loves and poetry of John Wilmot, the 2nd Earl of Rochester – could be pencilled on the back of an eraser.

Damn David Greenspan. If he'd kept his gob shut, Teri might not have had the spectacular meltdown which had provided our esteemed dean with the final nail in her academic coffin. And neither Mike nor I would be chasing our tails trying to find permanent cover.

'I didn't mean any harm,' David said afterwards. 'I was just being a bit mischievous.'

Mischievous? Downright provocative, I thought.

'I guess she wasn't very happy though when I said older women sometimes came across as sexual predators.'

'Probably not.'

'Especially if the object of their attentions was much younger.'

Oh Lord. Light the touch paper. Teri can be just a tiny bit touchy about age.

'And, I did raise the question of stalking...'

Bloody hell, David. If this is mischievous, heaven forbid, you ever get nasty.

'I tried to find her to apologise,' he said.

Huh! He should have tried harder.

I began to feel a little bit sorry for Teri, and it explained something else that had puzzled me. The country's not her natural habitat, she's more a high street and wine bar sort of girl and, though she'd made a good stab at feigning interest in Charlie and his goats, she hadn't kidded me. But, no wonder she'd sought refuge in Suffolk. Under similar circumstances I might have been tempted to do the same. Fingers crossed she found the fanciable man soon. She needed a confidence boost.

CHAPTER 20

TERI

Charlie woke us in the morning with mugs of strong tea. I prefer lemon in hot water, and Lee won't drink anything other than weak gnat's piss, but strong tea must be the rural way of doing things so I thanked him and asked what time it was as it looked dark outside.

'It's seven a.m. Come on, get up. We're off to the big house for the girls,' he said.

'I must go into town and get myself a new phone,' I told him as he pulled back the curtains.

'We won't have time today,' Charlie said. 'We need to catch the girls and load them, and Andrew's invited us to stay for lunch. Anyway, mobiles aren't much use round here – the signal's not great. We're as rural as it gets, and we don't have these new-fangled things.' He laughed as he backed out of the room, tugging his fetlock or whatever these country bumpkins tug.

I lay in bed while Lee used the bathroom. When she returned, she was dressed in her natty leggings and a huge fleecy jumper. She never dresses elegantly or well, but I didn't have her down as a country girl.

The bathroom was surprisingly large, given the size of the other rooms in the cottage, and at first, I thought the bulky, old-style, Victorian radiator was something retro that the boys had found in an antique shop. But no, it – and the white, cast iron furniture – were the genuine article: old and in need of replacing. There was no shower other than one of those plastic arrangements that grip onto the taps. And there was no underfloor heating.

How do these people live?

Luckily there was plenty of hot water and, as I lay in a deep bath, I was able to look out of the window, positioned at bath height at the bottom end of the room. There being no curtains or blinds, I had a direct view into the garden beyond until steam created a mist over the glass.

I lay back in the water and soaked my hair. I don't normally wash it in the bath, but there was no way I was risking the hand-held shower. As I rose up and forwards from the final rinse, a shadow moved across the window. Then a face appeared. I could just make out long features and a beard. Then whoever it was knocked on the window and moaned. I shouted 'What the fuck?' and screamed for Charlie. The face didn't move. I grabbed a towel from the floor by the bath, stood and tried to wrap it around my dripping body. It was too small to do a complete job, so I held it in front of me instead, leaving my backside exposed.

'What's up, sis?' I heard Charlie say from the other side of the door.

'There's a man outside the window…'

'A man?'

'Yes, you dumbskull – a man.'

I couldn't take my eyes off the misted face still staring in at me. 'Piss off, you pervert,' I yelled, grabbing the soap from the side of the bath and throwing it. 'Charlie. Go get the bastard.'

I heard Charlie call for Denis, then the sound of running feet across the living room floor and the back door opening. The face dropped away from the window, and I slowly backed out of the bathroom into the living room, clutching my towel to my chest, eyes glued to see if the Peeping Tom dared to appear again.

'Hermione,' I heard Denis shouting, 'you bad girl. You've scared our Teri half to death.'

Hermione? One of the bloody goats. 'For fuck's sake,' I said, still trying to see through the steam while backing further into the living room.

'You might want a bigger towel,' a man's voice said behind me and, of course, I spun round.

I did better than Charlie and Denis, managing to hold the towel in place with one hand while using the other instinctively to cover my bare buttocks. But of course, the voice had already seen those.

The man standing in front of me was grinning. A grin that crinkled his mouth at the edges. A grin in a craggy face, hardened and smoothed by the weather. Blue eyes that seemed to twinkle. White hair that seemed to explode in a cloud of tight curls. Tall and well-proportioned. Blue, denim shirt tucked into black, denim jeans. Heavy, mustard-coloured boots, surprisingly clean.

I notice these things in a man.

'Not that I'm objecting,' he said, 'but I like to get to know a woman before I see her completely naked. I'm Andrew, and you must be Teri.'

'I...' was all I could manage. I was standing stark naked but for a scrappy little towel, my body still damp and my hair dripping wet, hanging down in a tangled mess. My legs probably needed shaving. I hadn't brushed my teeth. Oh, go on then, last night's mascara was probably running down my cheeks.

My mouth was open in shock. I'd never seen such a gorgeous-looking god-like man. And I'd never looked so bad in all my life.

'I'll just...' I said, backing out of the living room towards my bedroom door.

CHAPTER 21

TERI

Dressed only in my small towel, I'd edged away from gorgeous and god-like and raced to get myself dry and dressed.

Lee came into the bedroom, laughing at me and making comments about how she couldn't understand anyone being scared of a goat. She kept getting in the way as I hunted for the hairdryer to zap my hair, wittering about Andrew in the living room, but I told her to go. I needed to concentrate, dab on mascara, lippy. No time to do the full works. Put on jeans, linen shirt, couldn't find the right shoes. Go back into the living room in bare feet. The natural look.

'Ah, that's better,' Andrew said as I reappeared. He looked up at me from where he was sitting on the sofa – appreciatively, I like to think.

'I was coming this way with the trailer, so thought I'd bring the goats. Save Charlie and Denis some work later.' Andrew moved his long frame forward and put his mug of coffee on the table in front of him.

'The other two went off down the field when I let them out, but Hermione clearly thought it was bath time.' He grinned. 'Sorry she gave you such a fright.'

The boys had gone into the field to settle the girls, Andrew told me, and Lee was up a hill looking for a mobile signal.

'She seems nice,' Andrew said.

Forget her, I thought. I was alone with gorgeous and god-like but couldn't think of anything to say. What on Earth was wrong with me; must be the country air.

'Yes,' Andrew said as though answering a question. 'I'm going down to Bottom Hill Farm to pick up some sheep…' As though that explained everything. I must have looked blank because he continued, 'That's why I had the trailer.' His voice became slow as though explaining higher maths to a dim child. 'Rather than come with an empty trailer…'

'Yes, I get it,' I said, finally finding my voice.

'Must have been a helluva shock – seeing a face in the window like that.' And the laugh he had obviously been suppressing since first seeing me naked and dripping, burst out, and he threw himself back into the sofa with the glee of it all.

'Sorry…sorry…' he spluttered, holding a hand out with the palm open towards me by way of apology. 'But it was funny seeing you standing there like Botticelli's Venus…'

Normally, I'd be insulted, angry, if someone made fun of me, but with this man I could only see the joke. Stop behaving like a love-sick cow, I told myself. Stop simpering. Do not throw yourself at this man.

'But you're all still invited for lunch,' Andrew went on, 'if you still want to come?'

There was nothing that would stop me. Not even three ridiculous goats.

CHAPTER 22

LEE

Andrew wasn't quite what I had in mind when I started fantasising about a new love interest for Teri. For one thing, he was married and I'd thought that, just this once, it might be a nice change for Teri to fall for someone who was free to fall for her.

It was the boots that were the giveaway – mustard-coloured, polished to within an inch of their soles and spotlessly clean. Any man with boots like those, who lives in the hen scratchings and sheep droppings and goat poo of Suffolk, has to have a woman tucked up at home making sure he doesn't traipse the muck around the house.

You'd have thought Teri, who believed cleanliness *was* godliness, might have put two-and-two together, but she was too busy rushing round the bedroom getting herself dry and dressed. 'What's the hurry?' I asked. 'Worried the goats will come back for a second look?'

She snorted. 'Did you see him?'

'Who?'

She rolled her eyes. 'The most gorgeous, god-like man in the whole universe.'

'Oh, you mean Andrew? Yes, the boys introduced me when he arrived with the goats – before Hermione began terrorising you. We were out in the orchard when you started screaming.'

I poked my head around the bedroom door to have another look at Andrew who was now slumped on the sofa.

'Don't look at him,' she screeched. 'He'll know we're talking about him.'

'Of course we're talking about him,' I said. 'It's what you do when a strange man catches you starkers in the living room. Or, at any rate, it's what I'd do. Not sure about you…'

Andrew looked up and saw me. I gave him a little wave. 'Hello.'

He waved back. 'Hello.'

I turned back to Teri and shut the door. 'He's not bad. But –'

'But, but…but nothing,' she said. 'I'm not looking a gift horse in the mouth.'

No, that would have been too much to expect. Clearly, she hadn't clocked the pristine boots.

'Now get out of here,' she said. 'I'm sure Charlie and Denis could do with a bit of help with the girls.'

'Stop pushing,' I hissed. 'And I don't like goats.'

'Who cares?' she replied, pushing harder and closing the door firmly in my face.

I gave Andrew another wave. 'She's putting some clothes on,' I said.

'Shame,' he said.

'Just making a phone call,' I said, pulling my mobile phone from the back pocket of my jeans. 'Won't be long. Well, I won't be long if there's no signal up the hill.'

'No rush,' he said.

There was every rush in the world. I didn't trust gorgeous and god-like as far as I could throw him, which, judging by the size of him, would not be far.

Hurrah, though, Denis had been right: there was a mobile signal at the bus shelter parked at the top of what passed for a hill in these parts. It didn't provide much protection from the wind, which was howling across the flat landscape direct from Siberia, because some idiot, who'd probably got bored waiting for a bus, had punched a hole in one of the glass panes, but it was better than none.

I felt almost girlishly excited as I retrieved my mobile and scrolled through my contacts book looking for Dan's number. Perhaps it was time to add him to 'my favourites' folder? I'd just started to change his status when Freddie Mercury belted out a couple of lines from 'Don't Stop Me Now'. Bloody Victoria; she'd been playing around with the ring tone on my phone again. Last week it had been Michael Stipe pushing an elephant upstairs, now Freddie Mercury was yodelling about having a good time. Good luck to him, I thought. Here in Suffolk I wasn't sure about my chances of anything similar.

It was Stella. 'Hullo,' I said, hopping from one foot to another to keep warm.

'I've been thinking,' Stella said. 'If you can't find anyone else to cover for Teri, perhaps I could…' She hesitated.

'Yes?' Please God, she was thinking what I was thinking. If anyone could step into Teri's shoes it was Stella Lastings, whose fondness for the seventeenth century poet and rake was matched only by Teri herself.

'I don't know if you're interested, but I could maybe fill an hour next week talking about the history and context of the Restoration poets,' she offered.

Interested? If she'd been standing in front of me I'd have kissed her.

'And, perhaps,' she said, 'I could follow that up with a discussion on Rochester's early life and loves?'

And she didn't see it as a stop-gap measure either.

'The week after I could cover the mid-life period and then we could start to look at individual poems and assess their impact on Rochester and his relationship with the king and society in general.'

And, she'd be more than happy to see the series of lectures and seminars through until the end of the academic year.

Whoopee! She'd taken the words right out of my mouth.

Of course, Teri would have spat blood if she'd known her arch enemy was stepping into her shoes. But she didn't know and, frankly, there was no immediate reason why she ever should. I certainly wasn't telling.

CHAPTER 23

LEE

Stella – and more importantly, Lord Rochester – sorted, I rang Dan. Just a quick phone call because there was rain on the wind and I was beginning to wish I'd worn a pair of gloves. And a woolly hat. And a second pair of socks. But silly me for thinking he might be even mildly interested to hear I'd finally put the Teri problem to bed. I mean, it wasn't as if I'd been fretting for weeks and weeks about the loss of our friendship or worrying myself sick about how we were going to fill her Restoration literature shoes. So, of course, I wasn't bursting to tell him we'd finally, properly made-up or that another Rochester-obsessive had stepped up to deliver her classes. Or, that the lewd looks Teri was casting in the direction of gorgeous and god-like suggested she might be having second thoughts about re-kindling passions for past loves such as either Dan or Declan. Which had to be a good thing?

Whatever made me imagine he'd find Teri's naked encounter with the goat in the window as laugh-out-loud funny as I did?

Or that he'd enjoy my description of Denis and Charlie's nude goings-on when we first arrived?

Silly me, too, for supposing he'd be as stunned as I'd been to discover Teri's dad had gone bust, cutting her off without a penny.

Whatever was I thinking?

Obviously, it was much more immediately important he vent his spleen about Victoria's new penchant for heavy, black eyeliner and purple lipstick. Not a great look, I agreed, but it was unlikely she'd applied it with a trowel as Dan suggested.

And, without being unnecessarily rude, I really didn't care that Sara didn't approve of Victoria's new boyfriend. Who was he, by the way?

'Dunno,' Dan said. 'Probably some spotty geek she picked up in a bar.'

And that was another thing. 'She's drinking far too much.'

I counted eight paces forwards and eight paces back between one end of the bus shelter and the other. 'How much is too much?'

He didn't know.

'Does she come home falling down drunk?'

'No!'

Then what the hell was all the fuss about?

'She's still a schoolgirl!'

I'd been one of those once and survived to tell the tale. No doubt, Victoria would come through unscathed too.

Unless she had a best friend like Teri, in which case, we perhaps ought to worry a little. Best not mention that to Dan.

My turn now to off-load. 'I just wanted to tell you…' I began. No such luck.

'I haven't told you about Finlay Baxter.'

No, but I had a horrible feeling he was going to do so.

'Finlay Baxter?' He'd mentioned him once or twice before.

'Flash bugger, almost straight out of journalism school. Thinks he knows everything.'

Clearly, Dan thought Finlay knew sod all.

'I've been asked to mentor him.'

Wasn't that a compliment of sorts?

Apparently not.

Someone thought it would be a good idea for 'the pup' to get a feel for the weekly political discussion-cum-chat show Dan presented from the station's Westminster studios.

I got the picture. Ridings at Westminster – daft name but I kept my opinion to myself – was one of those flagship programmes that garnered far more kudos than it deserved. Too much jaw-jaw, I thought, but was too tactful to say so.

'Doreen booked us both on the same train. Two bloody hours of him telling me how to ask killer questions.'

I could see it might have been a strain. Especially as Dan had been asking said killer questions since before Finlay was even a twinkle in his dad's eye.

'Conniving Scottish git,' Dan ground from between teeth almost as full of grit as a snow plough. 'He's obviously angling to get his fat bottom on my primetime couch.'

'Why else does he need a feel for my programme?'

It was a rhetorical question, which over the next twenty minutes, he answered at length.

Made a change though from listening to him moan about Victoria.

At long, long, long last, he ran out of grumbles and asked about me. Too late. 'I'm fine but the signal's a bit weak so I'll ring you back tomorrow.' It was good to talk but not right now when my fingers and toes were almost as numb as the paws on a ceramic dog. And, then, just as I'd hunched my collar more firmly around my neck – I'd wear a scarf next time – and taken a step or two back down the hill, Freddie Mercury started hollering again.

'Victoria.' I tried to sound pleased. No prizes for guessing this wasn't a social call. Sighing, I headed back to the meagre protection of the bus shelter.

'Lee, you've got to talk to Dad.'

I could guess what was coming next.

'He's ruining my life.'

That was one way of looking at it. Dan, no doubt, would claim he was saving her from herself.

'He's really got it in for my new boyfriend.'

A slight exaggeration, I thought, since Dan hadn't yet met the lucky fella.

'Oh,' I said. 'I didn't realise they'd been introduced.'

Victoria hesitated. 'That's the thing…they sort of have. And they haven't, if you get what I mean.'

No, I didn't.

'Dad knows him. But he doesn't know he's my boyfriend.' The pride in those last words was palpable.

Clearly, the spotty geek was more of a catch than Dan had given him credit for – or else teenage girls had changed a lot since my day, when spotty geeks were NOT any sort of catch.

Wrong: the boyfriend wasn't a geek and his spotty days were long behind him.

'I'm seeing'– Victoria paused for dramatic effect –'Shayne Brickham.'

'Shayne who?' The drama was wasted because I didn't think I'd ever heard the name before.

'The footballer.'

Nope, still didn't know him.

'Plays for the Jukes.'

I didn't feel significantly wiser.

'Their top goal scorer. Dad's interviewed him loads of times.'

Okay. I wasn't sure whether that was a plus or a minus.

'He's a bit older than me,' Victoria confessed.

That, I thought, would be a minus point.

'But, Dad's mad keen about the Jukes.'

Which would be a plus, if it was true, which I doubted since I'd never heard Dan even mention the Jukes in passing.

'So I wondered –'

'No,' I cut her off. 'I'm not getting involved. This is between you and your mum and your dad.'

'Leeeeee,' she wailed. 'I thought you were my friend?'

'I am. And that's why I'm keeping out of this.'

And, thankfully, at that point I lost my mobile signal.

CHAPTER 24

TERI

What to wear for lunch in the country? Pleased that I had brought a couple of dresses and heels, I chose a tight-fitting, low-cut number and my nude heels, and took extra care with my make-up. Lee walked into the bedroom as I was piling my hair on top of my head.

'Better up – or down?' I asked her.

She stood and stared, and I swear her mouth dropped open. Obviously thinking I was too gorgeous for words.

'My hair,' I said, explaining. 'Up like this – or down?'

'You're not going like that,' she said.

'Why not?'

'Well, don't you think it's a little over-dressed for the country?'

'We're going for a smart lunch at the main house,' I told her.

'Well, okay then.'

Charlie and Denis returned from their goat-tending, and I could hear them talking in the sitting room, so I moved through. As I entered the boys became suddenly quiet. Denis put his hand over his mouth and giggled.

'You're not going like that,' Charlie said, echoing what Lee had just said. The pair of them was clearly clueless about style.

'Why not?'

'Well…okay then.' Again, just like Lee – doubtful.

'Are you two not getting changed?' I asked, indicating the jeans and sweatshirts that they'd had on earlier for goat-moving.

Denis sniggered again, rather childishly, I thought, and Charlie laughed. 'This is the country, sis. We're dressed for rural life.'

'Do you think this is too much?' I asked, smoothing the front of my dress with my hands, although why I do that I don't know, given that I have no belly to flatten whatsoever.

'Er…no,' Charlie said. 'To be honest, you look fabulous, sweetie. It'll give the village something to talk about. Let's go.'

'Shall I drive?' I asked.

'Drive?' Denis said in a high-pitched voice that was nearly a camp scream. 'It's only up the lane.' I was beginning to find him a little irritating.

The lane turned out to be potholed, muddy and uneven. Even I could see that my shoes were entirely wrong for the terrain and my beige mac wasn't anywhere near warm enough, but I wasn't going to give Lee or the boys the satisfaction of my admitting defeat and going back to change.

I noticed that Lee, walking slightly ahead of me with Denis, was still wearing her leggings and fleecy jumper and seemed to have found some big, clompy boots as well.

'By the way,' I said, innocently, 'what's Andrew's story?' I hesitated to ask the important questions, like, is he married? Is he gay?

'Story?' Denis looked back at me over his shoulder. 'What do you mean, story?'

'Well, you know…where's he from? Does he have family?'

'You mean,' Denis said with a slight sneer on his face, 'is he married or is he gay?' He gave Lee a theatrical nudge on her arm. And she giggled back at him. The cow.

'No,' I said in mock indignation. 'I'm just interested, that's all.'

'Well, you'll just have to find out.'

God, that Denis was getting on my nerves. But I didn't have time to argue as one of my heels caught in a clump of mud and I fell forward, saving myself by clutching at Charlie who'd been walking beside me. Even so, I fell onto one knee.

Denis laughed, and I swear Lee was doing her best to suppress a smile as Charlie pulled me back up to my feet. I gave them all a filthy look and brushed myself down. The shoe was practically ruined; it was so clogged with mud that it was hard to see it had once been nude. 'Fucking countryside,' I muttered under my breath.

'Heard that,' Denis said, cheerfully, linking his arm through Lee's and setting off again with a swagger.

And fuck you too, I thought.

'Do you want to go back?' Charlie asked, eyeing my knee, which as well as being muddy was now bleeding slightly.

'No, it'll be okay,' I said, bravely. 'Let's go. I can sort myself out when we get there.'

We rounded a bend in the lane, and the house came into view. It was an imposing, square, double-fronted building with huge picture windows on the ground and first floors and smaller ones on the second. It looked Georgian and was probably listed. So this is where gorgeous and god-like lives, I thought.

And there he was, standing in the open doorway. I could almost picture a couple of Labradors at his feet and me by his side, welcoming our guests to a fabulous dinner party organised by Cook.

He started to come towards us and then stopped, staring at me. Before he could say anything, Denis dropped Lee's arm and scampered forwards and up to Andrew in what I thought was a rather fey way. They embraced, and Denis planted a kiss on his cheek. Surely gorgeous and god-like wasn't gay? Charlie did a gentle thump on his arm in greeting. Then Andrew moved forward and, pulling me towards him, gave me a kiss first on one cheek, then the other. 'You are the most extraordinary thing,' he said, eyeing me seriously.

I simpered in delight. Me! Simpering!

'First I see you wet, bedraggled and practically naked,' he said, 'and now here you are looking a million dollars but covered in mud. Never mind. Let's get you inside and we can look at that knee.'

I liked the idea of him looking at my knee but then, of course, Lee had to pipe up and say 'Hi, Andrew' and he was forced to break away to give her a perfunctory kiss on the cheek.

He turned back to me and smiled. 'C'mon in and we'll get you tidied up.'

Just the idea had me blushing. Denis must have read the look on my face because he snorted, but Andrew went on, 'I should be able to find you some slippers somewhere…'

It never occurred to me then to ask why he would have some slippers somewhere that would fit me.

CHAPTER 25

LEE

I hate it when grown women simper. Actually, I hate it just as much when teenage girls and old women simper. And I especially hate it when Teri gurns and gabbles and giggles like a Restoration virgin on her wedding night.

She'd have pulled a different face if she could have looked in a mirror.

But, who could blame her? Even I wasn't immune to Andrew's masculine charm, although I thought Charlie might have told her the truth about his marital status – sibling loyalty and that sort of thing – when she made a not-so subtle enquiry about significant others. Denis though butted in before he could speak. 'You'll just have to find out.'

What a bitch!

1. However, it probably wouldn't have mattered one jot if they'd come clean and admitted Andrew was very much married. Teri had *that* look in her eye – the one that screamed 'I fancy the pants off you'. Usually when she wore that look, the pants came off.

2. As ever her preparations were extensive. Her holiday wardrobe was a little lacking by Teri standards – it still knocked my actual real, at home wardrobe into a cocked hat – but she mixed and matched dresses and shoes and handbags and hairstyles and, crucially, underwear. 'Agent Provocateur or Coco de Mer?' she asked, holding up a pair of identical, and miniscule, bits of lace.

'Nobody's going to see your bloody knickers.'

'Oh, you never know,' she said. 'One should always be prepared.'

'In which case, I wouldn't bother.'

'What?'

'Save yourself a bit of time. Don't wear any pants.'

She considered for a moment; I swear to God she was taking the suggestion seriously.

'No,' she said. 'It would look too presumptuous.'

'It wouldn't look anything unless someone went looking.'

'Lee,' she said, widening her eyes and fanning her face with her hands, 'for a nice Catholic girl, you've got a filthy mind.'

Yes, I thought, but unlike you, I don't act on it.

Not often, anyway.

Eventually, after everything in her holiday wardrobe had been on and off the hangers at least a couple of times, she settled on a low-cut, fitted dress and a pair of nude heels. The dress was quite nice, although I didn't like the way it bunched around her stomach. Probably she was a bit bloated. Last night's evening meal had been an interesting – I use the word advisedly – combination of chicken meatballs, quinoa and curried cauliflower. It wasn't a recipe I'd be adding to my repertoire.

'Not sure about the shoes,' I said when she asked for an opinion.

'Why?' She pointed her right foot and then her left. 'I think they're rather gorgeous.'

'They are,' I agreed, 'but I'd struggle to walk round town in them let alone the country mile-or-so to Andrew's house.'

'We're not walking!'

I nodded. 'Denis insists it's just a hop and a skip.'

'So not a country mile – whatever that is.'

'It's further than you think.'

Teri gave me the look she sometimes directs my way when she thinks I'm being particularly irritating.

I shrugged. She'd learn. I, for one, wasn't making the same mistake twice. I added an extra cardigan, plus hat, gloves and scarf and two pairs of socks. Denis patted me on the back. 'That's my girl,' he said, opening the door and ushering Charlie and Teri ahead.

'Bloody hell,' I said, clapping a hand across my nose as I stepped outside after them. 'What's the smell?'

'Muck,' Denis replied.

I breathed heavily. 'I didn't smell it earlier.'

Denis pointed across the fields. 'Wind's changed direction. Andrew's man will have sprayed the fields this morning.'

Another reason my tenancy of the spare room would be short-lived.

Denis linked his arm through mine and, as we marched in front, nodded at Teri, who was tip-toeing delicately with a handkerchief pinched to her nostrils.

Sadly, I missed her tumble because Denis and I were engrossed in a discussion about the finer points of goat rearing. Finer points? Don't ask me, I was only half-listening but Denis was very animated. It wasn't much of a discussion either. More of a one-sided lecture which, not a moment too soon, was interrupted by wild shrieks from behind. We turned. Teri was genuflecting in the mud and clinging to Charlie as if he was God's own anchor. He, on the other hand, appeared to be fighting to cut loose as he slithered and slipped trying not to join her on his knees.

I'd have laughed but didn't quite dare. Denis had no such qualms. 'Ha, ha,' he roared, making no effort to help either of the stricken pair. Charlie, with a supreme effort, gained his balance and planted both feet securely on a soggy bit of grass. Teri was still hanging onto his arm and still on bended knee, swearing like a trooper. 'F***ing countryside. F***ing, f***ed up place.'

Breathing heavily, Charlie hauled her upright. 'Bloody hell,' he said as she swayed unsteadily against him.

'F***ing countryside,' she muttered again and glared at Denis, who was still giggling provocatively.

'That's a nasty graze,' I said, dragging a slightly grubby handkerchief from my pocket. Tiny dribbles of blood were wending their way down her leg and, without thinking, I spat on the hanky and dabbed at the cut.

She recoiled and snatched the cotton square. 'I'll sort myself out later.'

'Do you want to go back?' Charlie asked.

And miss a dalliance with Andrew the Adonis? 'Tut, tut, Charlie. Don't you know Teri better than that?'

Oops! I hadn't meant to say that last bit aloud.

'Pardon?'

Charlie looked perplexed. Teri narrowed her eyes.

'Perhaps you could borrow a pair of Charlie's boots,' I suggested. 'And maybe a warmer coat? I could nip back and get them.'

I'm not sure it was an entirely successful diversionary tactic.

'F***ing countryside,' Teri said again.

Sometimes, I think she is a bit lacking in imagination. I could think of at least a dozen other derogatory things to say about the delights of rural life. Or, perhaps she couldn't erase the thought of Andrew and sex?

'Heard that,' Denis said, linking his arm through mine again and dragging me along with him.

'Come on. They can wallow in the mire if they choose but I'm getting out of the cold.'

Andrew, credit where credit is due, was the perfect host. 'Come in, come in,' he said. 'Make yourself at home.'

And then he saw Teri, leaning on Charlie's arm and limping slightly, and there was a distinctly 'country' pong about her. 'Extraordinary,' he said.

He held her at arm's length and they air kissed. 'You have been in the wars,' he said. 'Let me help you out of your wet things.'

I knew what that meant – and so did Denis. He sniggered and raised his eyebrows. 'Oh my,' he said.

Oh my, indeed.

A good friend would have assumed the role of chaperone. Clearly I'm not as good a friend as I should be because I waved her off. If she couldn't take care of herself by now, there was nothing I could do about it. Besides, my mobile phone had synced with Andrew's broadband connection and my inbox was pinging fit to burst with new messages and missed calls. One was from Daddy. 'Ring me,' he said. 'I need a favour.'

A favour?

CHAPTER 26

TERI

The house, which looked grand and imposing from the outside, was equally impressive inside. At least, the west wing which Andrew had renovated was. He offered to take us on a guided tour. Charlie and Denis groaned.

'We've seen it all before,' Denis said, petulantly. That boy was seriously getting on my nerves.

'Well, you go into the drawing room,' Andrew said. 'Help yourself to drinks – I've left some wine in there.' He turned to me. 'Coming?' He reached out to take my hand. Lee, who'd been inspecting a large bookcase which ran along one side of the room, spun round and scampered towards us. 'Can I come too?' Typical of her to stick her nose in. She had my ex-husband and now she wanted gorgeous and god-like too.

Andrew grinned and said something about the more the merrier.

During a guided tour of the ground floor, he pointed out ornate plasterwork, shuttered windows, the billiard room, the boot room – a boot room? – and the galleried landing at the top of the first flight of stairs.

Lee was full of admiration. 'My word,' she said more than once as Andrew pointed out a frescoed wall and, 'Gosh, what a job that must have been…'

Every now and then Andrew would take my hand to pull me forward for a closer inspection of some arty brickwork or put his arm around my shoulders so that I could rest against him to examine the original picture rails in the high-ceilinged rooms.

I noticed he didn't touch Lee – mainly because she was rushing backwards and forwards inspecting this and that, running her hands along woodwork and saying 'Wow!' a lot.

We moved through the house and into a scullery at the rear. 'And that's the tour,' said Andrew, dusting his hands together.

'It's a wonderful house,' Lee said. 'I'm just going to pop back and inspect the books again. Do you mind?'

Mind? I couldn't wait for her to leave.

'It's a fabulous place,' I said, leaning back against an old stone sink and looking directly into those blue eyes.

Andrew moved towards me as I expected he would. 'You know,' he said, 'I think there is…' He bent closer, his face just inches from mine. I closed my eyes. His fingers rubbed gently just below my right eye. Strange thing to do, but I could go along with whatever he had in mind.

'There, got it,' he said, standing back. 'Bit of mud. Now, I must get on with lunch.'

Gorgeous and god-like must be gay.

****

Lunch was soup and sandwiches. There was no Cook. And the soup was out of a packet. The boys chatted mostly about the goats or the sheep that Andrew had collected earlier, with Denis changing the subject every now and then to mention some 'fabulous chandelier' or wonderful wallpaper he'd seen in town that would look lovely in Andrew's drawing room.

'Steady on,' Andrew said. 'I can't afford luxuries like that.'

'And neither can we now, thanks to Charlie's dad,' Denis said. I glanced at him and then at Charlie, who seemed not to have noticed the snide comment. 'I don't know what we're going to do. We're absolutely broke.'

'Perhaps you could get a job.' Denis looked at me. Daggers. Okay, Mister, I thought. I can play your game. 'Well, what's stopping you?' I asked. 'You're young, fit and healthy…'

'You don't understand,' Denis said, adopting a patient tone. 'Charlie and I are trying to make a go of it as smallholders.'

'What with just three goats?' I said.

'We have hens and we grow vegetables,' Denis said. 'And we sell eggs and stuff at the farmers' market.'

'Yeah, but not enough to make a profit,' I argued.

'Life's not always about making money.' Denis pouted like a child.

'Girls, girls,' Andrew said, flapping his hands. 'Play nicely. Now, coffee?'

'Sounds lovely,' I said, 'but shall I clear these things up first?'

Lee, who'd seemed distracted through lunch, offered to help, but I said, no, stay and chat to Charlie and Denis.

I leapt to my slippered feet – and, yes, they were a size too small but made of a soft blue velvet, so they stretched. I decided that whoever had owned them had left them and was probably long gone. A previous girlfriend perhaps? An ex-wife? Or a weekend guest who'd forgotten to take them home? The weekend guest was my preferred option.

'By the way,' I said as I reached across the table to collect the plates and bowls. 'These slippers are gorgeous. Whose are they?'

Denis sniggered. He knew what I was up to, and I hated him for it. I slammed the pile of plates back down on the table and rounded on him. 'Denis, have you got something to say?'

Denis leaned back in his chair and raised his hands, palms towards me as if to hold me at bay. 'Whoa,' he said as though reining in a horse. 'No need to be so touchy.'

Andrew stepped in. 'C'mon, let's get these washed up,' and he scooped up the plates and headed for the scullery.

'For God's sake, Denis,' I hissed, then followed Andrew from the room.

'You don't have to do this,' Andrew said, twisting on the hot water tap to fill the old, stone sink in the scullery. 'I can manage.'

'No, it's all right. I'd like to help.'

He squirted in washing-up liquid and jiggled his right hand in the water to raise suds. I've heard people talk about the atmosphere being electric, and now I knew what it meant. Andrew remained silent, but I could sense he was tense.

'I'm sorry, Andrew…' I began, not really sure what I had to be sorry about. But he suddenly spun round, stepped towards me, reached out his hands – the right one still wet – and pulled me into his chest, where he hugged me for a couple of seconds. I didn't say a word. He loosened his grip, nudged me gently back a couple of inches, looked at me questioningly and leaned in for the kiss I'd been wanting ever since first having seen him.

We pressed into each other; he ran his hands up and down my back, finally resting on my buttocks to force me in closer to his body. I slid one hand onto his chest and down to his belt buckle. 'God, you're gorgeous,' he muttered in my ear. He pulled me to the scullery door, opened it and we stepped out into a walled garden. He pushed me against the one patch of wall not covered in a trailing clematis, and ground into me, rubbing my backside with one of his hands while fondling my right breast with his other. He was kissing me in a way I can only describe as urgent.

I've had sex in many places: on kitchen tables, open-plan staircases, in a ship's galley, and even in the back of a car – an Audi rather than a Fiesta, but even so… But I've never before been thrust up against a wall and taken in the way Andrew now planned.

I thought about objecting. Goodness knows what the stonework was doing to my dress, but without wanting to sound Jane Austen, the passion was too intense. I wanted this man and I was getting him, even if it meant a closer encounter with trailing greenery than I'd ever had before.

CHAPTER 27

LEE

Bloody Teri and bloody Andrew. I was itching to get on my phone and find out what Daddy wanted and the pair of them insisted on hoicking me around the bloody house to admire the plasterwork and skirting boards and embossed wallpaper and antique lighting. Why? If I'd been in Teri's slippers, I'd have taken the chance offered by the grand tour to slope off with Andrew and treat him to a display of my Coco de Mer Brazilian panties. And matching bra. But, no. 'Come on, Lee,' she said. 'You know how much you love old houses.'

No, I didn't know. My daddy built new homes, and I liked houses that were warm and waterproof and with perfectly aligned walls and ceilings. And Georgian mansions where half the property is falling apart at the seams and the other half has been renovated by the sort of cowboy builder who wouldn't last two minutes in Daddy's yard are not my cup of tea.

'How interesting,' I said as Andrew bored for England about his frescoes and his finishes and his God-knows-what-else.

'Wow,' I said in an attempt to vary it a bit.

'That must have been quite a job,' I said, presented with the newly-restored staircase.

Dear God, throw me a thunderbolt please, and get me out of here.

Eventually, under pretence of going back to inspect the library – a couple of easy chairs and a pair of bookcases rammed with celebrity cookbooks and ghost-written autobiographies – I made my escape. Not a moment too soon. As I pulled the scullery door behind me, the two of them locked tongues.

I was sorely tempted to turn right back around and see who choked first. But, what the heck? Teri wouldn't be staying in Suffolk long enough to get carried away and fall in love, and Andrew looked far too canny, and too practised an adulterer, to get drawn into romantic entanglements.

****

I was spoilt for reading choice in what passed for the library. It was a toss-up between TV chef Gordon Ramsey's kitchen nightmares and travels to infinity and beyond with *Star Trek* and Shakespearean actor Patrick Stewart. Good old Patrick won – the pictures looked better. So I curled up in a chair, opened the book, dug out my mobile and called Daddy. The phone rang and rang and rang. No answer. Not even a voicemail message. Well, that wasn't a surprise. His mobile phone was so old it was practically pensionable and didn't have a voicemail facility. But, Daddy is a utilitarian phone-user. As far as he's concerned a phone is a business tool and should be answered promptly. So why hadn't he picked up? It was puzzling. And that was another thing: Daddy doesn't do telephone chit-chat. Social calls are as rare as rocking horse poo, so if he'd left a message demanding a favour, it must be something fairly important. So again, why hadn't he answered my call?

Logic told me Daddy would be on-site and probably with one of his suppliers or customers. That's what logic said. But old man not-an-ounce-of-common-sense-and-let-your-imagination-run-wild didn't buy anything so sensible. No, he'd got both Daddy and Mammy dead and buried and me and Fliss crying buckets at the graveside.

CHAPTER 28

TERI

'Bloody hell,' Andrew said, standing back to adjust his trousers. 'I'm sorry, Teri. That was NOT meant to happen.' He emphasised the word not. I could almost see the capital letters.

'Please, Andrew…' What the hell was I pleading for? 'Please don't say sorry. We both wanted –'

'Yes, but –'

'No buts,' I said, coming over stern mistress-like. 'I wanted to do this as much as you.'

'Yes, but –'

'I said, no buts.' I straightened the front of my dress, swiped at my bottom in the hope that would get rid of any clinging stonework and clematis, and reached out for him, but he turned back into the scullery. He was filling a kettle at the sink when I came up behind him and wrapped my arms around his waist. He put the kettle down on the drainer, swivelled and embraced me, rubbing his nose in my hair.

He broke away. 'Let's give our guests their coffee.'

Back in the drawing room, Lee was curled up on one of the chairs flicking through a book that she'd – rudely – taken from the bookcase. She looked very much at home. Well, she could forget that.

Denis leered at me. 'Now what have you two been up to?' he asked nasally and full of insinuation. 'Been doing a spot of gardening?'

I smiled at him in what I hoped was an indulgent expression. 'I fell over.'

'Seems to be your day for tumbles.'

Charlie, who'd not said much while the coffee was being poured, drank his quickly, put his cup down, stood and turned to Denis. 'Come on, we ought to get back to feed the girls.'

Feed the girls? I thought they ate grass.

Lee uncurled herself from the chair, and Charlie leant forward to take her hand and pull her up. She gave him a grateful smile. She does know he's gay, doesn't she? I thought.

'I'll follow you later,' I said. 'Andrew's asked for some advice on a recipe…' It sounded implausible to me too.

I didn't bother looking at either Lee or Denis as I could imagine Lee's disapproval and Denis' gurning face. Well, stuff them both. They can think what they like.

Andrew and I stood in the doorway to wave them off. The only missing aspect from the dream scenario was the pair of Labradors.

'Have you ever thought of getting a dog?' I asked as I followed Andrew back into the house.

'What…?'

'Never mind.' I moved towards him in as seductive a way as was possible in my muddy state of disarray. I wondered if there was a dry cleaners in town.

'Teri, I need to tell you something…' He looked at his feet. I instinctively glanced down too, but at the blue velvet slippers, and I knew what was coming.

'You're married, aren't you? And your wife is away at the moment?'

His guilt-ridden face said it all.

'Yes. And she's got size five feet?'

Andrew frowned. 'The slippers,' I said. 'They're hers?'

'Yes.'

'And you've taken your ring off.'

He looked at his left hand and wiggled his fingers. There was a pale mark where a wedding band would have been.

'Oh,' he said, sounding almost relieved. 'No, I didn't take it off deliberately, I promise you. I just don't wear it when I'm working around the grounds.'

'Ah, but you've not been working around the grounds today, have you, unless you call the bit of gardening we did earlier "working"?'

He looked sheepish.

'Oh, you bastard.' I said it gently, not angrily; it takes two to tango, and I hadn't sat this one out. 'And where's your wife now?'

'She's gone on a girlie get-together. She's due back tonight.'

Girlie get-togethers. It had been a long time since I'd had one of those. In fact, I don't know if I've ever been on one unless you count the evenings I spent with Lee.

Lee, my ex-best friend. Lee who is even now planning her wedding to my ex-husband. Lee, who like everyone else in my life – including this gorgeous and god-like man standing in front of me – has shafted me and let me down. I was suddenly overwhelmed with self-pity. 'Oh, for fuck's sake' was all I could manage. Andrew, the wimp, just stood there.

CHAPTER 29

LEE

Denis is really quite sweet. Charlie too, although like his sister, he's a bit lacking in empathy. Denis, on the other hand, for all his bitchiness, perhaps *because* of his bitchiness, is a very noticing sort of person. 'Come on, Lee,' he said after watching me deconstruct a smoked salmon and cream cheese sandwich. 'What's with the mess?' He lifted the paper serviette, under which, while the others were engaged in a dull as dishwater conversation about goats and smallholdings and the loss of Teri and Charlie's inheritance, I'd hidden the turds of cream cheese I'd scraped off the salmon with a teaspoon.

'Don't like cheese,' I muttered, gesturing towards the sandwich platter which ten minutes earlier had been loaded with poppy seed and multi-grain mini rolls of Wensleydale and apple, cheddar and chutney, brie and grape and, of course, cream cheese and salmon.

'Slim pickings,' Denis said. 'What about the soup?'

I cupped a hand to my mouth and pretended to retch. He smiled and stirred the brown mush in his bowl. 'Can't say I blame you.'

'My stomach thinks my throat's been cut,' I whispered.

'Shame our host is pre-occupied.' He nodded in the direction of Andrew, who was feeding Teri a grape. I pretended to retch again. Denis slapped my hand with his serviette. 'Now, now,' he said. 'I thought I was the bitch.'

I giggled, and Teri frowned at me. 'Is everything all right?'

'Yes,' I said, 'although I might head back to the cottage when everyone's finished.'

'Goodness,' Andrew said, looking at his watch. 'It's later than I thought.'

He started gathering plates and soup bowls. 'Coffee anyone?'

Teri jumped up. 'Let me give you a hand.'

Denis raised his eyebrows and whispered, 'I can guess what sort of a hand she's planning to give him.'

Yes, so could I.

'Actually,' I said, pushing back my chair. 'I'm not too bothered about a hot drink. I think I'll set off back now.'

'Hang on a bit,' Denis said, pulling me back into my seat, 'and we'll walk back with you. Charlie won't go anywhere until he's had his coffee, but the girls will need feeding soon.'

'What about Teri? We can't leave her here.'

'Of course, we can,' Denis said. 'I'm sure she'll find something to occupy herself.'

Yes, but it was to be hoped Andrew's lovemaking was a touch less cheesy than his sandwiches.

It was certainly quick. The pair couldn't have been gone more than ten minutes, fifteen at an absolute stretch, but when they returned with the coffee tray it was apparent from the look on Teri's face – cat who'd swallowed a canary, followed by a bucket of double cream – not to mention the wisps of greenery trailing from her hem, that they'd exchanged more than a chaste kiss or two.

I hoped they'd washed their hands before making the drinks.

Nobody lingered over coffee. Teri was clearly itching for seconds, and Denis had the girls on his mind and so, it seemed, did Charlie, since he downed his coffee in one long gulp. 'Better get back to the girls,' he said. 'They'll be feeling peckish.' I thought Andrew might have tried to persuade his guests to stay a little longer, but he harried us out of the door with the fierce intent of a sheep dog herding kittens. Perhaps, he too had an itch that needed scratching. But, no, he seemed almost surprised, and not best pleased either, when Teri insisted she'd stay behind to finish clearing up. The jerk.

The three of us were striding purposefully back down the lane, helped along by an obliging wind which had changed direction again, when my mobile phone started dancing a fandango in my backpack.

Damn! As ever, it had wormed its way to the bottom of the bag and my frantic fingers struggled to get a grip. Finally. 'Mammy,' I said, 'I've been trying to get Daddy –'

'His phone's gone kaput,' she interrupted, which, excuse me, is not a reason to make random phone calls to your eldest daughter.

'I'm not surprised. It's been on its last legs for donkey's years.'

'Don't make silly jokes,' she snapped.

Well, it might not have been a great joke, but there was no reason to get so sniffy.

'Speak to your father,' she said and there was a muffled mumbling and muttering before Daddy came on the line.

'Just a quick call,' he said. When were his calls ever anything but quick? 'Thought you ought to know I've got an appointment at the hospital tomorrow.'

What?

Nothing to worry about, he said, but the GP thought he should have a check-up.

'What sort of check-up?' I asked.

'Oh, this and that,' he said.

'What sort of this and that?'

But he couldn't, or wouldn't, be more specific.

'Would you like a lift?' I asked, fully expecting a refusal. Daddy hates being driven. Especially by me. He says I have no spatial awareness.

But today, he accepted the offer. 'Thank you,' he said. 'The appointment's at one thirty. Come for us just before one.'

But first I needed to get home.

CHAPTER 30

TERI

When I got back to the cottage, there was no sign of Lee or Denis, and Charlie was slumped on one of the sofas. He looked up and straightened as I came in holding the shoes formerly known as nude in my hands. Denis would no doubt have a dicky fit if I got mud on the carpet.

Charlie and I aren't what you'd call close. We didn't huddle together as children against our mother's alcoholism and our father's absence, but instead, escaped to our rooms to grow up within our own solitude. Dad's long hours at the factory left all three of us neglected in our own ways. Materially, we wanted for nothing. Emotionally, we found our own distractions. As we got older, Charlie was always lost in some book about livestock management or allotment holding, and I went out on the hunt for boys with poor old Lee tagging behind and complaining when I got off with the better-looking one.

Lee could never understand my family set-up and was horrified when I told her that I saw our housekeeper more often than I saw my parents.

She, of course, had her solid, caring, darling Mammy, Daddy and sister, and the four of them lived together in a tight little Irish-we're-poor-but-we-stick-together unit. Although they weren't poor, at least, not after Daddy Harper became the Harper of Harper Homes and built most of the new des res detached houses around our town. Darling Daddy Harper even built one for his Dear Darling Daughter. I once told her to sell it and buy a luxury duplex in my apartment block. 'Modern living,' I told her, but she pulled her frowning face at how anyone could consider getting rid of something constructed by her own father's calloused hands. Although, actually, he has men do the physical building now.

So, Charlie and I were never close, but he's the only thing I have for a brother, and I sensed he was not best pleased as I stepped, bare-footed, into the room.

I held up my hands, palms forwards. 'You don't have to say it.' I wasn't entirely sure what 'it' might have been, but guessed it was probably disapproving.

Instead, Charlie shook his head and apologised to me. 'I should have warned you,' he said. 'Andrew's a bit of a bugger.'

'What do you mean?'

'Well, he's not entirely what he seems.'

'Oh, I know he's married,' I said.

'Yeah, but that doesn't stop him. He'll shag anything given half a chance.'

'Oh, thank you,' I said, sarcastically, stepping over the rug to his sofa so I could sit next to him.

Charlie turned and faced me. 'No, I don't mean anything against you. I could see he was taken with you. But didn't you suspect anything as he was showing you round?'

'How do you mean?'

'Well, he only showed you downstairs, not the bedrooms. If you'd gone upstairs, you'd have seen that he had a woman living there.'

True, it had struck me. But I was so caught up in the gorgeous but god-likeness of the man that I didn't question my reservations.

'But, honestly, Teri. Anything in a skirt, that's Andrew.'

'Thanks, again.' I leant back on the sofa. 'Where are the other two?'

'Ah,' Charlie said as if suddenly remembering. 'Lee had a phone call as we were walking back – never knew you could get a signal on the lane. Something to do with her dad. She's had to go home. Denis has given her a lift to the station.'

That's typical, I thought. There'll be nothing wrong. She'll have got the hump because I went off with Andrew. She's so disapproving. Always has been. Well, at least I don't have to listen to her going on about it.

CHAPTER 31

LEE

Teri and I had spent close on eight hours in the car on our way to Suffolk, and it took me just three hours and fifty-five minutes to do exactly the same journey by train. And that included sprints between underground and over-ground rail stations at both Liverpool Street and Kings Cross. In the unlikely event Teri persuades me to join her on another jaunt to goat heaven, I'll let the train take the strain.

Mind you, the rail companies make you pay through the nose for the privilege. 'How much?' I screamed at the man behind the booking office counter. 'You want me to pay eighty nine pounds for a one way ticket?'

'No, no,' he corrected. 'Not eighty nine but eighty nine fifty.'

Heaven forbid I forget the fifty pence.

'It's cheaper if you book in advance,' he said. 'You could have got the same ticket for just over thirty-six pounds if you'd bought your ticket three months ago.'

Yes, and, if I'd known three months ago Daddy would need a lift to the hospital, I wouldn't have come to Suffolk in the first place.

'Just give me the ticket,' I said, slapping my debit card on the counter. The clerk indicated the card machine.

'I'd just better arrive relaxed, refreshed and ready to go,' I said.

'Sorry?'

I pointed to the corporate logo on the wall behind him. 'That's the promise, isn't it?'

He turned around, thick tufts of greasy, greying hair curled slightly over the edge of his collar. They matched the hair spouting from his ears and nostrils. If I was his wife I'd treat him to a decent haircut and a pair of tweezers. 'We'll get you there refreshed, relaxed and ready to go,' he read.

'I presume it's a money back guarantee?'

'I'd have to ask my manager.' He pushed the ticket and my receipt across the counter. Somebody, his wife, perhaps, needed to invest in a good nail brush. There was enough dirt under his fingernails to grow potatoes. And his uniform could do with a proper wash too – his jacket was emitting a musty left-on-the-washing-line-overnight smell. 'Would you like me to get him?' he asked.

'No thanks,' I said. 'I'll send him a letter if I don't find every mile awesome.'

'Eh?'

FML, I thought, he ought to spend a bit of time familiarising himself with his company's tag lines.

I held out the ticket he'd just issued. 'On a mission to make every mile of every journey awesome.'

'Oh,' he said. 'We do make grand promises, don't we?'

You could f***ing say that again.

And, I must stop swearing too – even under my breath. It was getting to be a bad habit, and sooner or later I'd slip up and swear in front of Mammy or Daddy. Or Dan, who was equally po-faced about bad language.

The clerk coughed. 'I think you'd better get a move on, Madame. That's your train pulling in across the bridge.'

F***! I grabbed my bags and ran.

****

Dan was waiting at the other end. 'Good journey?'

I shrugged. 'Well, I didn't want to kill Teri…'

He laughed. 'She's a dreadful driver, isn't she?'

'I wouldn't mind the speed,' I said, 'if she just kept her eyes on the road and her hands on the steering wheel.'

He wrapped an arm around my shoulders, enveloping me in a cloud of citrus and sandalwood, and dropped a kiss on the top of my head.

'Never mind, you're home now. Let's get these bags in the car, and we'll go for something to eat. Where do you fancy? L'homme-vert?'

No, not really. I wasn't dressed for L'homme-vert, which, as the name suggests is French and posh and pretentious and, even if I had been dolled up to the nines, I still wouldn't fancy it. I just wanted to go home and curl up on my settee in my pyjamas with a large glass of wine or two or three. On my own.

Fat chance.

Dan had decided I needed cheering up and, since dinner at L'homme-vert always cheered him up, was convinced it would cheer me up too. F***. F***. F***.

But, hurrah, God was on my side. The posh restaurant goblins had paid a visit and L'homme-vert had been closed down. 'Hygiene irregularities,' said the notice on the door.

I wasn't surprised. Last time I'd eaten steak there it had been so rare a good vet could have resuscitated it.

'Let's pick up a pizza,' I suggested as Dan scrolled through his phone trying to find a number for The Social Club, his second favourite restaurant.

'No,' he said, punching the keypad, 'you've had a trying day and you deserve a treat.' He held up a hand and spoke briskly to the maître d' on the other end of the line. 'Hi, Michael. Dan Caine, I don't suppose you could squeeze me and a guest in for dinner tonight.' He looked at his watch. 'We could be there in ten minutes.' A pause. 'Twenty, it is then. Thanks, Michael. See you shortly.' He grinned. 'Success.'

Or not, as the case may be.

But, he was trying to be nice – and he was certainly very trying – so I gritted my teeth and kept my fingers crossed that after dinner he'd drop me off at home and go back to his place.

CHAPTER 32

TERI

To be honest, I was quite relieved that Lee had gone home. It meant I wouldn't be tempted to tell her about what had happened at Andrew's – or with Duck's Arse. She wheedles things out of me when I'd prefer them to remain private.

It was nice to be a world away from Lee and Dan and Declan and everyone else.

I'd not been this happy since I'd had those two weeks with Declan a couple of months ago. Our affair had ended, largely because the bastard had been seeing other women, but there was something about him I couldn't resist, and I *didn't* resist when he turned up at my duplex one evening with that lost-puppy-look of his that always caused me to crumple. Why had I let him reach out for me, draw me into his chest, kiss the top of my head and then pull me gently to the bleached hallway floorboards?

He told me how much he'd missed me, how much he'd missed making love to me, how much he loved me. Then he told me he was back living in the marital home, describing the arrangement as economical rather than emotional as he couldn't afford to run a house, wife and kids, plus a bachelor flat on the salary he got at the *Evening Leader*.

Reason, experience, logic – all those – deserted me. I thought it was time I had some love and happiness in my life. And Declan spelt love and happiness.

Well, clearly, he didn't, and I should have known better, but for the next two weeks, we were like a couple of love-sick teenagers, meeting at every opportunity, walking hand in hand around lakes and having picnics in the park.

'I love you,' Declan had said.

'I love you too and I can't live without you,' I'd replied. And that was a fatal phrase, as I had found out when Declan's wife turned up at my duplex, so pregnant with twins that I thought her waters were likely to burst over the expensive floorboards on which her husband and I had so recently had sex.

Marnie, the wife, clearly spoke a different language to me in that she took the declaration 'I can't live without you' to mean that if Declan left me I would kill myself.

'You worried the life out of him,' the stupid cow said, collapsed on my living room sofa like a beached whale while I worried how she was ever going to haul herself back upright again. 'You should be ashamed of yourself.'

Well, I thought. It isn't me who should be ashamed, but her two-timing, lying, fornicating husband. Anyway, I'm finished with him completely. And to prove it, I've had a very nice fling with Duck's Arse and a very nice fling with Andrew. I don't want anything from either of them – I used them rather than the other way round. And it feels good. At last, I'm in charge.

CHAPTER 33

LEE

We've had a couple of cold snaps lately when I've really appreciated Dan's toasty body lying next to mine. But a hot water bottle works just as well and doesn't snore either. Sometimes, the noise is so bad it's hard to resist the temptation to stick a pillow over his head.

Dan said nobody else had ever complained, which I found hard to believe.

'Teri?'

He laughed. 'Teri? It'd take a nuclear bomb going off next door to wake her. Once her head hits the pillow, she's out like a light.'

That wasn't strictly true. Get her head on a pillow and she was up for all manner of shenanigans.

'No.' Dan was adamant. 'There were no complaints in the bedroom from Teri.'

Excuse me? Oh, yes there had been.

'What about the fluffer and the nose bleed?'

'How do you know about that?'

What a dumb question. 'Think about it, Dan. Only two people were in the room. You didn't tell me so…'

'I can't believe she told you about that.'

Why? 'Get used to it. Women tell each other things.'

'What sort of things?'

'None of your bloody business.'

'I think it is my business if you've been swapping notes with my ex-wife.'

The pompous so-and-so. Did he think we had nothing better to talk about?

'She wasn't your ex at the time.'

'And that made it all right?'

Yes, actually it did.

'And, I suppose you've been regaling her with stories about my snoring?'

He really did think he was our sole topic of conversation.

'No, but if she'd told me you snored louder than a steam engine in a long tunnel I might have thought twice about letting you into my bedroom.'

'Well, that's easily remedied,' he said. 'I'll move into the spare room.'

Why? Why? Why not just go back to your place for a few nights so I can have a bit of peace and quiet?

'I heard that!'

Great. Now he was offended. Clearly, I was supposed to soothe his battered male ego. Tough. Give me a good night's sleep and I might be up to it.

Of course, he didn't move back to his flat. Or the spare room. I think I was glad. Certainly, I was developing a new respect for Teri; she'd lasted almost a full year with Dan. Not sure I would.

Still, he had his good points. Like today, when I was trying to get ready for my hospital trip. I didn't have a thing to wear – and that's something I bet you never thought you'd hear from me. It was important to strike the right tone with my outfit, and I couldn't decide either on the tone or the outfit.

Dan, who wasn't due in work until noon, tried to be helpful. 'You're the chauffeur, not the patient,' he said. 'No-one who matters will even know you're there.'

Tactful, as ever. And clueless, too. Okay, I wouldn't get to meet the medics, except, perhaps, briefly in passing, but I would be part of team Harper, and, since doctors are only human, it was important to look like someone from the posh Primleys rather than the grubby Grimleys. Besides, there was Mammy to consider too. Like Teri, she is congenitally incapable of stepping outside the front door without perfect hair, perfect make-up and perfect styling. I'm pretty much immune to their tuts of disapproval over my own more relaxed dress sense, and, if I'm honest, I do like to wind them up a bit by wearing stuff that I know they think highly inappropriate on a woman of my age. Neither of them understands the appeal of my biker boots or faded denim jacket.

I could imagine the look on Mammy's face if I turned up in my usual gear, and it wasn't worth the grief. Besides, I can scrub up reasonably decently when the occasion demands, and today was an occasion that demanded scrubbing up.

But the scrubbing up was proving troublesome. 'What about this?' I asked Dan, pulling a deep purple, fitted dress from the wardrobe.' Or this?' I wondered, taking a silver and grey tunic off its hanger. 'Or there's this?' I held up one of my favourites, a green and navy spotted number. It looks better than it sounds. 'And this?' I picked up a blue drop-waist frock.

'I like what you're wearing,' he said.

'I can't wear jeans.' Honestly. Had he listened to a word I'd said?

'Stick a jacket on and you'll look smart casual.'

Hmmm! He could be so annoying sometimes.

'The dark blue,' he said, pulling a long jersey number from the wardrobe.

We both studied the figure in the mirror. 'Swap the shirt for a loose top,' he said. 'Where's that nice amber one?' Sometimes, there are advantages to a fiancé who is a self-confessed media tart with an eye for fashion.

He gave me a hug. 'Try not to worry,' he said. 'It's probably nothing.'

Yes, that's why Daddy's family doctor had sent off blood samples for testing and booked him in for a CT scan instead of giving him a prescription for the iron tonic which Daddy insisted would see him right.

'And don't forget your ring,' Dan added as I picked up the car keys and headed for the door.

Ooops! And there you have another of the elephants currently lurking in our living room. Anymore and we'll have enough to start an elephant sanctuary. Mammy and Daddy were aware I was 'seeing' someone but I hadn't yet got round to telling them that he was a household name –

in Yorkshire anyway – or that he was a twice-divorced man. I thought they'd probably like him when, and if, they met him and they'd definitely be impressed with his job as senior anchorman on our regional television company's flagship evening news programme. But Mammy, sure as hell, would have something to say about those two divorces, and, the longer I could put off hearing what she had to say, the better.

Fliss, who was in on the secret, advised coming clean. 'She's bound to find out sooner or later,' she warned.

Tell me something I don't know.

Dan too wanted to stop prevaricating. Between marriages he'd been quite a ladies' man, and initially he was mildly amused at being considered too 'hot' for my mother's taste. Increasingly, though, he thought it was silly. 'You're a grown woman,' he said. 'What's the worst that can happen?'

Good question and a daft one too. Dear, good, devout Catholic Mammy, who wanted only the best for her daughters, had been brought up to believe that what God had joined no man should put asunder. Without a shadow of doubt, she'd think a twice-divorced man was doubly damned, and she wouldn't consider Dan too hot for me; she'd believe he was heading for hot and hotter and that, in marrying him, I'd be consigned to hell-fire and damnation alongside him. And it would be her Christian – Catholic – duty to keep us apart.

Bottom line: I wasn't ready to face the hassle so that's why, after giving Dan, a quick kiss, I switched my traditional Irish Claddagh ring from the third finger of my left hand to my right.

CHAPTER 34

TERI

Denis was less triumphant than I thought he would be at my downfall – or having become a fallen woman with the man in the big house; all very Tess of the d'Urbervilles. He had his mind on other things.

The Norfolk allotment convention had been quite a success – despite Denis having returned home to find a dead Philomena. What with all the drama of a deceased goat, falling out with Charlie, rounding up the three remaining goats, leaving home, making up with Charlie, and me arriving with Lee, he'd not had time to tell anyone that he'd been made chairman of the Norfolk and Suffolk Allotment and Smallholding Society and that he was off to the N&SA&SS's office near Norwich to have meetings and sort out paperwork in advance of the upcoming Annual General Meeting.

Top of the agenda, apparently, was a campaign to attract new members, and Denis had been giving the enterprise a lot of thought as he drove Lee to the station. No doubt she'd have given him her academic input.

'What do you think of The Politics of Persuasion in Country Matters; Action in an Affordable Rural Culture?' Denis asked us over supper. Lee had definitely suggested that one.

I held my tongue. I didn't want to put Denis off especially as it would mean him disappearing to near Norwich – expenses paid – in a week's time, for almost a week, leaving Charlie and me to bond over the goats and hens. I was surprised at how much I was relishing having some time off with my little brother.

CHAPTER 35

LEE

'Wait,' Dan said as I headed out the door. He fumbled in his trouser pocket and withdrew a handful of loose coins. 'Here.' He tipped them into my palm. 'You're bound to need some change for parking.'

I kissed him. 'Thank you.'

Mammy and Daddy had their coats on ready and waiting when I pulled up just after half past twelve. Fliss stood by the back door, twiddling her thumbs.

'What are you doing?' I asked.

'I'm coming with you.'

I rolled my eyes. Typical. Even a trip to the hospital has to turn into a family charabanc trip.

'Don't blame me,' she said.

'I invited her,' Mammy said. 'Families should stick together.'

They'd have no choice when they got into the back of my car. It wasn't exactly roomy.

And, why couldn't Fliss have chauffeured the hospital run? There was no need for me to come hot-footing it back from Suffolk if she was on hand. I'd assumed I'd been recruited because she was busy with the kids.

Fliss rolled her eyes too. 'Leave it,' she mouthed.

Mammy buttoned her coat. 'Are you locking up?' It was a rhetorical question. Daddy always locked up. He didn't trust Mammy to do the last-minute checks he considered essential. Lights off: check. Kettle off: check. Gas fire off: check. Front door locked: check. Back door locked: check. Front door: double checked. Back door: triple checked.

Five minutes later we were buckled into my car. 'Right, let's go.'

'Nice car,' Daddy said, as we pulled out of the street.

'I like it,' I said.

Mammy poked her head between the front seats. 'Plenty of room in the back.'

'Could you sit back?' I asked. 'You're blocking my rear view mirror.'

'Good leg room in the front too.' Daddy fiddled with the adjustable bar under the seat.

Fliss squeaked as his seat shot back almost hitting her in the face. She tapped his shoulder. 'Move it forward a bit. You're squashing me.'

'Not sure I can,' Daddy said.

Mammy leaned forward again. 'Just give a little pull on that thing between your legs.'

I snorted. Fliss spluttered.

'What thing?' Daddy reached a hand under the seat. 'Can't find anything.'

Fliss groaned. 'It's the little bar you were playing with a minute ago.'

'Oh that.' The seat zoomed frontwards. 'Any better?'

'Thank you,' Fliss said.

Mammy had discovered the head rest could be moved up and down. 'This is a good idea. I can adjust it to support my neck. Very comfortable,' she approved.

Oh, the joys of travelling with my family.

'How's Teri?' Fliss asked.

I suppose a change of subject is as good as a rest, but I'd have preferred to steer well away from talking about Teri.

'Probably hopping mad,' I said.

'Oh no,' Mammy said. 'What have you done this time?'

Well, no need to ask whose side she was on.

'She wanted me to stay in Suffolk until the weekend,' I said. 'I didn't get time to say goodbye.'

And I hadn't phoned her when I arrived home to explain the sudden exodus either. Nor, come to that, had she called me, which could mean she'd been too busy with Andrew to notice my absence. Or, that she still hadn't replaced her mobile and didn't want to talk on the house phone when both Charles and Denis would be all ears. Or, she could have fallen out with me again. I crossed my fingers and hoped it was either option one or two.

CHAPTER 36

TERI

I was a little annoyed that Lee hadn't bothered to ring and apologise since taking off so suddenly. So the day after the fateful lunch with Andrew, I rang her from Charlie's landline.

When I danced the tango on my mobile, I not only broke the phone but lost all my contacts. Because I was so used to using speed dial, I never managed to memorise telephone numbers, but luckily, I was still old fashioned enough to have written some down in my diary – and Lee's was amongst them.

There was no reply from her home phone so I dialled her mobile. It took some time for her to answer and when she did, she must have dropped the phone because there was a clatter and I heard her saying 'Damn…fuck…damn', which isn't like her. Miss Proper Toes never swears and generally ticks me off when I do.

More clattering, then 'Hello? Are you still there? I'm in the car, at the hospital. Trying to bloody park and it's so bloody busy…'

That girl was seriously stressed.

'What's going on?' I asked.

'I don't know. I dropped Daddy and Mammy at the main entrance. Daddy's having some tests.'

Lee's dad? Tests? Surely not; he was as fit as an ox. Or should that be as strong as an ox? I drew breath to start asking questions, but Lee was rabbiting on. 'I said I'd meet them in the department – once I've found somewhere to park the damn car and I can't find anywhere…oh, wait…a woman's coming out of a space…must go…bye.'

And the line went dead.

Well, really. Why had Lee got to go too if it was just some tests? That family of hers. Always making such a fuss.

CHAPTER 37

LEE

I probably spent longer trying to find a parking space at the hospital than Daddy actually spent in the consulting room. Dropping him and Mammy and Fliss off at the main entrance, I headed towards the car park. Inevitably, it was jam-packed; I'd be lucky to find a space this side of Christmas.

Eventually, I did what other drivers were doing and stalked someone heading back to their car – a mum pushing an industrial-sized baby transporter – and crawled behind her until she stopped next to a four-by-four gas-guzzler which straddled two parking bays. Good. I'd have no trouble getting my little Mercedes A class in there.

She gave a half-wave as she transferred the baby into the back seat as if to say 'Won't be long.'

I smiled back. 'No hurry.'

We both lied.

My phone started ringing as I tutted and drummed my fingers on the steering wheel. Strictly speaking, I should have ignored it; these days speaking on your mobile behind the wheel of a car is almost as taboo as drink-driving. And probably carries a greater penalty. But, there's something about an unanswered phone. Suppose this was the one call that would change my life forever? The vice-chancellor of the university inviting me to join the board of governors? Unlikely. He didn't even know my name. The editorial boss at Parsley Academic Publications offering a job as head of their English Literature section? Even more unlikely. He also didn't know my name. Or, the National Lottery people telling me I'd won the jackpot? Unlikeliest of all, since I couldn't remember the last time I'd bought a ticket.

Odds on, this phone call, from a number I didn't recognise, was someone who thought I must be in need of new soffits and gutterings and drainage pipes. Which I wasn't.

Even so, the lure of the unknown beckoned and, besides, I was going nowhere fast. Mummy dearest was taking a month of Saturdays and Sundays to offload the transporter and associated baby paraphernalia into her boot. So, of course, I picked up and promptly dropped the phone under the passenger seat so recently vacated by Daddy. With an exasperated sigh, and a 'damn' and a 'fuck' and another 'damn' for good measure, I slipped the car into neutral and, like the contortionist I'm not, fumbled to retrieve it. I could hear someone on the other end saying 'Hello…hello…hello…'

'Hello,' I bellowed, finally plugging the elusive phone to my ear.

'Lee?' It was Teri.

Guess I could kiss goodbye to a life-changing offer. Unless she was planning to invite me back to Suffolk...

'I'm in the car, at the hospital. Trying to bloody park and it's so bloody busy…'

Now, if someone told you 'I'm at the hospital, trying to park', you'd reply 'Okay, catch you later', wouldn't you?

Not Teri. She wants Chapter and verse.

'What's going on?'

Where to begin? My father says he needs an iron tonic, his family doctor says he might need something stronger. For what? No-one has answered that question yet.

'I've brought Daddy and Mammy to the hospital. Daddy's having some tests,' I gabbled. On the other end of the line, Teri gasped, whether in sympathy or shock I don't know because, at last, with another nod and a smile, Mummy slammed the trunk lid, checked her make-up in the driver's mirror, adjusted her wing mirror, and, with another cheery wave, reversed out.

'Sorry…parking space…got to go…bye,' and I chucked the phone onto the passenger seat and nipped smartly into one of the spaces she had vacated, narrowly pipping the driver of a seven-seater people carrier coming from the opposite direction. Ha, I thought, no chance. The driver made a half-hearted effort to manoeuvre her mini-bus into the remaining space before giving up in disgust and, with much revving and crunching of gears, resumed her search.

I felt a little guilty. There was a bored-looking older child in the front passenger seat and three smaller ones belted into car seats in the back. I wouldn't fancy parking a mega-monstrosity with such a critical audience. Still, people with limited spatial awareness should drive smaller cars. Like me. Or have fewer kids. Or none. Also like me.

As promised, Mammy and Daddy had parked themselves on a couple of seats just next to the reception desk. Fliss was waiting at the revolving door. 'What kept you?' She pointed at Daddy, who, at first sight of me returning, jumped up and marched ahead. 'He's been chewing at the bit for the last ten minutes.'

'Couldn't find a space.'

'That's what I said. But he was convinced you'd got lost. Another minute and he was going to send me to look for you.'

I sighed. It was going to be a long morning.

Daddy had halted and was beckoning impatiently. 'What are you waiting for? Come on,' he said. 'We follow the red line.'

He strode on ahead as if he knew exactly where he was going. Perhaps, he did. Fliss and Mammy followed at a brisk trot with me ambling behind. I don't know why but I wasn't in a hurry to get wherever the red line was leading. I wished Daddy would slow down a bit as he seemed to be in an almighty rush to get wherever he was going. I shivered.

'Are you all right?' Mammy asked.

'Yes,' I said, 'why wouldn't I be?'

Gradually the blue, yellow and green lines taking patients towards other departments diverged from the red path. Daddy turned. 'Come on. Keep up.'

'Are you sure we should be following the red line?' Mammy asked. 'We've been walking forever.' We hadn't, but she was clearly becoming disorientated by the distinctive hospital smell of disinfectant, faeces and old people.

'Yes,' Daddy said. 'We're on the right track.'

But on track to where?

And then the line crashed into a pair of double doors, opening into a small reception area, with standard issue waiting room chairs lined up barrack-style against the walls. A nurse took Daddy's details, and we'd barely got bums on seats before a worryingly young-looking clinician called his name and escorted him towards the consulting room. Mammy stood up to follow, but Daddy gestured her to sit down. 'I've got my list,' he said.

'The list was my idea,' Mammy said. 'He's becoming a bit forgetful, so I told him to write everything down. All his aches and pains. And his questions too.'

'Good idea,' I said. But aches and pains? What aches and pains?

'He's tired all the time,' she said.

'Mammy. He's seventy-two years old. And he's still running a building firm. It's not surprising he's tired.'

She ignored me and tapped her fingers, ticking off the list in her head. 'The tiredness. Loss of appetite. The sweating. Temperatures. The pain in his side.' She put her head to one side, thinking. 'And he's lost a lot of weight too.'

Yes, if he'd been a woman, I'd have said he'd dropped at least a dress size. And he hadn't been overweight to begin with. But, neither of them had mentioned any of the other things before.

'It's time he gave up work,' I said eventually.

Fliss nodded. 'Spend more time with the grandchildren.'

I thumped her arm. 'Not so sure about that.'

Mammy ignored us. 'I think he's ready to finish too. But who'll take over? He can't just wind up the business. What will happen to the men he employs? And their families?'

We sat in silence. 'It's a shame we didn't have a boy,' Mammy said.

Hang on! You've got two lovely daughters. Okay, I'm biased, but what's not to like about Fliss and me?

'A boy would have grown up in the trade,' Mammy said. 'It would be Harper and Son, by now.'

Well, so sorry we're girls.

Mammy squeezed my arm. 'But we've been blessed with you and Felicity instead. And two gorgeous grandchildren and another on the way.'

She gave a delighted wriggle. 'If we could just see Lee happily settled...'

She didn't finish the sentence. The clinician man-child was shaking hands with Daddy at the consulting room door.

'All done,' Daddy said, buttoning his coat. 'Now, who's for a bite of something to eat? I'm starving hungry.'

Whatever happened to his lost appetite?

CHAPTER 38

TERI

Over the next few days I noticed that, for someone who was about to take on a major title within the allotment and smallholding fraternity, Denis did remarkably little around his and Charlie's enterprise.

Denis scooted off to town whenever he could to 'check out wallpaper' or 'look at a divine table lamp' and then he would return to ring 'potential clients'.

'Denis has this idea that he'd make a good interior designer,' Charlie explained. 'He has got a good eye for detail, you know, colours and styles.'

I looked around the stunning sitting room, loathing to admit he'd done a good job here.

'Oh, he'd love to do up the rest of the place,' Charlie said, 'but we just can't afford it now. I ploughed all my monthly allowance into buying the cottage first and then gradually bought more land. Neither of us has what you'd call a job with a salary but what with selling goat's milk, our fruit and vegetables – and with the odd bits of work Denis does – we get by.'

'What work does Denis do?' I asked.

'Oh, he knows a lot of influential people in Ipswich – people with money – and he's done the odd bit of work for some of them, you know, helping to choose a chandelier or wood flooring, that sort of thing. But he needs to get a really big job where he can show off his talents.'

Charlie was clearly proud of his boyfriend.

CHAPTER 39

LEE

My parents are not sophisticated diners. Daddy's business interests mean they've eaten more than their fair share of posh luncheons and dinners, but their tastes tend to simpler fare. Specifically, fast food chicken pieces and French fries. Except on days when Daddy pushed the boat out and ordered a chicken wrap.

It was more than a couple of weeks after his hospital appointment, and there must have been something about the four of us being together that made him ask Fliss and I to 'grab something to eat' with him and Mammy.

We'd gone to an out-of-town restaurant near a large DIY warehouse store. It was one of those places that markets itself as 'family-friendly'. In other words, it stank of pre-cooked fries and part-baked white bread buns and was heaving with fractious pre-school kids, dropping half-chewed chips and ketchup on the floor as they chased each other around and between the tables of less-than-yummy mummys, who really didn't care so long as they could get five minutes peace with a strong, black coffee.

Mammy pushed at the door. 'You can tell the food's good when there's always a queue at the counter.'

It wasn't a measure of excellence I'd have subscribed to but I said nothing as Daddy handed me a twenty-pound note and sent me and Fliss to order while he and Mammy secured seats. 'Aren't you eating?' he asked when I returned with his wrap, nuggets for Mammy and a double cheeseburger meal for Fliss, who'd already wolfed down several mouthfuls of chips as we walked back to the table. I slurped at my summer berry smoothie. 'No,' I said. 'Bit too early for lunch.'

'You don't know what you're missing,' Mammy said, tucking into her chips.

Daddy tilted his carton of fries in my direction. 'Want one?'

I shook my head. 'Mammy said you're thinking of retiring.'

He frowned. 'I'm thinking.' He took a bite of his wrap and chewed for a few minutes. His top dentures moved just a teeny fraction as he rolled the food around his mouth. How long had he been wearing dentures? I couldn't recall him even going to the dentist for a check-up, let alone having a headful of teeth removed and falsies fitted. Did I ever properly look at my parents? Probably not. I glanced at Mammy, who'd finished her fries and was dipping her nuggets into a mini pot of ketchup.

'I always save the best till last,' she said. She was in better nick than Daddy, who looked grey with exhaustion, but even so, there were new worry lines on her forehead, and her coffee-coloured hair had faded to a lighter golden brown, which looked nice but...

'When did you start lightening your hair?' I asked.

'When the grey roots started coming through faster than I could walk to the hairdresser's.' She pulled a thick strand of hair in front of her face. 'I've been going half a tone lighter every six weeks-or-so for over a year. What do you think?' She fluffed her hair and peered, squinty-eyed at her reflection in the restaurant window. 'I wasn't sure at first, but I don't think the grey roots are quite as noticeable now my hair's not as dark as it used to be.' She exhaled deeply. 'Time's catching up with me.'

And me. It was all very well Dan claiming to be too old for a second stab at parenthood, but if I didn't get a move on I'd be too old to have a first shot at it. Yes, Dan and I had some serious talking to do. Because if Dan didn't want to make me a mother, I'd have to find someone else who did. Just like that.

Daddy interrupted my musings. 'You know, I'm not quite as hungry as I thought,' he said, pushing his meal across the table towards me and Fliss. 'Do you want to finish it?'

Fliss shook her head. 'I'm full.'

I prodded the unsavoury-looking object. 'No thanks. I'm not a big fan of wraps. And this one looks a bit cardboard-ish.'

'Tastes it too,' Daddy agreed, dipping a fistful of fries in ketchup.

'But you like wraps,' Mammy protested.

'Not today,' he said, cramming fries into his mouth.

Mammy slapped his hand. 'Manners! One chip at a time.'

He winked at me. 'Now then, what's new in your love life?'

First Mammy. Now Daddy. Clearly, my lack of a significant other had been a topic for discussion.

I looked at Fliss, and she shook her head slightly. Not her, then.

I took the lid off my drinks carton and swirled the straw around the fibrous bits at the bottom. 'Well, there is someone,' I said. But they knew that already. I'd mentioned once or twice, ever so casually, that I'd been on a couple of dates with someone I'd met on holiday. Yes, I know, I was being economical with the truth, but Dan and I only became proper friends when we bumped into each other in Tuscany. Until then Dan's relationship with Teri had put him off-limits. Vice versa for him as well. And afterwards? Well, afterwards it was a different ball game for both of us. But this was neither the time nor the place to start explaining the semantics. 'But you might not like it. He's recently divorced.' I scrunched up the empty carton. 'Nothing to do with me,' I added, carefully glossing over the fact that my beau had notched up not one but two divorces. Best drip feed the difficult bits.

Mammy's reaction was unexpected. 'Children?'

Children? Where was the gnashing of teeth and tearing of robes as she bemoaned the godless daughter fraternising with a DIVORCED man? Never mind. I could live without the histrionics.

'Just one. A girl. Aged eighteen.'

She snorted. 'Have you met her?'

'Yes,' I said. 'She's very nice.'

She snorted again.

Daddy folded his arms and leaned back in his seat. 'Does he make you happy?'

'Yes.' I crossed my fingers.

He nodded at Mammy. 'At her age she's not going to find a man without some baggage.'

'No. But when you think of the chances she's had.'

Excuse me. I'm sitting right here in front of you.

'Water under the bridge,' Daddy said.

'Beggars can't be choosers,' Mammy finished.

Just a minute. 'I'm not quite beyond all hope.'

'No, but you're not in the first flush of youth either.'

Fliss clapped a hand to her mouth, whether in horror at the way the inquisition was going or to stifle her giggles, I couldn't be sure.

But dear God, with cheerleaders like Mammy and Daddy I might as well hang up my slippers once and for all. But, let's look on the bright side, this was going rather better than I'd expected. Who'd have thought my parents would be quite so pragmatic about my chances of happily ever after?

'I'm not in my dotage,' I pointed out.

'Will he want more children?' Mammy asked, changing tack unexpectedly.

'I don't know.' No point discussing that particular elephant in our living room with the present company.

'Would we like him?' Daddy asked.

'I don't know. I hope so.'

'What do you think, Fliss?' Mammy went off at another tangent.

We both hesitated. 'We haven't really discussed it,' I prevaricated.

'What about your friends? Have they met him? What does Teri think?'

Oh dear. That was a tricky one. What Teri thought didn't bear repeating. Not in polite society anyway.

'We haven't really discussed it properly either.' Now, that was an out-and-out lie, but better than telling the truth.

'But she has met him?' If there was a prize for persistence, Mammy would be a clear contender.

'Yes,' I said. 'She's met him.' And married and divorced him. And was all set to try and win him back until she discovered I'd beaten her to it.

'And she likes him?'

Hells bells. Why did it matter what Teri thought about Dan?

'You'd have to ask her,' I said. 'I know she was gob-smacked when she found out we were dating.'

All of which was true.

Daddy stood. 'I'm done here.' He helped Mammy into her coat. 'Perhaps we should invite Lee's young man round to dinner?'

Mammy nodded. 'You didn't tell us his name?'

Oh dear. I braced myself for the inevitable. 'Dan,' I said. 'Dan Caine.'

Daddy frowned. 'Do I know that name? It sounds familiar.'

I hesitated. It might've been better if I told them before they made the connection. 'He's...'

'Got it.' He snapped his fingers. 'It's him off the telly.'

'Yes.'

'Teri's ex-husband?'

Too late. Mammy had got there before me.

CHAPTER 40

LEE

I don't know what outraged Mammy most: the fact that I'd 'stolen' Teri's ex or that I'd bagged that lovely chap from the tea-time news programme. As I drove her, Daddy and Fliss back from lunch, she wouldn't let it go.

'Such a handsome man,' she said from the back seat of my car.

The inference being that a good-looking bloke wouldn't look twice at me.

'He and Teri were so well-matched.'

Shows what she knew.

'Why on earth would he leave that gorgeous creature for you?'

He didn't. She booted him out, and I picked up the pieces afterwards. Long afterwards.

'And how could a daughter of mine get involved with another woman's husband?'

The rhetorical questions were coming thick and fast. Fliss tried to put in a good word on my behalf. 'I'm sure Lee didn't do anything she shouldn't.'

'She's no better than a common tart.'

Now that was going a bit far. I straightened in my seat, but Daddy put a warning hand on mine and shook his head slightly. 'Leave it to Fliss,' he whispered.

Sadly, she struggled to get a word in edgeways. I caught her eye a couple of times in the rear view mirror and grimaced. Might as well be realistic; we'd more chance of rolling back the Red Sea than getting Mammy off her high horse. So, I did what I used to do during RE lessons at school when I got fed up of listening to the nuns droning on about sinners and saints and switched off.

Instead I found myself humming under my breath snatches of the Robbie Williams 'Angels' song. I wouldn't have minded having one of his angels blessing us all with a bit of love and affection.

'You haven't listened to a word I've said,' Mammy snapped as I pulled up outside their house. What did she expect? I'm not a medieval mystic who enjoys beating myself up over my many and varied misdemeanours. 'I'll talk to you later,' she promised, slamming the passenger door so hard the car rocked.

I looked forward to that.

Fliss opened the other rear door. 'Don't stress about it,' she said. 'She'll come round.'

Daddy too was equally phlegmatic. He paused before heaving himself out of the front passenger seat. 'She'll calm down in a day or two. She needs time to get used to the idea.'

I nodded. 'I know. But can you please tell her I did not steal Dan from Teri. They were long divorced before we started dating. And she dumped him. Not the other way round.'

I should have added, 'And for another married man too.'

Wait until Mammy heard the truth about Teri and Declan. That would knock the spots off her halo.

'I'll do my best too.' Daddy waved and walked slowly up the garden path, his shoulders slightly slumped. I wondered what the medics had told him he hadn't told us.

Before I could pull away, the front passenger door opened again. 'Someone needs to apologise to your friend for your behaviour,' Mammy hissed.

Personally, I thought I'd done enough apologising.

'So, I'll be giving Teri a phone call tonight to let her know how ashamed we all are,' she continued.

Good luck with that. She wouldn't find Teri at home, her mobile was broken, and I wasn't going to pass on Charlie's Suffolk number.

But it might be a good idea to call Teri myself. She'd want to know about Daddy. She'd always had a soft spot for him – and Mammy too.

Right now I had a soft spot for Mammy as well – in the middle of a very deep, very wet Irish bog. I hadn't realised though just how much Teri envied my loving, sometimes claustrophobic family until once, when she was very, very drunk – as in propped against the kitchen wall cuddling an almost empty bottle of bourbon – she'd confessed she used to fantasise sometimes about swapping families. 'I'd give a small fortune to have a mum and dad like yours,' she slurred.

'But you wouldn't want Fliss as a sister,' I'd teased.

'Yes,' she said. 'Even Fliss.' She'd looked a little sad. 'I wish I had someone to look after my back the way they look after yours.' But then she smiled. 'Good job I've got you.'

I remember feeling touched. It's easy to take your family for granted and, though, right now, Mammy wouldn't make my short list for parent of the year, I'd choose her over Teri's miserable cow of a mother every time. 'You can be my sister by adoption,' I'd promised – I was a little squiffy too; Teri didn't drink the bottle of bourbon all by herself. And we'd hugged and pledged undying love and affection, and whilst there had been plenty of times when her selfish, inconsiderate behaviour nearly drove me to fratricide, we'd shared so many highs and lows over the years – many of them involving fickle, unworthy men – that now it was inconceivable I shouldn't share my worries about Daddy.

Besides, I wanted to know why she'd never mentioned that Dan was a humungous snorer.

CHAPTER 41

TERI

I was quite relieved when Denis set off for his week in Norwich. And then we heard that his week had turned into two, because he'd persuaded one of the important allotment and smallholder society members to let him project manage the design of his new house.

'He's just bought this fabulous place in Cambridge, and it needs everything doing to it,' Denis told us when he rang one evening. 'I'm going to be up and down to London, choosing fabrics, lighting, tiles. I'm so excited.'

Charlie was pleased for him, of course. And relieved. 'He loves the goats,' Charlie said, 'but he's not that interested in getting his hands dirty. I hope this project comes off for him.'

I was more than happy – not so much for Denis, but for this temporary change of lifestyle for me.

I quite surprised myself by slinging the former nude heels in the bin and popping into Ipswich to buy trainers and wellies. Trainers and wellies! If I'd had a mobile, I would've taken a selfie of my legs in their rubber boots and sent it to Lee. She'd never have believed it was me; I always used to nag her about the things she wore. I can see now she dressed for comfort rather than style. I shouldn't have gone on about those leggings and baggy tops, especially now I'd left my dresses in the wardrobe and wore jeans and sweat shirts every day. I can't say how liberating it was not to have to consider what to wear in the morning, not to have to put make-up on. Every morning I tucked my hair into a ponytail to whizz out to collect the eggs, and what with checking on the goats, digging in the vegetable patch, helping Charlie build a fence, mend a gate and paint the outside window frames, the next two weeks flew by. And even though the rural lifestyle was playing havoc with my nails, I was happy as Larry.

Removed from work – farm labour excepted – and with very little internet, no shops and no delis nearby, I was loving this simpler life. I hardly gave my duplex, Declan or Duck's Arse a thought. Deep down, I knew I'd have to consider what I'd do when I went home. Seriously, what sort of job would I want? Was I going back to university lecturing? I must say, it had been a laugh, especially when I got to choose the subject – and my subject had always majored on John Wilmot, the 2nd Earl of Rochester and probably the most controversial poet within the restored court of Charles II.

But, for the moment, everyone – including Lord Rochester – belonged to a different place and time.

It was only when Andrew came by on his way to take some sheep to market or whatever that I wobbled. 'Want to come?' he shouted from his four-by-four. In my head, the old Teri laughed and said 'yes', hoping a trip to an auction would end in a local hotel room. The new Teri waved him away.

But I knew this country girl act wouldn't last. It had been fun but, seriously, could I sell my lovely duplex and buy a cottage in the outback? I'd get bored; there are only so many eggs to collect and so many window frames to paint. I needed the city life. I also needed a proper job. And I needed to sort things out with Lee, get back on an even keel with her. Okay, she's a pain in the arse what with her moralising, but she's always been my pain in the arse and I missed her. I also wondered what had happened about her father's tests, but reassured myself it would be something and nothing, as they say in the country.

One morning as I was sloshing paint, Charlie appeared with a mug of tea – I was getting used to drinking builder's brew from chipped mugs. He handed me the drink and said, 'Great news! Denis is home tomorrow.' Great for him, less so for me.

'Ah well,' I said. 'In that case, I might just take myself off home. Three's a crowd and all.'

'Oh, you don't have to rush off,' Charlie said.

'Yes, I do. I've been here long enough. Time to go back and face the music.'

I had no idea what would be playing.

CHAPTER 42

LEE

For goodness sake! I surveyed the kitchen and almost choked. How dare he! It was mid-afternoon and I'd finally got back from lunch with Mammy and Daddy and Fliss to find the kitchen resembled a mini-bomb site. Honestly, no exaggeration. Dan, whose Ridings shift started mid-morning, had clearly made himself a bite to eat before he left for work – a strong black coffee and a cheese and tomato sandwich, judging by the lingering whisper of dry roasted beans and the crumbs of cheese and splatters of tomato seed on the chopping board. The *red* raw meat chopping board. Not the *white* bakery and dairy product one. How many times had I explained to him the importance of using the right colour-coded board to avoid the risk of cross contamination? Once a day? Twice? Three times? More than enough anyway. He said it was too complicated to remember which board was which, so I'd pointed him in the direction of the laminated magnetic chart on the side of the fridge. He'd laughed. 'You're beginning to sound just like Teri.'

Here's a tip, Dan: if you want to endear yourself to your current partner, don't compare her to the previous model.

'If you mean she shares my concern that chopping boards are a breeding ground for harmful bacteria, then I'm honoured by the comparison.'

I know. Even as the words came out of my mouth I thought I sounded a bit of a plonker.

But my kitchen, my rules; except Dan didn't seem to grasp the concept of kitchen rules or, for that matter, any sort of household rules. I'm not – God forbid! – as anally clean and tidy as Teri, who gets seriously disturbed by a drinks coaster being slightly askew, but I do have standards. Standards which I'd learned at my mother's knee and which included a respect for basic domestic hygiene and a modicum of tidiness. Actually, Mammy took it slightly further than a basic respect since she and Teri were almost equally obsessive.

Dan, on the other hand, had been spoilt by his first wife, who thought she was a cut above getting her hands dirty so had a cleaner come in five times a week to polish and shine and tidy. As a result, Dan, and Victoria too, had forgotten, if they'd ever known, simple domestic hygiene. You know, little things, like the dirty underwear and socks making their own way into the washing basket or used towels picking themselves off the bed and folding themselves back on the towel rail.

In the kitchen their ignorance centred mostly on an inability to make a simple sandwich without leaving a pile of crumbs and debris from whatever they'd packed between the two slices of bread and an unwillingness to navigate the intricacies of the dishwasher. So, today the bread knife had been chucked into the washing up bowl – fair enough, it had a wooden handle and the dishwasher was a no-no – along with a pickle-smeared plate, a butter knife sticky with butter, and a drinks mug, all of which were swimming in the ground coffee dregs from the cafetiere which topped the pile. Nice.

Reason told me that in the great scheme of things a mucky sink isn't such a big deal, but I'd had a trying day and knew with absolute conviction that tomorrow or the next day or whenever Daddy's test results came through was going to be equally tough. And, in such circumstances, it's not unreasonable to telephone the dirty bastard who thought I had nothing better to do than follow him around cleaning up his filth and tell him where to get off.

Dan, however, disagreed. 'Calm down,' he whispered. 'I'm about to go on air with a trailer for tonight's show.'

'I don't care if you're about to interview the freaking Queen,' I screamed.

Actually I did care; I thought he should refuse to interview members of the Royal family on the basis I was a Republican and, if it came to a referendum, would vote to scrap the monarchy. Although I wouldn't be above asking him to get an autograph for Mammy who thought Elizabeth Regina was an absolute star.

'I'll tidy up when I get home,' he promised.

'So, I'm supposed to live in a pigsty until you can eventually tear yourself away from your precious studio?'

'Don't exaggerate. It's just a couple of pieces of dirty cutlery and a sandwich plate.'

'It's the principle,' I shrieked. 'And what about the coffee mug and your cafetiere?'

'I'll wash them when I get home,' he mumbled sotto voce.

Part of me felt a small measure of sympathy for him. I was screeching like a banshee, and he couldn't respond in kind because he was surrounded by work colleagues fixing the lighting and sound and whatever else it is they have to get ready for an autocue-reading media tart to advertise the best bits from the evening's show.

But mostly I thought he was a lazy, thoughtless git who was turning my beautiful home into a stinking hole.

'Look, I've really got to go,' he soothed. 'I'll take you out for dinner tonight and we can discuss it properly.'

Ha! He'd missed his guess if he thought eating in public would stop me venting my spleen. And I didn't want to be *taken* out to dinner. I was perfectly capable of taking myself wherever I wanted to go.

'Aagh!' I screamed as loudly as I could, hoping he was holding the phone to his left ear, the one in which he'd soon be placing his earpiece.

And, with that cheerful thought I hit the 'off' button and burst into tears.

In such circumstances, Teri is always the best port of call, but when I dialled Charlie's Suffolk number she'd already gone. 'Back in Yorkshire, darling,' Denis trilled. 'She preferred to be grim up north than spend another night under my roof.'

Frankly, I didn't blame her. I'd quite liked him, and Charlie was harmless enough, but the pair of them together could be a bit wearing; especially when they got all lovey-dovey and touchy-feely.

I forgot to ask though when she'd set off homewards.

Sighing heavily, the weight of the world resting on my shoulders, I dialled her apartment and left a message on her answerphone.

Not back yet or not picking up again.

I was still trying to decide whether I should clear up Dan's mess or leave it for him to sort out, when the phone rang. 'Hello,' I said, my voice still weepy-wobbly.

CHAPTER 43

TERI

I felt sad saying goodbye to Charlie and as he walked me to my car, he linked an arm through mine. 'It's been good having you here, sis,' he said, pulling me against him.

'It's been good for me too,' I told him, turning to give him a giant hug The last couple of weeks had been the longest we'd spent together since we both left home. We'd not talked much – there was plenty to keep us busy on the smallholding – and we seemed to have a silent pact that we wouldn't discuss our parents or what had gone on when we were younger. I can talk about anything – the past doesn't bother me one jot – but I wonder if it would have been too painful for Charlie who probably felt lonely and marginalised as a kid.

As I pulled into the parking area near my apartment block, my spirits lifted. It was lovely to be back at my duplex.

My style is minimal, but classy. I don't over-furnish or fill the place with the chintzy nonsense that Lee goes in for. She has books, photos and little knick-knacks spilling everywhere, including ridiculous little wooden hearts dangling on short lengths of string from cupboard handles, some with trite aphorisms written on them, such as 'A Hug a Day Keeps Loneliness Away'. What absolute drivel; the sort of pithy rubbish that people put on Facebook along with pictures of their pathetic cats.

No, all the stuff that Lee surrounds herself with just causes dust and you can't move for fear of knocking into something. Not that it would matter; she hasn't got anything of value.

Everything here in my duplex is well chosen for its antique or aesthetic value. The look is pale and subtle; clean and uncluttered. I find it calm and restful – monastically meditative. Lee calls it sterile.

I bought the flat when I landed the job at the university. That shyster, Edward Pranks, had given me the money for the deposit and my monthly allowance used to cover the mortgage payments. I never stopped to wonder where that deposit money came from or how Pranks had lifted it from the factory funds. He just said 'I'll sort it with your Dad' and I assumed Dad had sanctioned it.

And nor, until now, had I wondered how I was going to pay the mortgage. Think about that later. I was more than happy to get inside. I was looking forward to a long, hot soak and a relaxing evening with a bottle of white wine.

I unlocked the door and pushed it open carefully, aware that post had piled up just inside.

I stepped over the letters, put my keys on the hall table, ignoring the flashing light on the landline indicating seven answerphone messages, and dumped my bag on the floor.

Luckily I'd not reduced the heating when I left for Charlie's, so the flat was lovely and warm. But I'd forgotten to empty the fridge, and when I opened it, saw a carton of milk and some yoghurts which were well past their sell-by date. But there was also an opened, half-empty bottle of white wine. I reached for it and a glass from the drainer. I find it's better to drain glassware and crockery rather than rub them dry with a tea towel which contains all manner of germs.

I took a swig of the wine. It tasted acidic. I was desperate for a drink, but not that desperate. I emptied the glass and the bottle into the sink and got another white from the wine rack and put it in the fridge. Could I wait for it to cool? Unpacking first and then having a drink would have been the sensible option. But I took the bottle back out of the fridge, unscrewed the top and poured a small measure into the glass. It wasn't too bad temperature-wise. I finished the glass quickly – it had been a long drive and I needed a boost – topped it up and took the glass with me back into the hallway to collect my bag.

The light on the answerphone was still blinking. The thought of listening to all the messages was daunting, but I pressed 'Play' anyway and heard Charlie's voice with the message he'd left just after I'd set off for his place more than three weeks ago.

The second message was Charlie again saying something fatuous about how I must have set off.

The third message was from some smooth-sounding chap saying his glass and glazing company was looking for show flats in the area in which to install their windows and I deleted him, also the fourth caller who was offering to chase up a road accident I *might* have had in the last ten years.

Message five was a shock; it was Declan. 'Er…Teri. Hi. It's Declan. I know I'm probably the last person you want to hear from…' You can say that again. Delete.

Message six was interesting. It was Doreen, the meeter and greeter from the Ridings Today studio who I'd first met when Dan had invited me to watch him read the news.

D'reen, as she'd introduced herself, was one of those flowsy women of a certain age who wear tight, black, pencil skirts and white blouses with one-too-many buttons undone to reveal an unnaturally tanned, crepe-y cleavage and skin that's leathery and wrinkled. Doreen also acted as a sort of secretary to Dan, so I guessed before she had time to finish that she was ringing on his behalf. 'Hello, Teri. Can you call me, please?' Well, no, D'reen. I'm afraid I can't. I need time to think about my strategy with Dan. I don't want him to think I'm at his beck and call. Delete.

Message seven was Lee asking if I was back yet and could I ring her when I was. I took my glass back into the kitchen and topped it up. Any conversation with Lee needs reinforcing alcohol.

I did a last number redial, and she answered pretty quickly, saying 'Hello?' in a querulous, almost timid way.

'It's me,' I said impatiently. I can't be doing with people who adopt odd telephone manners. Just answer the bloody phone normally.

'Oh.' She sounded relieved, as though she was expecting someone else that she hadn't wanted to hear from. I'm quite perceptive like that.

'What's up?'

'Oh, it's just every time the phone rings I think it must be Daddy…'

I remembered then to ask how he was. She said he'd been having tests, and I said, yes, she'd told me that when I'd rung before. I asked if the results had come back, and she said, no, but they were all terribly worried. She sounded tearful. I told her not to worry, nothing bad was going to happen.

'You've got an over-active imagination and always fear the worst,' I added. 'You're just the same in my car. You imagine the worst that can happen and get tensed up.'

She started wittering about me being a bad driver. Me!

'When have I ever had an accident?'

'Maybe not an actual crash,' she said. 'But –'

'No buts,' I said. 'Not everyone drives everywhere in second gear.'

'I do not.'

'Do.'

'Don't.'

'Admit it, Lee,' I said, 'you spend too much of your life worrying about what might happen.'

'I do when I'm in the car with you. And God knows why you've never been nicked for speeding.'

Oh, she can be so catty.

'I have to go,' I told her. 'I've got work to do.'

And I put the phone down.

I went into the bedroom, unpacked, had a bath and a couple of return trips to the fridge for more wine, and then remembered the post. Several circulars, an official-looking letter from the university – my formal marching orders, I expect – and a couple of identical buff-coloured envelopes both marked as having come from the Fixed Penalty Office.

That bloody speed camera. The mercenary buggers. Well, they can just bloody wait for their money, I thought, and, without opening them, stuffed both letters behind a pale blue and white Turkish earthenware vase on the hall table.

Sure enough the university letter was a long missive, probably written with delight by those farts in Human Resources and signed by plonker Heron, outlining the terms of the ending of my contract, but importantly, showing how much I was owed in salary and holiday pay. And here was a surprise; I was supposed to have had two months' notice but, as my dismissal had been – cruelly – instant, the university would still honour its obligations and this month's salary, plus two further months and holiday pay would be coming my way. It was a relief to know I could make my mortgage payments for a while and have some spare cash for emergencies like shopping for new clothes. Or even a holiday?

Lee considers me a spendthrift in that as soon as I get any cash, I can find things to do with it, like buy a wonderful new leather tote or some shoes. What's money for, I ask her, if not to spend? But she is forever telling me I should 'put a little away each month' like she does, for her old age, I presume. Well, bugger that! Live for today, I tell her.

And that attitude was all well and good while I had an allowance from the factory, but now, even though Lee thinks I'm stupid with money, I can see I'm going to have to do something. Like get a job.

CHAPTER 44

LEE

I wish I hadn't bothered ringing Teri in the first place. Oh, yes, she very obligingly rang back, but her interest in Daddy seemed tepid at the very least. Once she'd convinced herself no news was good news, she broke in with a fatuous comment about how 'he was obviously in good hands' and that she was sure he'd be okay before launching into an account of how well things had gone at Charlie's. She'd turned into quite the country girl.

Exasperated, I tried to cut into her monologue about where to find the best wellies, and failed, although she did change the subject and instead started berating me for being 'such a God-awful passenger'.

'Pardon?'

'I'm not having you in my car again if you don't learn to control your nerves.'

'What?'

'Every time you get into my car I can feel you tensing up even before I've turned the ignition key.'

'I wonder why?' I asked.

'I can't imagine,' Teri said.

'Because you're an awful driver, and I'm waiting for you to kill the pair of us. Or some other poor sod.'

'And when was the last time I had an accident?'

'Maybe not an actual crash,' I conceded, 'but there have been an awful lot of close shaves.'

'Name one.'

That was easy; I started ticking them. 'The yellow school bus at the end of our street when we left for Suffolk; the tractor near Blacker Farm, also on the way to Charlie's; the left turn near the Knife and Hand pub you nearly missed because you were speeding…'

I imagined her holding up a hand in defence. 'Not everyone drives everywhere in second gear,' she said.

'I do not.'

'Do.'

'Don't.'

Hmmm…this conversation was going nowhere fast, and we seemed to have strayed away from the original topic of discussion.

'Admit it, Lee,' Teri said, 'you spend too much of your life worrying about what might happen.'

'I do when I'm in the car with you,' I agreed.

'And has any of it ever happened?'

Honesty compelled me to admit, yes, I and other road users were still in one piece. 'Not for want of trying,' I said. 'And God knows why you've never been nicked for speeding.'

Funnily enough that shut her up.

After that conversation I decided against sharing the story of Mammy's fury over my alleged treachery in 'stealing' Teri's ex-husband. She'd enjoy it too much.

Dan, bless him, came home suitably chastened and apologetic – although I would have preferred a chilled bottle of wine rather than a bouquet of lilies. The scent *is* gorgeous and they are lovely when they're in full bloom but it's amazing how quickly they start shedding their petals.

We decided against eating out. One look at my blotchy face – I'm one of those unfortunate women who don't cry prettily – and Dan cancelled the table he'd booked at The Social Club. 'Another time,' he suggested and instead we had baked beans on toast and scrambled eggs.

Sometimes, it does a media tart good to eat plain, honest fare.

Afterwards, he loaded the dishwasher. Shame he didn't quite stack the pans and crockery in the Harper-approved manner but I didn't comment. So what if the dinner plates were in the saucepan lid rack and vice versa?

Mind you, saying nothing nearly killed me.

He scored extra brownie points though by displaying an appropriate level of interest in the hospital trip – he actually turned off *Newsnight* so he could listen better – and was suitably outraged on my behalf when I told him about Mammy's tongue-lashing.

'Do you want me to have a word?' he asked. 'Put her straight about what happened between me and Teri?'

Good God. 'No!'

Talk about adding fuel to the fire. We'd need an army of fire fighters to douse the flames.

'You're probably right,' he agreed. 'Give her a couple of days and everything will be fine.'

'You don't know my mother,' I snapped. 'She's from Irish stock. They hold good grudges.'

'She loves you,' Dan said with the sweet reasonableness that was possibly his most irritating habit. 'She may not like you very much at the moment but she does love you. And, however much she likes Teri, she doesn't love her, so you win hands down.'

I growled and stomped off into the bedroom. I didn't need him to point out the bleeding obvious.

And, I still hadn't quizzed Teri about his blasted snoring. Calls herself my friend? She might have warned me.

CHAPTER 45

TERI

Despite a slight hangover, I was up bright and early the next morning with my laptop open on the kitchen table. I'd showered and put on a crisp, white shirt, some jeans and loafers. My hair was brushed and silky smooth. I hadn't bothered with make-up apart from eyeliner, mascara and some lippy; I wanted to feel professional. After all, I couldn't go job hunting – albeit via the internet – looking as though I'd just crawled out of bed. It was probably psychological; I felt I had to put on what Lee would call 'a face'.

That got me wondering about her. I'd been a little unsympathetic on the phone when she was telling me about her dad. Perhaps I should ring her again? But then I reasoned if it was anything serious she'd ring me.

Meanwhile, I had important work to do. But where to start? My career hadn't exactly shone so far; most of my jobs ended in some sort of disaster. I needed to do something that I knew a lot about and that I really enjoyed.

Ping! I had a lightbulb moment.

Job hunting suddenly didn't feel important. I rose from the table and moved into the sitting room and looked at the big, black box file on the floor by the side of the sofa. Lord Rochester was in there; enshrined in notes, essays, research papers, poems and my twelve-thousand-word MA dissertation. I'd considered dumping the lot along with all the other crap from university, but my libertine was just too important to ditch. After plonker Heron had so unceremoniously thrown me out, I decided Rochester, the randy old rake, would come with me. I'd not finished with him yet.

In fact, I was going to immortalise him in a book.

I opened the box file and rooted among the papers for the memory stick that I knew was loaded with all-things Rochester, strode back into the kitchen and plugged it into the laptop.

For the next few days, I worked and slept with Rochester by my side. I admit that I broke off from staring at either my notes or the laptop occasionally to pop into town and look round the shops, but writers say even when they're not writing, they're thinking about writing, and I was thinking about my Rochester book all the time. I have never been so obsessed.

I ignored the phone when it rang. I resented having to break off to go to the local supermarket to buy food. Rochester was hovering at my shoulder as I threw yet another ready meal into my trolley. I might be a trained chef – well, I did a catering course – but I had no time to indulge my skills.

I was writing.

Although, I wasn't writing as successfully as I imagined I would.

By the end of the week, I had written and re-written half a dozen drafts and had amassed just five thousand words of the great opus. What was wrong?

Writer's block. That's what it was. I needed a change of scene.

I pulled on my soft, tan, leather calf boots and slipped into a warm coat. I gathered up the laptop, slid it into my tote, collected my keys and left the flat.

I headed for Portly & Groops, one of the local delis which did strong, aromatic Americanos just as I like them.

I was going to write this book. Not at my kitchen table, but sitting in the warmth of a café, surrounded by buzz and atmosphere. Inspiration would strike, just as it did for what's-her-name, the one who wrote that book about that wizardy thing? Anyway, whoever it was, I was going to do the same.

****

The deli was buzzing, but not in a good way. It was crammed full of mumsies who'd dropped their precious darlings off at school and were now idling the day away with their remaining offspring too young for school or nursery, and chatting with other mumsies about mumsie things like how little Leonoria was doing in her private Latin tuition – and she's only four – and how Bertram never took to the bottle so was breastfed until he started school.

Oh please, I thought, feeling nauseous. I'm not at one with child-talk. When anyone announces that they're pregnant, my reaction is to say 'Oh hard luck' while everyone around me is cooing. I just don't see the attraction – all that belly rubbing for nine months, the pain of having your insides ripped out, and then the next sixty-odd years of having to finance the damn thing.

I negotiated my way around the various buggies that the mumsies had so conveniently left in the way of all the other customers, and found a table at the far end of the room.

The one other person in the deli who was not female, pregnant or posing with a baby, was the man sitting at the table next to mine, reading a newspaper that was spread out in front of him. He was quite old, certainly in his sixties. His face was baggy with a bulbous nose and he was balding, overweight and dressed as though for gardening in one of those fleecy tops with a half zip, scruffy chinos and old-man shoes that fasten with Velcro. What is it with geriatrics that they can't tie laces? They haven't got anything else to do so surely they could spend an extra second fastening a buckle. But no, shoe on, flip the Velcro, sit down in a chair and watch TV all day.

One of the waiters came over, and I ordered a black Americano. 'Do you want milk with that?' he asked.

'No, black,' I repeated. 'But I'd like a small jug of water on the side.'

'Hot water?'

'No cold.'

'Cold water?'

'Yes.' I suppressed the angry sigh welling up. 'To cool it.'

'Ah, no problem,' the twit said, writing the order in his little pad. Well, of course it's no problem, you idiot. This is a coffee shop; you serve coffee. Why should there be a problem?

I pulled the laptop from my tote and opened it. Balding and

overweight Velcro man looked up from his paper and tried to catch my eye. I just hate it when you know someone wants your attention and you simply can't be bothered. Why don't they read the body language: leave me alone? But no. Velcro man wanted to talk.

'You writing a book?' he asked as I tapped away on the keyboard. No, I thought. I'm milking a goat.

I looked up slowly and gave him what I hoped was an icy stare.

'I'm writing a book,' he said, undaunted. I caught a whiff of stale coffee fumes on his breath. He folded his newspaper and inclined towards me as if anything to do with his life and his Velcro fastenings was something I'd been waiting to hear all morning.

'Oh,' I said in as flat a tone as possible. It wasn't an expression of interest or even a question, but the man took it as a given that a woman alone in a café, writing on a laptop, was a kindred spirit and in need of his wisdom.

'Yes, it's about two men. What do you think of that? Unusual, eh?' He waggled a pair of thick, unkempt eyebrows as a sign of his creativity.

What was the deluded, old sod talking about?

'Yes, two men. Don't often find books about two men. It's usually a man and a woman, or a woman on her own. You know, chick lit stuff that you girls write.'

'I don't write chick lit,' I said, staccato-voiced, mentally kicking myself for responding. I guessed that whatever I said would be seen as encouragement.

He ignored my comment and went on. 'Yes, two men. In their sixties. They've both retired and play golf, and it's all about their friendship – they're not gay, by the way, if that's what you're thinking.' He leaned closer. I caught the stale coffee fumes again. The eyebrows wiggled.

'I wasn't thinking anything,' was all I could manage.

'Good. Because these two men have been friends from school and the book's all about the way their lives have gone on.'

'Have they done anything interesting with their lives?' I couldn't help myself.

'Well, they both went to school, they got married and got jobs. Then they retired and took up golf.'

'And what's the story?'

'Oh there's no story yet. I'm just sketching it out.'

'But if there's no story…'

'Oh, there will be. Inspiration will strike.'

I wasn't sure he should be so confident.

'Are you basing this book on your own life?' I asked.

'Well, yes. You've got to, haven't you? Write about what you know.' He tapped an index finger against the side of his bulbous nose as though imparting words of great secrecy and wisdom.

'And how much have you written?'

'Oh, I've not started writing. It's all in here,' he said, tapping the side of his head and wiggling the eyebrows one more time. 'I'm far too busy to actually sit down and write. Not like you ladies who can come in here and drink coffee all day.'

I stared at him, unable to form the words that would tell him what a time-wasting twat he was.

The waiter arrived with my coffee, and I imagined him erecting an invisible barrier around me to stop the physical attack I was planning.

Then the deli door opened, and I looked over hoping that one of the buggy mums was leaving and I could move to her vacant table.

Velcro man was speaking again, but I didn't hear what he said. I was too busy looking at who'd come in the door.

CHAPTER 46

LEE

Daddy telephoned the next day. Mammy was still spitting blood, he said, but she'd calmed down a lot after talking to Mrs O'Brien. Mrs O'Brien? Declan's mother? What on earth did this have to do with her? Nothing, of course – but she did dish the dirt about Teri and Declan. Mammy had been sworn to secrecy because although it was widely known Declan and his wife had 'experienced difficulties' the extent and nature of those difficulties was not quite so well known. I doubted either Mammy or Mrs O'Brien knew the full story either, but at least Mammy was prepared to concede I was not quite the harlot she thought. And Teri not quite the blue-eyed girl either.

But there was another matter Daddy wanted to discuss. 'If I have to go into hospital, I might need you to help out. Just for a week or two.'

Help out? With what?

'The business. Obviously,' he said.

Obviously? It wasn't obvious to me at all.

'We can't talk over the phone,' he said. 'Meet me for lunch?'

'Not chicken pieces and fries,' I said.

'Your office?' he suggested. 'I'll bring the sandwiches, you can make a brew.'

He arrived just after one, straight from the building site. He'd left the hard hat and donkey jacket in the car but clomped through the door in his steel-toed working boots. 'I'm afraid I've brought a bit of mud with me,' he said, looking back at the trail of footprints stretching down the corridor.

'Just a bit,' I agreed, thinking it might be a good idea to buy Frank the janitor a cheap bottle of whisky as a peace offering.

Daddy had brought us both tuna sandwiches. I fetched him a cup of tea from the staff kitchen and filled my water bottle at the same time. 'Nice little cubby-hole you've got here.'

'You've seen it before,' I said.

'I know, but every time I come I'm struck by what a clever daughter you are.'

Darling Daddy. I wondered if he knew how much the conviction, which he shared with Mammy, that their girls could rule the world if they just put their minds to it had helped propel me and Fliss forward. True, her career as a book illustrator was on a bit of a back burner while the kids were so young, but she was still the artist of choice for several of her publishing contacts.

'And you enjoy the job?' he asked. 'Don't you ever get fed up being bossed around by that Heron guy and what's-his-name?' He meant Mike Orme.

I was about to say 'no' when I remembered this morning's mandatory training session which Peter had organised for the senior management group. Two hours of listening to an HR suit offering tips and winkles on how to chair a successful meeting. I've chaired meetings that haven't lasted as long. And to add insult to injury, Peter, the one person in the group who really needed some lessons in that direction, had excused himself after twenty minutes because he had 'something important to do'.

'Mostly,' I said.

'Have you ever thought about being your own boss?' Daddy waved what was left of his sandwich in my direction, chucking crumbs all over the carpet. I mentally upgraded Frank's bottle of whisky from supermarket-own brand to a Scottish label.

'I suppose I might go for an executive role one day,' I said.

'That's years away,' Daddy said, 'if ever.'

What had happened to his belief that this daughter could rule the world?

He'd down-sized his ambitions. He wanted me to rule his world instead.

CHAPTER 47

∞

TERI

It was a shock to see Declan coming into the deli, not because it had been more than two months since I'd last seen him – and two months since the episode with his beached whale of a wife.

No, the shock was seeing him and thinking how startlingly gorgeous he was. I couldn't help myself; I felt a primeval pull towards him. The sheer sexuality of the man.

Stop it, Teri, I told myself. How could I possibly think like this after the way he'd treated me?

But I needed to think; how should I be with him? Should I smile when he sees me? Should I tell him to fuck off if he comes anywhere near? Should I get up now and walk out? Should I sneak off to the loo and spy on him from behind the toilet door?

He wasn't looking my way, but back towards the door, which had just opened again. He waved to the young woman who'd walked in, pink faced and grinning. There was something familiar about the way she flicked back her long, lank hair...

I remembered. It was Cassie, a junior reporter on the Evening Leader who I'd first met at the Peter Heron media networking event at university where Declan and I first got together.

The girl had clearly been besotted with Declan, giggling with delight at his jokes. But he'd sent her off on a breaking story – a tyre factory fire – to get rid of her. I'd been flattered at the time that Declan, the shit-hot news editor, chose me over a breaking story, but I've since learned that with Declan, it's all a means to an end. He'd say or do anything to get a woman into bed – any woman, anytime, anywhere.

And, as it turned out, he'd bedded Cassie too. I realised this when I saw them coming out of the Leader's offices one day. I'd followed them, obviously, because even though it was lunchtime and perfectly natural for a boss to take one of his underlings for a glass of lime juice and soda as part of the mentoring process, the way Declan had his arm around her shoulder and the way she looked up at him like a trusting puppy, said this couple were not discussing that day's news list.

I did some more mental calculations. Marnie, the beached whale was at least eight months pregnant now. Declan was about to become a dad for the zillionth time and what was he doing? Taking one of his conquests out for coffee. I got it! Sex with Marnie, beached and whale-like, would be out of the question, so Declan was making sure his penis stayed in working order by going back over old pastures. Unless, of course, he'd been stringing poor, young Cassie along all this time and their affair had not been halted so abruptly in the way ours had. The devious sod.

Declan indicated to Cassie to find a table while he turned and talked to one of the baristas at the counter.

For a moment, Cassie looked lost and unsure. She was clutching a brown satchel to her chest, steeling herself to push her way through the buggy forest to find a vacant table. She didn't look as fearless as I thought these reporter-types were supposed to be.

As she looked round the room, she spotted me and her face registered vague recognition. Her brows knitted as she tried to remember where she'd seen me before – was I someone she'd written about in the past, perhaps? She smiled a weak smile, took one hand away from gripping the satchel to half wave, made a step towards me and then caught her foot in the strap of one of the mumsie's baby bags which had been dumped on the floor. She faltered, wrong-footed herself and stumbled into the back of a chair one of the mumsies was sitting on, jolting the woman and the bundle of puke and mewling she had in her lap.

'Oh, sorry…sorry,' she said as she flapped about. 'Oh, God. I haven't spilt your coffee, have I?'

Flap, giggle, flap.

Oh Cassie, I thought. Get a grip. How have you got this far in life – junior reporter on a local evening rag – and yet don't have the confidence to tell mumsie to shift her arse and not leave her germ-encrusted nappy bags where people with a brain want to walk.

Cassie, reassured by the woman that all was okay in Mumsie-land, must have realised I wasn't someone she could put a name to and body-swerved away from my direction to an empty table by the window.

Now Declan looked round, scanning the room to see where she'd gone. His eyes drifted over my side of the deli. He did an exaggerated jump of mock surprise, shook his head vigorously in disbelief, and strode straight over to my table. Touching the back of the empty chair opposite me, he asked, 'Can I...?'

'Please yourself,' I said. 'But aren't you with young Cassie over there?'

He glanced back and waved at the puppy to stay where she was.

'It's good to see you,' he said, ignoring my indifference and plonking himself into the seat. 'Are you all right?'

'Of course I'm all right. Why wouldn't I be?'

'Well, you know...'

'Oh, you mean, having treated me like your sexual plaything, lied to me and then got your bloody wife to do your dirty work to get rid of me?'

Velcro man, who'd gone back to his paper when he realised I wasn't going to help with his bestseller, looked up again and pressed his eyebrows together quizzically, aware there could be something here for his next novel.

'I didn't treat you like a *sexual plaything*,' Declan said, putting emphasis on the ridiculous term I'd used. 'I'm offended you could think such a thing, Teri. And I didn't ask Marnie to do anything. She...sort of...found out.'

'Yeah, but you were there – waiting for her when she came to my flat. You didn't try to stop her. It was disgusting...'

Declan dropped his head. 'I'm sorry, Teri. I should never have put you through that –'

'Damn, fucking right, you shouldn't have.'

'But you don't understand the pressure I was under. It wasn't easy with Marnie, the kids – and the twins on the way.'

'And is that why you're taking solace in young Cassie now?' I suddenly felt protective of the silly, little girl.

'Wha…? No, Cassie and I aren't –'

'Oh, fuck off, Declan. Of course you are. It's as plain as day. You should be ashamed of yourself. How old is she? Seventeen?'

Velcro man looked from me to Declan and then across to Cassie.

'Well, actually, she's twenty-five,' he said. 'But I'm not having an affair with her…God, Marnie's due any day now; I wouldn't dare.'

Velcro man wiggled his eyebrows and snuggled back in his seat. He was enjoying this.

'Of course you'd dare, Declan,' I said. 'You dare to do anything when it comes to women – any women. You're a philanderer, a rake, a libertine.'

'A what?' Declan said, cocking his head in mock puzzlement.

'Oh, don't try and be clever. You know exactly what I mean – a lecherous bastard. 'My whole life's been shredded – by you, Dan, the university. Everything.' I looked down at my coffee cup and at the Americano getting colder. Three pounds ten wasted as you can't heat up cold coffee – it ruins the taste.

Declan must have thought I'd bent my head to cry because he reached across the table and placed a hand over mine, giving it a gentle squeeze. 'I know and I'm sorry,' he said softly.

No, my mind screamed. No, no, no. Pull your hand away. Do not leave your hand there. Do not look at him. Do not do this.

CHAPTER 48

LEE

'Why would you need to go into hospital?' I squeaked.

'I'm not well, Lee,' Daddy said. 'I may not have as much book learning as you or Fliss, but I know my way around the internet as well as the next man, and I don't need to be a medic to know that when I go for the test results next week the news won't be good.'

'Next week?' My voice had gone up so many octaves only a dog could hear me without wincing. 'That's pretty quick.'

'Yes,' he said. 'And that says a lot about how serious things must be.'

I was having trouble breathing. And it had nothing to do with my asthma. 'How serious?'

'You'll be the first to know,' he promised.

'I'll come to the doctor's with you.'

'It's probably better if Mammy and I go on our own this time.'

'If it's because of Dan…'

'No, no,' he reassured. 'But afterwards we'll probably need a little time on our own to gather our thoughts.'

'How will you get there?' I wailed.

'Lee, the doctor's surgery is just around the corner.'

I started to protest. It was at least a couple of corners and a good long stretch along the straights.

'We're perfectly capable of walking the half mile-or-so.'

'But why are you so sure it'll be bad news? And what sort of bad news?'

Stupid question. There was only one kind of possible bad news.

'Lee. Calm down.'

Calm down? That's exactly what Dan said when I'd phoned him to say Daddy was on his way over.

'Wait until you hear what your father's got to say before you start panicking,' he counselled.

Why? I much preferred to think the worst and deal with it in my head so I could face the reality with a modicum of control.

'Hold on,' he said when I tried to explain my rationale. I could hear him talking to someone else in the background. 'Yes, yes, won't be a minute…' He turned his attention back to me. 'I've got to go. Shayne Brickham has just arrived to do a pre-recorded interview, and I need to be in place before he comes out of make-up.'

Gee, thanks. Now I knew where I stood in Dan's list of priorities: several steps behind Shayne-bloody-Brickham.

'I'm sure your dad's going to be fine,' he offered, what he obviously thought was the perfect panacea. 'And what do you expect me to do about it anyway?'

Good job he didn't hang around for me to answer that question.

I didn't bother ringing Teri. I could do without another monologue on wellies and country living or my imaginative shortcomings. That's if she deigned to answer my call. Sometimes our friendship seemed a bit of a one-way street. How many times had I soothed and consoled over Declan and God knows how many other blokes who'd wangled their way into her knickers, and the first time I got my knickers into a twist over something really important she couldn't spare five minutes to lend a listening ear?

Yes, self-pity was in full throttle, along with selective memory. There had been plenty of times when Teri had delivered on my behalf – the Christmas abortion, for one – but I wasn't in the mood to give any credit where credit was due.

'So,' Daddy was saying, 'while the business can tick over for a week-or-two, longer term it would be a good idea if one of you had a bit of an overview.'

One of who? He was looking at me a little too intently for my liking.

'Dom's a good bloke,' he continued, 'and he can manage the day-to-day on-site work, but I'd feel happier if you could pop in now and again.'

Me? What did I know about running a building yard that Dom didn't? He'd been Daddy's second-in-command since I was in ankle socks.

'Fliss can't spare the time because of the new baby and though I hope Charles will continue to look after the books, he's not much good with his hands.'

Daddy had a gift for under-statement. My sister's husband needed help changing a light bulb. But what made him think I could spare the time? Hadn't he read the nameplate on the door? Lee Harper, Deputy Head of Teaching and Learning. It was no sinecure.

'I don't want to sell up,' Daddy said.

'No,' I agreed. 'The value of the business would dive bomb as soon as any buyer got wind of why you were selling.'

He nodded. 'That's one reason but it's never a good idea to do things in a hurry.' He leaned forward, slopping tea onto the floor. He bent and swiped at it with his hand, and then rubbed his palm along the arm of the easy chair on which he was sitting. At this rate, I'd have to buy Frank a bottle of his favourite single malt whisky.

'Can you get leave of absence?' he asked.

'What?'

'What do they call it? Sympathetic leave of absence?'

'Compassionate leave,' I corrected. It was obvious where this conversation was heading. 'How long?' I asked.

'Don't know,' Daddy said. 'Depends on what the doctor has to say. But I could do with you spending a bit of time with Dom getting to know how things work.'

'Might be tricky. The department is already one person short,' I said.

Daddy shrugged. 'That's the university's problem. Not mine.'

'I'll see what I can do,' I said, 'but no promises.'

'Good.' He stood to leave. 'Get yourself a pair of steel toe-cap boots over the weekend. Keep the receipt and I'll reimburse you. I can find you a hard hat. A donkey jacket too. It won't matter if it's a bit baggy. But I doubt we've got a pair of boots that'll fit your size fives.'

Size five-and-a-half actually. Six if it was a small fitting.

'Right, that's settled. Monday it is.' Daddy kissed me on the cheek. 'Bright and early. Dom doesn't like shirkers.'

Nor did I. But what time did the shirkers start, and how early was bright and early?

'Half past seven,' Daddy called as he marched down the corridor. 'And not a minute later.'

F***! That would mean getting up an hour earlier at least. I'd known for years the clock visited half past six twice a day, but I preferred to experience it awake just the once.

And where the hell would I buy a pair of steel toe-cap boots? Normally, footwear-related queries were Teri's domain. But I didn't think she'd be much use this time.

CHAPTER 49

TERI

We couldn't get back to my duplex quickly enough.
I'd looked into Declan's eyes and could see how sorry he was, how mortified that he'd hurt me so much.

'Those other women meant nothing to me, Teri. Nothing,' he'd insisted, sitting opposite me in the deli, refusing to let go of my hand even though I did try to pull away. 'I love you so much, but I'm afraid of my own emotions – how powerful they are,' he said. 'It feels like if I give in to my feelings for you, I'll never recover – and I can't do that to you.'

No, it doesn't make sense now, but then, sitting in the deli with Velcro man pretending not to listen, I understood everything Declan was saying. He was *afraid* of giving in to his love for me because it would change both our lives forever.

He'd pulled me to my feet and, letting go of my hand long enough for me to close the laptop and drop it into my tote, reached into his pocket to put some coins on the table for my coffee.

He signalled to Cassie. 'Urgent call – got to go,' he called across the tables. She might have believed it had Declan not been half-dragging me across the café towards the door. I didn't dare look at her.

As we stepped outside and the door closed behind us, Declan stopped, turned to me and yanked me into his chest. He hugged me hard then released me slightly to incline his face for a kiss. We grinned at each other and, without saying a word, set off at a run down the street.

As we ran, holding tight to each other's hand and stopping every few yards to kiss again, I thought of Lee and what her reaction would be if she could see us now, gambolling along the pavement like a couple of teenagers. She would be righteous and furious. I know, because that's how she has always been: disapproving of everything that I do when it comes to men.

She told me that she'd been concerned when I married Dan; some nonsense about how it was too soon, we didn't know each other well enough. I can see now she was jealous and would've done anything to stop the wedding so she could take my place. Well, it worked. Eventually.

And don't get me started on what she thinks about Declan. She has clearly never been totally in love with someone the way I am with him.

But why does Lee and her moralising tone keep sneaking into my head?

My apartment block is only a couple of streets up from the deli, and we burst through the communal entrance doors and raced up the stairs to the flat. Declan threw himself against the wall, panting as I fumbled in my tote for the keys. 'Come on, come on…' he urged, shoving himself away from the wall to reach out and stroke my back.

I struggled to insert the key in the lock, Declan took it from me and tried – and dropped the key. We doubled over, giggling with anticipation and delight. Could we make love here on the landing hallway, I wondered.

The phone started ringing on the hall table just inside the door, adding a sense of urgency, although I was buggered if I was going to answer a phone when Declan was here, desperate as I was for the frantic, uncontrolled love-making that I knew was about to happen. Declan and I had been here before.

I took control, pushed Declan back slightly, bent down to pick up the key and put it in the lock and turned it. The door swung open. The phone stopped ringing.

'Ah, it's good to be back,' Declan said, nudging me gently into the hallway. The phone started ringing again. 'Leave it,' Declan said. 'Come here…'

We'd made love on my bleached hallway floorboards several times before, and there was something about the familiarity of the scene that made me pause. Hadn't we always rushed to have sex anywhere, any place – and then Declan had literally buttoned himself back up, gone back home, back to work, back to another woman?

'Hang on,' I said, unable to think clearly, confused and flustered by Declan's desperate needing, the phone's insistent ringing and a wave of doubt flowing through me. Was that Lee's voice I could hear in the distance: 'Don't be such an idiot, Teri.'

Damn, that woman was in my subconscious.

I flapped my hands as though warding off Declan, the phone and Lee's disembodied voice in my head.

'No. Stop. Wait,' I said, as Declan moved closer, trying to drag me back into his arms and then, no doubt, onto the floorboards. And then what? Lusty, passionate, frantic sex. And then what? He'd get up and go. And then what? Was I going through all this again?

'No,' I said firmly, holding both hands up in front of me, palms raised towards Declan.

'Come on, Teri…what's wrong?'

'Everything's wrong with this, Declan,' I said. 'It's what always happens. It's sex, sex, sex, for you.'

'You've never complained before.'

'I know. But nothing's changed; we'll be back where we were before and that's all wrong. This isn't going anywhere…and,' I said, suddenly remembering, 'your wife is about to have twins.'

'So…' Declan said, but whatever he was going to say was interrupted by his mobile phone. He reached into his jacket pocket. Hah! I thought. My phone is ignored but Declan's is answered.

He looked at the name that flashed on the screen. 'Oh fuck,' he said. 'It's Marnie. I've got to get this.'

Oh charming. The man's wife rings when he's just declared undying passion for his lover and is contemplating sex on her wooden floorboards.

As he swiped open the phone, I grabbed his arm, turned him around and pushed him out of the open door. 'Get the fuck out of it, Declan,' I shouted as loudly as possible so that beached whale Marnie could hear and, as he staggered out on to the landing, phone pressed up against his ear, I heard him bluster, 'No, it's er…'

Well, I wasn't going to be an 'it's er…' any longer.

And I slammed the door shut.

Lee would have been proud of me.

Odd that she still hadn't rung to arrange a meet up. Obviously too busy playing happy families with my husband. Ex-husband.

CHAPTER 50

LEE

Every time I decide I'd be a million times better off without Dan and his dirty socks under the bed he blind sides me with a thoughtful gesture. Daddy was barely out of the door, and I was still staring dumbly at my computer screen, wondering 'what the hell?', when someone knocked at the door. Probably a student. There'd been a succession of them all morning, mostly ones who hadn't attended a single lecture or seminar all semester and who now wanted an individual master class so they could meet next week's essay deadline and secure the first-class mark they wanted so much they hadn't bothered to do a stroke of work. I'd have liked to tell them to sod off and read a few text books, but such a forthright approach was frowned upon by Peter Heron, who was fond of blathering about the importance of 'supporting students to become co-creators of their own education'.

'Come in,' I called, pasting a supportive smile on my face. 'Ms Harper?' asked a voice from behind a garden of blooms that filled the room with the scent of autumn.

'Yes?'

'Where would you like me to put these?'

I wasn't sure. The bouquet was too big to sit on the desk – unless I was prepared to lose sight of my PC – and it seemed churlish to relegate them to the floor. But there was nowhere else, so I moved the easy chair so recently vacated by Daddy to make room.

'Thank you,' I said to the delivery man who seemed in no hurry to leave. Of course, he was waiting for a tip. Teri would have told him to get lost – she didn't give people handouts for doing their job – but I felt sorry for the bloke. He was missing a front tooth, and the toe of one of his work boots was peeling away from the sole. I could spare a couple of quid.

'Thanks love,' he said, pocketing the change. 'Don't forget to read the gift message.'

I didn't need telling twice. I was dying to know who'd fork out for such an extravagant display.

Dan, of course. Who else?

'Thinking of you,' he'd written. Or rather, the florist had written on his behalf. Didn't matter, I sat and beamed for a full five minutes.

****

And now a dilemma: lipstick or no lipstick? I pouted at the reflection in the mirror. Lucky old Hamlet. 'To be or not to be...' His only worries concerned his existential existence. He'd be well screwed up if he had to decide if today was a lipstick day.

I'm not big on lipstick – largely because I've never quite discovered the secret of keeping lippy on the lips. 'How do you do it?' I asked Teri once. We were in the executive washroom – a habitat that reeked of cheap soap and strong disinfectant rather than academic learning – gowned and mortar-boarded, readying ourselves to sit through another rendition of the vice-chancellor's annual graduation 'you go out into the wide world as part of our University of Central Yorkshire family' speech. Tosh! I've heard it so many times I could recite it for him. You'd think he'd vary it a bit now and again.

'Do what?' Teri asked, making a miniscule adjustment to the angle of her mortar board. She pushed a stray hair into place and, pulling a shiny tube from a concealed pocket, leaned across the washbasin, face inches from the mirror, her mouth contorted into a Hannibal Lector leer. She coloured in with the patience and attention to detail of a Dutch master. It was beautiful to see.

I nodded at her reflection. 'Keep that stuff on.'

Teri shrugged. 'It's a knack.'

'No, honestly. What do you do that I don't?'

Teri paused her painting. 'Honestly?'

'Yes,' I said, sashaying the length of the washroom in exaggerated imitation of a catwalk model. 'I want to be a woman with lipstick, oozing confidence and glamour and sex appeal.'

'Fat chance,' Teri said.

How rude, I thought. But lipstick was for grown-ups, and I wanted a bit of her lipstick grown-upness.

'Seriously though. What's the secret?'

'There isn't a secret,' she said, opening the washroom door. 'Don't lick your lips.' She gave a little wiggle of her bottom as I followed her down the corridor to the ante-room where the rest of the great and the good were waiting for the ceremony to start. 'And ditch your granny bashers for a skimpy lace thong. It'll change the way you walk.'

That I could well believe.

I was thinking of that conversation now as I made an executive washroom pit-stop en route to gatecrash Peter Heron in his ivory tower. I'd tried to book an appointment, but Chrissie, who after years as a cog in the general admin team was now ruling the roost as his personal assistant, had been extremely unaccommodating.

She'd muttered and grumbled about squeezing me in at short notice. 'He's a very busy man,' she said, offering a ten minute slot two weeks on Tuesday.

'That's no good,' I said. 'I'll pop across now.' I could hear her squawking as I rammed the phone back on its hook. I grabbed my bag and keys and ran from the room. Best get out before she had time to call back. The phone started jingling as I locked the door. Too late, Chrissie, I thought. Not fast enough.

I'd guessed, correctly, that my hair would benefit from a quick brush and, since my eyes are my one really good feature, I slicked on another coat of mascara while I was at it. And lipstick? On balance, yes. I needed all the help I could get, and a bit of lippy grown-upness wouldn't go amiss. Fingers crossed I didn't lick it all off before I got to Peter's office suite at the end of the corridor.

Shame about the purple Dr Martens, though. They lacked a certain professional 'je ne sais quoi' but, at least, they'd be good if it came to stamping my feet.

Chrissie was waiting, arms crossed, ready to bar admission to Peter's open-plan reception area. 'I've made you an appointment for next week,' she said. 'I've managed to squeeze you in first thing Monday.'

'Still no good,' I said. 'I've got to be somewhere else first thing Monday.'

'It's the best I can do,' she said, inclining her head to indicate the conversation was closed, and I should go back the way I'd just come.

The cheek of her; it wasn't two minutes since she'd reported to me as the senior academic responsible for liaising with the departmental admin support group.

I'd have liked to give her a good slap – the older I get the more intolerant I'm becoming of inflexible jobworths – but, sadly, this was neither the time nor the place. Instead, I stepped round her. She grabbed at my arm – and missed. I don't know what she thought she was going to do. Rugby tackle me to the floor? Shove me back down the stairs? No chance. My rubber-soled Docs easily out-paced her stiletto slingbacks, and I was pushing open Peter's office door before she was even halfway across the room. She caught up, just in time for the door to thud in her face.

Good. Hope it hurt.

Peter lounged in his 'big boss' black, leather chair, scrutinising his face in a small hand mirror, a pair of nail scissors in one hand. Ugh! He was trimming his nose hairs. How revolting! I mean, I know it's something men have to do but not in public. Please.

'Damn!' A trickle of blood seeped from his left nostril. He swabbed at it with the back of one hand. 'I told Chrissie I didn't want to be disturbed.'

'Yes,' I said, 'she did tell me you were busy.'

'You made me cut myself.'

'Yes,' I said, 'but I wasn't expecting you to have a pair of nail scissors jammed up your nose.'

'They were not jammed up my nose.'

'No?'

'No!'

I'd been rehearsing the start of this interview, in between giving due consideration to the lipstick question, on my way across the campus and up the double flight of stairs to Peter's office. Things weren't going quite the way I'd expected. I glared at Peter and he glared back, before we both turned to the doorway where Chrissie was blabbering it wasn't her fault I'd managed to barge in.

Peter waved her away.

'I did not barge in.'

'Well, you didn't knock.'

I sat down.

'To what do I owe the honour of this unexpected visit?' he asked.

I ignored the sarcasm.

'My Daddy's dying,' I said. And burst into tears.

Strategically, the tears, which were *not* planned, were a good move. Peter's face took on the frantic expression of a goldfish gasping for breath in a puddle.

'My dear,' he said. 'What can I say?' In other words, Peter-speak for 'I'm out of my depth here. Please go and cry somewhere else.'

So, in between shuddering sniffs, I told him how to get me out of the room: two weeks compassionate leave, with the promise of an extension if it became necessary.

He pulled a dazzlingly white, cotton handkerchief from his trouser pocket, looked at it regretfully for a moment and held it out. 'Of course, as much time as you need.'

I scrunched the handkerchief between my fingers. It seemed a shame to contaminate such a beautiful object but, needs must, so I shook the pristine folds and rubbed my eyes, leaving black smears of mascara and smoky eye shadow.

Peter closed his eyes; he looked like a man who'd just been told by the dentist he'd have to have all his teeth pulled.

I gave a long, loud snotty nose blow.

CHAPTER 51

TERI

I sat down in the hallway, my back against the door, breathless. I half expected Declan to start banging on the door to be let back in. But that was not going to happen. I'd come to my senses where that prat was concerned. Who the hell did he think he was? And what sort of idiot did he think I was?

The phone had stopped ringing, and I couldn't hear any sound from the landing, so guessed Declan had jumped to his wife's beck and call. If she'd heard my parting message, Declan was in for a major row back at nappy towers.

The phone rang again. 'For fuck's sake.' I dragged myself up to my feet and stumbled the couple of paces to the hall table.

'Yes? What?' I said firmly, ready to give the double glazing or PPI salesman a good blasting.

'Teri?' a woman's voice said. 'I've been trying to get you for ages… it's D'reen.'

'Oh… D'reen?' Dan's meeter, greeter and sometimes secretary. 'I've been away,' I told her. 'Is it about Dan?'

'No,' she said. 'It's Richard. Richard Walker.'

'Who…? Oh Duck's… Oh, Richard.'

'Yes, he asked me ages ago to get in touch with you, but you've obviously not got my messages.'

'Ah, my mobile's broken and well…er…' I remembered she'd left a message while I'd been at Charlie's and I'd deleted it when I got back, thinking she was running errands for Dan.

'Yes, Richard seems to think you wanted to attend one of the conferences that he's organising and asked me to give you the details.

He doesn't have your number, otherwise, I suppose, he'd have called you himself.'

'One of the conferences…?'

'Yes. He said you'd been to the Digital Realisations of Mainstream Media event, and apparently you'd said you'd like to go to the next one, although I can't think why. Didn't think it was your sort of thing at all.'

Duck's Arse, the devious sod. He couldn't ask D'reen to simply arrange for me to meet him in a wine bar so he comes up with this belter.

'Oh yes,' I said. 'Synergetic Platforms is exactly what rocks my boat. When is the next conference?'

'Well, it was a couple of weeks ago. I told Richard I'd not been able to get hold of you, so he said, never mind. But I thought you'd want to know.'

'So…er…is he inviting me to the *next* conference?'

'No, he said if you weren't interested, he'd leave it –'

'Oh, but…I am…interested, I mean.'

'Well, I'll tell him when he's back.'

'Back?'

'Yes, he's just gone to China on a business trip.'

China? He works for little Ridings Today not World News. But, bugger. It would've been nice to see Duck's Arse again.

'If you're in touch with Richard, can you let him know I've been away, but I'm really keen to attend the next conference? Will you tell him? And give him my number – I know you're not supposed to give out home numbers, but I think we can both trust him.'

Okay, will do,' Doreen said, not suspecting a thing.

CHAPTER 52

LEE

I wasn't one hundred per cent surprised when Peter, rather peevishly, I thought, told me to 'keep his handkerchief'. 'I'll wash it,' I promised.
'No, no,' he said with the joie de vivre of a man who'd just swallowed a tumbler of malt vinegar and, insisting I take the rest of the day off, propelled me through the door with almost less delicacy than a pub landlord evicting a drunk at closing time.

Just to be on the safe side he escorted me to the lift and pushed the call button.

Talk about solicitous.

'Let me know how things go,' he said as the lift doors closed between us.

A little more sincerity wouldn't have gone amiss, but I couldn't quarrel with the result. Truthfully, I'd have preferred to sort out the mountain of loose ends stacked up on my desk before taking up Peter's very kind invitation to pack my bags and forget about the University of Central Yorkshire forthwith. But, on the basis it would have been churlish to do anything else, I posted an out-of-office message on my email account and headed for home.

I paused briefly in the car park to telephone Dan. I'd been so busy smiling at his flowers I'd forgotten to say thank you. No reply. Of course, he'd still be mid-interview, coaxing dressing room secrets from soccer-God Shayne. Poor boy. I could imagine Dan leaning forward, listening and sympathising, encouraging Shayne to be more and more indiscreet. Sometimes the ease with which journo Dan deployed his charm to persuade silly buggers like Shayne to jump through headline-scoring hoops worried me. It was okay with chumps like Shayne, who had agents and managers to protect them, but what about the little people, enjoying their fifteen minutes of fame, who said more than was good and sensible and who had to face friends and family and neighbours when the media furore died down? There was something not quite nice, I thought, about the way Dan put his desire for a scoop ahead of their need to be protected from their own silliness.

And, when did journo Dan switch off? Had he charmed me into a relationship that suited his needs more than it suited mine? Like his outright refusal to even consider a baby, which in the wake of Daddy's sudden illness now seemed more and more of a deal-breaker.

Peter had told me to go home and put my feet up – not sure how he thought that would help – but I needed a breath of fresh air, except, since it was raining cats and dogs and I didn't feel like getting wet, I decided to go for a swim instead. And, yes, I can see the contradiction – hard to swim without getting a bit damp – but it was thinking time, and there's something very therapeutic about the repetitive, Zen-like pull and kick of the arms and legs and the lapping of water around and across the body. And, dear God, I needed some Zen.

It was clear Daddy was dying. I don't know how I knew this. Just that I did. Perhaps, it was something to do with the way Daddy's eyes seemed to devour my face as if he was trying to drink me up? Or, the elaborate care with which he rescued a dunked chocolate biscuit from the bottom of a mug of tea? Or, the gentle way he lowered himself into a chair or pulled himself out again? Or, the slight tremble as he fastened his coat buttons or tied his shoe laces?

He seemed to have aged almost overnight. Good Lord, it didn't seem two minutes since he'd sacked me as his Saturday morning running partner because I was holding him back. I was flabbergasted, although, to be fair, I was ready to quit anyway. The running wasn't going well. We'd had a handful of problem-free excursions when Daddy had adapted his pace to suit my shorter strides, and then I was felled by shin splints in my left leg. The pain, jagged and intense, brought me to a standstill.

'You go on,' I told Daddy, collapsing in a heap on a memorial bench erected in memory of Alderman William H Banks. 'I'll be all right in a minute or two.' He waved and sped ahead, leaving me to hobble the rest of the way home. I watched him, wishing I was as light on my feet. But, never mind, I thought, he'll come and pick me up in the car when he gets home. Fool! He told Mammy I'd be a few minutes and went to golf as usual. Clearly, tee-ing off took priority.

Gorgeous Greenspan advised a proper stretch and warm up next time, but it didn't make much difference. I lasted about one hundred yards past old Willie's seat before conking out just outside the church, where I leaned against the wall, until the pain subsided enough to limp home.

Over the next couple of weeks, me and the wall became extremely well-acquainted until I got wise and arranged with Fliss to park her car in the bus lay-by near the church so I could hitch a ride.

We stopped off at Mammy and Daddy's house so I could collect my car. I planned to tell Daddy I was resigning as his running partner. But he'd already sacked me. He'd showered and rung his old friend Sean Walsh. 'He wants to improve his fitness so he's going to run with me instead,' he said. And, with a quick peck on the cheek, he picked up his car keys and left for the golf course.

I was not amused. But I was glad to get my Saturday morning lie-in back.

And now neither of us would be flying around the back lanes circuit; Daddy was already hobbling like a dead man walking.

I don't know whether Mammy knows, or Fliss, but I don't need to wait for the various test results or the next doctor's appointment to know my father is dying. And, as the water washed over me, I said it again and again in my head as I swam back and forth. 'Daddy is dying. Daddy is dying. Daddy is dying.' Thank God I was in the pool because nobody could see I was crying.

****

David Greenspan lounged against the reception desk, chatting up the duty receptionist, when, hair still wet as a rat's tail, I headed for home. My eyes were a little red-rimmed, but that was probably the chlorine in the water. I fumbled for my swipe card to get through the exit barrier, and David leant across the reception desk and pushed the release button. Always the gent.

'Hey Lee,' he began. 'What are you doing here? Shouldn't you be teaching your African-American literature class right now?'

'And shouldn't you *be* in my African-American literature class?'

'Touché!' He held up his hands in surrender. 'But I was lured here by a couple of clients, who offered double rates. It was an offer I couldn't refuse. What was your excuse?'

'Double rates?' I asked, ignoring his question.

'They're trying to tone up for an off-season sun-break. They'll never do it,' he said. 'I'm good, but not that good.'

'I'll vouch for that.'

We grinned at each other. David and I had dated briefly before he enrolled at university. It was an interesting experience.

'Coffee?' he asked.

I glared.

'Tea, then?'

I hesitated.

'Go on,' he said. 'You can tell me all about Teri. What's she doing now?'

Good question, although I wasn't entirely sure I ought to share her latest exploits. He'd also been the subject of her sexual attentions – unwelcome in his case; a first for Teri? – which indirectly led to the complaint about unprofessional conduct that provoked her dismissal. I checked my watch. I ought to be getting home but could spare half an hour, and it would be nice to off-load on someone who knew me warts and all. Well, not quite all my warts. Much as I'd enjoyed being a young man's love interest, I'd never felt comfortable enough to undress in front of David. I was as at home in my own skin as any woman my age could be but had never felt quite brave enough, or, let's be honest, randy enough, to get my kit off. David was patience personified; which was almost as much a relationship killer as my inhibitions. The real death knell though was his decision not just to study at the University of Central Yorkshire but to enrol as a student on my English Literature course.

Professionalism dictated we split – although we remained friends and, from time to time, still worked out together.

When I first trained with him, I'd fallen a little in love. Apart from his obvious physical attractions – *Baywatch* body with poster-boy face – part of his charm had always been his homeliness. He made no secret of the fact his main ambition was to settle down with a nice woman, who'd provide him with the requisite two-point-four children. Since Dan was proving such a let-down in that direction, perhaps I should consider the alternatives?

I made a mental note to run the idea past Teri.

CHAPTER 53

TERI

My reaction to D'reen's phone call surprised me. I'd not given much thought to Duck's Arse since he'd left me at the King's Hotel that night. It had been a one-off, I thought, and he'd gone back to his wife or whatever. But when D'reen mentioned his name, a warm glow of recognition surged through me.

Richard Walker certainly wasn't my type of man at all. I like them tall, fit, strong and six-packed – although I made an exception with Dan, my husband. Ex-husband.

Richard was more the comfy and cuddly type. A big bear.

Oh, stop it, Teri. And then I heard Lee, chuntering away inside my head again. 'He's probably after another afternoon of sex,' her disembodied and disapproving voice said.

Thank goodness I hadn't told her about my encounter with Richard. It's bad enough imagining what she would say having discovered I was having *another* affair with *another* married man without her moralising in real life.

Strangely, even though Lee has treated me so badly, I miss her. I'd never tell her this, but she really was the only real friend I ever had.

But enough of that silly bag. I had work to do and writing the life and times of Lord Rochester was not working as well as I'd hoped. I needed to find a job.

****

Vic Brennan sounded pleased to hear from me. I'd looked up the number of the University of West Riding and asked to be put through to my old tutor.

Vic, like me, was an authority on Rochester, and he and I had many conversations about the old rogue during our tutorials and then later when he supervised my MA into the life and work of one of the greatest libertines of all time.

'Hi Teri,' he said. 'What are you up to?'

Vic is a down-to-earth sort of chap, despite never having worked anywhere but in academia. He manages to avoid talking the language of tedious academics who spout nonsense about 'negotiating the text to juxtapose the binary'.

Despite his expert knowledge of his subject, literature of the seventeenth and eighteenth centuries, he expresses his intellect in an easy-to-understand way, making him one of the few lecturers who believes his students must comprehend what he's saying. Too many academics hide behind a verbal wall of confusing theory that leaves the listener baffled. To Vic, like me, philosophical waffling is anathema; plain speaking is what's needed.

The other good thing about Vic is that he never hit on me.

He must be gay.

But I don't fancy him anyway.

'You probably heard what happened?' I said.

'At Central?' Vic said. 'Yes, news of your er…'

'It's okay. Sacking's the word.'

'I was going to say departure.'

'Thanks. But, yes, there was a misunderstanding, and I'm not working there anymore. Just wondered if there was anything going at your end?'

'Hardly, Teri, given the circumstances.' Vic was nothing if not blunt. 'Sorry, but be realistic, even if there was a lecturing vacancy here, how could we take you on if you'd been "let go" by Central?'

'Is there nothing at all? I need a job; it doesn't need to be lecturing. I'm desperate.'

Vic went quiet on the other end of the line, and I knew he was thinking. He had a way of tilting his head to one side, looking up to the ceiling and pouting his lips, all the better to let in great thoughts.

'There is something, but you might not like it,' he said.

'Try me.'

'You'll hate it.'

'Go on.'

'It's a Student Consideration-Awareness Officer role. There's no teaching; it's purely support.'

'What, like counselling?'

'No, it's er...' Vic sounded hesitant. 'I'm almost embarrassed to talk about this; thought it was a ridiculous idea when it came up at a recent Developing Student Needs meeting.'

He took a deep breath. I waited.

'You know how students are nowadays – mollycoddled; told how wonderful they are when they're not; shielded from reality. They pay their fees and expect to get a service with a first class honours degree at the end of it for doing bugger all themselves. And they want to do it within a "victim-appreciative environment" where they are neither challenged, appropriated or upset. They can only study texts that they've approved, they can't take part in debates where there might be an opposing view to theirs, and they mustn't come into contact with any subject area that's too English, white, male, colonial or traditionally cultural.'

'You are kidding me?'

'No,' Vic went on. 'Think about it. If a student's been brought up to be mummy's best boy or daddy's little princess, and they've just had to snap their fingers to get whatever they want, and they've been told how clever and talented they are – when they're not – what do we expect when they arrive here like little emperors expecting to receive the attention and adulation that they've had all their lives at home? Well, our wondrous powers-that-be have bought it – the infants really have taken over the nursery – and we need a Student Consideration Awareness Officer to liaise with the kiddies to find out what they want, how they want it and when they want it.'

'You're right. It doesn't sound like my sort of thing,' I said.

'Told you,' Vic said.

'But on the other hand,' I said, 'I am desperate.'

'There's a job description and application form on the website,' Vic said. 'You'll need two referees – put me down as one. I'm sure there's someone at Central who'll provide the other. There must be someone there who's still speaking to you?'

'Oh, no problem,' I replied, not entirely convinced.

I put the phone down and it rang almost immediately.

CHAPTER 54

LEE

Thank heavens I had that cup of tea with David. Ten minutes in his company and I remembered the other reason we broke up. The boy's a crashing bore. He's obsessed with maintaining his perfect six-pack, which is understandable – I'm a little obsessed with it myself. It really is a thing of beauty. But, at what price? He eats like a medieval monk, works out like a US Navy Seal and drinks like a nun – no caffeine, no alcohol, NO bloody life.

Bet he even passes on the communion wine too.

'Have you thought about trying a de-caffeinated fruit tea?' he asked when I ordered my usual weak Earl Grey.

'No,' I said, beginning to fill the familiar craving for a large, dry white wine, which always seemed to overtake me in David's company.

I considered changing my order, but it's a gym and not a wine bar, and I know from past experience the wine is rarely properly chilled and often slightly corked. So I swallowed my tea as quickly as possible, made my excuses and scratched David once and for all off the baby-father shortlist. I couldn't risk spawning a beautiful but boring sprog.

But the encounter, as well as everything else that had happened, had left me in desperate need of something strong and alcoholic and, in such cases, Teri was always a reliable drinking companion.

And I had a lot to tell her.

CHAPTER 55

TERI

I chose the King's because it held memories for me – and you never know who might walk in. How I'd love to see Lee's face if viperish Victoria arrived with her latest blind date.

Lee arrived a couple of minutes after I'd ordered a bottle of Sauvignon and bagged a corner table. I didn't want her getting the wine. She has a palate for cheap stuff that tastes of gnat's piss.

'Go on then…' she said as she settled herself in the chair and leaned forward, eager to hear all my news. I started with Andrew, and she tried to make out that she already knew he was married.

But she was completely knocked out when I told her about my encounter with Richard. Of course, her first thought hadn't been for me; she was more concerned about what it might do to Dan's career. I felt like telling her that Dan could look after himself after what he – and she – had done to wreck my life, but I bit my tongue.

She started wittering about my track record with men, and I knew she was referring to Declan, so I took great delight in telling her how I'd recently resisted him and chucked him out of my duplex. She didn't react in the way I expected. She seemed distracted suddenly, picking up her wine glass and staring intently at the contents.

'Are you all right?' And then I remembered she'd been anxious about her father. 'How is your dad?' I asked, reaching out and gently stroking her wrist in what I hoped was a gesture of concern.

She raised her face. Her eyes were red-rimmed, on the verge of crying. 'Oh, Teri…' she started, putting her glass down and rummaging in her bag for a tissue. When she found one, she blew her nose noisily. Shaking her head as if to shrug off the emotion, she said, 'He's not well at all. I'm so worried about him.' She cast me a look so imploring I was lost for words. It must be serious for her to get so upset.

'What's wrong with him?' I asked. 'What've the doctors said?'

But she shook her head again. 'There's nothing specific – at least, not yet. We're waiting for test results. But Daddy knows something that he's not telling us, and I have this awful, horrible, shitty feeling…'

I couldn't believe this; Lee's dad couldn't be that ill, surely? This was big, strong, capable Mr Harper we're talking about. The man, I have to confess, I liked and admired more than my own useless lump of a dad.

'Anyway…sorry…' Lee said, wafting a hand in front of her face as if to clear away the tears and pull herself together. 'I really didn't mean to talk about this. Let's not worry until we know more, eh?'

I looked at her, doubtfully.

'No, really, Teri. Let's talk about something else. What's happening on the job front, for instance?'

I must say, I wasn't sorry to leave the subject. I hate talking about illness.

'Well, actually,' I began, 'there is something. I'd like to put you down as a referee for something at the University of East Riding.'

There was a pause, then Lee said, 'What's the job?'

'Oh, it's student counselling, that sort of thing.'

'It's what? Counselling students? Not lecturing?'

'Well, no. It's liaising with the little darlings to see how unhappy they are about being culturally appropriated. That sort of ridiculous thing.'

'It doesn't sound like something you'd enjoy.'

'It isn't.' But I explained it was only a stop-gap measure and that working on my Rochester research was going to be the big thing in my life. She looked surprised when I mentioned my unfaithful Earl. I was too bored to explain any further, so I dragged the conversation back to the counselling-students job.

'You're right,' I told her, 'it's not ideal. You know how I feel about mollycoddling the precious little squirts. Get some backbone and get on with it, is my mantra.'

'In that case, Teri, it definitely doesn't sound like your sort of thing, and you shouldn't apply for it.'

'What do you mean? Don't you think I'm capable of doing this pathetic job?'

'Frankly, no. And shush, don't talk so loudly.'

'Don't you shush me. I'm not talking loudly. Why'm I not capable?'

'Well, for a start, just listen to yourself. You're rude about students – you've never had any respect for them – you're rude about the job – you're already calling it "pathetic" – and I think you're wasting everyone's time going for a job like that. And, as to your research into Rochester, where on Earth is that supposed to get you? You're kidding yourself if you think someone is going to take a book by you on Rochester seriously.'

I'm used to Lee giving me lectures when she thinks I'm in the wrong. But that was vicious. I couldn't believe her complete over-reaction and, frankly, I wasn't going to be spoken to like that. I stood and slapped a ten pound note on the table and stalked out.

Thinking about it later, I reckoned she'd lashed out at me because she was feeling over-emotional about her father. So I put her name as a referee anyway.

I filled out the application form including plenty of empathetic statements about my belief in the need to protect students from mental challenge and harm. I'd show Miss Goody-Two-Shoes Harper.

I pressed the send button, and an electronic receipt came back, thanking me for my interest and saying applicants who'd been successfully awarded an interview would be notified by the end of January. Interviews would be held in March. Bloody hell! In three months' time? I know universities don't operate under the same time scale as the rest of the working population, but this was ridiculous.

CHAPTER 56

LEE

Teri had already bagged a corner table when I arrived. 'Sauvignon all right?' she asked. I'd have preferred a Muscadet, but Teri says it tastes like gnat's water.

A waiter arrived and plonked a bottle of Sauvignon and two large glasses in front of us as I slipped into the seat opposite Teri.

'Shall I pour,' he asked.

'No, we'll manage,' Teri said dismissively.

I watched as she sloshed the wine into our glasses. Then she pushed one towards me. 'Cheers,' she said.

'Cheers,' I said, waiting for her to ask about Daddy. But, no, she launched into a long account of her capers with gorgeous and god-like, aka Andrew, the four-by-four adulterer.

'You don't seem surprised about Andrew.' Teri took a long slurp of wine.

'I'm not. I told you he was married,' I reminded her.

'Yes, but how did you know?'

How? It was as plain as the nose on her face. 'Maybe it was the pristine boots. Or the lady slippers? Or, perhaps,' I suggested, remembering, 'the tan line on his ring finger?'

Yes, on a subliminal level that white band of flesh had been ringing alarm bells.

'Oooh,' she said. 'I never noticed that. Or,' she amended, 'at least, not until it was too late.'

'You're well shot of him.'

She nodded. 'But it was nice while it lasted.'

'Which wasn't long,' I pointed out.

'Too true,' she giggled. 'He'd barely got his zipper down than was pulling it back up again. Now, Richard…' She leaned forward and smirked. 'What a surprise.'

'Richard?' I said, genuinely puzzled. 'Richard who?'

'Richard Walker.'

'Richard Walker?' I repeated, dumbly.

'Yes, yes.' Teri twiddled with her watch strap. 'Richard Walker. Head of Ridings Today. Dan's boss.'

'I know who he is, but what's he got to do with you?' I asked. Then an awful thought dawned. 'You haven't…? You didn't…? Not with Richard Walker.'

Clearly she had.

She beamed in reply.

'God, Teri. Are you completely mad?'

She grinned and nodded furiously.

'Teri…' Words nearly failed me. 'When did you…where…? Oh God, Teri, you idiot. Me and Dan has been complicated enough. Dan and Richard is even worse.'

She stopped grinning and frowned as though she hadn't thought there might be implications to sleeping with her ex-husband's boss.

'Oh, it won't affect them,' she said, shaking her head. 'Anyway'– she looked down into her glass –'it was nothing; just a one-night stand. Here, in fact. We came for a Ridings Today lunch and then got a room.'

Her tone of voice implied 'what else could we have done?'

Said no? Kept your knickers on? But, no, that probably never even occurred to her as a possible option. But, after all she'd said about Duck's Arse, I struggled to picture the two of them in bed together.

I needn't have worried. Teri dotted the i's and crossed the t's.

'Oh Lee,' Teri laughed. 'I can read your face like a book, and you think he used me for gratuitous sex. Don't you?'

'Well.' I paused. 'You don't have the greatest of track records.' I was thinking of Declan. So was she.

She clutched my arm. 'I haven't told you about Declan yet, have I?'

'No,' I said, heart sinking. Please God, that wasn't back on again, was it?

'You'd have been so proud of me,' she said.

And, I would have been, if I could just erase the image of a naked Richard and his kettle-steamed buttocks. It seemed a bit of a step-down to swap demi-god Declan for the pantomime dame.

God forgive me. I was being as shallow as Teri; there was no comparison between the two men except Declan rather had the edge in the looks and attractiveness stakes. Were there any other stakes that mattered in the bedroom?

'But, wait until you hear this,' Teri said, 'I've been saving the best till last.'

FML! It was just like old times, swapping stories, exchanging confidences, giggling like a couple of schoolgirls locked in a sweet shop. And I hadn't thought about Daddy once.

The bonhomie didn't survive the next revelation; actually it never properly recovered after Teri finally got round to asking about Daddy. Quite apart from the fact that I started to tear up as soon as she mentioned him, I was bloody annoyed at the casual way she brought it up.

'But before I tell you – and Lee, you just won't believe it – tell me quickly, how's your dad?'

Tell her quickly? Words failed me so I rummaged for a tissue instead, and, since I couldn't find one, blew noisily into Peter's mangled handkerchief. 'Not good,' I muttered. 'We're waiting for test results…I have this awful, horrible, shitty feeling.'

I waited for her to say something sympathetic.

And waited.

Nothing. Not even 'Aw, I'm so sorry'.

So I changed the subject. 'Anyway…sorry…' I waited…no, still not a peep from Teri. 'I'd rather not talk about it. No point worrying yet.'

Now, if she'd given me a big hug, offered a clean tissue, mumbled empty platitudes or done anything except launch into more me, me, me…

There was no point beating about the bush. 'No.'

'No? What do you mean?'

For goodness sake, what did she think I meant? 'No,' I repeated. 'I can't, and I won't be a referee.'

'But, why?' Teri seemed genuinely puzzled.

'Because it's a daft idea, and Vic Brennan must have taken complete leave of his senses to even suggest it.'

'Oh, well.' She rolled her eyes. 'You never did like Vic –'

'I don't bloody know the man,' I almost screamed.

Actually, I knew him slightly; we'd met at various conferences and, despite Teri's histrionic descriptions of his oratorical lecturing style, he'd seemed a fairly level-headed sort of chap. An opinion I was now rapidly revising.

'It's nothing to do with Vic,' I said as patiently as I could.

'Oh, so it's me, is it?'

'Yes,' I said.

'Yes? What do you mean?'

Heads turned at the next table.

'Keep your voice down,' I muttered. 'People are looking.'

'I suppose it's all right for you to shout,' Teri hissed. 'And I don't care if people are looking.' She glared round the room.

'I didn't shout. Or, at least, I didn't mean to…it sort of popped out,' I said, trying to catch the waiter's eye. The sooner we paid our bill and got out of here the better.

But he seemed to have gone AWOL.

'Explain,' Teri ordered.

'Explain?' I wasn't sure what she wanted explaining. How well I knew Vic? Why it had nothing to do with him? Why Teri as a student support worker was just about the dumbest idea in the whole bloody world? Or, why I wasn't prepared to tell lies on her behalf?

'Why you won't be a referee. It's a perfectly reasonable request given the circumstances.'

What the hell was she on about? 'What circumstances?'

'Peter Heron. Mike Orme. You.'

She'd lost me completely now. 'I'm sorry,' I said. 'I'm not sure I understand.'

She carefully ran a finger under her lower lashes. Hell's bells, I thought. Don't tell me she's going to cry.

'I'm sure you could have saved my job if you'd really tried.'

Dear God. In what parallel universe did she live? Not even the Angel Gabriel could have saved her job after the shit load of shit she'd stirred up.

I scratched my head.

'Got nits, have you?' she asked sarcastically. 'Picked them up from the devil's spawn?'

She meant Victoria. 'Don't call her that. She's a nice kid.'

'I'm still waiting,' she said. 'Go on. Tell me why you won't be a referee?'

'Keep your voice down.'

People six tables away were now gawping.

'Just answer my question,' she said without lowering her voice one decibel.

'Because…' I tried to think of the best way to point out the bleeding obvious. She'd be a really rubbish student support officer because she lacked the necessary empathy and patience and eye for administrative detail required by this sort of forward-facing student role. Dear God, did I really say that? Thankfully no, I'd kept my thoughts to myself.

'Because I don't think you'd enjoy it,' I said.

'Why not?' she asked. 'I'm a very sympathetic and nurturing sort of person, and I think I'd enjoy giving something back.'

'Don't talk twaddle,' I said.

'I'm not talking twaddle.'

'I know, I know. I'm sorry.'

Why did I keep apologising?

'Because…' I tried a different tack. 'I don't think you'd find it intellectually stimulating.'

'I don't need a job that's intellectually stimulating,' she said. 'I've got my research.'

Research? What the hell was she on about?'

'Rochester,' she said. 'I'm still hopeful funding will come through to help me take it forward.'

'You can kiss goodbye to that idea,' I said, thinking of the research grant she'd sworn blind was in her pocket when she was first appointed as a senior lecturer. In fact, securing the bursary was a condition of her employment and, whatever else she may or may not have done, Peter Heron had been well within his rights to dismiss her when the money failed to materialise.

But once she'd got the bit between her teeth there was no stopping her. 'And, until it does, I'm going to plough on regardless. I'm going to make Rochester the new Duchess of Devonshire,' she said, referring to a recent academic tome which had been turned into a Hollywood blockbuster.

Well, you had to applaud her grand vision but, right now, it was more pressing to squash her student support ambition if for no other reason than to protect the poor bloody students.

'That's a great idea,' I said, 'but, in the meantime, I think supporting struggling students will bore you daft. You're used to more mentally demanding work.'

'Perhaps,' she conceded. 'But I'm willing to pay that price in order to give myself the brain space to work on other things in my own time. And it's not like you to be so negative. Or unsupportive.'

Talk about the pot calling the kettle black. How supportive had she been five minutes earlier when I'd tried to tell her my father was terminally ill? I'd have had more sympathy from a rabid dog. It would have served her right if I'd told her exactly what I thought. But I didn't because what was the point of starting another quarrel? So, I apologised again. 'I don't mean to be negative, but I really think you might find this too much of a stretch.'

That wasn't the right thing to say. I tried to make amends. 'You're more suited for…jobs that…working with people who…' Oh hell, I couldn't think of anything that might suit.

'You mean you don't think I'm capable of this pathetic little job?' she screeched so loudly, dogs three counties away whined in pain, and the waiter – who'd been missing a few minutes earlier – miraculously appeared behind the bar, looking in our direction. We'd be chucked out if she didn't calm down.

'Shush,' I said.

'Don't shush me,' she bellowed, scrambling for her bag and gloves.

'Will you or will you not be my referee?'

'No.'

She was on her feet and struggling into her coat.

'Call yourself a friend. With friends like you I don't need enemies.' She slapped a ten pound note on the table. 'I'll leave you to settle the bill,' she said, and flounced out of the bar.

Well, trying to keep the peace had worked *really* well.

CHAPTER 57

LEE

I'm not one who believes in allowing even a bottle of Sauvignon Blanc to go to waste so, after Teri stomped off on her high horse, I stayed and swallowed the dregs. Ugh! It had been possible to ignore the awfulness of the vintage when we were swapping confidences, but this wasn't a wine to savour alone. I called the waiter and ordered a large glass of Muscadet to wash the taste from my mouth. A couple of sips later, and taste buds almost restored, I thought about heading for home – and didn't think much of the idea so swallowed what was left in the glass in a couple of large slugs and ordered a refill. That one went down almost as fast as the first. There are some days when a good cuppa doesn't hit the spot quite as well as a cold glass or three of dry white wine.

Out of the corner of my eye, I could see a couple of lads – okay, gentlemen not quite in the first flush of youth – eyeing me with interest. One of them whispered something to his mate and raised a glass in my direction. Clearly, they thought a woman drinking alone must be in need of a man. I scowled in reply. Look in a mirror, fella! Call me superficial, but if I'm going to fall for a wine-bar Casanova it'll be one who doesn't need the help of a mirror to see his genitalia.

Reluctantly, I asked for the bill – probably best to go home now anyway while I could still walk in a straight line – and almost fainted when I saw the total. Hell's teeth, Teri's tenner didn't even begin to cover the cost of the ghastly Sauvignon.

The taxi driver was one of those jolly 'have a nice day' types who insisted on trying to drum up a conversation. 'Been anywhere nice?' For, goodness sake, you picked me up from The King's, you know I haven't been anywhere more than ordinarily nice. 'Got anything planned for the rest of the evening?' Yes, several more glasses of dry white wine; as many as it takes to dull the nagging agony consuming the pit of my stomach. 'Hubby'll have dinner on the table?' Yes, in the parallel universe where I have a husband or even a partner who can cook a meal without dirtying every pan in the kitchen.

'Oh dear,' he said as we pulled up outside the house, 'sounds like someone's having something of a humdinger.' A bit of an understatement, I thought. The front door was wide open, and the noise was so bad it was hard to believe a stuck pig wasn't bleeding to death in the hallway. I should be so lucky. Just in case the day hadn't gone badly enough, Dan and Victoria were having another difference of opinion.

Squaring my shoulders, and mentally donning a combat helmet and flak jacket, I strode confidently into the battle zone.

Well, they both seemed glad to see me. 'Lee,' implored Dan as I banged the front door shut. No need to provide the neighbours with any more entertainment. 'Please tell this stupid girl she can't go out looking like a street walker.'

'Lee,' begged Victoria, 'tell Dad there's nothing wrong with what I'm wearing.'

I guess, on one level, it was good Dan was so unfamiliar with the usual working garb of the Red Light district's prostitutes he thought Victoria was aping their style. But it was nevertheless slightly concerning she thought a black, cropped top, black, leather curtain pelmet skirt and ripped stockings constituted a good look. The black eyeliner and purple lipstick didn't add much either.

Who to placate first?

'Where are you going tonight?' I asked Victoria.

'It doesn't matter where she's going, she's NOT going out dressed like a whore.'

'I am not a whore!'

For pity's sake. Talk about waving a red rag in front of a bull. 'There's nothing wrong with her outfit.' I'm good at little white lies. 'And she's quite right; all the girls are dressed just like that. She'll blend in with the crowd perfectly.' I can be provocative too. 'So, where are you going?' I asked again, raising a hand to shush Dan.

'I'm meeting up with some friends from college.'
'Boys?'
'Yeah,' she drawled sarcastically, 'some of my friends are boys.'

Yes, I thought, but at least one of them is also a flash-git soccer player, who eats little girls for breakfast, and your dad, who gave him a grilling this afternoon in the Ridings Studio, would finish him off him on the barbecue if he knew what was going on.

But, today, at least, I had the little madam stitched up. 'That's okay then.' I smiled at her and turned to Dan. 'The kids'll be going to studenty-sort of places where they'll drink cheap beer and plastic-coloured shots, and the bouncers will chuck them out and send them home when they get too rowdy.

'And you needn't worry about them going on to any of the posh places where blokes in Armani suits might ply them with champagne cocktails, because in those clothes they'll never get through the door.'

Victoria glared, and I did a mental high five. Whoopee! I'd guessed correctly. She had a liaison with Shayne and, in her innocence, hadn't taken into account that the Goth look would go down like a bomb in the high-class joints he liked to patronise. Now she'd have to figure out how to explain her willingness to change into an outfit Dan might consider halfway respectable without actually giving the game away.

Even Dan might suspect a rat if she capitulated too easily.

'I'm not staying here,' she said petulantly. 'I'm going back to Mum's.'

Clever; she could scrub up there, and Dan wouldn't suspect a thing. There was just one little problem though...

'Could you give me a lift, Lee?'

'No can do. I've been to the King's with Teri, and I've drunk too much wine to risk driving.'

'Oh Teri...well if she's more important than me.'

The cheeky little so-and-so. What had I said to Teri earlier? 'She's a nice kid.' Not today, she wasn't.

But, tough, I wasn't risking my licence on her behalf.

'Dad?' she queried.

'Sorry,' he said, picking up his car keys and heading for the door. 'I've got to get back to the studio and, no I can't make a detour.'

Victoria stared in fury as he gave us both a cheery wave and shut the door behind him. 'What am I supposed to do? I'm going to be late for my date.' If she'd been just a few years younger she'd have stamped her feet.

I shrugged. 'Call a taxi? Call your mum?' Poor child. Talk about being stuck between a rock and a hard place.

CHAPTER 58

TERI

Lee was right. I'd applied for a god-awful job. Typical that the sanctimonious cow had seen it straight away.

Needing a coffee the next morning, I walked down to Portly & Groops for a reviving Americano. On the wide, low window ledge just inside the door was a stack of Evening Leaders, a newspaper I never read even while involved with Declan. I prefer my news in bite-size chunks on my mobile. And that was another thing I ought to sort out: a new phone.

The barista looked over and saw me eyeing the papers. 'Have one – they're free if you're buying coffee,' he said, adding in a quieter voice, 'No-one would buy that crap anyway – full of rubbish.'

I grinned, making a mental note to pass on the comments to Declan should I ever see that low-life rat again.

Underneath the Leader's front page masthead was a declaration in smaller type promising a more 'streamlined in-paper reading experience' but as I flicked through I could only marvel at the screaming hysteria of the headlines that held no relation to the banality of the stories beneath.

And the mistakes! I retrieved a pen from my bag and circled grammatical errors. Does no-one know the difference between 'their', 'there' and 'they're'?

No wonder they have to give this rubbish away. My streamlined in-paper reading experience was not matching the performance metrics the editorial idiots had set themselves.

Turning to the jobs pages at the back, I considered the receptionist's job at a local spot welding company when I recognised a logo. It was an ad for L'homme-vert, the most expensive restaurant for miles around. And they wanted an assistant chef. Well, this was more like it. Why waste my time ministering to the needs of dozy, over-protected students when I could be putting my catering course qualifications to good use?

It had been a while since I'd done any chef-fing, but it wouldn't take me long to get back into it.

L'homme-vert was a classy place; Dan used to take me there when we had something to celebrate, which wasn't often during our short, disastrous marriage. He'd known the owner, Jules Lestrange, and we'd always had an indulgent welcome and, I have to say, rather obsequious service.

Damn, no mobile phone to ring the restaurant, and it had been so long since I used a telephone box, I wouldn't know what to do. I'd have to go back to the flat and use the landline. Better, still, why not just go round to L'homme-vert now?

It was nearly lunchtime, but as I approached the restaurant I could see it was closed. L'homme-vert was one of those places that said 'typically French'. The building was double-fronted with two large bay windows painted green on either side of a green wooden and glass-panelled front door. The stonework was a washed-out green colour although you could hardly see it for the amount of ivy growing up and across the frontage.

The name 'L'homme-vert' was spelled out in a Monotype Corsiva font on a rectangular wooden sign nailed above the door to give it a 'French' look, although I think Mistral or even French Script itself would have been better. But, hey, the best French restaurant in the whole of the north of England didn't need my design input.

I approached the door and squinted through one of the glass panels. I could see a young man, possibly in his twenties, pulling chairs off the tables where they'd been piled while the floor was swept.

I rapped on the glass, and the man turned to me and waved his hands in a 'no-no' gesture to indicate – presumably – that they weren't open yet and turned back to the chairs.

I rapped again; I was not going to tolerate any pseudo Parisian arrogance. He turned again and with an exaggerated shrug of the shoulders strolled over to the door.

'We ees not opern,' he said in a cod French accent.

'Open the door, please,' I instructed. 'I don't want to eat, I want to speak to Monsieur Lestrange.'

Something in the authority of my voice persuaded him, and he made a big thing of sliding a bolt back and pulling open the door.

'Thank you,' I said, giving the impression that I'd been patient just about long enough. 'Can I see Monsieur Lestrange?'

'Why?' the insolent chap said, rubbing his hands down the sides of the big, black apron he was wearing over black trousers and a crisp, white shirt. You shouldn't really sweep the floor wearing the gear you're going to be waiting in, but I decided against telling him this.

'Is he here?' I asked.

'Non. He ees not, how you say, availible. But why you want heem?'

The guy was now sounding Spanish.

'I'm here about the assistant chef's job.'

'You ees a chef?' He had the cheek to step back, holding both hands up in a gesture of alarmed surprise.

'Yes, I am,' I said firmly, plonking my tote on a newly de-chaired table and turning to glare at him. 'Could you let the owner know I'm here?'

'I ees him,' the man said and then he suddenly turned away and half-bent as he put a hand up to his mouth and spluttered.

'Sorry, love,' he said, turning back to face me, his face blushingly pink – not a good look on a man. 'Couldn't help it – you look so indignant.'

'You're not French, are you?' I said.

'No, I'm Yorkshire. Sam Johnson.' He held out his hand to shake mine.

'What's happened to Monsieur Lestrange?' I asked, registering a strong, dry grip and a good-looking face. Too young though, even for me.

'Sold up, retired and gone back to Paris.'

'And you've taken over?'

'Yup. Bought the place six weeks ago and been making a few changes – there's only so much of the distressed French look I can take so I've given everything a coat of paint, put in a new kitchen – and now we're nearly up and ready for business.'

'And you're looking for a chef?'

He eyed me and pursed his lips. 'Sorry, love. You're too late; hired someone just the other day. You'd be amazed at the number of chefs looking for work.'

He registered the annoyance on my face and mistook it for disappointment because he went on. 'But I do need other staff, including a front of house person – and you look as though you'd be great in that role.'

I was about to inform him that I don't do front of house, that I was a qualified chef. Then I remembered Lee and her little saying about beggars and choosers.

'I'll have a think about it.'

'Well, don't think for too long. I've had lots of interest in the job, and I need to have someone in place by the end of the week.'

'The end of *this* week?'

'Yeah, we're opening on Saturday.'

CHAPTER 59

LEE

On balance, it's about a million times more likely that hell will freeze over before Teri and I achieve any sort of rapprochement. After the way she'd stormed out, she certainly wouldn't be in any rush to make the first conciliatory move and though, once Dan and Victoria had buggered off on their respective engagements, I did toy with the idea of ringing her to discuss possible alternative sources of employment within the higher education sector, I decided against it. Frankly, it would have been a waste of time, largely because, honestly, I couldn't think of any non-academic posts for which she might be suitably qualified – apart from joining the domestic services team. And, while, nobody could ever criticise her thorough approach to cleanliness, I rather thought she might balk just a little at the prospect of earning a measly seven pounds twenty-seven an hour as an entry-level cleaner.

Instead, I took a bottle of wine from the fridge and a wine glass from the glass cabinet and took myself up to bed.

I was asleep by the time Dan got home so it wasn't until next morning over breakfast that I told him about Daddy's suggestion that I should swap my academic gown for a pair of builder's overalls. I don't think he took it in properly. He was rather more concerned with tracking down his wayward spectacles which had gone AWOL.

Again.

A nicer woman than me would have joined him in scouring the house. But I did that the first time he mislaid them. The second time too. My enthusiasm for playing hunt the specs began to wane a bit at the third attempt and had completely vanished by the fourth. So, instead, I read my paper and finished my tea and toast, which was a bit mean, especially as I knew exactly where he'd find them. I'd spotted them when I took yesterday's newspapers outside for recycling.

But I thought he deserved to sweat a bit after his tepid response to my news about Daddy.

The words were barely words out of my mouth before he started wittering on about the up-coming RTS dinner. Bloody Richard Walker had issued a three-line whip: all senior executives, plus key 'talent', such as Dan, were expected to don their dinner jackets and schmooze for England. Or, rather, Ridings TV. Bloody cheek, I thought, especially as he was in the Far East and wouldn't be attending himself.

Dan, however, was more sanguine. 'He's a busy bloke,' he said, 'and the RTS is a big deal in our business, so it's legitimate for him to expect us to represent him.'

Bollocks! 'If it's that important he should have cancelled his business trip.'

'Not that simple.' Dan shook his head. 'He's got a lot of people to see, apparently. Business people. Chinese business people.'

'Oh?'

'Don't ask me. I don't know. I'm only the main anchor man – not privy to Richard's business dealings. In fact, now I come to think about it, I know very little about what he does when he's not at Ridings Today. But D'reen did let slip that he's dealt with some dodgy beggars in the past – and that he was planning to bang a few heads together in China. But I don't know why or what for. That's Richard for you.'

How interesting. And how much did Teri know? Not much; there's no way she'd have kept such information to herself. Shame we weren't speaking, I'd have loved to see her face when I told her…

'Don't you dare tell anyone,' Dan warned.

I considered. How serious was Teri about Duck's Arse? She'd laughed off their dalliance as a one-night stand, but if Richard was into something deeper and dangerous, she deserved to know the truth. Not that it was any of my business but still… No, why was I worrying? Teri and Duck's Arse? They didn't belong in the same picture. But I must tell Dan sometime; he'd find the steamy kettle story rather amusing. Only not right now; he was far too steamed up about his missing spectacles.

'Are you sure you haven't seen my glasses? I've looked everywhere.'

That was a daft assertion. If he'd looked everywhere he'd have found them. However, I'm nothing if not magnanimous. 'Try your shoe.'

He frowned. 'What?'

'Try your shoe.'

'I wish you'd talk sense.'

It would have served him right if I'd left it there, but I needed to get to the yard to meet Dom so I slapped my half-empty mug on the breakfast bar and, stomping off to the utility room, returned with the black, leather brogues he'd worn last night. His glasses were in the left shoe.

'Who put them there?' Dan asked.

Who do you think?

CHAPTER 60

TERI

It was more fun than I thought it would be. L'homme-vert opened on the Saturday night as Sam said it would, and I was installed as front-of-house meeter and greeter.

In my red JK Fennick dress and a new pair of nude high heels.

It wasn't the job I thought I'd be doing, but if you've got to have a front-of-house person, you might as well have someone who looks good and dresses well.

I'd not heard anything from Vic Brennan about the student-mollycoddling job, but that would only be a matter of time. Meanwhile, I'd decided to see L'homme-vert as a stop-gap – and enjoy it.

Two days earlier I'd been introduced to the chef, Louis, who remarkably *was* French, but not in that suave, sexy French way some French men are. He was overweight and not at all good-looking. Such a shame.

I'd also met Sam's wife, Zofia – from Poland – who was to help Sam and Louis in the kitchen, and the two waiters, Gary – from Lancashire – and Beniamin –from Romania.

We were quite an eclectic bunch, but we bonded over coffee and cakes as Sam went through arrangements. Well, that's to say, the rest of them had cakes; I really don't see the need to stuff your face with sweet things every five minutes.

Sam had invited friends, family and a few local worthies to the launch night and the atmosphere was buzzing. I half expected Dan to stroll in – as a famous face off the telly he was always being invited to parties and events – but when I mentioned it to Sam he said he'd tried to get Ridings Today to cover the opening but they'd been too busy.

'They'll be up to their arm pits in roller-skating ducks,' I told him. 'You know, the serious news.'

'But we've got someone from the Leader coming,' Sam said, 'and they've promised to do a review once we've been open a while.'

Sam sounded pleased, but I was more circumspect. The Leader had what they termed a Dishy Dining Out page every Friday in its What's Up and On section, written by someone called Cromwell.

I knew, because Declan once told me, that Cromwell wasn't a real person but a general byline name used to cover up the fact that any number of different reporters were sent out to eat at local restaurants and write up their experiences.

Most of the reviews were jolly 'Five Spoons' affairs – spoons being used to grade the food, atmosphere and service of whichever eaterie was under the spotlight. And most used tired and clichéd descriptions. 'My chicken was enlivened by a yummy white wine sauce while across the table my partner toyed happily with a pork cheek.' That sort of thing.

Occasionally a place would be given a measly One Spoon. Declan told me that the Leader was in collusion with most of the restaurants in that they offered a free meal – the free food being a way of supplementing the reporter's low wages – and in return the restaurant got a good review. But, every now and then, a restaurant would refuse to take part so a reporter was sent undercover, paid for a meal – claiming the cash back on expenses – and wrote a stinker.

'And that's somehow ethical?' I'd asked Declan.

'It's business – makes the world go round,' he'd said.

CHAPTER 61

LEE

It didn't take five minutes in Dom's company to confirm I knew as much about the building trade as he knew about teaching English Literature. Or that whatever he might think about shirkers he wasn't too hot at time-keeping. 'What time do you call this?' I asked when he eventually rolled up.

He glanced at his watch. 'I make it 7:42am. What time do you make it?'

Was he *trying* to be funny?

He unlocked the door to the management office – a glorified, and very draughty, garden shed – and flicked on the lights. 'Brrr, it's cold in here.' He turned the knob on a small portable electric heater. 'Soon be warm and toasty.'

He held up the kettle. 'Fancy a brew?'

I'd drunk Dom's milky, pea-souper tea before. 'No thanks.'

I stared out of the window at the empty yard.

'Where is everybody? I thought this place would be teeming with activity by now.'

Dom peered at his watch again. 'It's early yet. They'll be here by eight which is when they're due to start.'

What! Work didn't start until eight? Why the hell had I dragged myself from my lovely bed to get here for half-past seven?

Dom pulled out a chair and, indicating I should sit too, cleared space on the office desk for the grubby, old-fashioned workman's lunch box he'd been carrying when he first arrived.

'But first, grub time,' he said, biting into a white bread door-stopper of a bacon sandwich.

The kettle whistled on its little bottled gas hob. Dom inclined his head. 'Do you want to do the honours?'

No, but Dom's question was a rhetorical shortcut for 'if you've got nowt else to do, make me a cuppa', and it didn't seem polite to respond 'I didn't drag myself out of bed at the crack of dawn to become a builder's char-wallah'. Instead, I chucked a tea bag into a mug and topped it with boiling water.

'You might want to sniff the milk,' Dom said. 'I'm not sure how fresh it is.'

My stomach curdled.

'Where's Daddy?' I asked as Dom munched away.

'Boss never gets here this early.'

So, why did I need to be here so early?

'Not really sure why you need to be here at all.' Dom washed the sandwich down with a swig of scalding tea.

I watched in awe; if his mouth wasn't lined with asbestos he was in serious danger of third-degree burns.

He rubbed his bacon-stained fingers on his trousers and wiped his mouth on the sleeve of his grime-encrusted coat.

It's to be hoped his immune system was working overtime.

'Boss is practically a part-timer these days. We usually have a bit of a catch-up mid-morning. I tell him what we're doing, and he tells me to go-ahead and do it.'

What? That wasn't the impression we got at home.

Dom poured the last dregs of tea down his neck and then moved across to the sink and rinsed his mug under the cold water tap. He let the running water wash over his hands. 'He's been looking a bit peaky of late.' He dried the mug thoroughly with a tea towel that was distinctly the worse for wear, polishing it inside and out as if it was precious metal. I was half expecting him to hold it up to the light to check the shine. 'Is there anything I ought to know?'

Yes. No. Maybe? What was I supposed to say? Wasn't my place to tell; this was a conversation Daddy needed to have with him.

Dom dropped the tea towel on the draining board and put his mug back on its shelf. He stared into the sink. 'I'm guessing the answer's yes?'

I went and stood next to him. 'I'm not sure, Dom,' I said. 'We're waiting for some test results.'

He pulled a check cap from his coat pocket. 'Okay,' he said. 'I guess the priority is not to let Boss worry about things.'

He dropped a hand on my shoulder and squeezed slightly. 'Between us we can keep things ticking over.' He winked. 'It'll be interesting to have a lady Boss.'

That was one way of looking at it. But it was well meant.

'I'll keep you briefed,' he continued, 'just like I do with your dad, and if anything really major comes us, I'll give you a call.'

I put my hand on his. 'Thank you.'

Dom opened the shed door. 'Come on, Lady Boss. I've got work to do.'

Dear Dom, where would the Harper family be without you? Up the creek without a paddle – or without a business anyway.

CHAPTER 62

TERI

The restaurant opened Saturday evenings and Sunday lunch, closed Monday, Tuesday and Wednesday, but opened again for lunch and evening meals on Thursdays and Fridays.

And Sam was right – the place was getting busier all the time with the pre-Christmas bashes. Local firms would arrive for lunch at noon and still be knocking back the expense account Sauvignon at five p.m. by way of celebrating the festive season even though it was only mid-December.

Still it was one way of team-building, I suppose, although I'd never seen the point of wearing a stupid paper hat and getting rat-arsed with a bunch of people I work with – but didn't like – just because it was nearly Christmas.

Still, it kept me busy – and the tips were good. One business-type had come in with a group of underlings and lectured them on company policy. 'If commitment isn't there,' boss man said, 'it's a very powerful signal of the failure to commit.' But the thick-brained fool left three twenty-pound notes in the tip box for me and the rest of the staff.

While lunchtimes were mostly taken up with local business people, we did get the occasional couple coming in, including one chap who was trying to celebrate his wedding anniversary despite his wife's protestations that they didn't have to come here and spend so much when she could have done her 'chick pea and bulgur wheat dish' at home. I told Gary, the wine waiter, to keep filling the husband's glass. He needed it.

CHAPTER 63

LEE

Increasingly, I felt as if I could give a headless chicken a good run for its money. Sometimes I even felt as if the headless chicken had the better deal, at least its legs would give up the ghost sooner rather than later while I had no option but to keep going until…I was going to say until Daddy dropped, but even Teri wouldn't put things so bluntly.

Plonker Heron proved his utter cockwombleness almost immediately. Within days he'd rescinded his offer of compassionate leave on the grounds that 'we can't spare someone of your seniority at such a busy time of year, especially when we're already a staff member down'. Well, whose bloody fault was that? It wasn't me who'd pointed the finger at Teri and pushed her out the door.

I could have gone to HR and thumped the table and demanded my rights, but, frankly, after my first meeting with Dom it was pretty clear that as a builder's boss I made a very good academic. So, with Dom's agreement, I became an in-betweener, shuttling backwards and forwards between him and Daddy to keep the business cogs ticking over. But, goodness, it was exhausting; most days began with a pre-breakfast meet-up with Dom. He'd tell me who was doing what and where, provide a list of the supplies and fixings that were on order and where and when they'd be dropped off, and bring me up-to-date with progress on current and up-and-coming projects. I'd scribble everything down in a little notebook so I could report back to Daddy but, honestly, sometimes I wondered if Dom had been talking double Dutch since half the time my notes didn't make an atom of sense.

In theory, I was supposed to have a post-breakfast catch-up with Daddy but, since he'd changed the habits of a lifetime and didn't even get out of bed until the daytime TV presenters had settled their bottoms on their sofa, usually we chatted at lunchtime instead.

On the days I didn't have any teaching scheduled, I'd go over to Mammy and Daddy's house for lunch – well, I say lunch but I was the only one doing much eating. Mammy would pick at a sandwich, and Daddy would chase a bit of cheese and pickle around his plate for ten-minutes-or-so until he thought he'd clocked up enough food miles to make us both think he'd eaten a full feast.

As pretences go, it wasn't terribly successful, but there didn't seem much point in trying to force feed him.

Other times I'd send an email update – which was equally time-consuming. Either way, I'd catch up with Dom again when he returned to the yard at tea-time. He'd ask if Daddy had any specific instructions or questions and I'd say 'No, just do whatever you think best', so Dom would tell me what needed to be done and I'd say 'Right, that's what we'll do'. And then I'd go in the next morning, and Dom would tell me exactly the same things he'd told me the previous evening and I'd go back to Daddy and he'd say 'Whatever you think best' and I'd tell Dom and…I did suggest that perhaps Dom and I didn't need to meet quite so often, but Dom was horrified. 'Does me good to talk things over,' he said. I was flattered he thought me a good sounding board but, no, nothing of the sort. 'When I say it aloud I can hear in my head what Boss would say so I know I'm doing right.' So, he didn't really need me to scurry to-and-fro between him and Daddy? 'Well, I don't need it but it wouldn't be right not to keep him in the loop.'

True, but all these itty-bitty meetings were eating into my working day, and the only way to keep ahead of myself was to get up earlier and do an hour before breakfast and to burn the midnight oil, which made both Dan and Victoria grumble that I never seemed to have time for them.

Frankly, I didn't. But I didn't have time for me either.

The only person who didn't grumble was Teri; but that was because we weren't speaking again.

This time I was too tired to care.

And too grumpy.

Dan, I'm afraid, often got the rough end of my tongue. Sometimes I worried I was turning into a miserable old shrew, but, mostly, I thought it was his fault for winding me up. How hard is it, for instance, to put yesterday's newspapers out for recycling? Note the use of the plural: newspapers, as in every bloody copy of the print media that rolled off the nation's presses. I swear to God Dan never came through the door without a bundle of today's news tucked under his arm – do you have any idea how many supplements accompany the Sunday broadsheets? And the tabloids are almost as bad. Sometimes, I thought the ruddy things must be breeding; they were strewn across the living room carpet, spread across the dining room table and tucked behind the settee cushions.

I'd tried dropping a hint or two. 'Could you put the papers in the recycling bin when you've finished with them?' But I might as well have been talking to a brick wall.

'What did you say, Schnookums?' he asked once.

'What did you call me?'

Surprised, he looked up from his newspaper. 'Schnookums.'

'Schnookums,' I repeated. 'What sort of a word is that? It sounds like something a Hollywood diva would call a pedigree pup.'

He snorted indignantly. 'Well, it isn't. It's a people name. I heard a bloke on an American sitcom call his fiancé Schnookums and I thought it was kind of cute.'

'I don't.'

He returned to his newspaper. 'I was just trying to find a pet name for you.' His tone suggested I was being overly critical.

'No offence, mate, but keep looking.'

The newspaper rustled. 'You should look up the dictionary definition.'

'Pah!' I said and went into the kitchen and took out my bad temper on the wooden love-hearts, dangling on short lengths of rustic pink twine from the kitchen cupboard door handles. They'd been a gift from Teri. 'I saw these and thought of you,' she'd said. She didn't say what she'd thought but it can't have been complimentary. I pulled a pair of scissors from a drawer, snipped the string and chucked them into the trash can. It felt extremely cathartic. If I couldn't make Daddy better or get myself a baby or patch things up with Teri, I could, at least, reclaim my kitchen.

A 'charming' floral decoration – Teri's description, not mine – which had been gathering dust on the window sill followed suit, along with a 'cute' spotty dog oven timer – again, Teri's opinion, not mine – and a set of drinks coasters emblazoned with so-called 'witty' Yorkshire witticisms.

I was getting warmed up now. Next in the bin was a nursery rhyme wall clock – don't ask; a Toby jug – hideous thing; and a huge wooden pepper mill that hadn't worked properly since the day Teri had foisted it on me.

The bin was getting full but never mind. I was a woman on a mission: I was going to de-clutter the kitchen or die in the attempt.

Well, I didn't die but the de-clutter fairy – yes, there is one, she charges thirty quid an hour – would have been proud of me. And I saved myself over one hundred pounds in the bargain.

Dan, perhaps, sensibly steered well clear of the kitchen apart from once when he poked his head around the door and asked if it was okay if he made himself a coffee.

'No,' I said and, once he'd retreated, threw the half-opened packet of dark roast Arabica coffee beans which Teri had bought last Christmas into the bin. Not because I'm a bitch, but because, as everyone knows, once you can't smell the coffee, it's off. And whatever the smell coming from the packet, it wasn't coffee.

In fact, it was quite an eye-opener when I started checking best-before dates. Technically, I know tinned stuff like baked beans will stay edible practically forever, but there were a couple of cans lurking on a top shelf that were almost teenagers. And the fridge and freezer weren't much better. Who knew, for instance, that fresh sweetcorn will ferment if left in the bottom of the salad drawer for a fortnight? Or that hummus, which is basically chick peas and olive oil, will develop its own personality if left to linger too long? Or that even in the freezer beef burgers don't last for more than twelve months?

Clearly, I was a very bad housekeeper, and it was a wonder none of us had gone down with food poisoning.

It was very satisfying though to survey my almost minimalist kitchen.

Right now a lot of my life was spiralling out-of-control but, at least, within these four walls I'd regained some power back.

Unfortunately, I'd also managed to strip the place of anything that might have made a decent evening meal.

'Come on, Dan,' I said, dropping a kiss on the top of his head. I'd just Googled schnookums: *a person who is everything that is good in the world and nothing that's bad.* 'Let's go out to eat.'

CHAPTER 64

◦∞◦

TERI

When things are going well, why do people in charge of businesses need to make changes? It's change for change's sake; tinkering around the edges to give the business what they see as a boost. They see it as stimulating and motivational, but it's actually unsettling and demoralising.

I've never met a manager who hasn't done some sort of business management course and thinks innovation under some meaningless banner such as 'Breaking through Clouds to see Skies' is better than consolidating.

It was like that when I was teaching at the university. Plonker Heron couldn't bear to see us bumbling along smoothly with everyone knowing what their job was and how they were doing it. No. He'd get those numbskulls from Human Resources to download the latest training fad, and we'd all have to attend tedious, mind-numbing sessions on how to Improve Your Position of Positivity and Put Revolution on Your Radar.

I remember Lee muttering 'Wouldn't we be better off lecturing the students as we are paid to do?' which was a bit revolutionary for her as she's usually one for towing the academic line on educational initiatives. But Heron's stance was always the same on new modes of teaching and learning. He'd say something like, 'Taking part in thought showers might mean us kicking the kitten but, overall, we'll be going forward to embrace the paradigm shifts of pedagoguery.' I think it would have been closer to the truth if he'd said demagogy, but hey ho.

So when Sam said he'd done some 360-degree thinking, I was more than a little concerned. We were having one of our pre-lunchtime team sessions when he announced, 'We're going to do away with menus.'

Do away with menus? We're a restaurant for goodness' sake.

His idea was to hang blackboards on the far wall behind the bar and write the various dishes up in white chalk.

'But there'll be some people whose eyesight is not so good – and people in the window tables won't be able to see that far?' Beniamin said, reasonably.

'We'll give them little binoculars,' Sam replied, clearly having anticipated that question.

'What, everyone coming into the restaurant will be given some binoculars?' I asked, given that meeting, greeting and giving out of paraphernalia would be my job.

'Yup,' Sam answered. 'Or,' he continued, 'we ask for their phones and take a picture of the blackboard and then they've got a photo…'

'Oh, isn't that all a bit messy?' Gary said, the no-nonsense Lancastrian.

'And too trendy,' I said, backing him up. 'L'homme-vert is a classic French restaurant, our customers like things done traditionally.'

'We've got to get into the twenty-first century,' Sam said. 'Classic French or not.'

'And when they've got their little photo,' Gary said, 'do we still take their orders in the same way?'

'No,' Sam said. 'I'm doing away with your notepads and pens. Customers will text their choices direct to the kitchen.'

Louis, dressed in his cooking whites, looked up sharply. 'And how do I know what they've texted?'

'You'll have a mobile in the kitchen…' Sam began.

Louis sprang to his feet and thumped a hand down on the table. He was a stereotypical chef; full of emotion. 'No, no, no,' he said. 'I can't be cutting meat, stirring sauces, dishing up meals and looking at some ridiculous little phone message to see who wants what!'

'But –'

'No,' Louis interrupted, 'and it's not hygienic. Think of all the germs on a mobile phone…'

He was on to a winner there.

Sam thought for a moment. 'Er, well, yes, that's a point,' he said.

'I'll give it some more thought. Maybe get the customers to download a L'homme-vert app…'

'What's thees about a happ?' Zofia asked, sharply. She'd clearly been in on the blackboard idea, but hadn't been told about any apps.

'Well,' Sam said, 'we'd create an app and put all our menus on it, customers download it in advance and can pre-order their meals by email – so one of us would have time to make a note to give to Louis in the kitchen…'

I shook my head. 'I don't know many people who'd have the time or inclination to do that – and remember that little old couple who came in the other day? They've probably never bothered with the internet and wouldn't have a clue what an app was.'

'I think thees needs more thought,' Zofia said, reasonably. 'And look at ze time, we're opening in five minutes.'

'Business as usual?' Gary asked.

Sam sighed. 'Business as usual. For now.'

CHAPTER 65

LEE

Why, given everything I've said about telly luvvies and Hooray Henrys, did I jettison my principles and accompany Dan to the RTS dinner? Because…lots of reasons. Shall I list them?

One, Finlay Baxter: I was interested to meet the junior bogeyman. 'You'll be disappointed,' Dan warned. 'He's got the beginnings of a paunch, and his hair is greying at the temples.'

I raised a pensive forefinger to my mouth. 'Hmm…that reminds me of someone…'

Dan pulled at his waistband. 'I don't know what you mean.'

I think he did.

Reason number two: Victoria. Naturally, the RTS had invited one of the district's biggest personalities – I use the word advisedly – to present their top prize. Who? Shayne Brickham, of course, and, also, of course, despite all my entreaties, Victoria was determined to attend as Shayne's other half.

'Your dad will have a fit,' I'd warned.

But she'd simply tossed her head and said, 'Let him.'

Oh well, on her own head be it.

Nevertheless, in the interests of saving Shayne, without whom the Jukes hadn't a cat in hell's chance of staying in the Premier League, I decided to sacrifice myself and join Dan as his 'plus one'. I might also be needed to keep Victoria in one piece too.

And then there was reason number three: those Hooray Henry's, or rather, the guest list, which included some of the UK's biggest names in journalism and current affairs. 'I'm a big name,' Dan said when I mentioned I was quite looking forward to rubbing shoulders with one or two of his rivals.

'Not in my household,' I said, giving him a peck on the cheek to soften the blow.

And, finally, the real reason for donning the glad rags: the whispers that Dan was in the running for a prize.

'I ought to be there to hold your hand when you win.'

'Or, in case, I don't,' he said.

But, neither of us really believed he wouldn't be raising the trophy. Doreen, source of the whispers, was never wrong.

Even so, I nearly cried off at the last minute.

CHAPTER 66

TERI

Sam had no sooner got over his idea of blackboards and apps when he came up with his next revolutionary suggestion.

'We'll still have menus, but they'll be re-designed,' he said.

Instead of the traditional, thickly padded, red menu holders into which we'd slide sheets of paper with dishes written in black italics, we'd have long, thin pieces of card, folded in half – length ways – with the dishes printed in alternating red and green Comic Sans script.

'These cards will stand on the tables, nestled between the salt and pepper grinders and little mock milk bottles holding tiny bunches of flowers,' Sam said, gazing round we members of the pre-lunch team meeting.

We members of the pre-lunch team gawped back at him.

I was the first one to find a voice. 'Where would we get the milk bottles? And who would pick and arrange the flowers every day?'

Sam gave me a stony glare, but before he could answer, Gary stepped in.

'So, we wouldn't be handing out menus?'

Sam sighed impatiently. 'No. They'd be already on the tables.'

'So Teree would seat coostomers,' Beniamin said, nodding at me, 'and tell them to look at cards on table?'

'That's the idea,' Sam said.

'And then we take order?' Beniamin added.

'Ah, no,' Sam said. 'Not exactly.' He swept a self-satisfied smile around the table. 'When the customer has chosen from the card, they simply raise it in the air and wave it.'

Each of us looked back at him, dumbfounded.

'Good, eh?' Sam grinned, leaning back in his seat and folding his arms.

'But…?' Gary tried to verbalise the problem. 'So we have customers waving menus…er, I mean, cards…in the air?'

'And we keep watch until someone waves?' Beniamin filled in.

I saw Zofia giving an almost imperceptible shake of her head. She'd obviously been told about the menu cards but perhaps not about the waving-them-above-the-head idea.

'Sam…' she began. 'Do you theenk ze customers would want to do waving?'

'And won't the cards get a bit tatty, left sitting on the table?' I added. 'And then being waved willy-nilly by all and everyone?'

Sam unlocked his arms and straightened himself up for the fight. But before he had the chance to speak again, I hit him with something he'd not thought of.

'And the colours, Sam,' I said. 'Red and green?'

'What about them?'

'They're the colours of the Italian flag – red, green and white,' I said, feeling slightly superior.

'Well,' Sam snapped back, 'let's make them red and…I don't know… yellow?'

'Spanish flag,' I said.

'Well, what bloody colour do you recommend?' Sam said.

'Well, the French flag is red, white and blue – tricolour,' I said.

'No way,' Sam said. 'That's too like the British flag.'

'I sink we leave eet for now,' Zofia said, rubbing Sam's arm in either sympathy or pity. 'Sink about it some more, Sammy. But for now, let's get these tables ready.'

CHAPTER 67

LEE

I was dithering over which of my extensive collection of evening gowns – all two of them – would be most suitable for the evening's shindig when Daddy telephoned. He didn't have much to say. He had advanced renal cancer. The medics said chemotherapy and everything else they could throw at the cancer could prolong his life by six months, maybe a year. Daddy wasn't interested. He wasn't afraid of dying – that's the benefit of being a devout Catholic – and the treatment would compromise his quality of life. He preferred to get on with things and get the dying over and done with; personally I'd have liked a little more rage against the dying of the light, but I resisted the selfish urge to press him to go for chemo and the rest of the works. His life, his death.

Dressing to impress didn't seem terribly important anymore.

'Stay at home,' Dan said as I wept on his shoulder.

'No,' I said. 'I might as well keep you company.'

'I'll stay here with you,' he said, realising I couldn't bear the thought of sitting home alone.

'What about your prize?'

'Doesn't matter.'

I said nothing for a few minutes. 'No,' I said, pulling away. 'I'll get ready. There's no point you getting into a row with Duck's Arse…'

'Bugger Duck's Arse,' he interrupted.

I laughed. 'Bet you wouldn't say that to his face.'

'I'd never call him Duck's Arse to his face,' he said, drawing me close again. 'And I don't think you should either,' he added.

'No,' I agreed, blowing my nose into what was left of the tissue I'd been using to dry my eyes.

Dan gave me his handkerchief. 'So,' he said, 'what are we going to do?'

'Staying home won't change anything,' I said. 'Daddy's dying and I need to learn to live with it.'

Not, perhaps, the best frame of mind in which to attend a party, but it was the best I could lay my hands on.

****

We headed straight for the bar and elbowed our way to the front of the raucous throng fighting for the attention of the staff.

I plonked a twenty-pound note on the counter. 'I'll have a dry white wine.' The barman reached for a regular-sized glass. 'A large one,' I added. He swapped it for a bigger one. 'And fill it to the brim,' I ordered, when he stopped pouring halfway up the glass. He looked at Dan, who glanced at me. I glared at the young man. He topped up the drink.

'And you, sir?' he asked.

'I'll have a small one,' Dan said.

We leaned against the bar and spent a companionable couple of minutes watching the other guests. There was a lot of effusive air-kissing and extravagant hugging. And the frocks! One girl wore a glittery gold dress so short and so low cut it was little more than a belt. 'I'm wearing it in the ironic way,' she announced as though it was all right to show off your knickers if it was done for a properly pseudo-intellectual reason. Sounded more like the sort of thing an academic would say rather than a luvvie.

And then the guest of honour made his appearance. Damn it! I'd forgotten to warn Dan.

'Victoria,' he yelped as she entered the room on Shayne's arm.

Thank heavens for small mercies; she looked sweetly pretty in a slim-fitting red frock. And she'd ditched the black eyeliner and purple lipstick. Definitely an improvement. She waved and joined us at the bar, Shayne ambling along behind her. He was supposed to be one of those rare creatures, a footballer whose brains weren't just in his boots, but, frankly, he looked like an amiable, over-grown teenager, whose feet were slightly too large for the rest of him. 'Hello Dad,' Victoria said. 'Have you met

Shayne?'

Of course he had. The boy spent so much time in the interview chair at Ridings TV they were practically bosom buddies. That'd change now he'd been outed as Victoria's date. He could score a hat trick for the Jukes every day for the rest of the season and he'd still be the bloke who wasn't 'good enough for my daughter'.

Shayne, of course, was oblivious to his reduced status. 'Dan'– he held out his hand –'nice to see you here, mate.'

Dan ignored him. 'What the bloody hell are you doing here?' he hissed at Victoria. Shayne's mouth dropped. He wasn't used to being cold-shouldered; usually he was the centre of attention. 'Is there a problem, mate?' he asked.

'I'm not your mate,' Dan snapped.

'Hey.' Shayne held up his hands. 'Steady, mate.'

'Dan, leave it for now.' I tugged at his arm. 'She's here. We don't want to make a fuss in front of everyone. We'll talk about it when we get home.'

I took the champagne flute pressed into Victoria's hand by a passing waiter. 'And keep off the booze,' I said, downing the fizz in one slurp. 'I'm watching you, so behave yourself.'

Her eyes flickered from me to Dan and back again. She licked her lips and dug her fingers into Shayne's arm. Dan and his shouty-outbursts were water off a duck's back. She'd never seen me get mad before. Come to that, neither had Dan.

'Come on, love.' Shayne put a proprietorial arm around her waist. 'There's my old pal Finlay over there. Let's go and say hello.' If he'd wanted to wind Dan up even further he couldn't have found a better way to do it.

Thankfully the MC was tapping the podium microphone and urging the assembled 'ladies and gents' to take their seats. We were at one of the top tables near the mini stage. A good sign? I gripped Dan's arm in encouragement, and he grinned as we sat down, and then, almost immediately, flinched as someone came up from behind and clapped him on the back. 'Ah, Danners. I see we're on the same table. Unnervingly close to the stage, eh?'

'Lee,' Dan said, 'let me introduce you to Finlay Baxter. I'm sure you've heard me mention him.'

'Oh, yes,' I said, 'you've mentioned him. Often.'

Finlay smirked. 'I hope he hasn't said anything too awful.'

You can hope, I thought. He was everything Dan had said he was – young, gauche and far too full of himself. And with the beginnings of a paunch too, although I couldn't spot any grey hairs.

After half-a-dozen similar encounters with a mixture of old hacks and young wannabes, I was ready to gnaw my own arm out of sheer boredom. Roll on home-time.

And then the compère, a local comedian who'd made his name playing panto dames, jumped on stage to introduce the interminable awards: Best Regional News Programme; Best Regional Reporter; Best Director; Best Grips Driver and so on and on and on.

I watched Dan. He nodded in agreement at the nominations, he applauded as the winners were announced and he laughed at the witticisms in the acceptance speeches. But he didn't relax. He didn't get up to congratulate winners as they came off stage, merely waving back if they acknowledged him. Otherwise he held himself tight and straight.

And then it came to the top award: Lifetime Achievement.

'We have someone very special to present this very special award,' the compère said. 'The award is the crème de la creamery…' – brief laughter – '…of the television world and tonight to present it is the crème de la beautiful game…' – general laughter and some whooping from Finlay – '…yes, it's Shayne Brickham.'

And Shayne bounded up on stage to take the mic.

Dan groaned. 'Why's he doing this?'

Finlay, sitting opposite us, was whooping even more in encouragement. 'C'mon, Shayney,' he yelled.

Peering to read from an autocue box at the edge of the stage, Shayne began. 'Tonight's award goes to someone who is so well known, he…'

Dan bristled at the 'he'. It meant his opposite number at the BBC – someone he referred to as a 'gobby' woman – hadn't got the award.

Shayne continued, '…needs no introduction. So I'll not bother…' Shayne dropped the hand holding the mic down by his side. Lots of laughter. He brought the mic back up to his face and went on. 'He's a man of many talents, a family – sorry, a familiar – face both on screen and off.'

Dan straightened his shoulders. I put a hand on his thigh and gave a gentle squeeze. He was concentrating too hard to turn and smile.

Shayne continued, screwing his eyes to better read the autocue. 'He has worked tiredly – sorry, tirelessly – in the industry for many years, using his nose for news to be at the cutting edge of …'

Dan had moved forward to the edge of his seat and was rubbing his hands along the tops of his legs as if to prepare himself for the handshakes to follow.

Shayne came to a stop. 'Er,' he said, 'there's nowt else coming up…'

A technician leapt on stage and gave the autocue a gentle kick. 'Ah, it's come back,' Shayne said. 'Where'd I got to?'

'Oh just get on with telling us who it is,' Finlay yelled, waving a wine glass in the air.

Shayne grinned at him. 'And the winner of this year's Lifetime Achievement Award is…Finlay Baxter.'

And that would have been that if Victoria hadn't pulled one last trick. She'd kept a wary eye on us during the evening, and while Shayne was handing the glassware to Finlay amid lots of handshaking, she came over to our table.

'Should have been you, Dad,' she said, nodding in the direction of Finlay who was now launching into a speech about how proud and humbled he was and how he'd not been expecting this when there were so many more 'experienced veterans' in the room.

'We're off now,' Victoria said as Shayne approached. She gave us both a peck on the cheek. 'See you tomorrow?'

'Most definitely,' I said.

'Think we won on points there,' I said, as Shayne stepped aside to let her exit ahead of him.

'You mean, *you* did.' Dan leaned in, and for a brief moment our foreheads touched, he squeezed my hand and we shared a fleeting kiss.

'Are we going?' he asked.

We were approaching the exit when a waiter came hurrying across. 'Sir,' he said. 'Madam. Your daughter left her handbag.' He held out the long, strappy, gold purse Victoria had been dangling from her shoulder when she arrived.

'Are you sure?' Dan frowned at the glitzy thing. 'It doesn't look'– he hesitated –'very Victoria-ish.'

I took the bag from the waiter's outstretched hand. 'Did you check for ID?'

'Just a quick peek,' the waiter said, looking at a spot above my head. 'There was a school bus pass. Miss Victoria Caine.'

'That's Victoria,' I said, snapping open the clip and poking inside. My eyes met the waiter's. Like me, he knew the significance of the small, plastic bag and its powdery, chalky white contents, squashed into an unsavoury lump at the bottom of the bag. Oh dear.

CHAPTER 68

༄

TERI

On the Friday of the weekend before Christmas we were fully booked. Sam warned us all that the Leader was sending someone over to do a review that night – as if we didn't have enough on our plates.

'Just do your best,' he said in a kitchen pep talk, 'and give them the same high-quality service you give everyone – except even better.' He winked.

Throughout that day the phone rang with people hoping to get a last minute booking, and although Sam and I scanned the reservations book looking for spaces, there was no way we could fit them in. 'Damn the Leader,' Sam said. 'They're taking up a table for two and not paying anything either.'

'I tried to warn you,' I said. 'By the way, do we know who's coming from the Leader?'

'Someone called Cromwell – and a partner. That's all I know.' He laughed.

'Well, the partner will be either Henry or Charles,' I said, but Sam didn't get the historical reference so I left it there.

I saw that he'd given them Table Four, the table in the right-hand side window bay and one of the most popular ones for diners who liked to see and be seen by people inside and outside the restaurant.

After a busy lunchtime session, we were gearing up for the evening diners, when Sam took a call from someone cancelling their seven p.m. reservation for that night. They'd booked Table Six – the one in the left-hand side window bay. As he put the phone down, it rang again immediately. 'Yes,' he said, 'as it happens, we do have a table that's just come free. It's for seven p.m. – is that okay? Ah, good. For two? Name of? Contact number? Great, thanks. We've given you Table Six. See you at seven.'

He scrawled a name in the book. I usually check entries so that when diners arrive I can welcome them personally. But as I went to check, the door burst open behind me and a party of eight booked for six-thirty practically fell through the door. They'd obviously been making a day of it and had started celebrating early. It was all hands on deck.

So it wasn't until the door opened again just before seven and two people stepped in that I realised I should have made more of an effort to see who the last-minute bookers were.

CHAPTER 69

~~~

LEE

I don't want to dwell on Daddy's diagnosis or on his imminent death. It's miserable and horrible and serves no useful purpose except to make me cry. Again. So, I mention it when necessary but, otherwise, it was always in the background of my thoughts. However, life goes on and, even when you think your heart is breaking, nice things can still happen. Although, let's be honest, there was nothing nice happening right now. But life was certainly going on – Victoria was well and truly in Dan's bad books.

Crime number one was turning up at the RTS dinner.

Crime number two was turning up at the RTS dinner with a 'flashy git of a philandering footballer' – Dan's words not mine.

And crime number three was being caught in possession of an illegal substance. Strictly speaking, of course, she hadn't been caught in possession since she'd left her handbag, and the drugs, behind when she left the dinner, but Dan was in no mood for semantics. If he'd been a hanging judge poor old Victoria would have been swinging from the gibbet before morning had even thought about dawning. But, since that option wasn't available, his second preferred choice of action was to march straight down to the cops and turn his daughter in.

'Don't be silly,' I said, watching the taxi that had just deposited us at the front door drive off in pursuit of its next fare. 'You're too drunk to drive to the police station, and I'm not calling another taxi at this time of night.'

'I'm not drunk,' Dan said, peering narrow-eyed at the front door key which refused to slither home.

'Yes, you are,' I said, elbowing him aside and successfully navigating the door lock and stepping into the hallway. 'You don't think you're drunk because you're too drunk to know you're drunk. But anyone who isn't drunk would know straight away that you're drunk because you actually sound quite drunk. And, if you turn up drunk at the police station with a stash of cannabis in your hand you'll be locked up before you can say "I'm not drunk". Savvy?'

Dan scratched his head. 'No,' he said. 'Maybe... I don't know. You lost me somewhere around sounding drunk and being drunk.' He thought for a moment. 'I certainly don't feel drunk.'

'There's feeling and feeling,' I said, helping him over the doorstep. 'You'll feel it in the morning.'

Which he duly did and which was doubly unfortunate because we woke at half-past six to loud banging on the front door.

'Hell's bells.' I leapt out of bed and, grabbing a towel, raced into the shower.

Dan squinted at the bedside clock, groaned and pulled the duvet over his head. 'Tell whoever it is downstairs to go away.'

'You tell them.' I poked my head round the door, trying not to dribble toothpaste onto the bedroom carpet. 'I've got a breakfast meeting with the senior management group, and I need to see Dom at the yard first. Pound to a penny, it's Victoria. And it'll be you she wants to talk to not me.'

Dan snorted. 'I'm sure she'd much prefer talking to you.'

I pulled the duvet from him and slung it on the floor. 'She might, I wouldn't.' I put the toothbrush back in my mouth, and dribbled some more. 'And she's your daughter not mine.'

'I thought this was supposed to be a partnership?'

I peeked back round the door. 'I'm reviewing the terms of engagement...'

As expected, Dan's version of the conversation-cum-shouting match between him and Victoria differed enormously from Tory's version. Both though can be summarised as: 'He/she is selfish and self-centred and doesn't care about anyone else except him/herself.'

'Tautology,' I murmured.

'Eh?' Dan said.

'Someone who is selfish and self-centred doesn't care about anyone else.'

He raised an eyebrow – how I wish I could do that! Teri was also an exponent of the arched eyebrow. I wondered if she and Dan had ever had eyebrow face-offs? I'd have asked but he'd already stomped out of the room.

Victoria was equally sniffy when I suggested Dan was as much sinned against as sinning. 'I don't know what you're talking about,' she said and went home to Sara's house.

She was back on Saturday morning with an apology bunch of flowers. 'Sorry for waking you up so early the other morning, but we went on to a club after the dinner and I thought if I came to your house my mum wouldn't know I'd stayed out all night.'

Dear God, the girl was perennially optimistic. 'Dan does talk to your mother, you know.'

'I know,' she said. 'But there's no reason for him to tell her I didn't get in until getting-up time.'

No reason? Sometimes I wondered what planet she inhabited.

'I mean,' she continued, 'he hasn't said anything about the…' Her voice trailed off.

'No. We both thought we should have a chat with you first.' Actually we both thought nothing of the sort, but Dan had been persuaded, reluctantly, to hold fire. 'He's not here now, is he?' She looked around the kitchen as if she expected him to jump out of a cupboard.

'He got called into the studio for a live interview.' Bloody politicians. If they're going to get arrested for drunk-driving, like our local MP, why did they have to do it at weekends?

Victoria settled herself on a bar stool. 'Good, I was hoping we could have a proper chat.'

'Don't get too comfortable,' I warned. 'I'm going for a walk with my dad in half an hour.' Walk? A stroll round the park's rose garden was the best we'd managed last time we'd had an outing.

'Awwwww… Can't you cancel?'

I could but I wasn't going to – nor did I propose telling her why. She'd be sympathetic and kind and, right now, sympathy and kindness was more than I could bear.

So, in a bit of a rush, she told me what she hadn't yet told Dan. The drugs belonged to Shayne Brickham – well, I knew that already. Only an idiot – Dan? – could have thought otherwise. He'd put them in her bag for safe-keeping, and she'd pretended they were hers because he was worried – he was worried! – the club chairman would put him on the transfer list if the drug habit became public. And who was the club chairman? Richard Walker, man of many fingers in many pies. What an interesting kettle of fish this was turning out to be?

Dan was also apologetic although his penance [sic?] was dinner at L'homme-vert. On the whole, I'd have preferred to stay in since I'd promised Victoria I'd bring her father up to speed with her latest revelations and home seemed a better place to break bad news than a posh restaurant. But, hey ho, Dan insisted, so we donned our glad rags again, called a taxi – we practically had an account with the firm – and headed for the city bright lights. I was still rehearsing my opening line – 'Dan not only is your daughter dating a flashy, philandering git of a soccer player, but he's also a druggie' – when we pulled up at the restaurant. Dan paid the taxi driver – we seemed to be using so many taxis lately it was almost worth investing in our own chauffeur – and held the door open so I could go inside ahead of him.

So, lucky me. I got first sighting of our maître d'. Thank God, I'd worn the new Milano wool, soft coat Dan had bought for my birthday. For once, I properly looked the part of a TV luvvie's partner.

CHAPTER 70

TERI

Of course, I don't know why I was surprised. L'homme-vert was Dan's favourite restaurant, and it was actually quite unusual that he'd not been in before. And here he was, stepping over the threshold, confident and suave, dressed in a dark-blue, cashmere overcoat. I was so busy staring at Dan that I hardly noticed Lee. She'd come in slightly ahead of him with head bowed, looking uncomfortable as though she didn't want to be there.

I wondered if they'd had a row. Wouldn't be surprised; Dan could be an irritating man. He and I were always having rows when we were married. Well tough tit, I thought, watching Lee in what looked like that ridiculous black duffle coat she always wore. You stole him from me and made your bed – now lie in it.

But damn, damn, damn. Why hadn't I prepared for something like this?

I stood erect and frozen at the lectern we use as a meeter-and-greeter station, the reservations book open as though a bible from which I was going to read a passage. I glanced down and saw, in Sam's handwriting, 'Caine x 2. Table 6. 7pm.'

I had to go over, welcome them, take their coats and lead them to their table.

Dan, standing tall and authoritative – and looking not a little impatient – was casting around for the spot of service I was supposed to be providing.

Lee looked up from grappling with the toggles on her coat and spotted me. Her left hand shot up to her mouth, and she reached out with her right to grip Dan's arm. She continued staring at me as Dan turned back to her. She said something I couldn't hear and Dan turned to look at me. I've read in cheap novels about people's eyes locking, but never really experienced it until now. Dan's eyes fastened on mine, and for a moment I think neither of us could look away or think of anything to say or do.

I was about to move forward when the door flew open again, and two people burst in – a man and a woman – bumping Lee who was standing rooted and blocking the entrance.

'Wooah,' the new entrant said, giving Lee a conciliatory pat on the arm by way of apology for pushing her. 'It's cosy in here.' Then he noticed who she was. 'Lee,' he said. 'Bloody hell, fancy seeing you in here – and Mr Dan Caine too.'

And then he looked my way. 'Fucking hell,' he said in genuine surprise. 'It's Teri…'

Of course. Cromwell had arrived, and it was Declan with his little puppy Cassie.

What had I expected?

CHAPTER 71

LEE

I stepped back as soon as I saw Teri. 'It's okay,' I said to Dan, lowering my head. 'You go first. The staff know you better than they know me.'

Which was a great big whopper since the place was under new management, and none of the new team knew either of us. Apart from Teri, who knew both of us very well indeed.

I needed time to think. I'd had lots of imaginary conversations where I told her she was a colossal prat and an almighty pain in the backside, but, it's one thing rehearsing a speech and quite another delivering it in front of a room full of other people. And, inappropriate too since, as our waitress, she'd be at a disadvantage what with the customer always being right.

I shouldn't have worried. Teri might have returned to her epicurean roots, but she'd taken care not to swallow any of that tosh about servility and deference. She gave me what I can only describe as a boiled-cabbage look. Clearly, time had not been a healer. If I'd have been a worm crawling out of a hole in the ground, I'd have hot-footed it back down under. But, I'm not a worm.

I reached out to nudge Dan's arm. 'Look who's here,' I hissed, and he turned and saw Teri. I went back to fiddling with my coat buttons. Beautiful buttons. Nothing quite like them.

Before Dan had a chance to do or say anything, the door behind us flew open and I was shoved in the back and catapulted forward by two customers who'd hurried in to escape the winter cold. My fault; I shouldn't have been blocking the doorway.

FML – oh God, I really *must* stop swearing – it was Declan.

'Bloody hell,' Declan said. 'Fancy seeing you here.' He leaned across to give me a peck on the cheek.

'And Mr Dan Caine too.' He held out a hand in greeting.

I'm not sure if he was being deliberately provocative, but you've got to admire his chutzpah.

But before Dan could make a move – either to bat the hand away or pummel it like an old friend, we'll never know – Declan dropped it back to his side.

'Fucking hell,' he said. 'It's Teri...'

I caressed my buttons. Now the proverbial was really going to hit the fan.

CHAPTER 72

TERI

'Come on, Teri,' Sam said, stepping up behind me, 'get that lovely arse of yours into gear. People waiting.' He only dared speak to me like that when Zofia was safely in the kitchen and out of ear shot. He clearly fancied me, but I wasn't giving him any encouragement. Yes, he was young, fit and hot, but I liked little Zofia, and I didn't want to see her get hurt.

The gentle nudge he gave me in the back had the effect of unlocking my knees and propelling me towards my ex-husband, ex-best friend, ex-lover and a giggling puppy. The last four people in the world I wanted to see and all looking expectantly in my direction.

I moved to Dan and Lee first, while Sam leapt towards Declan and Cassie.

'Hello, Dan,' I said, my voice stiff. 'Let me take your coat.'

'Thank you,' he said, not taking his eyes off me as he slipped out of the cashmere to reveal a cream, linen jacket, pale-blue shirt and dark-blue chinos – a combo that always looked good on him. I hung the coat over my arm – it was new and felt expensive – and indicated Table Six.

'Would you rather we left?' Dan asked, finding his voice at last.

'Don't be silly,' I said. 'You're here now, you might as well enjoy the evening.'

'But…I…we… We honestly didn't know you were working here or we wouldn't have come –'

He was interrupted by someone on the table for eight calling his name. 'Hey. You're that Dan Caine, off the telly.'

The table for eight turned as one and looked at Dan, and he inclined his head in greeting. Oh how he loved an adoring public.

Lee, who'd gone back to un-toggling herself, seemed cross at the intrusion.

Yes, I thought. I remember that feeling: never being able to go anywhere in public without some idiot member of the public asking 'Who's reading t'news tonight?'

'Out for a meal, are you?' asked the table-for-eight man.

'Something like that. Enjoy your evening.' And Dan turned his back on his new admirers to look at Lee. 'What are you doing with that bloody coat?' he said just as she managed to free herself.

'It's okay, I've done it.' She started taking the thing off.

I told them Gary would be over to take their drinks order, and spun on my heel to walk away, all the while ignoring Declan, who was hissing at me in a stage whisper. 'Teri…? Teri, what are you doing here?'

Hanging up Dan's coat, I resisted the urge to delve into the pockets. Why? What would I be searching for? A memento from the time he and I were together? I went back into the restaurant and slipped into the kitchen.

Sam, who'd been slicing bread, stopped and raised his head. 'Everything all right? I sense something of an atmosphere.'

'You can say that again,' I said. 'It's only my ex-husband on one side of the room and the man I left him for on the other.'

Dear little Zofia took a couple of steps towards me, concern written on her face. 'Oh, Teree,' she said. 'Would you rather not work tonight? We can manage.'

'No, we bloody well can't,' Sam said. 'It's all hands on deck.'

'Sam.' Zofia pointed a warning index finger at him.

'Sorry, Teri,' he said. 'Go home if you must. But I'd really appreciate it if you could stay. Can you manage?'

'Of course. Don't worry about me.' And I strode back into the restaurant.

CHAPTER 73

LEE

Teri, who'd seemed rooted to the spot, suddenly jerked and moved towards us while another waiter strode over to Declan and his woman friend. Not his wife, I realised.

'Teri,' Dan said, his voice curdling with the sort of faux-politeness he employs when welcoming politicians whose views he doesn't quite trust onto his politics show. 'Fancy seeing you here. Would you rather we left?'

My hand flew to my mouth. How rude! I tore my eyes away from my buttons and risked a glance at Teri. Yes, she recognised the tone. Her eyes narrowed, but, all credit to her, she pinned a polite smile on her face. I could guess what she was thinking though – and if Dan had had even the foggiest idea he'd have adopted a defensive position immediately.

I put a restraining hand on his arm. 'Don't,' I muttered. 'She's probably embarrassed about being caught out waiting on tables.'

He arched an eyebrow – God, he was so sexy when he did that!

He slipped off his coat and handed it to Teri. She took it, and hanging it over one arm, stroked it with almost as much love and attention as I was giving my buttons. She gave another glue-tight grin and, with a tilt of her head, indicated a table in the window. I might as well have been invisible. Good job I had those buttons to keep me occupied.

Dan started to say something about how we wouldn't have come if we'd known she was working here but was interrupted by someone from a table full of diners who yelled across the room, 'You're that Dan Caine off the telly.' As one, the other diners turned to look.

Dan was usually pleased to be recognised but tonight he was irritated. 'Enjoy your evening,' he said, tightly, hopefully dismissing them.

Teri strode off. I went back to fiddling with my buttons. The safe option. But then Dan snapped at me. 'What are you doing with that bloody coat? Hasn't anyone taken it?' Doh! Daft question. Would I still be wearing it if one of the waiting staff had put it on a hanger?

'No,' I said. 'Doesn't matter I'll hang it on the back of my chair.'

CHAPTER 74

TERI

Gary had taken drinks orders from both Dan and Declan, and Beniamin, who'd given menus to Dan and Lee, was now at Declan's table.

I strode over to Table Six. Dan and Lee looked up expectantly, and Lee started to rise from her seat. 'Teri…' she began, but I held up a hand to interrupt whatever snivelling apology she was about to give and she sank back down.

'We're recommending the cassoulet tonight or the sea bass,' I said, adding under my breath, 'served up with a big dollop of dog's do and treachery.'

'What was that?' Dan asked.

'Served with dauphinoise potatoes and home-grown vegetables,' I said.

'Look, Teri.' Lee managed to find her voice. 'If this is awkward for you, we'll go.'

I noticed she'd hung her duffle coat over the back of her chair so that it draped on the floor. The coat already looked old and dusty, so I didn't bother offering to move it.

'Why should it be awkward?' I asked. 'You two have come here, no doubt, to celebrate something wonderful in your fabulously happy lives. I happen to work here as I lost my job and need to do something to keep body and soul together. Why on earth should it be awkward that I now have to stand here and serve you?'

I turned to walk away and was aware of Declan jumping up from his chair at Table Four and coming over to pull on my arm.

'Teri…?' he said. 'What are you doing here?'

'Oh for fuck's sake,' I said, rather too loudly as the table of eight stopped their celebrations aware that something more exciting was going on in each of the restaurant's windows and were nudging each other to listen.

'What is it with you all?' I said, addressing Dan, Lee and Declan, and curling my hands into fists in a vain effort to curb the anger welling up. 'I'm working here, not that it's anything to do with any of you.'

And then I thought, well, actually, it is. I'm only here working as a glorified waitress because of you people. Until I got involved with any of you I was a successful career woman with a happy life. Even as that thought whizzed through my brain, I knew the bit about successful and happy wasn't entirely accurate, but decided not to let the facts get in the way of a good rant.

And then I saw red. My ex-husband, the woman who'd stolen him from me, my ex-lover. They were all to blame for the position I now found myself in.

'Quite frankly,' I said, 'you've each done your bit to damage me – and so now you're here to gloat. Well good fucking luck to you, you smug, self-satisfied load of bores.'

The table for eight prickled in their own silence.

Dan stood and moved towards me, holding his hands out as if to keep the peace.

'Teri, please…' he said.

Now I had Dan to the left of me, Declan to the right.

'Push off, Caine,' Declan said, 'She doesn't need you.' And he put his own hand out as if to bat Dan away but accidently made contact with a cream linen sleeve.

'Don't you push me,' Dan said.

'I'm not pushing you,' Declan replied. 'I'm telling you to back off.'

'Dan,' Lee said, a warning note in her voice. She rose quickly and stepped forward but caught a foot in the hem of her trailing coat and fell forwards into Dan's back. Dan tottered and regained his balance, but not his composure. Angrily, he turned to Declan. 'This is your fucking fault, you snivelling bastard.'

'Wha…?' Declan was, for once, lost for words.

'Is everything all right here?' Sam asked, stepping smartly into the breach. 'Please, ladies and gentlemen, come back to your tables…let Gary here pour your wine…' Gary was concentrating intently on unscrewing a bottle of Merlot.

'It's on the house tonight,' Sam added.

'I don't want free bloody wine,' Dan said, 'and I don't want to sit here with that twat sitting opposite me.' He indicated Declan, who thrust his chest forward and inched towards Dan.

'Oh, I'm a twat, am I?'

'Always have been and always will be, you sad little newspaperman.'

'And you're just a made-up television tart,' was Declan's response.

'Who are you calling a tart?' Dan exploded.

I must say, the level of argument was pretty childish, but the table for eight were enjoying it and one or two of the occupants joined in. 'Yeah, go, Dan boy, go.'

Their encouragement – and, no doubt, the word 'tart' – hit a nerve and Dan did something I'd never thought him capable of.

He hit Declan.

It wasn't a big hit. It didn't even knock him down. But it was enough for Declan to sway, swear and take a swing at Dan. He, too, made contact – it was more of a feeble glance off the chin – but Dan staggered back against Table Six, ricocheting into Gary innocently waiting to pour the Merlot. The opened bottle spun out of his hand, spewing a fountain of red wine down one of Dan's expensive linen sleeves.

'Okay, lads, enough.' Sam jumped between them with both arms outstretched to keep them apart.

'Look what that bastard did to me,' Dan said, looking down at the cream sleeve now decidedly red. He moved towards Declan, but Sam and Gary each grabbed an arm and stopped him. It was like a scene from a movie.

'I think you should all leave,' Sam said. 'You first.' He nodded at Declan.

'With pleasure,' Declan said. 'I didn't want to eat in this pseudo French flea pit anyway. 'C'mon, Cassie.' And Declan pulled open the door, striding out with Cassie scampering behind him.

The table for eight roared their approval.

'Now, you.' Sam turned to Dan.

Dan was about to say something, but changed his mind, gave an exasperated and loud sigh and stomped to the door.

Lee hovered, and turned in my direction.

'And you can shut up,' I told her before she had a chance to speak. She gave one of the ever-so-concerned looks that she saves especially for me.

As the door closed behind them, Sam rounded on me. 'You'd better go too.' And then as an afterthought, he added, 'To be honest, you've been nothing but negative all the way along. I've never liked your attitude – and now you're causing fights in my restaurant.'

I was about to object – nothing but negative? Just because I objected to his silly little mock milk bottles. My mouth must have dropped open, because Sam lifted both hands, palms towards me as if for silence. 'And don't bother coming back,' he said.

The table for eight booed. They didn't want to see me go, bless them.

I walked home, replaying the events in my head, going over what Sam had said about my negative attitude. Negative, me? For goodness sake. But of more particular note, I thought about the way Dan leapt to my defence. The way he'd hit Declan. The way he'd snapped at Lee. It was patently clear: Dan was still in love with me.

He'd clearly never got over the fact that I left him for Declan, and the pent-up anger towards the man who'd cuckolded him erupted tonight. In spectacular style.

I've had men fighting over me before, but verbally, never with physical action and never with such a passionate outburst. Poor Dan. He obviously never got over me or what Declan and I did to him.

Interesting.

And poor Lee when she realises she's not the love of Mr Dan Caine's life.

CHAPTER 75

LEE

It's a shame Dan had taken such a high moral tone with Victoria over her 'philandering druggie boyfriend' because it rather put him on the back foot when Victoria popped round to show us the early morning, online news headlines. Yes, the morning after the evening you've been snapped having a fist fight with the ex-lover of your ex-wife is not a good time to get high-minded with your daughter – again!

It's even more of a no-no if you're fretting about missing the early train for London and are having a minor panic about getting to the Westminster TV studios for the ten a.m. briefing.

And, worse, when you're refusing to acknowledge you'd have missed the train completely if darling daughter hadn't chosen to hammer on the door twenty minutes before you need to be in a taxi if you're going to have a cat in hell's chance of making the 7:05am train.

Poor Dan.

Nevertheless, it's a pity he asked her how she managed to get to our house so early. 'The buses aren't running yet?' he asked. 'Are they?'

He took a swig of coffee and pulled a face. 'Lee,' he said. 'It's about time you learned how to make a decent cup of coffee.'

'Why?' He was lucky I'd got up and made him a drink at all.

But another thought had occurred to him. He turned to Victoria. 'I hope you didn't get a taxi here. Because if you're frittering your money away on cabs –'

'No,' Victoria said, no doubt feeling pleased with herself. 'Shayne dropped me off.'

Oh dear!

It was like a red rag to a bull. Thank goodness the clock was ticking, because it didn't leave him much time to pontificate about the general awfulness of young Mr Brickham, and what a bad influence he was and what was she doing getting lifts from 'that goon' at this hour?

Dear God, Dan! What do you think she was doing?

They were still shouting and bawling at one another – Dan running up and down the stairs, chucking last minute toiletries and underwear into his overnight bag, Victoria two paces behind – when the taxi driver tooted outside the house. Victoria, quite legitimately, I thought, pointed out that Dan was hardly an exemplary role model. 'Have you seen the Leader's website?'

No, he hadn't.

Victoria whipped her mobile phone from the back pocket of her jeans and, faster than you can say 'I just happened to have this handy' was soon scrolling through yards and yards of pictures, snarky copy and screaming headlines of the TV NEWS HOST PUNCHES LEADER BOSS IN ROW OVER DISHY EX-WIFE variety.

Not good.

But, at least, Teri would be happy. She'd like being described as dishy.

And there was quite a nice background snap of me too.

'Your hair looks nice,' Tory said, squinting at the screen. She giggled and pointed at the caption. 'Look at this.'

I peered over her shoulder. The picture caption was a Leader classic: 'Caine's new partner – university boffin Lee Harper, doyenne of the Harper Homes building empire.'

I snorted and so did Victoria. I'm not sure whether I was most tickled by the 'university boffin' moniker or the 'building empire doyenne' one.

Dan, understandably, was not quite as amused.

'Good God!' He looked a little sick – but that might have been last night's booze. He'd opened a bottle of Scotch when we got home and had rapidly downed more glasses than were good for him.

He groaned and scratched his head and took a deep breath.

'Well,' he said, 'talk about making something out of nothing...'

He didn't sound terribly convincing – even to me. And Victoria certainly wasn't going to be side-tracked. 'It's all very well being snotty about Shayne,' she said, 'but *he's* far too mature to get involved in a public brawl.'

I frowned at her. No need to be priggish. And she was on dodgy ground too because Shayne had a reputation for being a 'dirty' player. Declan – now why would I have been discussing football with Declan? – had once told me Shayne wasn't the best player in the Premiership but he was good at stopping those who were. I'd looked puzzled; football was double Dutch to me. 'He kicks their legs from under them,' Declan explained. 'There's more than one player who's had their career cut short by a Brickham tackle.'

He didn't sound nice to me.

While I'd been musing, Dan had finished his packing. He was still lecturing Victoria – a diversionary tactic to save thinking about those worrying pictures.

What was Duck's Arse going to say when he saw them?

Instead, Dan, TV brawler, made himself comfortable in his zealous dad shoes. 'I don't need advice from a chit of a girl about how to behave in public.'

Especially, he added, when said girl was running around – and doing God knows what else – with a man who was, in his humble opinion, virtually a child molester. And a criminal drug-dealer.

Talk about hyperbole; I was almost lost in admiration at his ability to make mountains out of mole hills. He couldn't have done it better if he'd been a bona fide tabloid hack.

'I'll talk to you when I get home,' Dan shouted as he galloped down the drive towards the waiting car. I waved him off. Victoria stuck out her tongue. 'Hateful man,' she said.

'Oh no,' I said. 'That's not fair.'

Ding dong! I'd rung the bell for the start of the Lee vs Tory fight. *She* couldn't believe I was siding with HIM! *I* couldn't believe she was turning into such a little Madam. 'I am not a little Madam,' she screamed.

'Oh no?'

She stamped her foot. 'I'm not staying here to listen to this.'

'Okay,' I said, opening the front door.

She hesitated.

'No,' I said, closing the door. 'You can't go home because your mother thinks you spent the night here. And if you go home this early she'll know you didn't.'

Victoria said nothing.

I sighed. 'Has anyone had the birds and the bees talk with you?'

She gave me the look teenagers reserve for adults they consider to be congenital idiots. 'I'm not a child.'

'No?'

'I'm not going to get pregnant if that's what you mean.'

Well, that was reassuring – I think.

Victoria mooched around the house for a couple of hours and then popped her head around the office door to announce she was heading home. She put her arms around me and, resting her head on my shoulder, squeezed hard. 'I'm sorry I'm such a brat.'

I wrapped an arm around her and rubbed her head. 'You're not a brat,' I said. 'Well, not all the time...'

She laughed and pulled free. 'See you tomorrow,' she promised.

On balance, I thought, I'd prefer it if I didn't. These early morning shenanigans were becoming a bit wearisome. The front door slammed behind her, and I returned to my emails. Peter Heron's policy papers were every bit as dire as I'd expected. The man was incapable of using one word where half a dozen would do instead. But I ploughed through and added some comments and suggested amendments and then carried on through the mountain of routine stuff that had collected in my inbox. There was a particularly interesting request from Vic Brennan.

CHAPTER 76

TERI

Cheered by the thought that it would only be a matter of time before Dan and I were back together again, but aware I needed to look for another job, I went to Portly & Groops the next morning to check out job vacancies in the free copies of the Leader.

The first thing I noticed was the front page headline. 'TV STAR IN FROGS' LEGS FISTICUFFS' accompanied by a picture of Dan taking a swing at Declan with Lee in the background looking shocked.

Someone on the table for eight had taken pictures and a video with their mobile phone and sent them into the Leader. For any readers wanting to know more, the story was also posted on the paper's website, Twitter, Facebook and Instagram.

I stared at the newspaper. Poor Dan.

But why had Declan allowed it to be splashed across the front page of his own newspaper? After all, he was in the picture too; the Leader's news editor being punched by a local TV celebrity. It didn't look good for him either.

The barista glanced over at me. 'Sounds like a right old ding dong,' he said, nodding towards the paper in my hands and laughing.

'You can say that again,' I said, not laughing.

I needed to do something about this – after all, it was partly my fault – but what?

Then it struck me. 'Cancel the Americano,' I called across to the barista. 'Gotta go.'

I raced up the street to L'homme-vert.

I knew Sam or one of the others would be in and getting ready for tonight and sure enough, as I peered through the glass panels on the front door, I could see Sam sitting at a table folding long bits of card lengthways. He was trying out the new menu idea, the twerp. Sitting next to him was Zofia, arranging little bunches of flowers. I couldn't see any mock milk bottles.

I rapped on the glass. They both looked up. Sam saw me, said something to Zofia and shrugged, but Zofia leapt to her feet and moved quickly towards me.

She slid back the bolt and pulled the door open. 'Come in, poor Teree, come in.' She yanked me by the arm, and I stepped into the room. I think she'd have given me a hug if I'd not backed off. I can't bear all that huggy huggy business.

'Are you all right?' Zofia asked.

'Of course she's all right.' Sam didn't give me time to reply. 'It's us I'm worried about.'

We both glared at him, and he had the grace to look chastened.

'Well,' he said, shrugging again, 'it doesn't look good, does it? We've now got a reputation as somewhere to come for frogs' legs and fisticuffs.'

I winced at the reference, but Zofia wafted the tea towel she was holding in his face. 'Oh, do not be so hysterical,' she said. 'All publicity ees good publicity. Isn't it, Teree?'

Well, not for Dan it isn't, I thought, but smiled weakly.

'Look, I'm so sorry about last night,' I said. 'If I'd realised Dan was coming in I'd have been better prepared. And then when Declan walked in too…well, you can imagine. It threw me completely off balance. But I never thought the two of them would attack each other.'

'Well, yeah. Okay,' Sam said, looking down at his knees, 'apology accepted.'

'Good boy,' Zofia said, laughing at him.

'But don't think you're having your job back,' Sam said. 'I can't take the risk. And, as I said, you were very negative about my plans…'

I eyed the pieces of folded card, but decided it was best not to say anything. They did look a bit scrappy, though.

'No, that's okay,' I said, thinking, actually, that's not okay. I still need to earn some money. 'I haven't come begging for my job. I've come for Dan's coat. In all the…er…shenanigans, he left without taking it. I thought I'd get it for him.'

'Okay, help yourself. You know where it is,' Sam said, indicating his head towards the cloakroom.

The coat was a dark blue, soft cashmere, and I gave it a couple of strokes as I carried it over my arm and back to my duplex.

I laid it carefully over the sofa and imagined Dan sitting there, wearing it. I checked the pockets. I had to make sure nothing was likely to drop out. There was a receipt for petrol and a used train ticket from London to Leeds, but nothing else. What was I expecting? An un-posted letter declaring his love for me? A poem he'd written as an ode to Teri?

I changed into another of my JK Fennick dresses. I do find their style suits my figure. This one is in a startlingly bright royal blue which sets off my blonde hair perfectly. I re-did my make-up and stepped into my nude heels.

One last check in the full-length mirror. Perfect.

The coat and I drove to Lee's.

This is where my life gets back on track, I thought. No more Declan. No more Andrew. No more Duck's Arse. It was Dan and me from now on.

****

Lee answered the door. She looked tired and sad, but not altogether surprised to see me. Perhaps the poor girl had realised what had happened. Dan had obviously told her last night that he still had feelings for me. This would devastate her, I knew. She'd never been lucky with men. But enough of that, I thought. This is about me. And Dan.

'Is Dan here?' I asked even before Lee had time to speak.

'Er... no.'

'Is he due back soon?'

'Er...no.' She sounded cagey. I'd assumed he was living at Lee's now, but maybe he wasn't. Interesting!

'He does live here, doesn't he?' I demanded.

'Not exactly.'

Not exactly? Now what could that mean?

'Are you expecting him?' I asked.

Instead of answering she reached forward to the coat I was holding. 'Hang on.' Lee had found her voice. 'Is that Dan's coat?'

'Yes, but don't worry, I'll give it to him when I see him.'

'What do you mean?' She sounded confused – and a little cross. Then she sighed and gave me another one of the looks she keeps especially for me – the oh-for-goodness'-sake-what's-going-on-now look. 'Teri, come in.' She stepped back to let me into the hallway.

'Tea?' she asked, moving into the kitchen.

'No thanks, I don't want any of your weak muck. Coffee if you've got it.'

'Get the cafetiere and the ground coffee's in there,' she said, indicating a cupboard. It was almost like old times when I would go round to her house and know where everything was – the bottle opener and the wine glasses generally.

'How are you after last night's little escapade?' Lee asked, pouring boiling water into a mug and holding an Earl Grey tea bag a few inches above it.

'Life's been better,' I replied. 'Although I can't exactly remember when.'

'I know how that feels,' Lee said quietly. Ah, I must be right: Dan had dumped her.

She dunked the tea bag in the boiling water for a nanosecond and tossed it in the bin. My stomach lurched at the thought of all that blandness.

'I applied for that job.'

'The student counselling?'

'Yes. I know you don't approve but I need a job –'

'I've been asked to supply a reference,' she said.

'Oh, that's come already, has it?'

She looked at me closely, and her face softened. 'Teri, is that really the sort of job you want?'

I was about to tell her that, no, it wasn't. Previously I'd have gone into great detail about why I didn't want the student-mollycoddling job, and we'd both have laughed about the fact I was even considering it, and Lee would have made other suggestions, and I would have taken her advice.

I was tempted to open up and talk to her about everything – the failed romances, the failed jobs, the failed family life, the speeding tickets – but as I turned towards her we both jumped at the sound of the front door being wrenched open and slammed shut.

'That fucking, bloody, God-forsaken bitch of a woman. I'm going to fucking kill her.'

It was Dan.

Lee tottered quickly into the hallway. 'Dan…what's the matter? What are you doing back?'

'I've been suspended,' he shouted angrily, 'and all because of that fucking, bloody woman…' and then he looked beyond Lee and saw me.

'What's she doing here?'

I moved forward, but he held up a hand to ward me off.

'Keep away from me, you stupid bloody woman. I've lost my fucking job because of you.'

'Dan, calm down, please.' Lee reached out to hold one of his arms. He shrugged her off.

'Got as far as Grantham,' Dan said, staring at me, eyes blazing. 'Then some stupid little squirt from human resources rang and said I was suspended. And all because of that fucking woman.' He stabbed an index finger in my direction.

'Bringing Ridings Today into disrepute. Not good for the studio's reputation. Can't have our main presenter getting involved in street brawls.' He reeled off the misdemeanours. 'Not only that,' he almost spat out, 'but they've got that fucking little cretin Finlay Baxter to stand in for me. I got off the train at Peterborough and got the next one back to Leeds, and Finlay-fucking-Baxter is now on his way to Westminster to do MY JOB. Happy now, are you?' He glared at me.

This was clearly not the time to have a discussion about how much he still loved me.

Dan stormed from the kitchen and went upstairs, muttering and swearing under his breath. He behaves as though he lives here, I thought. But does he?

Lee glanced at her watch. 'Damn,' she said. 'I've got to be somewhere

– meeting Mammy and Daddy. Can I give you a lift anywhere?'

'No,' I said. 'I've got my car…shall I stay and try talk some sense into Dan?'

Lee looked at her watch again. 'It might be better if you didn't.'

She gave me a weak, apologetic smile, grabbed her bag, unhooked a bright poppy-red, waxy sort of coat – hideous – from the hall stand, yelled up the stairs to say she was going out and ushered me out of the door.

I sat in my car, making a great pretence of checking the rear view mirror, giving Lee time to drive away from the house and up the road. Once her tail lights disappeared around the top of the estate, I got out of my car and walked back up her Harper Home path.

CHAPTER 77

∞

LEE

I'd barely waved Victoria off before there was another knock at the door. 'What's she forgotten now?' I wondered as I went to let her in. 'I'm going to have to get you a key.'

Hell's teeth. 'What are you doing here?'

'That's a nice way to greet your best friend,' Teri said.

Best friend? With best friends like Teri my enemies could take a sabbatical.

'I was hoping to speak to Dan,' she said when I didn't answer.

'To apologise?'

'Er... no.' She sounded cagey.

Why?

'Is he due back soon?' She peered over my shoulder. 'He does live here, doesn't he?' she asked. Rather rudely, I thought.

'Not exactly...'

She looked puzzled, waiting for me to elaborate. I didn't.

'Are you expecting him?' she demanded.

I ignored her question and then noticed the coat she was holding. 'Oh,' I said, 'is that Dan's coat? We thought we'd left it in the taxi.'

I reached out a hand, expecting her to release it. Instead she stepped back.

'Yes, but don't worry, I'll give it to him when I see him.'

Yep, she was definitely up to something. But, what?

'Are you going to invite me in?'

Put like that I could hardly say no. I looked at my watch – I'd arranged to meet Mammy and Daddy. 'I've got an appointment later,' I said, 'but, yes, a quick cuppa would be nice.'

Silly me, she was already in and heading for the kitchen. Looking for Dan?

She'd be lucky; he wasn't due back until tomorrow tea-time.

I followed her down the hallway. 'Do you want –'

'No thanks,' she said. 'I'll make my own.'

She tossed the coat over the back of a chair and opened a cupboard.

It was almost like old times – Teri helping herself, making herself at home.

'About Vic Brennan,' I said. 'He's asked me for a reference.'

'Oh, that's come already, has it?'

Yes, I thought, and I told you categorically I didn't feel able to act as a referee.

She frowned. 'You are going to say nice things, aren't you?'

Nice things?

I could say lots of nice things about Teri – honestly, yes, I could – but that still wouldn't have made her the right person for the job. 'Are you sure this is really what you want?'

Her shoulders sagged a little, and she reached out and stroked Dan's coat on the chair next to her.

Bloody hell, I thought, it's Dan you want.

She looked suddenly very vulnerable – my heart ached for her. Sorry, love, he's taken. I'd have said something, but suddenly the front door was wrenched almost off its hinges. 'That f****** bloody God-forsaken bitch of a woman. I'm going to f****** kill her.'

It was Dan – no prizes for guessing who'd provoked his ire.

'Well,' Teri said, when he eventually stormed upstairs in a hail of f*** words and other expletives. 'I've never seen him so worked up before.'

Dear God, I swear she was turned on. No bloody chance, I thought, and shepherded her out of the front door, which was still just about functional.

She declined a lift into town and pointed at her own car parked a little further down the street.

'I'll be all right,' she said.

I gave her a quick hug. 'I'm sorry. We never got a proper chance to talk.'

She said nothing but gazed at me and then back at the house.

Idiot! I ought to have the word 'stupid' tattooed on my forehead. I was shuffling round the back garden with Daddy when the penny dropped. Of course, Teri waited until I was out of sight and then went back to have her heart-to-heart with Dan. I hoped it was just a heart-to-heart and there weren't any other body bits getting close to one another. Dan wouldn't do that, would he? Teri would. 'All's fair in love and lust' was practically her motto. And, if she'd convinced herself that Dan was secretly nursing a broken heart? But, not in my house? In my bed?

Daddy smiled. 'Penny for them?'

I shook my head. 'Nothing important.' Which was true, whatever Teri and Dan may or may not have been doing, there were other more immediately pressing concerns to hand.

Daddy seemed to have gone downhill at a rate of knots. It was as if the terminal diagnosis had been the permission he needed to give in to the aches and pains, which he now conceded had become 'something cruel'.

'We need to talk,' he said, leaning on my arm.

'Yes?'

'I'm dying, you know.' It was the first time he'd properly said it. Before he'd spoken abstractly about 'a terminal diagnosis' or 'the doctors aren't optimistic' or 'things won't get better'. You didn't need to be a genius to know what he meant, but he'd never actually said 'I'm dying'.

'I know, Daddy,' I said. 'I've known for a long time.' And I had, ever since I'd followed him down the hospital corridor when he went for those first tests.

We shuffled some more. 'Nice roses,' Daddy said, inhaling the scent. 'I've always liked yellow roses.'

And I promised myself, 'I'll make sure there are yellow roses on your grave.' Instantly I hated myself for thinking him dead already.

But, in a sense, he was to all intents and purposes a dead man walking, because, eating scones and jam and cream and sipping tea under the back veranda, it was clear that mentally he'd already moved into the next world.

'Might be an idea to think about a new car,' he told Mammy. 'You'll find one with an automatic gear shift much easier to handle.'

She said she was more than happy with the car they already had, but he poo-pooed her. 'Much too big for you to use as a run-around,' he said. 'And you don't want to give up driving completely. It's very limiting if you've got to depend on other people for lifts.'

I didn't like to point out that she'd pretty much given up driving years ago and didn't seem to have any problem depending on people for lifts. Although without Daddy, the car pool would be down to just me and Fliss. Perhaps I should encourage her to get back behind the wheel?

But Daddy had already settled that problem and had moved on to me. 'About the yard,' he said. 'Mammy and I have decided the business should be signed over to you and Fliss as joint partners. Dom can look after the day-to-day stuff – God knows he's been practically running the place for the last couple of years. You'll need to give him a new job title though – gaffer doesn't quite cut the mustard – and a pay rise to match.

'Maybe when Ritchie's a bit older,' he speculated, 'it would be nice to think one of the family was in the trade.'

Thank heavens he'd given up on his 'and daughter' plan. Harper and grandson sounded much more plausible.

'And I've been thinking about...' He paused. '...afterwards.'

Afterwards? Wasn't this all about afterwards?

'I don't want to be buried,' he said. 'Make sure I'm properly dead and then cremate me. No fuss or flowers either.'

'A requiem mass and then cremation. And no bawling or weeping and wailing.' He wagged a finger in my direction. 'Mammy'll be fine. She's a strong woman,' he said, 'but you're as soft as a goose-down duvet. I warn you, no waterworks. I'll be watching.'

That was me told. Please God, I could cope.

CHAPTER 78

TERI

Dan answered the door and looked dumbfounded to see me standing there.

'Don't say anything,' I told him. 'I just need to talk.'

He sighed but moved aside to let me into the hallway where we both stood, awkwardly, avoiding eye contact with each other.

'Look, I just want to say sorry,' I started. 'I should have behaved better. If I'd only checked the bookings I'd have seen you and Lee were coming to the restaurant. And I would've been better prepared. As it was, you took me completely by surprise. It was such a shock to see you. And then when Declan came in with that stupid, little reporter of his… well, things just boiled up in my brain. It all came to a head. And then Declan started playing up and you stepped in – which I thought was so magnificent of you – like a knight in shining armour. I realise now how angry you must be with me – and Declan. But I hadn't realised how much we'd both hurt you. And it made me see that you still have feelings for me and, Dan, I still have feelings for you. You'll never know how much I –'

Dan interrupted to tell me to 'Shush' and he reached out and led me into the sitting room. He pulled me to sit down beside him on the sofa.

'Teri…Teri…' he said, shaking his head.

This is where he leans forward and kisses me, I thought.

'Teri…how can I put this? Yes, I was angry with you and with that little newspaper runt. But it's not because I still have feelings for you… well, yes, I will always have feelings for you, but not in the way you think. I'll always be fond of you…'

Fond?

'But I thought we'd cleared all of this up…we were disastrous for each other; we've both agreed that. Our marriage was a mistake; we've both agreed that too. And now I've met someone I really, truly love – I can't tell you what she means to me, because I've never felt like this before about any woman and I can't even put it into words.'

'You mean Lee?' I said, not even trying to disguise the surprise in my voice.

'Yes, of course, Lee,' he said, impatiently. 'Last night was a fiasco – but it wasn't all about you, Teri. There's things going on at work, with Victoria, and yes, between me and Lee and, yes, things have been building up for you, but you're not the only one who's had problems to deal with recently.'

'Oh, I'm sorry. You poor –'

'You don't have to apologise. As I said, it's not about you, Teri. Last night was the catalyst, but you and Declan were not the cause. And now I've let off all that steam, I've got some thinking and apologising of my own to do – starting with Lee.

'And you,' he said, his voice sounding stern, 'have some thinking to do about your own relationship with Lee. She's the one person who has stood by you all these years, bailed you out of one problem after another, defended you, stood by you – and look how you treat her.'

'Yes, but she –'

'No buts. She's been worried sick about you, and now her father's dying and she needs a friend –'

'Her father…?'

'Yeah, if you stopped looking inwards at yourself all the time, Teri, you'd see that other people are going through tough times too. Think about that for once in your life.'

CHAPTER 79

TERI

I drove back into town. I'd got a lot of thinking to do. I'd known old man Harper since Lee and I first became friends at sixth-form college, and he – and Lee's mammy – had always been good to me. Perhaps they didn't realise the scrapes I used to try to drag their precious daughter into, because they always seemed pleased to see me when I turned up on the doorstep.

But Mr Harper, who'd created and built up Harper Homes, was an amazing man – tall, strong, successful. He couldn't possibly be dying.

I felt an overwhelming sense of sadness. I really thought that I'd care more if something happened to Mr Harper than if it happened to my old man, the useless git who'd put our entire future into the hands of that shyster, Edward Pranks.

I pulled up on the double yellow lines opposite Portly & Groops. The high street was busy with Saturday shoppers, and I couldn't be bothered driving along to the car park, but I needed a strong Americano and wouldn't be long and, besides, there were never any traffic wardens out on a weekend.

A constant stream of cars flowed past preventing me from opening my door – one driver honked his horn and wagged a finger, full of his own traffic-directing importance. 'Oh, get a life,' I mouthed at him.

Finally, there was a gap in the traffic, and I pushed open the door to step out only for an idiot driving a shiny black Jaguar to come screaming along, screeching to a halt at the last minute, missing by inches my car door and my extended right leg.

'You stupid bloody cow…' I heard him say, having taken time out from his rage to wind down his passenger window to better show me his mad-motorist face.

I stared. He stared back.

'Jim,' I said in surprise.

'Teri?' he said.

Jim bought me an Americano to calm my nerves. Nearly having my right leg sliced off by a shiny black Jag had been unsettling.

He'd persuaded me to move my car to the car park where we both parked up, and we walked back together to Portly & Groops.

'It's good to see you, Teri,' he said. 'And I'm glad we bumped into each other…'

'Almost literally,' I laughed.

'You know Richard's been trying to get in touch?'

'He's not tried very hard.'

'Well, he's had a lot on and you're not an easy bird to get hold of.'

I must do something about that mobile phone.

Jim was one of those skeletally thin, wiry sort of men. It was hard to put an age on him; the skin on his face was creased around the eyes, but otherwise his features were taut as though he'd been sandblasted. I imagined him being tough as iron; a lightweight boxer, for instance, whose size belies his strength. But he had a way of listening intently as I talked, leaning his head to one side and gazing at my eyes – not in a sexy way, more considering and calculating.

We drank our coffee, and I felt myself relaxing. When Jim asked what I'd been up to, I found myself going over the edited highlights of my catastrophic life so far.

He wasn't too interested in tales of love in the Suffolk countryside, and I didn't go into detail, but he perked up when I mentioned the steel factory.

'That belongs to your dad?' he asked. 'I always thought Pranksy owned it.'

'You know Pranksy?'

'Well…yeah. Long story…but we've met once or twice…'

So I elaborated. Told him the story of how Pranks had inveigled himself into Dad's trust and literally cleaned us out.

Jim nodded thoughtfully. 'Sounds like Pranksy.'

'How do you know him?'

'Well.' He frowned. 'Done a bit of time. Met old Pranksy first time round in Armley nick.'

'What? You've been in prison?'

'Yeah.' He gazed down at his coffee cup cradled in his long, bony fingers. 'Was a bit of a bad boy – nothing serious, just twocking a few cars, doing them up, selling 'em on, that sort of thing.'

'Twocking?'

'Taking without consent – of the owner. Nicking them.'

'Oh, Jim…'

'Oh, don't worry. It was all a long time ago, and as I said, I've done me time. The Jag's Richard's by the way. But he lets me keep it to drive him around. It's all legit.'

'But how do you know Richard?'

'Another long story, but he used to visit me in the nick, and he promised to help me when I got out. And he did – gave me a job – and here we are. I owe him everything.'

Old Duck's Arse. Talk about a man with a past.

But before I could ask how Richard came to be prison visiting or why Pranks had been in jail, Jim had pulled out a little notebook from his coat pocket and was leafing through it. 'Yeah, Pete Danvers…he'll do…' he muttered to himself.

'Do what?'

'Don't you worry about it, pretty lady.' He looked at his watch. 'Better be off…now make sure you park properly next time. See you soon.'

And he jumped to his feet and headed for the door before I could say anything else.

CHAPTER 80

LEE

I'm not going to talk about what happened when I got home. It's private – but I suppose it wouldn't be a breach of confidentiality to admit I cried a little when Dan said he'd told Teri he couldn't live without me and that he'd never felt that way about her. Ever. It made me realise how lucky I was and how precious Dan had become and…oh no, excuse me, pass the sick bucket. I'm making myself feel queasy. Let's just say Dan and I agreed we were having teething problems, but they wouldn't kill us, and we'd grow out of them. And, though I wasn't entirely convinced the Teri elephant would never visit the bedroom again, she wasn't flapping her ears quite as much as she had before. More importantly, it looked like the baby issue, the deal-breaker, could be negotiable. I'll take that as a good starting point.

First, however, there was the Vic Brennan question: did I consider Teri a suitable person to take up a student consideration awareness role at his university?

Academic integrity demanded a degree of honesty and, having already 'helped' Teri secure one university post, I was a bit reluctant to stick my neck out again. It was a question of reputation. When she'd joined the University of Central Yorkshire, it had been my championship that had put her on the shortlist, which was fair enough. But it wasn't fair of Teri to lie about having landed a thirty thousand-pound research bursary into the lives and loves of Rochester, which as we subsequently discovered, wasn't even worth the paper the research contract wasn't written on.

And, that's the rub: I'd believed the research contract was genuine and had supported her job application on that basis. And Peter and Mike had also believed it, and so had Rochester-enthusiast Stella Lastings, who was also on the interview panel, and we'd all been made to look extremely silly when the bursary didn't materialise. Peter's fury over what Teri dismissed as a 'minor deception' wasn't the only reason he'd taken huge delight in booting her out of the university – but it had been a big part of it.

It was also the reason I was hesitating now. That and the fact that it's one thing to fudge a reference to put in a good word for someone applying to answer phones in a washing machine call centre, but I couldn't, in all conscience, put pen to paper – or fingers to PC keyboard – and promote Teri's virtues as an ideal candidate for any sort of student-support role.

I wanted to help her – really, I did – but what about the poor bloody students who'd be coming to her for help? Ten minutes of Teri and they'd be permanently damaged goods.

In the end, I rang Vic and spoke off the record. 'Yes, my boss dumped her for numerous alleged misdemeanours but, hell, Vic, you know Peter...' Sure, he knew Peter and loathed him. If anything, the fact Peter had fired Teri was a big plus. Further, I told Vic frankly that since he'd taught Teri for three years he must know what he was getting, and if he wanted a support worker with a robust attitude, who certainly wouldn't be wrapping students in cotton wool, then Teri was his woman.

Vic said he was grateful for my honesty. He thought a tough-love approach was called for, and I agreed Teri would deliver that in spades. Not, perhaps, the most glowing recommendation, but truthful and, at least, I hadn't contributed anything in writing that could later be used in evidence against me.

CHAPTER 81

TERI

I'd been thinking a lot about what Dan said. No, not about me looking inwards at myself all the time. I don't know where he got that idea from; I'm always thinking about other people.

Look how I've helped Lee over the years; no-one's done more for her than me. Who organised that abortion for her? Me. Who helped her style her little house that Daddy Harper built for her? Me. She didn't like the idea of furnishing it in grey as I advised, but she loves those little nickety-nackety things I buy her – photo frames in the shape of a Scotty dog, lavender pouches to put in her undie drawer. Can't stand the things myself.

And who helps her with her dress sense – because, let's face it, she doesn't have much of that? I tried checking once that she had enough transitional pieces to take her from summer to autumn, and she looked at me blankly, and then said she'd got plenty of cardigans to put on if it got cold. Cardigans?

No, I'd been thinking about what Dan said about her daddy. He couldn't possibly be dying. What a shock. Lee had told me he'd been having tests and she was worried, but she never said how serious it was. She must be beside herself; she's a real family person and is probably going through hell. No wonder she's been acting so unreasonable with me lately.

I bought her a card. Not an 'In Sympathy' one – he wasn't dead yet – but a blank one with a picture of a bottle of wine and two glasses on the front. Tasteful.

I couldn't think what to write. 'Thinking of you…' and 'Sorry to hear…' didn't sound right so I simply wrote, 'Call if you need me. And I'll bring the wine. Love Teri x' and left it at that.

I didn't want to deliver it by hand and risk seeing either Lee or Dan. For a start, Lee would get all gushy and girly, and I couldn't stand that. And for seconds, I was a little confused by Dan's reaction when I told him I still had feelings for him. He's 'fond' of me, he said. But he actually loves Lee more than he's ever loved anybody – even me. Or Sara, his other ex-wife.

Well, win some, lose some.

So I decided to post the card. I'd pop down for a stamp and maybe call in at Portly & Groops for an Americano.

And then wished I hadn't. The local council had put up the high street Christmas lights back in September – it's obviously cheaper to do it then – so I was used to seeing those, but the deli was playing Christmassy pop songs and the place was heaving with late afternoon shoppers, loaded down with carrier bags full of presents and rolls of jolly wrapping paper.

Christmas. What's it all about? I know it's a religious occasion celebrating the birth of Christ. But the rest of it: turkeys, sprouts, crackers, soggy puddings and far too much cream.

Over-eating, over-drinking and over-spending on tat that no-one wants – unless, of course, you've been given a gift list from which to choose, despite the fact you'll not be able to find half the things on the list, and when you do, you'll buy the wrong colour. Luckily, you'll have kept the receipt so the recipient can join the greedy, mad-eyed crush on Boxing Day to take the damn thing back for a refund.

'Oh, but it's all about the children,' the daft and delusional say. What? You stuff your kids with too many sweets, cakes and those Belgian chocolate biscuits that someone thinks is a good idea for a present – as if wrapping a cardboard box of biscuits in paper makes it more interesting – and you wonder why they're sick.

No, I've never enjoyed Christmas.

I downed my Americano and stepped back out into the street only to have to press myself back against the door as a party of about fifteen people swarmed along the pavement in a tight lump.

'Oy, oy, oy. It's a boy, boy, boy,' shouted one of the revellers. 'And don't forget the girly whirly girl,' another screamed in delight.

These bloody stag dos, I thought.

And then I saw Declan in the middle of the throng. Coatless, tie undone, eyes glazed, arms outstretched, big grin on his stupid face. Clearly pissed out of his head.

And then the glazed eyes focussed and he saw me.

'Teri, Teri, Teri…' he slurred, and the throng opened to allow a passage through which he lurched towards me.

'Teri, the love of my life,' he yelled. 'See this beautiful woman, you lot.' He swung around, arms still outstretched, to address the throng. 'She loves me and I love her.' He turned back to me and added, uncertainly, 'You do, don't you?'

I noticed the throng looking even more intently in my direction.

'Er, Dekkie…you coming, or what?' asked one from inside the pack. Dekkie?

'Not without this beautiful lady,' Declan said, falling against me so that I was pressed even harder against Portly's door.

'Get off me, Declan,' I hissed, trying to push the drunken lump away. One of the group emerged and pulled at Declan's arm. 'C'mon, Dekkie. Sorry, love,' he said, turning to me, 'we're celebrating. His wife's just had twins…he's had a bit too much to drink.'

As if that wasn't obvious.

'Fuck my wife and her bloody twins,' Declan shouted, shaking his pal off and sounding suddenly angry. 'It's this woman I want. Teri.' He reached out, groping wildly. Portly's door flew open behind me, and I fell backwards into the hot and loud, musical deli, and onto its Italian-style, black-and-white tiled floor. Declan landed on top of me and, as I lay trying to push him off, I was aware of Slade blasting out, 'Merry Christmas, Everybody.'

CHAPTER 82

∞

LEE

It would be nice to report the 'Teri Meyer question' as well and truly put to bed. But nothing is ever pure and simple where Teri is concerned. For one thing, she didn't seem to have replaced her mobile, and she never seemed to be in to answer her landline.

Dan thought I should write her off as a dead loss, but you can't just call time on a friendship that's lasted at least a couple of decades without wanting to save it. Can you?

I couldn't anyway.

And, without being overly melodramatic, Teri's held my hand through every life crisis I've ever faced, and while Dan's sympathy over Daddy's impending death was much appreciated, it didn't quite fill the gap left by Teri's in-your-face assumption that nothing was so bad it couldn't be cured by another glass of wine. Or two.

Put it like this: where Dan asked whether I really NEEDED *another* glass of wine, Teri would have asked if I wanted to open another bottle?

There was a world of difference between the two approaches, and I knew which I preferred.

Besides which, Teri had known and liked Daddy for years and years, and my loss, in a different way, was also her loss. Dan, with the best will in the world, hadn't got a clue what I was losing.

Yeah, people say 'I can just imagine how you're feeling'. Sorry, no, you imagine as much as you like, but you have no idea of the pain until it actually comes along and smacks you in the face. So, I was doubly hurt by Teri's continued cold shoulder. Didn't she love Daddy even a little bit? And me?

But Daddy, having made up his mind to die, wasn't hanging about;

after five or six days as a hospice day visitor he'd been promoted to a boarder and, a fringe benefit of half a lifetime as a fully-paid up Catenian, he was also given a private room.

'You're very lucky,' he was told by the nurse who checked his blood pressure and dished out medication. She was a busy little woman, slightly stout with an old-fashioned 'shampoo-and-set' hairstyle, who'd introduced herself as charge nurse Williams – 'call me Lindy, short for Linda' – and said she'd be responsible for managing his care. 'Most newcomers spend a few nights in a twin room before getting a place of their own.'

Well, I was sorry they had to wait for their upgrade, but what was lucky about being admitted to a hospice? It's not a holiday home.

And, however hard they'd tried to make it feel like one, with an ensuite shower and bathroom, a couple of easy chairs, a sofa and a small dining table, nothing could mask the hospice smell of sick and blood and pus, seeping through a shroud of antiseptic. Lindy straightened a couple of cushions. 'While you're well enough you can get up and eat at the table.'

Or, to put it another way, until you're actually about to peg out you can sit at the table like a normal person.

'And there's a nice view of our Peace Garden.' She indicated the large bay window. Thank you, I thought, we can see that for ourselves. Clearly, Lindy was a woman with a talent for stating the bleeding obvious.

I sat on the sofa, suddenly exhausted. 'And you've got a comfy bed settee.' She was beginning to sound like an estate agent trying to persuade us to rent what in letting terms would be considered a bijou bed-sit. A bed settee? 'In case your wife wants to stop over, later on,' she told Daddy.

It didn't take a genius to read the sub-text.

'It's all part of God's plan,' Daddy had said once when I complained about it all.

Some bloody plan, I thought. Not that God took a blind bit of notice.

Fliss and the kids arrived almost before Daddy had unpacked his toothbrush – scrub that – before Mammy had unpacked his toiletries and other stuff. It was like a hurricane arriving. Ritchie, who'd had a growth spurt, was talking nineteen-to-the-dozen, and Fee, who'd stopped being a baby and become a bona fide toddler, tried to climb onto the coffee table. Ritchie helped her up, and Fliss pulled her back down again.

'Sit down, the pair of you,' she said.

Ritchie scrunched up on the bed, nearly pushing Daddy over the edge, and started telling him about the dispenser of sanitising gel at the top of the stairs. 'It's so people don't bring germs in,' he explained. And then he saw the garden outside and jumped off the bed. 'Can I go and have a look?'

'Later,' his mother said. 'We're here to see Pops.'

'Pops won't mind,' Ritchie said, confident his grandfather would understand his burning desire to explore. 'He can come with me?'

'I'll come,' I said. I needed a break.

We collided with Dan in the doorway. He'd just come from a meeting with his editor and looked like a cat who'd swallowed a saucer of cream.

'Sorry,' Ritchie said, who, not being part of the audience demographic for Ridings Today, didn't immediately recognise the newcomer.

'Hello, Ritchie,' Dan said.

'Wow.' Ritchie was impressed. 'How do you know my name?'

'We met at the bowling alley,' Dan reminded him. 'You, me, Lee and your little sister and –'

'The big girl, Tory,' Ritchie exclaimed. 'He peered behind Dan. 'Is she with you?'

'No.'

'Oh, I liked her.' The implication being he could take or leave Dan. 'What are you doing here?'

Well, the short answer was meeting Pops before he died, and the long one was…exactly the same.

Oh God! Daddy was going to die, wasn't he? And much, much sooner than later.

'Why are you crying?' Ritchie asked.

'Because…' I said. 'Just because…'

CHAPTER 83

TERI

The throng managed to prise Declan off me after our unexpected entrance into Portly & Groops and dragged him away, but I could still hear him calling out for me as they rounded the corner at the bottom of the high street. One of the party – a young lad, possibly what they call a cub reporter – stayed behind to check I was okay. 'Sorry about that,' he said. 'Declan's our news editor, and he heard at lunchtime that his wife had –'

'I know, don't bother telling me,' I interrupted. 'She's had her fucking twins.'

The cub took a step back and raised his eyebrows in surprise at my angry tone. 'Er...yes. We all went for a drink at lunchtime and it...er...'

'Went on all afternoon,' I finished for him. 'And why isn't your wonderful news editor at the bedside of his beached whale and mewling brats?'

The cub hadn't finished looking surprised so carried on looking surprised.

'Oh, forget it,' I said, impatiently. 'Go and enjoy yourselves. It's Christmas.'

Declan rang the following day to apologise. And to beg me to meet him for a Christmas drink.

As if.

I'd prepared myself for spending another Christmas on my own. Let's face it, apart from a couple of times I'd spent the so-called festive season with Lee, that's how it had always been.

Declan would be pulling crackers with the whale, Lee would be cosying up with Dan – and hopefully the feckless daughter would be there to cause her usual chaos – Charlie and Denis would be in loves-ville in Suffolk, Andrew would be in his manorial home perhaps having bought his wife some new velvet slippers, Duck's Arse would be…? What? Where would he be and who would he be with?

On a whim, I rang D'reen at Ridings Today. 'He's still in the Far East,' she said. 'It's a business trip with a holiday tacked on. He's not back till second week of January…'

Alone it is then. Ding Dong, Merrily on High.

CHAPTER 84

LEE

Dan joined Ritchie and me in the hospice garden. There was a distinct chill in the air but the borders held winter at bay with a host of late-season flowering plants – elegant anemones and statuesque salvias framed by hardy plumbagos, whose spectacular red leaves provided a striking contrast to the vivid blue of their flowers. Here and there bird tables dotted the lawns and somewhere nearby a woodpecker hammered on a dead tree.

We followed a wide, flat wheelchair friendly path, which looped via a mini-woodland into a copse of telegraph poles set at crazy angles. Ritchie spread his arms into aeroplane wings and, with a loud, droning hum, zig-zagged backwards and forwards. I leaned against the tactile trunk of a birch tree and savoured the minty, wintergreen scent. Perhaps I, too, needed to live in the moment?

Abruptly, Ritchie dropped his wings. 'Look,' he exclaimed, 'a fox.'

And a family of deer and a pair of badgers as well – exquisite wooden sculptures bringing the woodland to life. Ritchie stroked the littlest fawn. 'Aren't they cute?'

He raced off again, excited to see what lay around the next corner – a sizeable pond where he and Dan practised skimming stones across the surface. Inevitably, it ended up as a competition to see who could get the most bounces from flat pieces of shingle carefully selected for shape and size from the garden paths. Ritchie was just nudging ahead – a lucky fluke, and nothing at all to do with the fact I was refereeing and making up the rules as I went along – when an orderly asked them to stop. 'Makes the koi carp nervous,' he said.

Yes, I can see how it would be a bit distracting to have small pebbles dive bomb your water lilies and bulrushes.

'And we prefer to keep the stones on the path rather than in the pond,' Mr Jolly added. 'They block the filters. And kill the fish.'

Yes, well, you'd have thought that with his job he'd be used to the dead and the dying.

We all pulled suitably solemn faces and continued our walk. Ritchie made a beeline for a large monkey puzzle tree. 'It's just asking to be climbed,' he said. He stood on tiptoes and strained towards the lowest branch. 'Give me a lift,' he begged. Dan bent and was just about to heave him up when the orderly appeared again. I wondered how long it had taken him to perfect his penchant for turning up when you didn't want them.

'Those trees aren't meant to be climbed,' he said.

I'd have argued – those branches looked very inviting – but I had a horrible feeling that Ritchie might climb up with relative ease but would struggle to get down again.

And Dan wasn't dressed for rescuing small boys from trees.

Instead we went and sat in the cafeteria where the light grey and lavender décor was clearly intended to calm and relax. Shame about the lingering odour of boiled cabbage and fried liver and onions, but the white-haired volunteer behind the counter obligingly allowed Ritchie to sample all three flavours of ice-cream – vanilla, chocolate and strawberry – and entered into a spirited and knowledgeable discussion of each before he finally settled for a vanilla cornet and a can of lemonade. I'd have preferred something stronger, but Ada behind the counter said she was clean out of dry white wine. I settled for a weak Earl Grey tea instead, and Dan had a mug of something that might have been coffee but equally might not. 'Tastes a bit as if something died in the pot,' he said.

It was a hospice, after all.

We'd come in separate cars, so I had to wait until we got home to hear his news. He'd been bursting to spill the beans but didn't want to say anything in front of Ritchie and the others. Especially Mammy, who was, embarrassingly, and somewhat surprisingly, star-struck.

'I've never met anyone from off the telly before,' she said.

You're not meeting anyone from off the telly now, I'd thought. He's

OFF the telly. Ha, Ha. You've got to laugh, haven't you? Best antidote to grief. And better than weeping and wailing like a banshee, which was the only other, self-indulgent, option.

I gave myself a mental shake and a stiff telling-off. 'There are no such things as banshees. Stop being a drama queen and cut the crap.'

There, that had told me. Not sure how well it would work though; most of the time I felt as if a molten lump of grief had lodged in the pit of my stomach, and the only way to get a modicum of relief from the ache was to spew it up.

Mammy was speaking to Dan. 'I don't think we've seen you on the news lately.'

'No,' he said. 'I've been on a little break.'

'Don't think much of your replacement – whatisname? Baxter Finlay?'

'Finlay Baxter,' Dan corrected.

'He's very young,' Mammy said, 'and he talks a lot of rubbish.'

'He'll learn,' Dan said. 'He's a nice boy and tries hard.'

Was I hearing things?

Dan winked. He knew something I didn't.

Back home, I'd barely picked the post off the doormat when Dan spun me up and down the hallway in a mock-Highland reel. 'Hurrah for the wonderful Doreen.'

I laughed. His enthusiasm was infectious. 'Why am I paying homage to another woman?'

'Can't you guess?'

Yes, he was back at his anchor desk. He'd only been gone for half a week but already Doreen, Richard Walker's secretary, was fed up to the back teeth with customer complaints.

'Customer complaints?'

'Her words not mine,' Dan said. 'They're all customers and if they don't buy our products we're all dead in the water.'

'And?'

'And they don't buy Bullshit Baxter.'

Nor were they shy about telling Doreen he was a ham-fisted twerp.

'Her inbox has been clogged with emails from viewers,' Dan said.

'Why are they telling Doreen? It's nothing to do with her.'

'But as Richard's PA his mail all comes to her first for filtering.'

Seems her filter couldn't stand the strain. She'd telephoned Duck's Arse and told him to lift Dan's suspension. NOW. Or else.

Dan, of course, was cock-a-hoop. 'One in the eye for age and experience.' Huh! With his age and experience he should have known better than to deck Declan in the first place. But I was glad he wouldn't be moping around the house anymore.

One less thing to worry about.

'Let's go out to dinner,' he said. 'L'homme-vert?'

'Dan! No!'

It would be deliberately provocative. I showed him the card that had come with the morning's post. 'It's from Teri,' I said.

A peace offering? Or a truce?

CHAPTER 85

TERI

I'd just about resigned myself to spending the festive season on my own – again – when I thought of Lee nestling up to Dan in front of a Bing Crosby black-and-white movie and a thought struck me.

Why don't I invite them round to my duplex? I know – a ridiculous idea. But part of me wanted to show them both what they're missing by trying to obliterate me from their cosy, little lives. The other part of me didn't want to be alone again. Although I'd never admit that to anyone.

I rang Lee's mobile, and it rang for ages before she answered – and then in a whispered 'Hello'.

'Lee, it's me and I've had a fantastic idea. You're going to love this…'

'Teri,' she said ever so quietly, 'I'm at the hospice.'

'Oh God, he's not…'

'No…no. He's –'

'Oh good. Listen, I was thinking about Christmas and how we've had such fun when we've spent it together…'

And then a thought dawned, and I must say it was inspirational. 'I realise you're at the hospice with your dad and probably don't have much time to think about Christmas, so I'm willing to organise something for you here – and Dan, of course. But not the devil child, obviously.

'I could do a goose – who likes turkey anyway? And I'll do some fabulous chocolate pots – much better than Christmas pudding. I'll sort out the wine. You won't need to do anything – except turn up and enjoy yourself. How about that?'

Lee was so quiet on the other end that I thought we'd lost connection.

'Teri, I'm sorry,' she said. 'It's very kind of you and a nice thought.

But I can't…we won't… Daddy isn't…'

And she started to cry.

'Lee…?' I couldn't think of the right thing to say; I was lost for words. It really was serious, then. I know what Dan had said, but I hadn't really believed things could be this bad. Mr Harper was dying. I had an overwhelming sense that Lee needed me.

'Do you want me to come over?' I asked.

There was a pause. Then Lee said something about yes, she did, but now's not a good time as all the family was there and she'd like for me to come over when it would be just her and me and her dad. And, rather than be offended, I realised what she meant. She wanted the three of us to have some special time. Before Mr Harper died.

We arranged that I'd go over the next day. I put the phone down. And I cried.

CHAPTER 86

~~~

LEE

Poor Teri. Her heart's in the right place – as in somewhere to the left of her lungs and just below her left breast – but, my goodness, her timing's awful. Although, credit where credit is due, you've got to admire her chutzpah.

Yes, Teri, I thought, it's only two minutes since you were trying to seduce my fiancé, of course, we'd love to come to dinner. NOT!

Maybe next year, when the dust has settled a bit, I might be up to pulling Christmas crackers with you on one side of the table and my fiancé, your ex-husband, on the other. But not this year – not when Dan, who reads the news headlines for a living, has been hitting the headlines after you created a humdinger of a scene in a popular, local restaurant which resulted in a brawl with your ex-lover.

And, most emphatically not when my father is heading for death's door and is buckling his skates so he can get there even more quickly.

So, sorry Teri, I know how much you'd love to show Dan just what he's missing – and there'd certainly be plenty to talk about over the goose and chocolate pots – but, the answer's no thanks.

'It's very kind of you and a nice thought,' I started, 'but I can't...' And I stopped; I couldn't say it. I just couldn't say it out loud. 'We can't come because my daddy is dying.' So I burst into tears instead – which hadn't been my intention but did, at least, stop her gabbling on about the merits of goose and the benefits of roasting potatoes in their fat.

By the time I pulled myself together she'd had another bright idea. 'Do you want me to come over?'

Honestly? Not really; I didn't have the energy to tip-toe around her bruised ego. Nor, as it turned out, did I have the energy to tell her to 'bugger off'. 'That'd be nice.'

'We could have some quality time together.'

Clearly, she didn't know much about whiling away the hours in a hospice waiting for someone to die.

'That'd be nice,' I repeated.

CHAPTER 87

TERI

St Thomas More Hospice had been a privately-owned manor house until forty years ago when a local alderman bequeathed the place to the town for conversion into a sanctuary offering care for the dying. I read the brief history, displayed on a poster in the foyer, while I waited for Lee to collect me.

I'd never been to the Thomas More before; no reason to, thankfully. But then I'd always thought hospices were where you went to die. Another poster, however, told me they weren't. St Thomas More provided 'personal and holistic end of life care as well as offering emotional, psychological and practical support to patients and their families'.

I was just about to read on about the Care Quality Commission's rating when Lee appeared through a doorway at the other end of the foyer.

'You made it, then…' she said, unnecessarily.

'Yes, but, are you sure…' I began. 'I mean, is your dad okay to see me?'

'He's looking forward to it,' Lee said, putting an arm through mine and pulling me through the door and into a short corridor.

Halfway down, she pushed open another door and stepped inside. I followed her slowly and carefully. I hate hospital visiting. All those sick people.

But the room was a surprise, it didn't smell of disinfectant or pee like some hospital wards; it was light and airy thanks to two enormous windows, and the walls were painted in a fresh, lemon colour. There were even pictures of country scenes around the room.

I tried hard not to cast my eyes over anything else, certainly not the oxygen cylinder in the corner and something that looked like a wheelchair with a potty in the seat. Get a grip, Teri, I told myself. Lee scampered to the far side of the bed and was in the process of pulling a chair closer to her father when she looked up and indicated for me to do the same on my side of the bed, but I remained standing. To be honest, I couldn't move. Was this really the lovely Mr Harper?

He was propped in a semi-sitting position. Through the thin coverlet – in a darker shade of lemon; not hospital white – I could make out his thin form. He'd always been a big, muscular man – well, a builder would be – but now he appeared frail and wasted. I was glad to see he was wearing a grey tee-shirt, which seemed more normal and reassuring than those old-man pyjamas some poorly people wear, but even so, he was half the size and weight of when I'd last seen him. His once handsome face was now sunken and craggy.

He gazed at me, and I was momentarily alarmed that his eyes were almost blazing but realised they were watering, and the winter sun, coming through the windows, was making them shine. He raised a thin, bruise-mottled arm towards me, and I couldn't help staring at the cannula attached to it, held in place by two plasters and being fed from an overhead bag containing clear liquid.

Lee followed my gaze. 'Morphine,' she said in answer to my unspoken question.

Mr Harper ignored her. 'Teri…' he said, holding his arm out towards me. I thought he wanted to shake hands, so I stretched out my right arm. He caught my hand, swung his left arm over, stacked his other hand on top and pulled me towards him. I was right up against the bed now with my knees pressing into the mattress.

Without taking his eyes off me, Mr Harper inclined his head slightly towards Lee and said, 'Sweetheart. Why don't you go get us some tea – and none of that witch's piss you drink.'

Lee, who'd just got herself organised, putting down her bag, unravelling one of her voluminous pseudo-silk scarves, said, 'Oh, right…' and despite my trying telepathically to tell her to stay, she went.

Mr Harper, still playing hand-over-hand with me, squeezed hard. I was surprised at the strength in those long, bony fingers of his. He suddenly let my hand go and dropped his arms as though the effort had been too much. The cannula wobbled. Oh, God, I prayed it wouldn't fall out.

'I'm glad you came,' he said, pulling the coverlet up to his chest. 'Lee's told you things aren't too good? That I haven't got long? Probably weeks rather than months.'

'Yes,' I managed. This was all too surreal. I was hoping for a quick hello, a chat about the weather and then a promise to come back again soon. Not a prognosis.

'Lee's mother and I have always been fond of you,' Mr Harper said, which was a bit of a surprise given that Mrs Harper had sometimes pursed her lips disapprovingly when I'd gone round for tea as a teenager and regaled the family with stories about my latest boyfriends. 'We know you haven't always been the best of influence on our little girl,' he said, probably reading my mind. 'No, don't look surprised. You know as well as I do that you've got her into some scrapes. But you always seemed to get her out of them as well.' He chuckled to himself.

Just what was he alluding to? Did he know about her stealing Dan from me? Her abortion? Her affair with Mike Orme?

If I appeared puzzled, Mr Harper ignored it because he had more to say. 'But you've always looked out for her …'

'Well, she and I…' I started, but Mr Harper hadn't finished.

'My wife's a strong woman, and she's going to rely on our two daughters when I go. They'll do her proud. Fliss? Well, Fliss has her husband and her children. She'll be all right. But Lee? I know she's with Dan now, but he doesn't know her that well yet. She'll need someone strong. Someone who knows her inside out. Someone who'll know when she's putting on a face and trying to be brave. Because she's not brave at all and, to be honest, she's the one I'm worried about the most – how she'll be when I'm gone.'

'But, Mr Harper…' I tried. No, he had more to say.

'Teri.' He lifted an arm and waved away any objections I might have. The movement pulled on the cannula tube and made the overhead bag wobble. 'I'm asking you to look after her for me. Make sure she's okay. You'll know better than anyone when she needs help. Be there for her. Will you do that for me?'

'So, what did you and Daddy talk about in there?' Lee asked as we walked round the memorial garden – the plants paid for by the grateful relative of a former patient, or so I read on a sign attached to the trunk of a small tree. Lee had one arm linked through mine as we strolled up and down the path. There wasn't much path; it was a small memorial garden.

'Oh, you know,' I said, 'this and that.' And then I pulled away from her and bent to take a particular interest in a shrub on the edge of the path. 'Ooh, look at this…sage,' I said, trying to sound knowledgeable although the fact was written on a little label attached to a lollipop stick. 'Smells like sage too.'

CHAPTER 88

∞

LEE

Yes, the inevitable had happened: Teri had completely lost her marbles. One minute she was blethering on about the best way to stuff a goose and the next she was extolling the wonders of sage that – wait for it! – looks and smells exactly like sage. Probably tastes just like sage too.

'Not sure sage is the best accompaniment for goose,' I said.

She rubbed a couple of leaves between her fingers. 'Goes nicely with pork loin and a marsala sauce though.'

'Mmmm...' I inhaled the scent. 'Not too keen on pork. Bit fatty.'

She nodded. 'Can't beat a nice bit of crackling.'

Dear God, anyone listening to us would think we hadn't a care in the world.

We did another circuit of the garden. 'We're booked in for Christmas dinner here,' I said.

'Here?'

'Yes, three courses for family and friends. And residents.' At least, those residents whose digestive systems were still in working order.

'Sounds nice.'

'Turkey and the trimmings.'

'You don't like turkey.'

I laughed. 'I don't like Brussels sprouts either but they're on the menu.'

Teri punched my arm. 'You should invite me and I'll eat your sprouts.'

'Okay.'

'What do you mean, okay?'

'If I asked you, would you come?'

'Are you asking?'
'Yes.'
'Okay.'
'Okay?'
'I'll come.'

Well, it was good to know I wouldn't need to eat my Brussels. They gave me terrible wind.

CHAPTER 89

TERI

How could I tell Lee what her father had said to me? I couldn't. She'd fold up. I must say, when Mr Harper asked – told – me to look after her, I almost filled up myself. I managed to hold it together until we got out into the garden and then, against a border full of herbs, it suddenly seemed too much and I felt my eyes filling up. Taking an unexpected interest in sage was a clever distraction, but then Lee started wittering about it not being good with goose and a slight irritation overcame my need to cry.

We somehow got talking about Christmas dinner at the hospice and, lord above, she managed to persuade me that I should join her, her family and her dying dad for turkey and all the trimmings.

Well, it would be better than spending the day on my own – again. Wouldn't it? And I must be one of the few people in the world who loves Brussels sprouts.

CHAPTER 90

LEE

We were playing Grandpa Buckaroo when Teri arrived. She was looking very festive – and, if I'm honest, a little overdressed – in a red, knee-length off-the-shoulder cocktail frock and a staggeringly high-heeled pair of red suede shoes.

Richie stared. 'Aren't you scared of toppling over?'

It was a good question, which she didn't deign to answer because she was too busy glaring at Victoria, who was also in red, but sporting a much more practical pair of black patent pumps.

I hugged her and, as we exchanged air kisses, whispered a warning. 'Don't you start.'

Her mouth twisted into a moue of disapproval. 'Don't you find her even a little bit irritating?'

Truthfully? Occasionally, yes, but there was no way I'd ever admit as much to Teri.

She smiled; sometimes she knows exactly what I'm thinking.

Fee had toddled over and was stroking Teri's toecaps. 'Pretty,' she beamed up at Teri who did her best to plaster a 'you little cutie' smile on her face.

I grinned. *I* knew exactly what she was thinking: get your grubby mitts off my shoes! Fee, the little sweetheart, tugged at the hem of her dress. 'Carry, carry...' she bleated, lifting her arms beseechingly.

Teri grimaced. I think the last time she was this close to a small child, she'd been one herself. And she most definitely wouldn't want Fee and her buckled shoes anywhere near that gorgeous red gown. I pushed her into a chair and plonked Fee on her knee. 'Sit still, darling,' I said, unfastening the first buckle. Fee chuckled and wiggled her toes while Teri sat bolt upright, like a mannequin in a department store window, frozen with horror at having a miniature human perched on her lap. Fee leaned comfortably into her, one hand caressing Teri's skirt. 'Pretty,' she repeated.

'Cupboard love,' I told Teri. 'Red's her favourite colour.'

'Then why isn't she snuggling up to the devil child?' she hissed.

'Who knows? Perhaps she senses a kindred spirit?'

Teri glowered and jiggled her knees. If she'd hoped to unseat Fee she was out of luck. Fee thought this was a new game and dug her fingers into the folds of Teri's dress. 'Faster, faster. Make the horsey go faster.'

Teri flinched and brought the horse to an abrupt halt. But Fee's palms smacked at her legs. 'Faster,' she commanded, and Teri, who up to now had been denied the pleasure of being bossed around by a pint-sized tyrant, was forced to obey. I sensed she was already beginning to think she'd have been better off home alone.

Ritchie meanwhile had returned to his game; he'd lost interest in Teri as soon as she'd sat down, thus removing the possibility she might fall flat on her face. Poor Ritchie; he'd learnt to take his fun where he could find it since there wasn't much to keep him entertained at the hospice. That's partly how Grandpa Buckeroo came about. It worked on the same principles as the board game only Daddy was the donkey. He was spending more and more of the day asleep, often, as now, lying on top of his bed, propped up by a couple of pillows. Once his snores had reached the gently rhythmic stage, we'd take it in turns to plant small toys, borrowed from the children's playbox in one of the day rooms, onto his sleeping frame. We'd count how many bits and pieces we could balance on his belly and shoulders and in his thinning hair. We gave each other points: one each for Lego and jigsaw pieces, two for miniature toy soldiers or action figures, which were a bugger to stand upright on the uneven terrain of Daddy's tummy; and three points if we managed to sit a family of farm animals on his forehead – which didn't happen often.

Great skill and cunning was required; Daddy was a light sleeper at the best of times so the toys had to be deposited gently…gently…which didn't come naturally to either Ritchie or Fee who both had the grace and dexterity of a bull in a china shop.

The fun came from watching the toys bobble up and down to Daddy's breathing, waiting for the moment when he'd give an almighty snort and shock himself awake, sending everything flying.

'How many points did you get this time?' he'd ask as Ritchie and Fee chortled as if every game was the first one.

But Fee had other things on her mind now. She wriggled off Teri's lap and grabbed her hand. 'Need a poo.'

Teri's jaw dropped so far and so fast she almost bruised her toes. Clearly, she didn't welcome her nomination as poo champion.

Fliss jumped up. 'I'll take her,' she offered but Fee wasn't letting go of her new best friend, and, believe me, Teri was doing her damndest to prise herself free.

'Just go with her,' I advised, 'and give me a shout when…'

'Don't worry, I will.'

She might have shouted but, sadly, I didn't hear because Fee refused to use Daddy's private bathroom and instead insisted Teri take her to the ladies room at the end of the corridor where she thought it was a hoot to waggle her wet fingers under the warm wind of the hand dryer. This was, in her eyes, a far superior experience to using the coarse paper towels which were all that was on offer in Daddy's facility.

Teri was chalk-white when they returned, and there was a large wet stain on one of her shoes. I think there might have been a slight falling out because Fee ran straight to her mother and, from the safety of her knee, stuck her tongue out.

'What happened?'

'What didn't!' Teri shuddered. 'I thought you were coming to rescue me?'

'Sorry.' I tried to look penitent but I don't think I succeeded too well because Teri scowled.

'Yes, well…' She was breathing more easily now. 'First she made me kneel on the floor and hold her hands.'

I nodded. 'She likes a bit of encouragement.'

'A bit? Since when did you become queen of the understatement?'

I grinned. 'Go on…'

'Then I had to put my hands on the top of her head…'

'…and help push the poo out?'

'You've done it before? Why didn't you warn me? I thought you were my friend?'

I shook my head. 'I wish I'd been a fly on the wall.'

'I wish you had too. I'd have swatted you with the toilet roll. Did you know I'd have to wipe her bottom?'

'For goodness sake, Teri. She's barely out of nappies. Of course, she needs help to clean herself up.'

'I didn't know. At least not until she hopped off the loo, and dribbled all over my left foot' – ah! The water mark – 'and presented her bottom as if she were a randy bloody monkey.'

What a beautiful picture.

'Don't you dare laugh,' she ordered.

Too late.

She pulled a sulky face and then allowed a small smile to steal across her face. 'I suppose it is a bit funny,' she conceded.

Personally, I thought it was bloody hilarious.

It was the start of a slightly surreal day. The kids had been a little hyper when they first rocked up at the hospice each clutching their favourite Santa toy – in Ritchie's case a radio-controlled car with flashing lights and an ear-shatteringly loud beeper – but they calmed down after Victoria took them for a run around the gardens. And, once Mammy confiscated Ritchie's new wheels, the rest of us were able to relax. I wished she'd also taken possession of Fee's new doll, which had wide, staring eyes and a disturbingly demonic grin. Fee seemed to like it, but the doll freaked me out.

Victoria grumped a little when she realised we weren't exchanging family presents until after dinner. Dan had bought her a new mobile phone, and she was itching to get her fingers on it.

'Why do we have to wait?' she wailed.

'It gets the after-dinner washing-up done quicker,' I explained.

'How?'

'We're not allowed to open the presents until the plates and pots have been washed and tidied away. Everyone mucks in to help.'

'Except me,' Mammy butted in. 'I've done the cooking so I put my feet up and watch the Queen's speech on the television.'

Probably the reason why the rest of us preferred to be dealing with the dirty dishes.

'But, you're not doing the cooking, and we're not doing the washing up.'

True, but…

'Or are we?' Victoria added, blanching at the thought of the mountain of crockery that would be needed to serve today's one hundred-or-so guests.

'Surely they use dishwashers?' Teri splayed her manicured fingernails. It had been some time since *they'd* been immersed in soap suds.

But at least she and Victoria agreed on something.

I think they were also in agreement on the awfulness of Christmas Mass, which had to be moved from the chapel into the cafeteria to accommodate the larger than usual congregation. It was an unfortunate change of venue, because the serving hatch separating us from the kitchen was only partially closed so we could follow the progress of dinner from chef's clattering and banging and the ever-stronger smell of Brussels sprouts and pigs in blankets.

Not that the priest allowed himself to be distracted. He was the sort of high-church celebrant who, given his choice, which, mercifully, he wasn't, would have conducted the entire service in Latin. Instead, he compromised by entering in a puff of incense, followed by a column of altar servers, accompanied by every bloody verse of 'Oh Come all You Faithful'.

I particularly hate hymns with a chorus.

It got worse, long, long, long before it got better. We sang everything that could be sung – the Kyrie eleison, the Gloria, the Sanctus, every bit of the Eucharistic Prayer that had ever been set to music and Christmas hymns at every pause in between. It wouldn't have been quite so bad if the congregation had sung in tune. Dan, in particular, made an especially awful racket. I'd always thought he had a halfway decent voice, but that was when his efforts were accompanied by a shower of hot water. Without the benefit of soap and a sponge he was distinctly off-key.

Teri covered her face with her hands. Was she praying? Probably. I know I was. Please God, shut him up. Nope, she was laughing silently.

'Oh dear,' she whispered. 'A lifetime of Sundays standing shoulder-to-shoulder while he belts out the Gloria.'

I shook my head. 'This is his first and last Mass with me.'

Teri patted my hand consolingly. 'Sorry, dear, he's loving the theatre of it all. You've got a convert there.'

And they say God works in mysterious ways.

Mass finally over, it was all hands to the deck to re-dress the dining room in its rightful clothes. Dinner was…well, I think you really have to like turkey and pigs in blankets and Brussels sprouts to properly enjoy Christmas dinner. And Teri lied: she didn't eat my sprouts.

CHAPTER 91

TERI

I had doubts about attending the Harper Hospice Christmas Event. I mean, Dan and his devil child would be there, to say nothing of the whole Harper clan with an emaciated and sickly man attached by a perilous cannula to an oppressive-looking, overhead drip as the centrepiece. I considered ringing Lee to say I wasn't coming, but she'd be disappointed and, to be honest, she needed cheering up, and I'd be the only one there who could do that.

After a glass of wine in the bath – well, it was Christmas morning – I decided I should do her a favour and go. I chose a red cocktail dress and matching red, suede shoes to appear festive, even if I didn't feel it, and made my entrance.

They were all there. I noticed Dan first, sitting at the far end of the room with a newspaper open – although where he got a paper on Christmas Day is beyond me. It was probably yesterday's. He looked up and gave a tight-lipped smile and nod of the head. Yes, and a very happy Christmas to you too, I thought.

Mrs Harper was sitting next to him, watching a small crowd, which included Lee and the devil child, gathered around Mr Harper's bed. They were placing things on the lemon coverlet under which his thin body seemed to have shrunk even further. Odd, but presumably some Harper Christmas ritual.

Lee peeled away from the group and came over to give me a hug and was followed by her sister's boy who stared at my shoes and made some crude remark about me falling over. Stupid child.

Victoria turned and stretched her mouth into a forced smile. She was wearing the same red dress she'd had on for her first date with Shayne

Brickham. Obviously been unable to con her father out of money for a new frock.

After the hellos and seasonal greetings, which included Dan – reluctantly – Fliss and her husband –enthusiastically – coming over to give me a kiss, I realised the smallest kid was approaching. Small children are like cats in that they know when you don't like them and make a beeline for you. I hate cats.

It turned out that for no other reason than she liked the colour red, the kid decided my red dress was the one she wanted to sit on. I wondered briefly whether she had a nappy on and whether it was safe to have her on my knee.

My plan to bounce the kid up and down until she felt sick and had to get off failed. 'Do it again!' the creature screamed. I spotted Dan watching with a sardonic grin on his face.

My philosophy on life is that if things *can* get worse, they generally do. And they got worse for me when the wretched child announced she wanted to go to the lavatory – and I was the one to take her. For goodness' sake. What do these mothers teach their brats? You can't bring a child up to ask a total stranger to take her to the toilet. I know I wasn't a total stranger; I'd met these two kids before when I'd been at Lee's and Fliss had brought them round, deluding herself that Lee's friends were somehow interested in Lee's nephews and nieces. Which I wasn't.

And then things got worse. The child didn't want to use Mr Harper's en-suite, which would have been the sensible option given the proximity of the type of people, i.e. the parents, who could help if the situation started getting out of hand. No, the child wanted to wander down the corridor to a Ladies' where she washed her hands and dried them under the hot air dryer TWICE BEFORE going into the cubicle.

Once inside, she refused to shut the door, leaving it wide open while she struggled to climb onto the seat. I had to lift her and plonk her down. Then the instructions started: kneel down, hold hands, put hands on top of head, and push.

When she'd successfully evacuated the contents of her bowel, she hopped off the toilet seat and artfully dribbled over my left red, suede shoe. How did she do that? How did she pee after pooing?

'You stupid child,' I snapped. 'Look what you've done.'

She regarded me. Unused to grown-ups shouting at her, she was unsure whether to be frightened or defiant. 'Couldn't help it,' she mumbled.

'Well, it's time you tried,' I said.

But instead of trying anything, she turned and invited me to wipe her backside.

'And you shouldn't get cross,' she said, folding her arms and stamping a foot as I reluctantly grabbed a load of toilet tissue. 'Santa doesn't like little girls who get cross.'

'And that's a load of rubbish,' I said, trying to clean the girl up without getting too close. 'Who told you that? A man, I expect. Men always make up stories to make girls behave the way they want them to.'

'Santa's not rubbish and he's not a made-up story,' she said, quietly ignoring the feminist points I'd been trying to make.

'Huh!' And before I could stop myself, added quietly, 'And if you believe in Santa, you're an idiot.'

I hadn't expected her to hear that last bit, but, of course, she had. She turned to face me with as much indignation as a toddler could gather and shouted, 'I'm not an idiot and I do believe in Santa. SO THERE.'

With some dignity, which was impressive given the circumstances, she hoicked up her knickers, said she was going to tell Mummy of me, and stomped off towards the door of the Ladies' and waited while I straightened up and moved over to open it for her.

Back in the room, the kid went straight for its mother but, to give her some credit, she didn't drop me in it. Dan looked at me, then at the child, and back to me and twitched his newspaper up in front of his face. I swear he was laughing behind it. I motioned to Lee to come to the far end of the room and told her that if she ever put me in that situation again, it would be the last she'd see of me. She seemed to consider the prospect.

The rest of Christmas Day was taken up with the devil child whining about wanting her present NOW while the other two had theirs taken off them for making too much racket.

The Mass was a melange of noise from the hymn singing, the priest's intonations and the clattering of the kitchen staff in the next room getting turkey and all the trimmings ready.

All I could think about was getting through this – and getting on with whatever lay ahead in the New Year. Surely I was due some seasonal cheer?

CHAPTER 92

TERI

'Do you know someone called Peter Danvers?'
Dad didn't bother with any preliminaries such as 'Hello, Teri, it's your dad here…you know, the dad who never bothers to ring you unless it's bad news about the factory going bust…'

Nor did he bother with 'Hello, Teri, did you have a nice Christmas?'

Which is a shame because I could've told him I'd NEVER had a nice Christmas, thanks largely to him dispensing season's greetings at the pub and my useless mother spending hers getting blotto on the cooking sherry and taking to her bed to weep while the turkey burned.

Charlie and I would stay in our rooms playing with whatever expensive toys we'd been bought by Mr and Mrs Meyer as an alternative to good parenting until the housekeeper – who tended to pop in to check we were still alive – called us to eat whatever she'd been able to salvage from the charred festive trimmings.

No, my father simply dialled my number – out of the blue, two weeks after Christmas – and asked if I knew someone called Peter Danvers.

'You sound like a detective,' I said.

'Yeah. The detective who rang me sounded like a detective too,' Dad said.

'The detective?'

'Yeah, from the fraud squad.'

'Fraud squad?'

'Stop bloody repeating everything I say.' Dad sounded impatient. 'Apparently, this Peter Danvers says he knows you.'

'Me?'

'According to the fraud chap, yes. This Danvers person is some sort of petty crook, and the police have been watching him for some time, and he got stopped at Calais last night with a boot-load of counterfeit stuff – perfume, jewellery, designer handbags…that sort of thing.'

My mind raced. Had I ever bought a fake designer bag? Surely not. I always buy the real thing.

'Anyway, some sort of deal was done because this Danvers is only small fry but he knows bigger fry.'

'But where do I come into it?'

'Danvers says he knows you and that you're looking for Edward Pranks. And Edward Pranks is, apparently, bigger fry.'

'My God! I honestly have not been looking for Edward Pranks – and I certainly don't know anyone called Danvers.' I thought for a moment.

Then a mental light flicked on.

'Oh. Hang on.' I took some deep breaths to calm myself. 'Peter Danvers? Pete Danvers. Yes. I've heard that name recently. It was Jim, talking in Portly & Groops. Jim got out a notebook and looked something up – and then said something like, "Pete Danvers. He'll do…"'

'Well, whatever he's done, he's done good. He's put the fraud squad in touch with our Pranksy.'

'Wha…? You mean, they've caught him?'

'Not yet, but it's only a matter of time,' Dad said. 'The detective didn't go into too much detail, but this Danvers chap has given them an address in southern Spain where Pranksy is living. But he reckons Pranksy is due a visit back to Blighty any day soon – his mum's dying – and they'll be able to nab him as he steps off the ferry. With any luck, they can freeze his accounts, and although I doubt we'll get everything back, it should be a good chunk of what he stole from us.'

CHAPTER 93

LEE

I don't want to damn Christmas with faint praise but, all things considered, it wasn't as bad as I'd thought it might be. Unfortunately, things went downhill afterwards. While Daddy got steadily weaker, Victoria was living up to her devil-child moniker and Dan was tying himself up in knots trying to put a dampener on the Brickham romance which, despite his best efforts, continued to blossom. He'd been forced to temper his initial nineteenth-century 'hands-off my daughter' stance because, by now – Richard's orders – the Jukes hotshot had become a Ridings Today rent-a-quote. At least a couple of times a week he'd join Dan on the news sofa to express his opinion about whichever soccer non-event was making the headlines.

'Don't do the interviews,' I urged when Dan came home – again – fuming about the latest bon mots from 'thick-as-a-brick Brickham'.

Dan looked at me as if I was a couple of sandwiches short of a picnic. 'And let Finlay do them?'

No, that would never do. Instead, Dan gritted his teeth, chatted to Shayne as if he thought he was a soccer pundit par excellence and demonstrated a skill for acting that in different circumstances might have qualified for an Oscar nomination.

I don't think Shayne, who had adopted the local habit of referring to Victoria as 'our lass', deliberately set out to wind him up but he certainly succeeded. 'Aye up, mate,' he'd greet Dan, slapping him on the back with the sort of joviality that went down a treat when he was buying post-match drinks in the members-only bar at the Jukes stadium, but didn't generate quite the same bonhomie on our doorstep.

'I'm not your bloody mate,' Dan would fulminate behind his back as he followed Shayne into the living room.

'Tell our lass, I'm here, will you?' he'd tell Dan.

'I'm not your bloody servant,' Dan would mutter on his way to the bottom of the stairs to bellow, 'Your date's here.'

And she's not your lass,' he'd add sotto voce, before asking, 'Can I get you a drink?'

A double-measure of rat poison, perhaps?

Personally, I thought Shayne was more-or-less harmless, although sprawled in an easy chair in the living room his legs seemed to occupy a disproportionate amount of space. He'd apologised quite nicely over the RTS mishap too. 'Don't usually touch stuff like that but, sometimes, you know, it's hard to unwind after a game,' he said as he waited for Victoria to put the finishing touches to her make-up.

No, we didn't know.

'Mr Walker'd be hopping mad if he found out.'

I thought he might be rather more than hopping mad.

'Learnt my lesson though. I'm clean from now onwards.'

Not entirely sure I believed him. Dan definitely didn't.

'So, you won't say anything to Mr Walker?'

Now that's what I didn't understand. I couldn't care less whether he smoked dope or not, but if Dan wanted him playing the field elsewhere, why on earth didn't he have a quiet word with Richard as he'd first planned to do? 'What, and have Victoria screaming at me?'

I don't know why that bothered him. Victoria was always screaming at him about one thing or another.

'Or have every Jukes fan in the county screaming for my blood?'

Why? Wasn't him who'd sold Shayne the drugs.

'And have Richard screaming at me when the loss of his best goal scorer means the Jukes slump to the bottom of the league?'

Seemed he was in a no-win situation.

That didn't mean he was reconciled to the relationship; just hadn't worked out yet how to terminate it without terminating his relationship with his daughter.

Victoria's mother didn't help much. She'd welcomed Shayne with open arms. 'Such a good-looking young man,' she'd cooed. 'And so talented.'

And rich too.

Mind you, her relationship with Victoria wasn't exactly hunky-dory either. 'It's not nice when your mother flirts with your boyfriend,' Victoria told me.

I could imagine.

'And she goes all giggly and silly when he's around.'

Just like her daughter?

'And she's always finding excuses to come into the room when we're alone together.'

Didn't seem to occur to Victoria her mother might simply be checking up on her.

'And it's embarrassing the way she insists on watching TV with us.'

What's embarrassing about that?

'She sits real close and keeps putting a hand on his thigh and running her fingers up and down his leg.'

Yeuch!

So Victoria and Shayne kept popping over to our house and, somehow, we lumbered through the holiday season and into January and Victoria's mock A-level exams and her results – which, I guess you could say were commensurate with the amount of effort she'd put into them.

Dan waved the results paper under her nose. 'What do you expect when you spend more time partying than you do studying?'

'I did loads of revision!'

'When? I never saw you revising.'

'That doesn't mean I didn't do any.'

He slapped the report on the table. 'Well, you can't have done it properly. Look at those grades. Two Ds and a C. Those aren't the marks of someone who revised thoroughly.'

'The right questions didn't come up.'

'You need to revise more than two bloody questions,' he shouted.

She burst into loud sobs.

'There's no point crying,' he yelled. 'Do some bloody revision.' And he pointed theatrically upstairs.

'What? Now? It's months until the next exams.'

'I don't sodding care.'

She looked at him at with the sort of loathing I usually reserve for a glass of curdled milk.

'And if you think you're going out tonight you can just think again.'

Oh great! Friday night supper with a moody teenage brat. Just what the doctor ordered.

'You can't stop me, I'll go back to Mum's house. She understands me.'

That wasn't the impression I'd got the last time I'd spoken to her mother. 'I don't think I'm cut out to be the mother of a teenage girl,' Sara had moaned. 'It's nothing but me, me, me –'

I thought at first she was talking about herself.

'Always wanting more.'

She *was* talking about herself; she was forever demanding extra money from Dan to cover this or that unexpected expenditure.

'And the tantrums if she doesn't get her own way.'

I was thoroughly confused. Tory's angry spats were insignificant spittles of rage compared to Sara's mega outbursts when Dan refused to bankroll her latest fashion fad.

'A handbag!' he'd exploded when she'd requested a top-up to cover the cost of the new designer tote she'd bought as a treat 'because I was feeling a little down, darling'.

'It would be cheaper to buy my way into heaven.'

Technically, I thought he was probably wrong – Jesus had expressly pointed out the impossibility of buying a place in the clouds – but it didn't alter his conviction that if he didn't save his daughter from going to hell in a handcart no-one else would.

'She's a teenager in her last year at high school,' I reminded him.

'And?'

'It's a stressful time.'

'Tell her to get rid of that good-for-nothing boyfriend. That'll ease the stress.'

It was like talking to a brick wall.

So, between her mother and her father, Victoria was stuck between a rock and a hard place with neither of them prepared to cut her even a smidgeon of slack.

'You don't understand,' Dan said when I tried to broker a truce between them. 'I'm not saying you don't care about Victoria, but you'd feel differently if she was your child.'

Ouch! Any more tactless comments like that and he'd be joining Victoria in the doghouse.

But Dan was worrying unnecessarily on at least one front and, given how much he complained about tripping over Shayne every time he turned around, you'd have expected him to notice he hadn't tripped for at least a couple of weeks.

Yes, Shayne was history and had been since mock-exam Friday. He'd been quite philosophical when Victoria telephoned to tell him her ogre of a father had grounded her until further notice. 'No worries, babe,' he said. 'I'll see you when you're let out on parole.'

He might have been joking, but Victoria wasn't amused and she was downright furious after photos of him appeared in the Evening Leader with his arm draped around the shoulders of a pretty blonde in a tight, red dress.

'She looks a bit like you,' I said, when Victoria showed me the paper's double-page spread. 'Except for the hair.'

'Is that supposed to make me feel better?'

Probably not.

She begged me not to say anything to Dan, or her mother. 'Mum'll tell me I'm stupid to dump him for something so trivial, and Dad'll just say it serves me right.'

I couldn't speak for Sara but Dan, I thought, was more likely to smack the two-timing, worthless so-and-so into the middle of next week. Not a good idea. Duck's Arse had only just forgiven him for the fracas at L'homme-vert. Another punch-up, especially one involving his team's top player, would go down like a lead balloon.

'Even if I don't tell your mum and dad, they're bound to find out sooner or later,' I said.

'I know but I'd rather pick my moment.'

'But won't they wonder when you stop going out?'

'I haven't stopped going out.'

'Oh?'

No, she and her best friend Laura were having a great time painting the town red. 'We don't do anything really naughty,' she said. 'But sometimes not having a boyfriend can be quite fun.'

Clearly, she wasn't as broken-hearted as I'd first thought.

Except now, a couple of weeks later, she was crying buckets. 'I've missed a period,' she wailed.

Shit!

CHAPTER 94

TERI

My fingers shook, and I couldn't quite catch my breath as I put the phone down on Dad and rang the Ridings Today studio. The shock of my father's news coupled with how nervous I felt about ringing Duck's Arse – er, Richard Walker – was almost too much to bear.

I asked to be put through to Richard Walker and darling D'reen answered. 'Oh, hi, Teri,' she said. 'He's in a meeting.'

'Please, D'reen. Get him out. I must speak to him. It's desperately urgent.'

'Hey, Teri. What's the problem?'

'It's life or death, D'reen. Please, please…'

'Hang on,' she said. For a moment I could hear a tapping noise in the distance as if someone was typing on a computer keyboard, then the sound became muffled as D'reen put her hand over the receiver.

The background noise unmuffled, and I heard Duck's Arse's voice. 'Put her through.'

So he hadn't been in a meeting at all; D'reen was obviously in his office and screening callers.

'Teri? Hello.' And there was that lovely plumply warm voice that I hadn't heard since he'd nearly burned his buttocks over a hotel kettle and catering tea bags. 'I've been hoping you'd ring.'

He'd been hoping I'd ring! Why hadn't he bothered ringing me?

I was about to make some indignant comment, but something strange was going on. A surge of warmth ran through my chest and down into my tummy. It wasn't a panic attack; it was a lovely, cosy feeling, and, however breathless I'd felt before, the feeling intensified. Bloody hell, I thought, I'm behaving like a love-sick teenager. That, or I've been transported into a Mills & Boon novel.

'Richard,' I managed.

'You sound out of breath,' Richard said.

'No, no. I just…' What in God's name was wrong with me? 'I just wanted to talk to Jim.'

'Oh bugger,' he replied. 'There was I thinking you'd rung to talk to me.'

'Well, yes. And no. I need to speak to Jim to thank him.'

'Ah, you've found out then?'

'You know about it?'

'Of course I do,' Richard said. His voice was flat and reasoned as though it was obvious he knew about everything.

'Are you behind this as well?'

'I'm not behind anything,' Richard said, his tone heavy and serious. And then his voice lightened. 'I like to think of myself in front all the time.' And he laughed, then went on, 'Now, you and I need to talk properly. I'm tied up here for the next couple of days, but meet me at the King's on Friday at six and you can tell me what you've been up to. See you then.'

And the smug bastard put the phone down.

CHAPTER 95

LEE

Marvellous. It wasn't even the end of January, and I had headless chickens chasing headless chickens. The daily meetings with Dom were still topping and tailing my days, although, increasingly, Dom and I cut out the middle man and left Daddy out of the decision-making. Most of the time he was so woozy with morphine, he barely knew what day of the week it was.

You didn't need a medical degree to know he was slowly slipping away from us.

But there was no time for melancholy, not with thirty-six final-year dissertation proposals taking root on my desk alongside forty-nine essays from second-year students exploring alternative forms of narrative, all of which should have been marked last week.

But weren't, and probably wouldn't be marked next week either.

In addition, Peter was chasing a three-thousand word contribution to a faculty report he was putting together on the impact of deadlines on the mental well-being of students. Judging by the quality of the essays I was marking, students would fret less about deadlines if they actually took the trouble to read the set texts. But, I suspect that wasn't the response Peter required.

And Teri wanted a 'proper' chat – what's that when it's at home? Bloody hell, we're always chatting, she's on the phone every day checking on Daddy or ringing to let me know she's visited and 'no change'. I bloody know there's no change; he's my father, after all, and I've practically taken up tenancy rights at the hospice. *I'll* call *you* if there's any change!

And, as if Teri and her 'chats' weren't enough, I'd also got to work out how and when to tell Dan his darling daughter was up the duff with the bastard spawn of a randy footballer.

'Couldn't you have timed this all a bit better?' I asked God one evening as Daddy dozed intermittently.

'Nothing to do with me,' God replied. 'Free will and all that jazz.'

How flippant.

'Really?' I queried. 'And here was me thinking you pulled all the strings.'

'No need to be sarcastic,' he said.

'Well, it would make it easier on the rest of us if –'

'Stop whining,' he ordered. 'You could get some marking done while your father's asleep.'

He's always got to have the last word.

So, I didn't tap dance with enthusiasm when I got a call from Deidre O'Connell from the Association of English Educators, trying to add to my to-do list. She's a nice enough woman, but she lives and breathes the AEE and I can't say I felt particularly interested in her tale of woe. So what if they were having trouble spending a thirty-thousand-pound research bursary? They should be so lucky.

'About Teri Meyer,' Deidre said.

'What about her?'

'We've asked her to resubmit an application she made a couple of years ago.'

What had that got to do with me?

'You were named as a referee on the original application.'

Oh, yes? First I'd heard of it.

'I was?'

'Yes,' Deidre said. 'We're hoping to fast track the application and hoped you'd be able to supply a reference post haste.'

Cheeky beggars.

I hesitated.

'It doesn't have to be very long,' Deidre coaxed. 'Just some lines on Ms Meyer's suitability, her academic track record, research background – you know the sort of thing.'

I did indeed.

'We wouldn't be looking for more than five hundred-or-so words.'

What? Five hundred words? Not even a spin doctor could spin Teri's research profile that far.

'Okay,' I said.

I've always liked a creative challenge.

And, it would take my mind off other things. Temporarily, at least.

CHAPTER 96

TERI

The phone rang in the hallway. I was getting used to the landline; perhaps I wouldn't bother getting another mobile. The freedom of not having to check a Smartphone every two minutes, looking for texts, Twitter, Instagram and inane Facebook messages.

But the landline doesn't have caller display, which is a drawback. And I wouldn't have answered it if the caller's name had flashed up.

'Hi, Teri. It's me.' The 'me' was Declan.

'Oh, for God's sake, Declan. What do you want now?'

'Is that any way to talk to the love of your life?'

'Look, Declan. Get this into your thick, stupid head. YOU ARE NOT THE LOVE OF MY LIFE. YOU ARE PROBABLY NOT THE LOVE OF ANYONE'S LIFE. PROBABLY NOT EVEN THAT BEACHED WHALE OF A WIFE OF YOURS. PLEASE PISS OFF AND LEAVE ME ALONE.'

And I slammed the phone down. That's the other positive that landlines have over mobiles. Slam a mobile down and it'll probably break. A landline, however, is much more resilient.

The phone rang again almost instantly. I snatched it up and shouted, 'What don't you understand about Fuck Off?'

'Oh,' a woman's voice said at the other end. 'I think I must have the wrong number.'

'Yes, you must,' I snapped. 'You can fuck off too.'

Damn unsolicited calls.

I turned to go back into the sitting room. The phone rang again. Something made me hesitate. Declan couldn't be so thick-headed as to try again, surely?

I picked up the receiver cautiously and, disguising my voice, said, 'Hello, Teri Meyer here. How can I help?'

'It's Deirdre O'Connell from the Association of English Educators,' the woman said, who, just seconds ago, I'd told to 'Fuck off'. Please, please, don't let her recognise my voice.

'Oh, hello,' I said, bright, friendly, interested, certainly not in a 'Fuck off' way.

'Did your phone ring a couple of minutes ago?' Deidre asked.

'My phone? No. I don't think so. No.' Please, please, let her believe me.

'My mistake,' Deirdre said, briskly. 'Must have rung the wrong number. Anyway,' she went on, business-like, 'we've a proposition for you.'

Me? A proposition? The Association of English Educators?

'Two years ago you applied for an AEE bursary.'

'Yes, I remember.' Of course I did. A grant was up for grabs for a researcher to produce an academic volume on an historical character from the Renaissance period. There had been some small print about why that particular period had been chosen, but I'd ignored that and decided that my old Lord Rochester would be in for a chance at the trophy. And best of all, the grant was worth thirty thousand pounds.

'Well, I shouldn't say this, but the researcher who won the grant has let us down,' Deidre said.

'Oh dear.'

'And we're looking to start the process again.'

'Oh really?'

'We were looking again at your application —'

'You kept it on file?'

'Well, yes, of course. It was very impressive. Lord Rochester is an interesting subject...'

You can say that again, especially if you find sodomy, buggery, incest and general licentiousness interesting.

'...and we wondered whether you would care to resubmit your application so we could consider it again in light of the current circumstances.'

I thought about the box file in the sitting room in which the Earl of Rochester had been lying in wait to leap into the book I'd tried to start writing.

'I remember you wanted eighty thousand words?' I said, doing a mental calculation and adding up the number of words from my MA dissertation and my attempt at a book.

'Yes. We need it that length with a view to publishing.'

Publishing. Oh my.

Ah, there was one problem.

'I remember one of the requisites was that the applicant had to be working in higher education?'

'Well, yes. Of course. We can't accept works of this length and magnitude from just anybody. They must have an academic track record; we must be assured they can negotiate the textual context and deliver a thesis to the standards required.'

She was beginning to sound like Peter Heron.

'Why?' she added. 'You are still working in academia?'

'Yes, of course.'

'And where are you working now?'

'Oh…the University of West Riding…' Well, okay, I would be very shortly, albeit in a student-mollycoddling role, but, hey ho.

'Well, put it all in the application,' Deirdre went on. 'The form's on the website. We'll look forward to hearing from you.'

I had to ring Lee. It was more important than ever that she gave me a good reference for that damn job. Thirty thousand pounds was at stake.

CHAPTER 97

LEE

Daddy was going downhill rapidly. The morphine was killing the pain – and him too. He was sleeping more and more, and half the time he didn't know whether any of us were there or not. Except for Mammy. He tossed and turned painfully if she wasn't close by so she'd hardly been home since Christmas. Fliss and I brought her clean clothes and picked up the mail and watered the house plants. It wasn't much, but it was the best we could offer.

A couple of times I stood guard while she sneaked a quick shower in Daddy's bathroom. Strictly speaking she wasn't supposed to use the facilities – patients only – but the staff turned a blind eye so long as we weren't too blatant about it.

Fliss and I spent as much time as we could with her but, inevitably, she sat in that hateful room for hours on end, hands clasped around her rosary beads, with only her thoughts for company. Not for one moment did her faith in God waver. Me? I sometimes thought I hated him. And everybody else who thought they could cheer me up with inane comments such as 'he's had a good innings' or 'we've all got to go sometime'. Thank you very much, but I'd rather he didn't go just yet.

'And I bet you won't think seventy-two is a good innings when you hit seventy-one,' I told Dan who'd been daft enough to voice that particular piece of idiocy.

'No, but –'

Exactly!

But, and here's why I couldn't bear it when people tried to put the end into perspective, sometimes the tension of waiting for 'THE END' was so unbearable I almost wished it would come so we could get it over and done with and let the real hurting begin.

It was a wobbly time – understatement of the year – and the Victoria question added to the worry. Much against my better judgement I'd agreed to say nothing to either Dan or Sara just yet. Victoria said she wanted to consider her options first; she didn't say 'I'm thinking about getting rid of the baby so they never need to know'. But that's what she meant.

I wondered about ringing Teri. She'd organised my abortion – maybe that would be the best solution this time too?

I was mulling over that one when my mobile rang. Probably Teri, but of course, I couldn't find the phone which was buried in the bottom of my bag, and I didn't know for sure it was only Teri and I almost sobbed thinking it would go to voicemail before I could find it and Mammy would think I wasn't waiting and ready to rush to be by her side and…oh, the relief when I found the phone, saw Teri's number in the caller box and Teri said 'Hello'. She sounded a bit brusque but who cared? It wasn't Mammy, and Daddy wasn't dead – yet.

'Hello,' I croaked.

'Just ringing to see how your father is.'

Dying, I thought. But that was a bit too blunt. 'Not so good.'

'Is this a bad time to call?'

'No, no. It's good to hear from you.' It wasn't. God knows what she wanted to chat about – and it was to be hoped he cared because right now I didn't. I had enough on my plate and, even if I hadn't, my mind was on the other side of town, wondering what was happening there and was Mammy trying to ring and why wouldn't Teri get off the bloody phone and leave the line free? It was clear Daddy wouldn't be around much longer. And I was desperate not to miss the goodbyes.

I'm afraid I might have been a bit abrupt, possibly even rude, to Teri. Hell, be honest. I was downright rude, but I couldn't be bothered wasting time on small talk. I may, or may not, have reassured her about the job reference – can't remember. I don't think she mentioned the bursary. She'd probably forgotten she'd used my name in vain for that application too.

Was it her idea to meet up on Saturday? Or mine? Again, my mind was a blank. But the date was barely agreed, and she was still chirruping on about something and nothing when I put the phone down. Cutting her off mid-call was getting to be a habit, and one I needed to break otherwise our friendship would be irredeemably broken.

CHAPTER 98

TERI

It wasn't entirely appropriate for me to visit the hospice every day – I knew Lee was down there with her mother and sister, and I didn't want to get in the way. It had been good having some private time with Mr Harper – and in a funny sort of way, Christmas had been good too.

But I'd ring Lee most days mainly to check how she was doing.

And of course, once I'd heard from Deirdre O'Connell, I couldn't wait to tell her she was going to have to give me a damn good reference for the university job now that my Rochester research grant rested on it.

I took a deep breath and dialled her number.

The phone rang several times before she picked up. 'Hello?' she said, her voice tentative and wobbly.

'How's things?' I asked. 'How's your dad?'

'Oh. He's…' She sounded tearful. 'He's not so good today…'

'Oh, Lee. I'm sorry. Do you want me to come round?'

'No, it's okay.'

'Look, Lee,' I said. 'The reason for my call – as well as to ask about your dad, of course – I was wondering about that reference you were doing for me? I've tried ringing Vic Brennan, but he's not back at university yet. You academics get long holidays.'

She was silent for a moment.

'Hello?' I said, wondering if she'd not heard.

'Yes, I'm here.' She sounded a little impatient. 'I spoke to Vic before the Christmas break, if that's what you mean.'

'Oh, good. A lot's resting on me getting this job. I've got the chance of a –'

'Teri. Sorry to cut you off, but I'm not in the mood to talk right now. Can we meet later? Look, Dan's going off for the day with Victoria on Saturday – I'm not going with them. Why don't you come round and we can have a proper chat?'

'Oh, he's still doing the brat bonding?'

'Oh, don't be like that, Teri. See you Saturday?'

'Yes. Okay then. Saturday.'

But before I could think about re-bonding with someone who was my oldest and best friend – despite her stealing my ex – I had Friday night to look forward to.

****

I planned to spend the whole of Friday getting ready. Whatever Duck's Arse wanted to tell me, I had to be looking my best.

I booked in at Vanilla Pod, and Sasha went to work with her Luxury Radiance Facial and Express Spa Manicure.

I was glowing by the time I returned to the duplex – and found I'd got visitors.

I hadn't recognised the four-by-four in the parking bay next to mine, but as I stepped out of the lift on my floor, there they were: Charlie and Denis. And Andrew. Grinning like idiots.

'Surprise, sis.' Charlie laughed coming over to plant a kiss on my cheek. Denis felt he had to kiss me too and then Andrew loomed, gorgeous and god-like and, even though I turned to offer him a cheek, he nudged my chin with his fingers so that his lips landed on mine. He winked and grinned.

'What are you boys doing here?' was all I could manage as they danced and chattered around me. 'Wait, wait,' I instructed, pushing Charlie aside so I could get my key in the lock. 'Tell me all. Inside.'

Charlie and Denis were on their way to Harrogate where Denis was representing his Norfolk and Suffolk Allotment lot at some event or other. Denis was on expenses, and he and Charlie were booked into one of the town's smartest hotels.

Andrew had come along for the ride as he'd never been to this part of Yorkshire but had arranged to meet up with some sheep farmers in Swaledale on Sunday. Meanwhile, could he bunk down in my spare room?

Denis was almost wetting himself, sitting with his arms hugging his knees as Andrew's request unfolded. Charlie stared out of the window.

'I can't afford Harrogate's hotel prices,' Andrew reasoned. 'But if it's a problem, I could find a little B&B.'

I thought of Andrew, in my spare room, his gorgeous and god-like frame folded into the single bed while I lay in the next room in a king-size De Luxe, and I knew where we'd both end up. And I knew how wonderful it would be.

And didn't I deserve a little wonderfulness after another lonely Christmas?

It would mean postponing my meeting with Duck's Arse at the King's tonight. But then what had he got in mind?

Was it a meeting? Was he planning to bring me up-to-date with the Edward Pranks investigation?

Was it a date? And if it was a date, would it be a case of soft, cuddly sex and then he disappears back to his wife, whoever or wherever she might be?

Let's face it, Duck's Arse hadn't bothered to get in touch; too busy swanning around the Far East. And it sounded as though it was Jim who'd done all the investigative work into Edward Pranks' whereabouts.

No, Duck's Arse and his intentions would have to wait. I'd ring D'reen and get her to tell him I was busy.

I turned to Andrew and looked directly into his gorgeous and god-like face.

I must have stepped out of my body for a moment, because I heard someone who looked like me, sounded like me saying, 'No. Sorry, you'll have to find a little B&B.'

I don't know what was going on, but Lee would have been proud of me.

CHAPTER 99

LEE

I've learned a lot about myself over the last few weeks. First, I'm nowhere near as tolerant as I used to think, because one of these days I'll kill Dan if he doesn't remember to raise the toilet seat.

Two, I'm good at keeping secrets. Once upon a time I'd have blabbed Victoria's news to all and sundry – well, Teri, at least – almost before the pregnancy testing kit had delivered a positive result. Now there's a thought: has she actually *taken* a pregnancy test, or is she getting her knickers in a twist just because she's a few days late? Why didn't I ask?

Three, I'm not as dependent on Teri as I used to be. I wouldn't swap her as a best mate, but Dan – despite his disgusting toilet habits – has nudged ahead in the pecking order.

And, finally, I'm really rather shallow – not quite in Teri's league but much closer than I'd have believed possible.

How do I know? What's the evidence?

Let's start with the weighing scales, or rather let's not start with them since I don't own any. But I know I've lost weight since Daddy became ill because all my clothes are hanging better. At least half-a-dress size better, and if things carry on as they are, before the month is out, I'll be a whole dress size smaller. And, in spite of everything, I take enormous pleasure in this.

Dan, of course, has noticed the incredible shrinking Lee and is worried. He thinks I need to take care of myself – why? If Daddy's got to die I'll take whatever positives I can from it.

Nevertheless, Dan keeps trying to come up with little ways to cheer me up – so far these have been confined to a surprise dinner at L'homme-vert – frankly the surprise was they let us over the threshold; a bouquet of flowers delivered to work – yes, encouraged by the success of his first bouquet he'd repeated the gesture with the Yorkshire equivalent of the Hanging Gardens of Babylon in a wicker basket; and, most recently, a trip to the theatre to see *Les Misérables*, currently on a nationwide tour. If I wasn't miserable before the show started I was certainly ready to slit my wrists long before the end. It was grim almost beyond belief.

However, having established I'm a cultural philistine, it seems Dan is branching out in other directions. I overheard him and Victoria conspiring in the hall the other day.

'I'd like to do something special,' Dan said.

Whisper, whisper, whisper.

High-pitched squeak from Victoria, quickly smothered. More whispering and a muffled laugh, again from Victoria. They came into the kitchen, looking smug and self-righteous, itching for me to ask 'What's up?' But, I decided to ignore them although I wasn't above dropping a few hints – an overnight stay at a good spa or tickets for a show I'd really like to see. *The Full Monty*, perhaps? Or *Mamma Mia*? Both of which were also on tour.

See, shallow. My daddy is dying and I'm consumed with material greed.

Anyway, they took themselves out for the day on what was clearly a dress rehearsal for the main event. This was a little worrying; you don't need a practice run for a spa visit. Or even to see *The Full Monty* or *Mamma Mia*. So what exactly were they planning? Well, if they're daft enough to think bungee jumping or white-water canoeing or abseiling would cheer me up, please God, they come home with a broken arm and a leg apiece.

Serve them bloody well right.

CHAPTER 100

TERI

The clock in Station Square, opposite the King's, struck six as I approached the hotel.

I didn't want to be early – don't want to seem keen – and I didn't want to arrive exactly on time. I wanted to keep him waiting.

My stomach fluttered, and not for the first time that day. Why was I feeling so nervous? Hell, why was I putting myself through this? I could, right now, be drinking cocktails in Harrogate's swankiest boutique hotel with Charlie, Denis and the gorgeous and god-like Andrew. And then gorgeous and god-like and I could be on our way back to my duplex…

No, Teri. Stop right there. This is where things change. You've got Duck's Arse waiting just beyond those doors with whatever proposition he has for you, and you have to find out what that proposition is.

Whatever it was that happened between you and Duck's Arse – in this very hotel two months ago – was something unlike anything else.

No, I didn't know what I was talking about, but I had never felt like this about anyone before. Me. Teri Meyer. Going gooey about a man.

What would Lee say? She'd say 'No' to Andrew. Definitely. But what would she say to Richard Walker?

Oh bugger it. I'm going in.

The last time I was in this bar, Lee and I had rowed. I can't remember what it was about, but I do remember her being sanctimonious and awkward about something.

Tonight the place was buzzing with Friday fizz drinkers; the after-work six-o-clockers who were still on an adrenalin rush from sitting at their computers all day checking their Facebook status and ordering from the on-line shopping sites.

I saw Duck's Arse sitting on a stool at the bar, half turned so that he could watch people coming in through the door from the foyer.

He saw me as soon as I stepped over the threshold. I've read in cheap chick lit books about hearts lurching and feeling breathless, but, bloody hell, my heart lurched and I couldn't get my breath. Was it a panic attack?

I took a deep breath, gave myself a mental shake, shifted the tote on to my shoulder and strode across the room.

Duck's Arse slid off his stool and came towards me with one arm extended.

I detected a change in him. Something different about the way he seemed; less arrogant, less powerful. He was tanned, which was nice; he'd lost a bit of weight, which was good.

Then I realised. The duck's arse had gone! The little tufts of hair that used to peak above his forehead were no more. The hair was flat and cut short.

In the time it took me to take all this in, he'd reached forward, placed his fingers under the tote straps and pulled it gently from my shoulder. I remembered that gentle touch, and I swear my legs wobbled. Get a grip, Teri.

He set the tote on the floor, held out both his hands, took hold of my arms and pulled me towards him the better to kiss me, first on one cheek and then the other.

A double kiss on the cheeks. Not passionate; a bit of an everyday greeting. Was this how he greeted all the women? Was this a business meeting? I mean, if it was a date, wouldn't he have kissed me on the lips?

'Hello, Teri,' he said, quietly and seriously and studying me.

Then, picking up the tote and handing it to me, he steered us both to a corner at the far end of the bar where a small table had a 'Reserved' sign on it. A bottle of Chablis sat in a cooler alongside two glasses.

'Hope you don't mind?' he said, indicating the wine. 'I seem to remember this is your tipple?'

He still hadn't smiled. Or said how gorgeous I looked. Or asked how I was.

Wine or not, this was obviously a business meeting. Bugger.

We sat. He took the wine and poured it into the glasses, nudging one across the table in my direction. He didn't speak, and I couldn't think of anything to say.

I took as large a glug as I dared without it looking as though I was desperate for a drink. He took a sip of his, looking at me over the top of his glass. He put it back down on the table, still looking, but still not smiling.

I couldn't bear this.

'Richard,' I began, 'I...'

But what? What did I want to say to him?

'No, hang on, Teri,' he said, holding up a hand to silence me. 'I've two things to tell you...no, three. Three things to tell you – and then, I promise you can say whatever you want.'

My heart thumped. I felt sick. I leaned forward for my glass and took another drink.

'First,' he said, 'the police have got Pranks.'

'Wha...?'

'They got him last night at Calais. The stupid bugger thought the border patrol would be so busy dealing with refugees and chasing illegals that he could slip through unnoticed. But they've got him on money laundering charges and seized his bank accounts.'

'That's fantastic –'

'Hang on, there's a long way to go yet. Pranks has got a long list of creditors and your dad will have to join the queue.'

'But...?'

'But he should get a sizeable chunk back.'

'Oh, God...thank you –'

'No, it's thanks to Jim. He got Danvers on the case. One thing I'd ask, though, is that you don't mention either Jim or Danvers during any interviews or dealings you have with the police or Fraud Office.'

'Of course. But –'

'The second thing,' Richard went on, ignoring me, 'is that when we last met' – he gave a little cough – 'I was...sort of...married.'

I sat up straighter.

'No, don't look at me like that,' he said. I hadn't realised how deeply

I was frowning. 'I've never had what you'd call a serious relationship…'

'Except for a sort of marriage,' I interjected.

He ignored my comment and went on. 'Sure, I've had girlfriends and I even lived with someone for a while. But nothing ever came of anything. That changed three years ago. I went to China – business trip. But I met a woman there and…well, it was like Las Vegas, I suppose. We both got very drunk and I…er…we…er…decided to get married.'

'What, there? In China?'

'Yup.'

'Was it a legal ceremony?'

'As far as I was concerned it was. Obviously there's a process you have to go through, but Chunhua – that's her name – knew what we had to do. I was able to download the authentication forms that I needed from a Chinese consulate website, and Chunhua organised the ceremony in her local admin office. It wasn't really a ceremony, more like fifteen minutes of signing forms…'

'But –'

'No, let me tell you. As soon as we came out of that office, Chunhua started to put pressure on me. She wanted to come back to Britain with me, but there's no automatic right for a foreign spouse to enter the UK.

'I had to come home, but there was no way I could bring her. I felt bad about it and promised her I'd do what I could, but on the plane coming home, I started to have doubts. Why had I let myself get so drunk? Why the hell had I married her? I know, I know. I'm an arsehole.'

'Did you tell anyone back here?' I asked, thinking that Dan had never mentioned Richard having a Chinese wife.

'No. Apart from Jim, I never told a soul. Too bloody embarrassed.'

'But did you keep in touch with her?'

'Oh yes. And I did try to get her over here, but we never seemed able to get the right paperwork in place. About six months later, I went back and this time she really did put the pressure on. She introduced me to her six brothers and insisted that I help them get to Britain too, and, at that stage, it all got a bit threatening and I knew I'd been had. She'd married me for one thing – and it wasn't my startling good looks.' He managed a weak smile. 'Anyway, I went back again last September – with Jim this time – without telling Chunhua we were coming. And we did some digging around.

'It turns out that Chunhua wasn't Chunhua but Chunhua's best friend, Chenguang. The woman I married had used her friend's documentation because she'd done this before – hitched up with a foreigner and tried to get to Britain. If she'd used her own documents – the hukou they call them – they'd have shown she was already married. How she thought she'd get away with it, I don't know. But poor sap, me, fell for it.'

'And is it sorted now?'

'Yes. I had to go to China on football club business immediately after I'd…er…last seen you. But I stayed on over Christmas to get the "marriage" annulled. It was tricky, not least because I had to avoid Chunhua – or whatever she calls herself – and her so-called brothers. God knows what they'd have done to me if they'd seen me. But thanks to the British consulate and a disapproving Chinese admin official, all the documentation was voided.'

'Does Chunhua – or whatever she's called – know what's happened?'

'Oh, I think the Chinese authorities will have been in touch with her. She'll know by now that she is no longer Mrs Walker – not that she ever was.'

He breathed out. At last, he seemed to relax, leaning back in his chair, looking at me.

'Well?' he said.

'Well what?'

'Well, do you forgive me?'

'For what?'

'Well, I wasn't exactly honest with you, and I had to leave fairly abruptly after our last encounter…'

I should have agreed and said, yes, that was rude. I should also have started firing a million questions. But I just looked back at him like someone gone soft in the head.

Richard was talking again. 'I had to leave that night because we'd got an important signing at the Jukes, and as chairman, I had to be there and couldn't get out of it, much as I wanted to. But'– he sighed and looked down –'I also thought I wasn't being fair to you. I needed to get my

Chinese shambles sorted out before I committed myself to anyone else.'

'Committed?'

'Yes, Teri. This is the third thing. I don't know how to say this other than to say it – and you can believe me or not. Whichever. But I'm in love with you. Have been since the first time I saw you in the Ridings Today gallery looking fan-struck over my star presenter, Dan Caine.'

'But…?'

'And then at the RTS dinner, you looked so lonely sitting at that table while Dan was cavorting round with his television chums. But there was nothing I could do, was there? You and Dan were an item – you married him, for goodness' sake. I couldn't muscle in and, anyway, you wouldn't look at someone like me when you had Dan.'

'I…'

'I saw you and Dan at other events, but I kept my distance. And then the day you came into the studios to have a row with Dan I decided to kidnap you. Well, whisk you off to a television conference. I hope you enjoyed that, by the way?' He was grinning now. 'But that night I had a crisis of conscience and, as I said, I felt I couldn't take it any further.'

'Oh…'

'No, let me finish. Despite my best intentions, I did try to get in touch, but your damn mobile wasn't working and Doreen tried getting hold of you and couldn't…'

'I was away.'

'I know that now, but at the time I thought you were avoiding me so I thought, okay, that's it then.'

'But, you said you're in love with me.'

'Always have been. Always will be. Never been surer of anything in my life. What do you say, Teri?'

I looked at him and smiled. 'I'm so glad you got rid of the duck's arse.'

CHAPTER 101

~~~

TERI

Richard insisted on driving me home after our meeting/date. I invited him in, but he said, no, he wanted me to think over what he'd said, but he'd come round on Sunday – if that was all right – and we could see how we both felt then.

I wanted to shout that I knew exactly how I felt; I mean, what have all these tummy flutterings and heart palpitations been about? Why had I ditched the chance of a weekend with gorgeous and god-like Andrew? Why had I never felt so certain of someone as I did about Richard?

My God, Teri. You're in love with Duck's Arse.

Wait till I tell Lee.

****

Closing the door of my duplex, I strode over to the sitting room window and looked down on the car park to watch Richard's Jaguar nudge out into the road. He must have given Jim the night off.

I wanted to fling myself down on the sofa like a moody teenager. I wanted to hug myself. I wanted to dance. I wanted to tell someone that Richard Walker, MD of Ridings Today; chairman of the Jukes football team; probable prison visitor; friend of the ex-cons; solver of family financial crisis; so-called ex-husband of scheming Chinese woman; and all round lovely, soft and cuddly man was in love with ME.

My mind had never been so alive.

I should ring Dad, Charlie and my mother to tell them what had happened to Edward Pranks.

I should get Rochester out of the box file and complete the AEE application.

I should look at those bloody buff-coloured envelopes – there were four now, stuffed behind the pale blue and white Turkish earthenware vase on the hall table. The last two were threatening court action if I didn't pay my speeding fines. And if I pay up, I'll get points and probably lose my licence.

CHAPTER 102

LEE

I was in the shower and had just worked the shampoo into a rich lather when the landline rang. 'Yes,' I said, dripping water and shampoo suds into a slurpy puddle. It was Mammy. 'Daddy,' she said. 'Not long.'

'Fliss?'

'No. Will you?'

'Yes. Be there soon.'

No more waiting. Time for the finale to get under way.

Poor Fliss. Nothing is ever straightforward when you have to factor young children into the equation. Charles was playing golf. 'What if he's in the middle of the course and doesn't have a signal? What if he doesn't get here in time and I'm too late?'

'Bring the kids with you. Charles can collect them from the hospice.'

'I don't know…'

'Pack some games and colouring books. I'll pick you up in twenty minutes.' And I put the phone down quickly before she could stress any further.

I was half-dressed before I remembered my hair was still full of shampoo suds so I stuck my head under the bathroom tap and rinsed as best I could. There was a bit of a flood in the bathroom. I didn't really care. I slicked on some spray-in conditioner and a slither of mascara – and the rest of my clothes – and I was done. So what if I looked like an oik?

Fliss jumped into the car almost before I'd pulled on the handbrake. 'No kids?' I asked.

'Maisie, next door,' she said. 'She offered to have them until Charles can get home.'

I put the car into gear and pulled away. I nodded in the direction of my bag on the back seat. 'Can you reach my phone? I forgot to text Dan,' I said. 'Message him for me.'

She stretched and scrabbled, reaching backwards for my bag. She rooted around, pulled out my wallet, a packet of tissues and, finally, my phone.

'What shall I say?'

Dear God. I knew she was distressed but this wasn't rocket science. 'Tell him Daddy's dying and to get his butt home as quick as he can.'

She sniffed. 'I'll phrase it a bit more politely.'

I didn't care how she phrased it so long as she phrased it.

Message sent, she went to tuck the phone back into my bag.

'Can you ring Teri too?' I asked. 'We're supposed to be meeting up today. I need to cancel. You'll have to ring her landline – it'll be in my contacts – she's not replaced her mobile. The idiot.'

****

Daddy was no longer sleeping. Instead he'd segued into a drug-induced coma. There was more morphine flowing through his veins than blood. Mammy sat in a chair next to him, rubbing his hands between hers, and matching her breaths to his. But she breathed silently, while his breaths came and went with a deep rasp and whistle that grated on the ears and the nerves. I'd have given anything to shut it out, but I prayed it never stopped.

'The nurse said his body was beginning to shut down.' Mammy flicked back the bed sheet. 'Look, his feet are mottling.' The brain was shutting off the blood supply to the extremities to protect itself. She massaged his fingers. 'Eventually –' She didn't finish the sentence. There was no need.

It was one of those beautiful, crisp winter days you sometimes get in late January, like an unexpected gift before the dreariness of February creeps in. Lovely day, I thought, staring out of the window, surprised I could still appreciate the beauty of the scenery. In the corridor outside, the tea trolley rattled to a halt at our door. There was a muffled rat-a-tat-

tat and charge nurse Lindy poked her head into the room. 'Anyone want a cuppa?'

'Not for me,' I said, staring intently at a red robin foraging for grubs in the undergrowth opposite. I didn't turn around, one glance at her sympathetic face and I wouldn't be able to keep the grief in check.

Fliss joined me. Tears rolled down her face. 'We've been lucky.'

I sniffed and swiped my nose with the back of my hand. Lucky? Lucky? Lucky our Daddy was dying? 'With luck like this we don't need bad fortune,' I said.

Fliss rested her head on my shoulder. 'It's hard but if you can just accept how ready he is to move on.'

'But it's so unfair.' I swallowed, but the lump in my throat just wouldn't go away.

'Oh, Lee,' she sighed. 'If you could just believe. Even a little –'

'It's not about believing,' I protested.

'But, it is.' Fliss sounded very earnest.

'No, it isn't. I just don't always agree with God.'

Fliss laughed.

'You can laugh but I definitely don't agree that now's a good time for Daddy to die. And you'll never convince me otherwise.'

She opened her mouth.

'No,' I said. 'I'm not buying that tosh, and I'll never stop wanting him back.

'I don't think any of us will,' Fliss sighed.

We stood in silence for a few minutes.

'Mammy's been worried about you,' Fliss said at last. 'You've looked so peaky these last weeks.'

'That's because I've got a lot going on.'

'You sure? You haven't been at Mass these last couple of Sundays, and Mammy's terrified you're going to leave the church and marry Dan.'

Well, I probably would marry Dan at some point but I didn't see why I needed to become a heathen to do so. Or why missing Mass once or twice so I could have a Sunday lie-in was such a big deal.

I hugged her. 'Look, I'm never going to be a really good Catholic. Not like you and Mammy. I just don't buy into all the bells and whistles.'

Fliss laughed and shook her head. 'There's no need. Sometimes being a good enough Catholic is good enough.'

'Well, it's the best I can do.'

'Girls!' Mammy's anguished voice cut across the room.

Daddy's breathing had changed; it was heavier and deeper, shuddering through his fragile frame. Mammy bent and caressed his cheek while Fliss took one floppy hand in hers and stroked his fingers.

'Hail Mary, full of grace…' I murmured frantically, trying not to count the seconds between each gurgling breath.

The gaps seemed to get longer and longer.

Suddenly – silence.

Mammy's mouth formed a voiceless scream. And then another painful, juddering breath.

'Oh God,' I pleaded, 'make it stop.'

But life went on: the medicine trolley made its squeaky progress down the corridor, doors banged as nurses dispensed the drugs and visitors arrived bearing gifts and news of life outside and the minutes dragged on as Daddy laboured to leave the world.

And, finally, silence endured: Daddy died at 2:30pm, just four days before his seventy-third birthday.

CHAPTER 103

LEE

Here's something: real dead bodies don't look anything like the dead people you see onscreen. Except, perhaps, for those on the news? But they've mostly died violently so there's lots of unlovely blood and gore and twisted, mangled limbs. No, they bear little or no resemblance to corpses like Daddy; people who've died in their beds and who are also not pretty, but in a different way.

TV and movie-dead people, on the other hand, and despite the best efforts of the make-up artists, look far too healthy to be dead. Their skin's not quite the right shade of coffin grey and their mouths and eyes are tightly, peacefully shut. Even in death they look human. Daddy didn't. He looked like a not-very-good copy of the man he used to be.

Funny, isn't it, the things that go through your head at times of stress?

I don't know how long we stood staring at Daddy's inert figure. 'Shall we say a prayer?' Mammy asked.

So we did and wept and prayed again and wept some more and then I went to find Lindy, who kindly and efficiently shooed us from the room so she 'could dress the body'. I almost laughed out loud at the thought of her man-handling Daddy out of his pyjamas into a suit and tie.

She'd been speaking metaphorically; when she called us back in, the bed sheet had been pulled up to Daddy's chin. His eyes were closed and his mouth too. I presumed she'd taped it but never worked out how.

We huddled together and stared at Daddy, etching his already unfamiliar features into our memories, trying to delay the moment when we left the room and he would stop being ours and instead become the property of the mortuary and ultimately the undertaker.

Mammy stepped forward and, kissing her fingers, brushed them across Daddy's lips. 'Shall we go?' she asked.

Go where? There was paperwork to be completed: forms to sign and certificates to be issued.

Lindy pulled the curtains around Daddy's bed. 'Get yourselves down to the cafeteria,' she ordered. 'A nice cup of tea will do you good and I'll come down and find you in a few minutes when we've finished up here.'

Finished what? I didn't dare ask.

We squirreled ourselves away at a corner table, avoiding eye contact with the other customers who'd know from our red-rimmed eyes that death, who'd be paying them a call eventually, had knocked at our door first. We stared blankly at each other.

What next?

A jubilant message from Victoria, of course, complete with dancing emojis and multiple exclamation marks. 'My period has started!!!'

Really, Tory, they're not called screamers for nothing. Less is more.

Hope she'd had tampons with her though.

My stomach gave a sad, little jump. In one way it was a huge relief, but I was surprised at how remorseful I felt that Victoria's tiny blob was a blob no more. Realistically though we were well out of it – imagine the Leader headlines? 'Brawling TV presenter's teenage girl carries bastard baby of Jukes footie hero.'

Didn't bear thinking about.

Or worse: 'TV news frontman brawls with Jukes ace goal scorer, father of his unborn grandchild.'

Declan would have had a field day.

'Pardon?' Fliss said. She was holding hands with Charles, who'd arrived post haste from the golf links. He looked a bit of a twit, if I'm honest, in his pink Pringle sweater and checked golf trews. But, at least, he was there. Where the f*** was Dan?

'Nothing,' I mumbled. 'Just wondering what's happened to Dan? He should have been here by now.

I looked at Fliss. 'You did send the text, didn't you?' She could be a bit of a cauliflower brain sometimes, and pregnancy had not improved her cognitive abilities.

'Of course I did.'

I pulled out my phone. 'He hasn't sent a message. And there's no missed calls from his number. All I've got is a text from Tory.' Which, as I looked at it again, had been sent several hours earlier, soon after she and Dan left home.

Mammy, whose rosary beads were spilling through her fingers, looked up. 'What about Victoria? Is she coming with Dan?'

'I don't know,' I said. 'It's an old message.'

'What does she say?' Mammy persisted.

'Nothing much.' There was no way I wanted to share the contents of Tory's text.

'She sent it this morning just after they left. I didn't notice it before.'

'I hope she's enjoying herself,' Mammy said.

More than we are, I thought.

'I'm sorry,' Fliss said, peering over my shoulder at my phone, 'the message didn't send.'

'What?'

'Look. The one to Dan.' She pointed at my phone and the 'message undeliverable' receipt. 'I'll try again.' She took the phone from me and pressed resend. 'Nope,' she said after a moment. 'It's bounced back again. Is there something wrong with his phone?'

'No,' I said, cross I hadn't noticed the non-send before. But, I suppose, I'd had other things on my mind.

'I'll text Victoria,' I said.

Nothing. That message bounced back too.

'That's not right,' I said. It's silly, I know, but my stomach lurched so far south I'd have tripped up if I tried to stand.

Please God. Don't do this to me. I can't bear it.

CHAPTER 104

LEE

It's hard to think rationally when your stomach is tap dancing in your throat. Dan's phone is always switched on ready for the next scoop. So what the hell has happened that his phone has gone dead?

'His battery's probably gone flat,' Mammy said.

But, no, Dan's phone is his professional lifeline. He always keeps it fully charged. Ditto Victoria. Facebook, Instagram, Twitter – she'd be a social pariah if she didn't know what was going on every minute, every second of every day.

Clearly, there'd been a terrible accident, and he and his phone, and Victoria too, were splattered across some godforsaken country road miles from anywhere. A much more likely scenario…I'm a widow before I've even been wed.

Fliss too was letting her imagination run wild. 'Or their phones might have been stolen,' she said, 'and the thieves have taken their sim cards.'

'Now, why would they want to do that?' Mammy asked.

But that's exactly what she said at bedtime when Fliss and I were youngsters and were absolutely certain Dr Who's Daleks had nothing better to do than float up the stairs and EXTERMINATE us as we slept.

'Now, why would they want to do that?' she'd ask. 'Haven't they much bigger fish to fry. Like Dr Who?'

But we remained unconvinced. And, even if the Daleks didn't get us, what about the Cybermen? They had legs so they'd find the stairs a lot easier to navigate.

In retrospect. I'm surprised we were ever allowed to watch *Dr Who* – especially as we spent so much of the show peering at the TV screen from the back of the settee.

But I digress, an accusation that could never be levelled at Mammy, who could be drearily prosaic. 'I expect they're out of range of a mobile signal.'

Yes, that must be it. But where could they be?

High in the sky in a hot air balloon.

Of course.

First place you'd think to look for an idiot man planning a treat for his beloved. But in what parallel universe did he think I might enjoy a ride in a flimsy basket thousands of feet above ground?

Not the same one I inhabited.

He'd need to think again about his 'treat'. Perhaps I should send him a memo about picking up on hints? 'Hey Dan, what do you think about tickets for *The Full Monty*?' Or, 'Have you seen this advert for the new Volcanic Spa in Harrogate? Two for the price of one, weekends in February.'

Or maybe I should just begin the conversation with a health warning. 'Listen carefully, Dan, you are about to receive a massive hint…'

It probably wouldn't work.

Dan and Victoria came back to earth, and within reach of a mobile signal, several hours later, flushed with enthusiasm and dying, I use the word ironically, to tell me everything.

They were mortified when they heard about Daddy.

'Lee,' Dan said, wrapping me in his arms. 'You poor love.'

Victoria hovered helplessly. 'Shall I make you a cup of tea?' I gave her a look. 'Or open a bottle of wine?'

What do you think?

CHAPTER 105

LEE

It's a sad day when you're too sad to properly enjoy a glass of wine. But I seemed to have lost my taste for it. I blame Teri. She came round with a bottle of Chardonnay as soon as she heard the news. It was Sunday morning, and Dan had only just left to take Victoria back home. 'I know it's a bit early in the day,' she said, pouring a large glass, 'but this will make you feel better.' Of course, it didn't, but, then, God help the palate of anyone who feels better after a glass of Chardonnay.

She meant well but after the first sip I pushed the glass aside.

'Not in the mood,' I said.

I guess there's a first time for everything. Perhaps if she'd brought Muscadet?

'I can't imagine how I'd feel if it was my dad,' Teri said. She blew her nose so noisily I thought her ears might pop. She took a long swig from her glass. 'It must be so much worse for you.' Another long nose blow, followed by another gulp of wine. 'I mean your dad was nice. And you actually liked him.'

Whereas her dad?

'Mine's a selfish old git,' she said, reaching for a refill.

Yep, tell it like it is, Teri.

'I'm not sure I'd even bother turning up for the funeral,' she said. 'Charlie definitely wouldn't.'

No surprise there, either.

'Funny,' she said. 'My brother's called Charlie and your brother-in-law is Charles. Coincidence, eh?'

Coincidence? 'Just one of those things,' I said, wondering how much she'd had to drink before she arrived at my house.

She saw me frown. 'I'm not drunk,' she said, 'except perhaps with happiness.'

I laughed. I couldn't help it. It was so typical of Teri: my father's corpse had only just taken up residency in the morgue and already she'd moved on to talking about herself.

'See,' she said, 'I told you a glass of wine would help. Look at you, laughing already.'

My stomach gave one of the little flips it had been doing at intervals ever since I'd kissed Daddy goodbye for the very last time.

'I've got so much to tell you,' Teri said, 'and there's a little favour I need to ask too.'

CHAPTER 106

TERI

I stared at Lee. 'What do you mean you won't help?' I demanded. 'What sort of friend are you? All I'm asking is that you take three of my measly points. All you have to do is say you were driving my car that day. Where's the harm? I'll pay the bloody fine if it's the money you're worried about.'

'It's either that, Lee, or I lose my bloody licence and won't be able to drive. Think about that. Lee.'

I was trying to be patient with her, but she had that ridiculous look on her face that she adopts when she's feeling sorry for me: tolerant. And, frankly, I found her attitude patronising.

Now was not the time for her pathetic moralising. Okay, I'd been speeding. Yes, thank you, I know one shouldn't but not everyone can afford the time to crawl round at a dying gnat's pace. And whoever heard of going slower than thirty miles-per-hour on a straight road in broad daylight? Those sanctimonious shits who put posters up on lampposts with pictures of snails and 'Slow Down' in large letters obviously have no driving experience.

Well damn them.

And damn that bloody camera on the A615. But it's happened and if Lee doesn't help now, I'm up shit creek.

****

Lee

I'd been so pleased to see Teri when she turned up with her bottle of wine – less pleased about the Chardonnay but you can't have everything. And she'd said some really sweet things about Daddy and what a lovely man he was – or had been. But, while I could see the attraction of Duck's Arse – a satisfyingly large bank balance – I hoped she realised what she was doing. Richard, as I guess I *must* start calling him, would certainly shower her with material comforts and indulge her every whim – which she'd thoroughly enjoy. But, he was no pushover and he'd make mincemeat of Declan or any other would-be contenders for her affections. And Teri too if she tried to play those games again. Maybe that was what she'd needed all along? Someone who'd look after her and bail her out when she got into trouble?

That was certainly what she was after now – only it was me she expected to do the bailing.

'No,' I said. It wasn't too long ago that a top MP, now an ex-MP, and his wife had been jailed for a similar offence. If that's what they did to MPs, what would they do to Teri and me? And I didn't think jail would agree with either of us.

****

Teri

Lee was being all pious and prissy. 'I'm sorry, Teri,' she said, shaking her head. 'But it's against the law.'

'Oh, don't be ridiculous,' I countered. 'Lots of people do it. Look at…' My memory failed. 'There was some politician who got his wife to say she was driving so she got his points –'

'Yes, and they were both sent to jail,' Lee said.

'Yes, but,' I said, 'who's to know? We could say there was just you and me in the car, and I was letting you drive. You've always wanted to drive my car; it's so much better than that silly, little run-around you have. Although goodness' knows why you don't get a BMW like Dan's.'

'What I drive is neither here nor there. And leave Dan out of this.'

'Oh, here it comes. I'm not allowed to talk about my ex-husband now.'

'Oh, Teri. Don't be childish. Of course you are. But Dan's got nothing to do with this. You've asked me to break the law on your behalf, and I'm simply not going to. You got yourself into this mess, and now you must face the consequences.'

****

Lee

Actually, no, Teri, I've never wanted to drive your car. It's too big, too flash and I don't like the colour.

And, she knows I'm a rubbish liar. How many times did she despair in the past of my ability to follow through on a little fib about a boyfriend or missed homework?

No good either her pointing out that I don't actually have to lie.

'It's just a bit of form-filling,' she said. 'I'll fill it in to say you were driving, and the DVLA'll send the speeding notice to you and you'll just have to tick the box to say you were driving. No lying involved at all.'

She sounded almost triumphant.

'And, if you want, I'll tick the box for you so you don't even have to do that.'

She'd got it all figured out. 'And better yet,' she continued, 'you don't even need to get any points. You've got a clean licence so you'll be offered the option of a speed-awareness course instead.'

Oh thanks. I seemed to remember Teri had done one of those courses a couple of years back. She'd moaned for England about the tedium. 'That's four hours of my life I'll never get back,' she'd said. 'I wish I'd paid the fine and taken the points.'

Well, now she could and the driving ban as well.

I felt sorry for her, and the driving ban would be inconvenient, but she'd got herself into this little cauldron of trouble, and she wasn't getting me into it with her. Besides Duck's Arse employed a full-time chauffeur.

She didn't need a licence.

'I can't,' I said. 'I would if I could but...it's breaking the law. That's really serious. And friends or not, I don't think it's the sort of thing you should ask.'

****

Teri

How rude. How unkind. How heartless. How typical of Lee. After all I've done for her.

I stormed out. Funny how often I storm out of Lee's. And then I thought about what her father had asked me to do, and I realised I shouldn't be mean to her. I mean, her dad's just died and she's feeling like hell. I'll have to apologise.

I looked at those bloody brown envelopes again and wondered what the hell to do. A chilling thought struck me: I could be sent to jail. I wondered if Richard could help – he's had some experience of criminals and prison visiting if what Jim told me was right.

But, what to do about Lee? What I should do is go straight back round there and make sure she's okay. I could get some flowers. No, maybe not flowers. She's had plenty of those recently what with friends hearing about her dad and sending bouquets.

I decided to take some Prosecco. A glass of bubbly always goes down well, but I'd run out and would have to nip down to the off-licence.

Remembering what Jim had said about parking safely, I headed for the car park on the main street, but as I began to pull in, I noticed a familiar figure on the other side of the road. It was Lee, moving purposefully along the pavement.

I turned my head to see where she was going and spotted her nipping into Craven's Chemist; then some idiot coming out of the car park honked his horn for me to get out of the way as I was blocking his path and holding him up for a nanosecond.

I parked and dashed down the street to Craven's. I'd sneak up on her and surprise her as she was deliberating which mascara or whatever to buy. I'd obviously tell her the best make-up for her colouring and then we'd have a hug – she's touchy-feely like that – and go for a late afternoon drink. So excited by my plan, I forgot about the Prosecco.

I peered through the glass-fronted door and saw Lee at the far end by the counter talking to an assistant. I went in and crept up until I was almost touching her. Over her shoulder I could see she was holding a long, thin, blue box. Toothpaste?

She put it down and pushed it slightly towards the assistant, and I was able to see it more clearly and the words, in bright red. 'Pregnancy Test – over 99% accurate.'

'Blimey, Lee,' I laughed as she turned, startled. 'Who the hell are you buying that for?'

to be continued

ACKNOWLEDGEMENTS

We are so grateful to all those people, friends and family, who have offered us support and encouragement during the writing of this book. So many of you have shown an interest, and it's impossible to name you all, but we're sending our heartfelt thanks.

We must, however, give special mention to a small number of people who have been particularly patient: Kevin, Geoff, Meg, Annie and Dandy.

Thank you too, to our amazing publicist, Jeni Cropper, and the equally amazing Anne Cater, who organised our blog tour.

As writers we draw a lot of inspiration from snippets of conversations that we overhear when we're out and about – at the supermarket, in cafes and restaurants, on the bus or train. Thank you to all those anonymous people who have inspired us more than they'll ever know.

Thanks too to our friends who remain our friends even though they know we're always listening – especially the lovely ladies of the Knitwits knitting group and Edie's book club.

We'd also like to mention all our author and blogger friends on Twitter and the various Facebook writing groups that we belong to, in particular members of Book Connectors, The Book Club, Books for Older Readers and Authors, Writers and Readers. You've been a great support.

We're grateful too to the fantastic team at Lakewater Press, especially our publisher Kate Foster; our editor, Rebecca Carpenter; and Emma Wicker for the wonderful cover design.

And of course, thank you, you fabulous ladies, Teri and Lee.

ABOUT THE AUTHORS

Sue Featherstone and Susan Pape are both former newspaper journalists with extensive experience of working for national and regional papers and magazines and in public relations.

More recently they have worked in higher education, teaching journalism – Sue at Sheffield Hallam and Susan at Leeds Trinity University.

The pair, who have been friends for twenty-five years, wrote two successful journalism text books together – ***Newspaper Journalism: A Practical Introduction*** and ***Feature Writing: A Practical Introduction*** (both published by Sage).

Sue, who is married with two grown-up daughters, loves reading, writing and Nordic walking in the beautiful countryside near her Yorkshire home.

Susan is married and lives in a village near Leeds, and, when not writing, loves walking and cycling in the Yorkshire Dales. She is also a member of a local ukulele orchestra.

They blog about books at www.bookloversbooklist.com
You can find both Sue and Susan on
Twitter: @SueF_Writer and @wordfocus